MICHAEL _____ thrillers in the 1970s under the pseudonym Michael Sinclair, but stopped writing novels when he became the Queen's Press Secretary, a position he held for a decade. He now combines writing with a wide range of business interests, dividing his time between Edinburgh and London. Michael Shea's new novel, *The British Ambassador*, is now available in hardback from HarperCollins.

'Entertainingly written . . . Michael Shea knows whereof he writes. He has not forgotten how to make his readers turn the page.'
Sunday Express

'[Michael Shea] packs the novel with the kind of insider information that you won't find any-where else. A smart, sharp thriller.'   *Maxim*

'This suspenseful and highly readable tale of political intrigue and conspiracy is very reveal-ing about what goes on behind another of the nation's 'thrones' – the political one that is based at 10 Downing Street.'
Manchester Evening News

'A yarn of corruption and clawing ambition'
Birmingham Evening Mail

'An entertaining romp'   *The Times*

By the same author

SPIN DOCTOR
THE BRITISH AMBASSADOR

MICHAEL SHEA

SPIN DOCTOR

HarperCollinsPublishers

HarperCollins*Publishers*
77–85 Fulham Palace Road,
Hammersmith, London W6 8JB

This paperback edition 1996
1 3 5 7 9 8 6 4 2

First published in Great Britain by
HarperCollins*Publishers* 1995

Copyright © Michael Shea 1995

The Author asserts the moral right to
be identified as the author of this work

ISBN 0 00 649322 X

Set in Linotron Sabon

Printed and bound in Great Britain by
Caledonian International
Book Manufacturing Ltd Glasgow

To Mona, Katriona
and Ingeborg

'Nations would be terrified if they knew by what small men they were governed.'

Charles-Maurice de Talleyrand

'The battle for the mind of Ronald Reagan was like trench warfare in World War I; never have so many battled so hard over such barren terrain.'

Peggy Noonan, former speechwriter to President Reagan

FORETASTE

Strong, confident males, prosperous and gregarious, most of them attended by a well-turned-out partner or trophy woman. Influents to a man; shot-callers, not slot-fillers. A now ennobled ex-Secretary to the Cabinet, once the most influential man in Britain, sits, framed in his gilded box, with a Treasury Knight, the Editor of the *Sunday Times* and the Chairman of Kleinworts. Big men, and small men turned great by their PR handlers; the powerful, the would-be powerful; all are on display, all benefiting from the business largesse of Royal Opera House tickets, that peculiarly British lubricant in the machinery of national decision-taking. The Mandarin Class is at play.

Around and below them are more of the same: lawyers, bankers, industrialists, media manipulators, their patrons, their clients, their gofers, their protégés. Here and there, a scattering of career women sit among the wives and mistresses of public life. The auditorium is the stage; the audience the players. A rustle of programmes draws attention to those who are bent on finding the story-line and the singers' names with which to lard their interval conversations. High above, in the Gods, the real opera buffs wait in expectation.

Towards the back of the pit, amid a mixed party of business and political figures, Dr Mark Ivor and Lord Shand sit together. Unlike the others in the group, neither has a partner with him. The peer, an aloof and icy figure from the extreme right of the party, is a man with a savage intellect, a mission, a clear-cut vision of right and wrong; the other is a professional strategist, a spin doctor, of whom it is said that the only views he has of life are those of his clients.

At the interval Lord Shand steers his companion through the chattering classes towards the Foyer Bar. They collect glasses of Covent Garden's best dry white, then move away to a quiet corner.

'I'd welcome your input,' Lord Shand began.

'How serious is it?' asked Dr Ivor.

'We've just identified the problem,' responded Shand curtly. He took a sip from his glass and his lip wrinkled with distaste. His was the sort of face that was seldom free from some look of censure.

'That means you've got nowhere,' Ivor smiled helpfully.

'No, we've got somewhere. A very junior minister — Soper isn't Cabinet material — and a girl who's either the wronged innocent she pretends to be, or a protégée of someone like Max Clifford, who wants to pay off her mortgage before she's twenty-two.'

'With the money the tabloids are offering . . .'

'We think she's the latter, probably acting alone, but we need more facts about her.'

'What kind of facts?'

'What d'you mean?'

'Known facts; proven facts; indisputable facts; media facts; created facts?'

'Created? I don't understand.'

'Of course you do. Facts can be created. The press demonizes, or trivializes, or sensationalizes with "facts". You want the *Mail* to run a headline "*Tories pressurize PM over ministerial sex allegations*". It can be done. It's still easy to find Tories with grievances, who think they're safe enough to pontificate about other people's morals. All I do is provide the link where none exists. Bingo. A fact is born.'

'You do that?' Shand was impressed despite himself. A true aristocrat, an autocrat of steely right-wing views, he looked the part. Hair parted to the right of the centre, brushed down

2

hard, public school-style; a chin just short of being weak; a long, arrogant nose; a lean body, towering and cynical. 'No wonder *The Times* called you the British Machiavelli,' he added.

Ivor shrugged dismissively. 'Journalistic cliché. It's just a matter of giving the right push at the right time. As the Scots say, a lie's halfway round the world before the truth's got its boots on. A good created fact moves even faster. Spot a promising one; pick it up, and run. With care, it's embedded in the press cuttings files from then on.'

'You're advising the Ramsay Smythe Consortium?' asked Lord Shand.

'Correct.'

'You have time to help me too?'

'Always time.' Ivor paused.

'So what should I do?'

'Is it true?'

'Of course it's true,' said Lord Shand dismissively, abandoning his half empty glass on a side table.

'What does the Prime Minister think should be done?'

'The PM's in a state. He doesn't think. Brogan, the Party Chairman, tells him what his views are.'

'Harsh.' Ivor turned to look at the peer who stood regarding arrogantly the lesser mortals who thronged around him in the foyer.

'A real fact.'

'What does Brogan want?'

'He's got no time for Soper — too much of a friend of mine, but he wants the woman out of the way. Gently but firmly. In the state the party's in, he doesn't need another scandal.'

'Why don't you deal with it?'

'Brogan keeps me right out. He thinks I'm a neo-fascist.'

'And are you?' Ivor laughed emptily as the first bell signalling the end of the interval sounded.

'When we have as weak a political leadership as we have at the moment it is the men and women in the ante-rooms of power, the civil servants, the faceless advisers, people like you and me, that are needed.'

'Even strong leaders need advice . . .' Ivor hesitated, surprised by the vehemence with which the other man expressed himself. 'Look how much Margaret Thatcher relied on her inner team — Bell, Powell, Ingham.'

'A different ball game now.'

'More important. Fighting for access, for patronage, for the mind —'

'If the man has a mind. Soper is an ally. I don't want him to have to resign. Can you help, Dr Ivor, or does it run counter to your beliefs?'

'I'm a fixer. I've no axe to grind.' Ivor looked down, idly flicking through the pages of his programme.

'A man with no beliefs can be dangerous.'

'I have beliefs —'

'Which are?'

'I believe in making things work.' Ivor paused. 'Yes, I'll help.'

'In return for . . . ?' asked Lord Shand.

'I want access. What are *you* getting out of this?'

'The same as you. You're my key.'

'Frank of you. It's a vicious game. Getting access.'

'We don't assassinate people any more . . . unfortunately. No coups.' Lord Shand turned and began walking towards the door leading back to the amphitheatre.

'Coups don't need guns or revolvers. Words are sometimes enough,' said Ivor, tailing behind.

'In politics words can be deadly, even if they don't actually kill.'

'Correct. The victims don't die. They shuffle off into the retirement homes of politics. It can be quite comfortable in your House of Lords I gather. Anyway, all politics end in failure.' Ivor forced a smile that was not returned.

'People can die without bleeding . . . The wounds don't always show.' Lord Shand looked down at him, eyes narrowing with caution or suspicion. 'What is your fee?'

'For this sort of exercise? Price of an air ticket, and . . . I told you what I want.'

The peer looked at Ivor with something bordering on dislike. In the background, the Opera House bell rang again.

1

Just after midnight, on his way home from a black-tie dinner at the Savoy, Dr Ivor pulled over and stopped at the late-night news-stand by Victoria Station. He got out of his Volvo and, selecting some coins from his pocket, bought the first editions of *The Times* and the *Daily Mail*.

Back in the driving seat, he turned on a reading light. Even without it he had seen the front-page banner in *The Times*: '*Right wing united over defence cuts*'. The *Mail* had it inside. '*Rebels demand a say*' was their headline above a story about infighting between the left and right wings of the party. But all that could wait. Ivor quickly flicked through the pages until he found the Dempster gossip column. His planted story, with its whiff of more scandal to come, was tucked away as a tailpiece. Ivor tore out the page and tossed the rest of the paper onto the passenger seat. He punched a number into his carphone. It rang several times before a voice sleepily answered.

'Sorry to ring so late. The item – it's in Dempster. She's taken the bait. It seems to have worked.' He began to read. '"The down-market tabloids are fighting over a story involving a senior government figure and a young lady . . . The politician, a popular and widely respected figure, who is married to the daughter of one of the oldest and most distinguished –"'

'Get to the nub of it.' The testiness in Lord Shand's voice was unmistakable.

'"The young lady in question is believed to have flown abroad to an undisclosed destination accompanied by a hack from one

7

of the papers, in order to work on her story away from the pressures of —"'

'Good,' the dry voice at the far end cut in again.

'Are you sure it's good?'

'It's what we wanted,' said the peer.

'Things take on a momentum of their own. We need to monitor —'

'Then play it carefully. We only have one chance.' The line went dead.

Five days later, at eight forty a.m., Dr Mark Ivor was walking into Victoria Station to meet Sir David Brogan, the Party Chairman, off the Brighton train. He had walked from his nearby flat in Ashley Gardens, knowing that Sir David would have his chauffeur and car waiting as usual in Lower Belgrave Road. They would travel together; they had a lot to talk about. Choosing the right media spokesman for the party and getting him in place well before the run-up to the election was critical. Ivor had one or two names for Sir David to consider.

Then the bomb went off. A deafening bang, a moment's shocked silence, the sound of broken glass cascading from the domed roof, and then came the screams. He looked across the crowded foyer in horror. People started running in all directions as the police began to clear the station. A young officer bellowed hysterically at some bewildered French students. Ivor walked quickly forward and tried to explain that he was meeting someone important. The policeman shoved him rudely back. Ivor shrugged and moved quickly away. Brogan would probably not get through either. He would have to catch up with him later. A bloody nuisance.

An hour later he heard that Brogan had been killed in the blast. His chauffeur, who had gone to meet him off the train and had been carrying his weekend suitcase for him, also died before the ambulance got to the hospital. Two other passengers were dead and seventeen wounded. Ivor, despite his usually icy self-composure, was deeply shocked. A moment earlier and . . .

8

Poor Brogan. A tower of strength in the party, if a bit of a boor. Poor Brogan's wife. Bad news for the party. Bad news for the PM. Good news for the right wing. Particularly good news for Lord Shand.

The bomb story meant that there was little room for other items in the next day's editions. Only a few carried a short agency report from Bangkok. Yet another British woman had been arrested trying to smuggle drugs into Thailand. Her companion, a journalist, had claimed only to have met her on the flight. They released him after a few hours. No one, not even Nigel Dempster, made the connection. It was very much later that they realized who the girl was, but life had moved on by then and the media are fickle: they buy the kiss-and-tell stories but then they show little sympathy for the one who sings.

Special Branch were first off the mark. They turned up un-announced at his office just before lunch. His secretary, Deborah, had gone out, but Ivor had cancelled a social get-together out of genuine shock, and opened the door to let them in.

'Sir David Brogan had a diary entry. Today's first item: your name.'

'Correct. I was at the station to meet him.'

'Why didn't you —?'

'How the hell . . . Sorry, I mean . . . I was there when the damn bomb went off. I wasn't allowed through. So I came straight here. I've only just heard from his office that . . . that it was him. It could have been me.'

The policemen stared at Ivor. 'Yes, sir. Sorry, sir. You must be very shocked.'

'Has anyone claimed responsibility?'

'No warning. Nothing. We don't believe it's Irish related. Not any more.'

'Then who?'

'That's why we're here, sir. Trying to find out. Not to speculate.'

'He always came up by train on a Monday, didn't he?'

'No, sir. Varied his journeys a lot, as he should. Only his secretary and him had access to his diary,' said one of the officers.

'Who would know about *your* engagements, sir?' asked the other. 'Could we . . . could we see your diary?'

'By all means. But there's nothing in it. It was an important meeting for me. I didn't write it in because no way was I going to forget.'

'No one else would know?'

'No one – apart from Deborah, my secretary . . . I don't think.'

'Think harder, sir. If you don't mind . . .'

They had just left when Ivor had an urgent phone call.

'You've heard about Brogan?' asked Lord Shand.

'I was bloody well at Victoria to meet him!'

'Sorry . . . I . . . look . . . defuse that other thing, the Romanian story that Ramsay Smythe dug up. It's too dangerous at the moment, it's overkill. If people made the link – right-winger Soper off the scandal hook, and others getting screwed, along with Brogan going – it could look like a –'

'Plot . . . ?' said Ivor quietly. 'Look, I'll see what I can do. But the Opposition may already be onto it.'

'I'll talk to their Whips. They won't do the dirty just now, surely.'

'It's . . . the pain is that Smedley's got it. He's so crazy the Whips won't be able to hold him.'

'Stop it if you can. Otherwise . . . God, what a bloody catastrophe!' For once Lord Shand appeared to lose his cool.

He got to the House as quickly as he could to watch from the Strangers' Gallery, but he missed the inevitable tributes paid to Brogan from all the party leaders. It was a sombre, well-behaved place for once until, later on, Eddie Smedley MP stood up to question the minister, Peter Maltby. Looking down at the floor of the House, Ivor thought once again how badly designed it was: view and acoustics were both poor and there were not enough places on the long green benches for all the MPs to sit when, as now, something of import was about to happen. He watched as Maltby stood at the Dispatch Box, unusually nervously shuffling through his brief. Maltby, a tough fighter on the left wing of the party, had always been so sure of himself, so ambitious, so confident, so anti-everything, position, title, breeding, for which Shand stood.

The question came, gentle at first, lulling him, encouraging Peter Maltby to drop his guard. He managed a grim smile for the benefit of the television cameras. Then the unexpected came, whistling like a stiletto between the ribs, and just as deadly. The minister knew the answer but was unprepared for the question. 'Had he . . .' – Smedley was unperturbed by the aftermath of the bombing and ignored the shouts of outrage and calls to withdraw – 'had the Minister, when a junior member of the government in the Ministry of Defence, been in receipt of secret sums of money from a certain communist government?'

There was uproar in the House. The Speaker suspended the sitting for tempers to cool.

When the MPs reassembled, Smedley, who looked very pleased with himself, was repeatedly asked to withdraw his question, but refused.

Slowly Maltby stood and the House fell silent. Instead of grasping at the usual parliamentary device of saying that he would make a statement to the House later, to give himself time to clear his thoughts, he started skating straight out onto thin ice, slipped, then fell headlong. While MPs on his own side sat in embarrassed silence, those on the benches opposite bayed for his blood.

In the Strangers' Gallery, Ivor thought once again about the validity of the late Iain Macleod's remark that the best time to kick politicians was when they were down. Lord Shand would not be pleased.

*

Mrs Topping had it coaxed out of her by the woman police sergeant. She had the sort of far-reaching voice, punctuated by sobs, that the officer found hard to take, but eventually the whole story emerged. She had dropped off her children at the school gate and then driven the half mile down Belfrey Lane to the ivy-covered house at the end. She made it stridently clear to the policewoman that it wasn't a housekeeping job she had, let alone cleaning. She was doing Peter Maltby and his wife a favour by keeping an eye on the house for them, putting on the heating, sorting out the laundry and stocking the fridge for their all-too-brief weekend visits. Such a busy life; who would be a politician, or a politician's wife? No time to themselves, no privacy, never out of the public eye. Mrs Topping was doing a public service, she declared, making life just that little bit more comfortable for them.

She had parked the car at the side of the lane, opened the gate and walked up the short drive to the house. She always did it that way rather than try and turn the car on the small patch of gravel between the lawn and the house. She wasn't very good at turning the car, nor parking for that matter. Mr Topping had always teased her about how she'd ever passed her test.

Mrs Topping had been carrying a large wicker basket of groceries, almost thirty pounds' worth, including a few luxuries she'd never have bought for herself. They'd left her a list last weekend and asked her to stock up. The drink order was being delivered separately. She got to the front door, put her basket down on the ground and began searching for her key. It was then she had noticed that the heavy outer door wasn't closed, then that she had felt the first prickle of apprehension. There had been a number of recent burglaries in the village. She knew she had locked that door and that the Maltbys were not due down until the weekend.

Mrs Topping pushed open the door. The inner one was locked. Thank goodness. She must have made a mistake, after all. On her last visit she had been in such a hurry to get back to the cake she was baking. She put the key in the mortise lock. It wouldn't go in. She bent down and peered through the keyhole. There, quite clearly, she could see a key facing towards her. The door was locked from the other side. How silly. They must have come down unexpectedly, and yet . . . no car. She rang the bell and waited. Nothing happened. She rang again. Nothing. Mrs Topping went on a journey of exploration. She walked round the house. Everything was quite normal: curtains drawn back, even in the drawing room, where . . . where she had, she distinctly remembered, closed them so that the sunlight wouldn't bleach the pretty inlaid rosewood table that stood in the bay window.

Mrs Topping peered in through the window and looked round the room. Everything appeared to be as she had left it. But wasn't that a man's jacket on the sofa? The door from the drawing room into the hall was open. She knew she had shut it. She could make out the stairs and there, at the bottom, someone appeared to be lying. She knocked on the window, and Peter Maltby turned to face her. Such a kind and thoughtful man. A good constituency MP too, who read the lesson so beautifully at the Christmas service. But this was a side of Mr Maltby that she had never seen – unshaven, a wild-eyed apparition. Even through the windows she could see he had tears running down his face. He waved at her and mouthed something. He was trying to get her to leave. He had a newspaper in one hand and in the other . . .

What happened next was not entirely clear. One window shattered in a blast of shotgun pellets. Then she saw the blood running down the window panes like droplets of red rain . . . Mrs Topping knew that this was the time to put an end to independent action. She turned and, with a commendable lack of panic, hurried back down the drive to the car.

Many hours later the ambulance drove off with the minister's body. The house was swarming with police. An expert was examining the shotgun. The woman police sergeant escorted Mrs Topping out of the gate. The crowd of press and cameramen jostled around her. Tight-lipped, Mrs Topping was returned to her family and to a very late supper. Things would never be quite the same again.

* * *

The lead-up to the destruction of Peter Maltby MP had also been watched by the deeply unattractive figure of Fred Cree of the *Independent*. He had been in the Press Gallery by chance, but as he was busy working on a big arms-for-the-Middle East scandal, he had put the scene out of his mind — until the news of the suicide broke.

After brooding about it, Cree slouched in to see his News Editor.

'We've got plenty of people working on that story. Stick to defence, Cree,' was the muttered response.

'I've only got the one line I want to pursue: who put Smedley up to it.'

'He dug it out himself.'

'Far too stupid.'

The News Editor paused. He didn't like Cree, but then few people did. 'OK. But the arms story is still your first priority.'

Cree wandered back to his desk and started telephoning. Eventually he tracked down the MP.

'I've said all I'm going to say to the bloody press,' snarled Smedley. He sounded as if he had been drinking.

'I think you ought to see me, though, Mr Smedley,' whined Cree. 'You see I think you were used. To get rid of one more on the left of the party. See what I mean? Duped. I'm sure you don't like people doing that to you . . .'

2

October, and the party conference was in full swing. High above the uninspiring row of potted plants on the platform and the municipal 'No Smoking' signs, a strident blue banner proclaiming 'The Right Team to Run Britain' billowed gently in the hot air generated from beneath. It took on a life of its own, swelling and puffing up as the keynote speech reached its 'we will be defeated neither by terrorism nor by the Opposition' climax. It subsided only after the long-drawn-out ovation for the leader spluttered to its close and the huge hall emptied.

It had been a long, sticky four days in badly ventilated surroundings. Four days of constituency workers and their ilk come down from the hills to cheer success and shoot the wounded. Four days of empty, earnest speeches from the floor. Four days of proceedings dampened by a suicide and the assassination of Brogan but invigorated by the unity generated by these same events. Four days of the stuffed rows of platform people, nodding in time to the speeches, programmed when to applaud for the TV cameras, listening without listening, dreaming of power. Four days of even tighter security checks: everyone frisked, sniffed, metal-detected. Identity passes dangled on chains round every neck; constant police warnings overrode all the proceedings. There were TV monitors everywhere. In the background, suspicious wives also monitored: the comings and goings of pretty secretaries and research assistants had to be scrutinized as much as any potential terrorist.

The conference was over for another year. The political élite pushed and shoved toward taxis and trains and cars to take them home to the shires or the suburbs. But in a corner of the Terrace Bar a die-hard cabal of tabloid journalists lingered on, lubricating their talents, having long since filed their copy. Political plaudits and political obituaries were already set and ready to go.

In the opposite corner, Lord Shand stood with Dr Mark Ivor. The peer reached into an inside pocket, produced a white envelope and handed it to the other man. 'It was nasty for a while, but in the end I'm content. Maltby was a pain. Brogan was a pain. Soper I can use.' His voice was distant.

'You use a lot of people . . .' Ivor was unusually subdued.

'I regret nothing, you know. We on the right need to be strong.' His whole manner was emotionless; only a slight tremor gave the hint of inner tensions. 'And you, Ivor? I hope I can continue to rely on you.'

Ivor shrugged. 'I did what you asked. What you paid me to do.' Suddenly the atmosphere was chill. The two men nodded, then turned away from each other with no word of farewell.

Close but not too close to the tabloid men, the brief meeting between Shand and Ivor had had an audience of two: a barrel-chested man from *The Times*, sitting with his colleague, Fred Cree of the *Independent*. They had matured together in the Lebanon in their roving correspondent days, when both had been leaner and fitter men. Cree had not stayed long: twenty-four hours to be precise. He had developed a heavy dose of the runs, he said from food poisoning, others said from fear. Whatever, Cree thereafter had been able to dine out on stories of his time as a war correspondent.

The *Times* man looked half asleep, eyes hooded under heavy brows. But he was alert. He spoke first. 'Know them?'

'Shand. That man gives new meaning to the word arrogance. Hauteur personified. He's gone far – almost unnoticed. Until the assassination. Could he be the next Chairman?'

'Possibly. Too far to the right perhaps, and then the party may not like having one from the Lords. In any case, he prefers working behind the scenes . . . That's two of them.'

'What d'you mean? Who was he talking to?' Cree played the innocent. He knew precisely who the other man was.

'Dr Mark Ivor.'

'So that's Ivor. Well, well. Too smooth by half. Don't like the type.'

'Feeling will be mutual. Doesn't like journalists unless he can use them.' The *Times* man paused. 'You saw . . . ?'

'An envelope changing hands?'

'Ivor's pay-off.'

'For what?' Cree was fishing hard.

'Only guessing.'

'What?'

'Helped Shand's right-wing friends.'

'Peter Maltby's suicide did that.'

'Right.'

'You don't mean . . . ?' Cree showed amazement.

'Trust me. Think it through. Smedley's question.'

'That was Ivor?'

'It's his style. Dirty tricks. This time it went too far even for him.'

'You don't mean . . . ? What about my Lord Shand?' Cree's tone was mocking.

'He's a political thug behind all the breeding. And clever. With Brogan gone he'll be even happier. Now he'll want in on the act. Give the PM some spine.'

'But the PM's speech this year was one of his best as far as the right are concerned. They were over the moon.'

'And who wrote the key bits?'

'Not Shand?'

The *Times* man shook his head slowly. 'Not yet. Give him time.'

'Ivor . . . ?'

'He's good at the rabble-rousing slogans. Gets the party back-woodsmen cheering to the rafters.'

'Sloganeering doesn't produce consensus.'

'I know that. But Ivor's contacts followed it up with a lot of whispers in the wings.'

'Maybe he deserves his pay.' Cree was feeling pleased with himself. His colleague from *The Times* was feeding his so-innocent questions on cue, confirming what he had already guessed. There was the makings of a great story. All that was lacking was the small matter of proof.

At that moment Ivor reappeared briefly in the bar and saw the journalists watching him. The *Times* man lifted his glass in a mock toast. Ivor returned a cheery wave.

'The bugger doesn't even blush,' said the *Times* man admiringly.

3

Ivor immersed himself, mind with body, into a state of total relaxation. It was a key ability he had developed after a long-forgotten sixties catastrophe, to insulate himself against useless worry, conscience, pain and self-recrimination; others had recourse to alcohol or drugs or analysts. A long-remembered flower-power girl, with bead-plaited hair and a mystic training from some oriental guru, had taught him this and much more about physical release and inner peace. From her he had learned that people who think their work is terribly important are the first to have breakdowns. His eyes were opened then as they were open now, but, from the comfort of his executive seat, he took in nothing of the wing-tips as they seemed to brush the ice from the fir trees that clung to the sides of the mountains, or of the wider view through the lens-like windows of the Ramsay Smythe Beechcraft.

Out there, below the level of the mountains, a filigree of late November mist had draped itself over Lake Geneva. Beneath the small plane, the path of a river twisted a steel ribbon across the green chequered valley. It reached towards tiny clusters of orange and russet villages, then on to the obscene white chimney stacks of a cement works pouring its pollution up into a clear sky. In the furthest distance, caught by the light of the setting sun, facets of snow and ice shone brilliant on the fierce white teeth of the Alps.

After the allotted five minutes, as the plane pulled higher on its route back to London, Ivor gently eased himself back into his reality, and recalled a day well spent. In the aftermath of the death of Brogan, he had seen the party conference swing well to the right, and as his political clients had less need of him he was free to arrange his session with the Swiss and Frankfurt bankers. The mistakes had been out there waiting to be made, but there had been surprisingly little fallout after Peter Maltby's suicide – after all, the dead man had been a Romanian spy – and the media witch-hunt had not materialized. Ivor had had time to give his full attention to the immaculate gnomes of Zurich, and, more importantly, to his biggest industrial client, the thug and bully, Mr Ramsay Smythe.

The meeting, to an outside observer, would not have suggested a unity of minds or purpose. On one side of the table had sat effortlessly superior bankers, Swiss and British, in their well-cut suits and Jermyn Street shirts. On the other had been the group he was advising, led by Ramsay Smythe, a clutch of self-made men, steely-eyed, tough, ready for a fight, with accents to match. No public schoolboys. No peers of the realm on their board. And Ivor himself, holding the ring, on the lookout for tactical elephant traps, watching that Ramsay Smythe, as always mercurial and aggressive, did not flare up and spoil things. Not that the bankers were fragile flowers. They could see big fees whether or not the planned take-over bid of the Sigmont Corporation, the huge Dutch-German building and engineering conglomerate, succeeded. They knew that secrecy was crucial, that if anything leaked out, all options would be off. A large part of British and European industry was about to come into play: the Sigmont group of companies was a tasty target that would mesh in well and profitably with the Ramsay Smythe empire, and many people would profit, particularly those around that table. Now jugulars were being eyed. The chances of an agreed bid, a friendly merger, were slight. The bankers were key players. The stakes were astronomical.

The meeting had gone well. Minds had met. Strategies were agreed upon. Fees were negotiated. From now on, everything and anything, legal or paralegal, everything that would not be found out, that would not lead to the Monopolies & Mergers

Commission getting upset, everything was fair game. Dirty tricks would be deniable. Dr Mark Ivor would see to that.

Ivor was the only passenger on the private flight. He had his instructions. Ramsay Smythe and his team were staying on to work on the financial details. The plane would go back for them. Despite his experience of luxury over the past few years, he still felt a twinge of Calvinist guilt at being cosseted, alone in space, with only the pilot and co-pilot between him and eternity. He reached into the mini-bar and helped himself to a glass of mineral water, dictated a few letters into his pocket memo, including one to Lord Shand on the proposed shape of the new party political broadcast, then he slept.

He awoke as he sensed the plane's descent towards Blackbushe. Reluctantly he reached for the folder of action papers that the day's negotiations had forced him to neglect. He skimmed through them. Nothing that wouldn't wait, except the *Telegraph* profile. A jokey note from his hyper-efficient secretary, Deborah, was attached to it: '*Mostly old hat . . . Few nasty truths I can spot . . . she didn't ask me for my views*' (three exclamation marks followed) '*. . . but not too bad.*'

Had Deborah's views about him been forced out of her — any freely expressed ones would have been considered a gross act of betrayal — they would have been largely complimentary. For her, a thin and rather shapeless unmarried woman in her early forties, he was unobtainable, and therefore she kept that side of him out of her mind. But she would still have described a personally agreeable and vibrant employer whose eyes were his most striking physical feature, whether they were looking at or through you. Despite his dangerous reputation, he had a sociable charm and attentiveness that appealed particularly to women. He listened as well as he talked; listened and was seen to listen. But he had a low boredom threshold, and eventually it showed. That, as much as anything else, had created the several enemies that he had. He was a man who knew that first judgements of people took a lot of shifting and he was always alert to the effect he had on others. To Ivor, self-presentation should be economical but immaculate because everyone, cynic and non-cynic alike, reacted to image, was affected by it, until sufficient time had passed for maturer judgements to prevail. Deborah would have summed up her employer as someone who exuded that imperious aphrodisiac which was the self-confidence of a man of influence.

Ivor skimmed the article with a remote feeling of apprehension, though to the outside world he had little about which to feel vulnerable. He was perceived as hard, even vicious; seldom did he stop to admit, even to himself, that deep inside was a hidden matrix of small insecurities. The woman who had written the article had been persistent in trying to interview him. He presumed she must be young, judging by her perseverance and the number of exclamation marks that she, like Deborah, kept using to make her point. She had strained his secretary's customary sangfroid by her failure to take no for an answer; the guardian of his strict ordinance of privacy had just managed to remain civil, explaining that he was unavailable for interview, that he never talked on the record to the press, that he never discussed himself, that in any case he was abroad, was in conference, was on holiday – this on the third or fourth telephone call. On one occasion Ivor had been standing right next to her in the apartment that doubled as his office in an anonymous mansion block in Victoria. Deborah had stone-walled like a mason.

To satisfy her editor, the journalist had resorted to what most of her ilk did: it was a scissors and paste amalgam of old press cuttings, padded with gossip and hearsay . . . and exclamation marks. He recognized many of the phrases, the old clichés wheeled out once again. Even the photograph, under the headline 'Power Broker for the next Millennium', was several years out of date. It wasn't that the profile was inaccurate. He never rejected undeserved praise and was flattered by the repetition of stories of his successes, including a straight lift from another recent piece in the Telegraph about how he had helped manipulate the party conference and bring the right wing into prominence. It was all there about his impressive client list, his female conquests.

Somewhat exaggerated on the latter. Not so many. Not quite so many.

He read rapidly, spotting how the journalist had also drawn heavily on an old 'Insight' profile. 'Middle class teachers as parents . . . from an undistinguished West of Scotland town . . . a minor public school . . . a scholarship to Oxford where a good second in PPE had set him on the inevitable but grubby road to a career in politics or perhaps journalism. Even then,' the article suggested, and here came the plagiarized phrases from the clipping file, 'he suffered fools badly . . . hated working under anyone . . . wanted to be his own man.'

Was it really true, Ivor wondered as the aircraft touched down on the Blackbushe runway, that he 'was reluctant to compromise'? Was it true that he had 'deliberately shunned the posturing route of all aspiring young politicians and struggling journalists who had had to sell their integrity, their beliefs, their ideals, for a front-page lead or a few extra votes at the hustings'? It hadn't been like that. But it would do for the history books. He read on.

'Dr Mark Ivor needed to know where he was going and how government worked, so after completing his PhD at Harvard, he sat the Civil Service Administrative exams and passed interviews and syndicate tests with flying colours. Graduating effortlessly into the Treasury, he spent a full ten years, with a two-year secondment to the Cabinet Office, working on budget forecasting and departmental estimates, before ending up in that crucial position of economic influence, as the Private Secretary to the Financial Secretary. There,' readers who had lasted that long were told, 'he learned about the often devious mechanisms of governmental power-broking and worked long hours negotiating with departmental budget controllers. He became the key arbiter between his brilliant fellow Treasury civil servants and their less gifted political masters. He now lived among the sort of politicians who had so much ambition in their blood that it would only be removed by embalming fluid . . .' From where, Ivor wondered, had the young journalist stolen that phrase?

The Beechcraft taxied to a stop. The co-pilot appeared and opened the door. Ivor folded the newspaper. He would read the rest later. There would be no surprises. It would be gossip all the way, those traditional journalistic substitutes for facts.

On his drive into London he brooded on the one thing that had jarred, the sentence that 'he would go to any lengths in his desire to wield power . . . that the ends justified the means, that this motivated him above all else.' How wrong! Almost libellous. He never went to extremes; extremes caused problems, created crises rather than solved them, brought self-destruction on the perpetrators. Nor was he after power. He wanted influence, the ability to play people, to get them to do things they did not necessarily want to do. He liked working without force or deceit, by subtly persuading others that certain courses of action were in their own best interests. That's why he was enjoying getting Lord Shand into Downing Street, into the Prime Minister's confidence. He enjoyed operating behind the scenes, never on a floodlit stage. When he was forced to think about it, his view of himself was as a facilitator, a lobbyist, a negotiator, an arbitrator and only occasionally as a power-broker. He hated being defined in print, which was why he never gave interviews and avoided being quoted. The first rule of politics was that public statements had to be justified later; they led to rigid positioning; they removed flexibility in negotiation. That was his advice to clients; he stood by it for himself. That and a bit of mystery, keeping the other side guessing, was crucial in the influence game. He put the article out of his mind. If that was the worst the press could say . . . But at that stage Ivor knew nothing of the painstaking enquiries of the unpleasantly determined Mr Fred Cree.

Even if he had known where to look, where the evidence once had been, Fred Cree would not have been able to find it. The small town newspaper that had carried the story had long since ceased publication. Later, sometime at the end of the sixties, all its records had been incinerated. The two or three bound copies in the local West of Scotland libraries each had, if anyone had bothered to look through those long-forgotten tomes, one page of one particular day's edition removed sometime in the past by a young man determined that nothing in print would be there for future researchers to uncover. The police file on the accident, there was perhaps still a police file, would have lain buried in a cellar full of many more important archives. There was just one copy of the press cutting, brown and fading, in a sealed envelope buried at the back of a file in Mark Ivor's safe.

Even Ivor would have taken time to find it. A few forgotten column inches. A photograph of an older, bearded man. The story of an accident of a youth and his father hillwalking, and about the son having to run for miles for help when his father had slipped over the cliff ledge. If he had found the article Fred Cree would still never have guessed at what motivated the boy, now the man, and what drove his deep-seated need to succeed. Even if he had discovered that the father had not died but lived long in a vegetative state, alive but not alive, in a house for incurables, unvisited and unloved, but still exerting a heavy black power on the son. Long after the eventual death and an unattended funeral, the shadow remained.

Ivor's self-imposed limits on how ethically to play things had first been seriously undermined several months earlier at a lunch with Ramsay Smythe at Wiltons in Jermyn Street. It was late July. He remembered they had sat in one of the panelled mahogany alcoves, facing each other across the starched tablecloth. Generous plates of smoked salmon with meanly sliced brown bread and butter were consumed amid the low tones of their conversation. A waiter in a long white apron appeared, briefly and remote, to pour the Sancerre.

Ramsay Smythe had long been among his best clients. More honestly, he was one of the best payers. He telephoned infrequently for a word of advice, for a letter of recommendation, for a slant on a useful contract. Otherwise Ivor had been required to keep him informed on certain aspects of government legislation particularly as it affected Eastern European trade. The Ramsay Smythe account was a nice little earner. Yet Ivor had always been uneasy about it, not only because it was so highly profitable for so little work but also, more importantly, because he knew so little about his client. Ignorance always made him cautious. And the money he was being paid might just turn out to be a substantial set of handcuffs for some future service. Recently all that had changed: the workload in the run-up to the bid for the Sigmont Corporation was enormous. But he still knew too little about his client.

There are always questions asked and few answered about a certain type of self-made man. The world is less curious about inherited wealth. You've got it and that's all there is to it. Ramsay Smythe fell somewhere in between. He was, if external trappings were anything to go by, very wealthy indeed, running his own private Beechcraft and with houses in Mayfair, Gloucestershire and New York. He had spoken unguardedly once about having been left a legacy by a rich relative, but the source of such real wealth must have been elsewhere. One answer had to be Eastern Europe, particularly Romania where, long before the collapse of the Ceauşescu regime, he had spent a disproportionate amount of his time.

A more immediate problem Ivor always had with Ramsay Smythe was over his appearance. This was particularly high-lighted in a hyper-conservative setting like Wiltons. He had a huge shaved head like some villain in a James Bond movie, or some First World War German officer, an unfortunate image further embellished by an indeterminate foreign accent. He was of an age that would have justified his throw-away claim to have earned his spurs in some long-forgotten anti-Communist East European uprising, but the whole effect, even when he was being as amusing and charming as he could be, was distinctly offputting. The old *Fawlty Towers* warning 'Don't mention the war' became an impossible game of 'Don't look at the bald dome'. As a result, when he was with Ramsay Smythe, Ivor untypically spent most of his time staring at his plate, his notes, or into space.

His client was a man who kept a low profile, usually avoiding such fashionable restaurants. He was known to a few City men as a pre-eminent fixer of East—West commercial deals, but that was that. Photographs in his wallet, by contrast, indicated a pleasant, domestic life, a dumpy wife and two adolescent children who lived in the country; she had never been around when Ivor had been present.

Their low-key, matter-of-fact meetings until now had always been at his Green Park apartment or at the same corner table at a very simple little Italian restaurant on the Pimlico Road. This was an altogether different occasion. The bombast and stress level were high.

'You know how many bloody billions this Sigmont deal is worth?' The accent blended badly with the subdued Wiltons setting.

'Tell me.'

'It's private. Even to you. Peter Maltby's being bloody awkward. As the minister responsible in the Department of Industry, we told him in confidence, out of courtesy. Now he's threatening to refer it.'

'I think —'

'Let me finish. Talk when I ask you to talk. If he does that, we're stuck for at least another year. Know how much that'll cost me?'

Ivor looked across at his companion, his expression camouflaging a rapidly accelerating concern. As Ramsay Smythe ladled salmon into his huge mouth, an errant smudge of brown bread and butter stuck messily to his lower lip.

'I pay you to sort out this type of thing. Go pull some strings. Or are you too busy playing around with Shand and the party?' His client stared at Ivor, waiting for him to blink.

'Other people are involved. It's not just Maltby —'

'Excuses . . . Look, I want real pressure put on him. The real stuff.' The breadcrumb on the lip danced up and down in irritation.

'Which is?'

Ramsay Smythe lowered his voice. 'A whiff of character assassination.'

'That's not my style, I'm afraid.'

'Afraid, eh!' his client mimicked. 'I know more about you and your ethics than you think. I'm not talking about sex, women, mistresses . . . that sort. Rumour has it that, unlike most MPs, Maltby's happily married. No. I want to increase the pressures on him. I know about the man. He was in property too, and real estate dirt tends to stick like dog droppings on your shoe.'

'I'm listening,' said Ivor. He felt increasingly uneasy.

'Pressure. That's what I want. He's doing a poor job at the Department. Everyone realizes that. He's from the Brogan school, blocking the right wing, Shand and the rest, getting a fair crack with your friend the PM.'

'I advise caution.'

'Caution!' Ramsay Smythe exploded. 'Whose side are you on? Maltby, for all his left-of-centre pretensions, is an arch snob. He sneers at people like me. That upper-class bray. No. It's time for a Cabinet reshuffle. Get a stalwart like Alexander in his place, and that would be very good news for the bid, and for your fee. And give the party more balance. I know Alexander. Been my guest at the Wimbledon finals. So, go to it.' The breadcrumb, damp and disgusting, fell off onto the tablecloth.

'I'll look into it.'

'Look into it? There's no time to look. Drop your other poncing commitments. Like do it bloody today, or I'll take my trade elsewhere.'

'True, Number Ten aren't happy with him.' Ivor tried to keep cool. 'But the PM doesn't want a reshuffle right now. Move Maltby, and you've got to have the musical chairs bit. The party conference is just over the horizon.'

'I know all that, Ivor. Look: go see bloody Peter Maltby. Tell him how many jobs my bid will create.'

'I'll get that message to him.'

'Tell him,' Ramsay Smythe's voice dropped low, 'if he doesn't, then there's a nasty Romanian secret about him waiting to ooze out of the woodwork. I have good sources in Romania. There's a lot of dirt hidden in the old *Securitate* files about some quite important people over here. Including Maltby. I'm of the Jimmy Hoffa School, Ivor. I do to others what they do to me, only worse.'

'Are you serious?' Ivor had laughed, despite himself.

'Never more so.'

'What secret?'

'Extremely unpleasant. I want you to get the proof.'

'That's blackmail.' Ivor paused. 'How can I –?'

'Don't be so prissy, Ivor, it's the facts of bloody life. You, above all, should realize how lonely it is on top of integrity mountain.'

'This one isn't for me.'

'You're serious? My turn to ask.' His whole shaven head appeared to redden. '"*Government minister was on Ceauşescu's payroll*" would make a good headline even though that Commie's long dead and buried. The past can haunt very effectively. There's someone I want you to see.'

Ivor tried to play for time. 'For the party's sake then, the PM is worried . . . I might just . . .'

'However you dress it up for your conscience, *Dr* Ivor,' sneered Ramsay Smythe. 'But ring this man now. Here's his phone number.'

He recalled how unwilling he had been, but he had, nonetheless, rung the number Ramsay Smythe had given him, which had led him to a gaunt, dilapidated building close by Leicester Square. After the prolonged and sullen dampness, the rain had suddenly found strength and slammed down, washing rivulets of grime from the windows, streaking the once-white sills. Outside, under a low, leaden sky, Charing Cross Road was as drab as it could be, the detritus of the littered weekend swilling in the gutters or being pounded into grey slime by passing traffic.

Ivor stared disapprovingly around the bare waiting room. It lacked even the faded quality of some run-down doctor's surgery.

Paint peeled from the walls where a past water leak had blistered and rotted the plasterwork. The wooden chairs and the lopsided table were covered by a film of untroubled dust. It was not reassuring. But he did not have to wait long. Walt Tesco, private investigator, breezed in almost immediately, exuding a generous twin dose of seedy bonhomie and halitosis. He was small and round, compressed into an ill-fitting suit and rumpled shirt that was fastened round the folds of flesh at his neck by a black tie that might just be a clip-on. To make up for it, behind the pebble glasses and the unmemorable button nose, Tesco's eyes sparkled, matching a smile of brown, stained teeth.

His office, into which Ivor was ushered, was cluttered beyond reason with files, printouts and old newspapers. In one corner an antique wooden filing cabinet spewed papers from every drawer and crevice. On the walls, as if they had been pinned to camouflage the damage caused by the same water that had sullied the waiting room, an erratic line of framed and browning photographs of unidentifiable groups of smiling people stared out through the grime. What the hell was he doing here? This wasn't his style – nor Ramsay Smythe's.

Tesco brushed assorted junk from a chair to allow him to sit down. He settled himself opposite and peered at him through the piles of paperwork on his desk. To one side, a large cardboard box revealed the evil-looking remains of a long-abandoned take-away pizza. On the other, incongruously, was a book on the anti-Ceauşescu revolution in Romania.

Their conversation began uneasily.

'What are you looking for?'

'Mr Ramsay Smythe asked me to . . .'

'Ah . . . him. I might have guessed.'

'You have some information.'

Tesco laughed. 'I have lots of information. It's how I manage to eat.'

'From Romania.'

'Ah . . . that stuff. Yes I have some files.'

'How much do you cost?'

'Ramsay Smythe never worries about that.' Tesco paused and beamed. 'Big fish?' he asked.

'Big fish,' responded Ivor uneasily.

'Then big money, of course. Now, tell me who.'

That was back in July. Had he known then how things would be working out now, in early December, Dr Mark Ivor would have been far from relaxed. The strains of the suicide, the bomb and the party conference had blown over and were forgotten in a public life of short memories. But the hero of war-torn Beirut, Fred Cree, was still on the trail. He walked into his editor's office one morning just before the daily strategy meeting.

'Mark Ivor: I've got him.'

'Yes,' said the editor without looking away from the computer screen on his desk.

'He's also retained by the Ramsay Smythe Consortium.'

'As reported very fully in yesterday's business pages.'

'I've traced a man called Walt Tesco. A bit of cash and he talked. Small-time fixer, with access to the Romanian material. Ivor set the minister up via that MP, Smedley, because the minister was trying to refer the Ramsay Smythe bid for the Sigmont Corporation.'

'And then the Prince of Wales and the Archbishop of Canterbury got involved . . . Look, Cree, I'm not interested in bloody conspiracy theories.'

The editor still did not look at the other man.

'This could be important.'

The editor stood up slowly and at last faced the other man. 'Look, Cree. That suicide is history. The Ramsay Smythe Consortium bid is strictly an ongoing business story. You failed to deliver on the Middle East defence —'

'We ran two days —'

'Of scissors and paste agency material.'

'I tell you —'

'No. I tell you. We have a serious political vacuum in this country. A cypher as a Prime Minister, some strange advisers floating around Downing Street, a non-existent Opposition, falling circulation figures, proprietor breathing down my neck, and, oh yes . . .' The editor paused as he suddenly remembered something. He reached over and shuffled through some papers in his in-tray. He pulled out a sheet of figures and thrust it towards Cree.

'Your last three months' expenses.'

Cree went white.

'I was putting off talking to you while you kept out of my way.'

'If there's any problem, Kevin, I'm sure I can explain –'

'One problem . . . ten problems. The Finance Department have been through these receipts like effing ferrets. Bills for hotels never stayed in, plane tickets. Was this an effing family holiday or something? On your business credit card – Jesus . . . A meal for four at Langan's and the restaurant has no trace –'

'I can explain. I –'

'Don't bother. Don't bother at all. Just clear your desk. Like in the next hour. We'll deduct any money owing from your final pay slip.'

The editor sat down and turned his full attention to his computer screen.

Dr Mark Ivor was only tangentially responsible for Fred Cree's abrupt sacking from the *Independent*. But with a man like Cree, a deep and bitter intent festered and grew from these small beginnings.

Around sixty people packed the small conference room at the Edinburgh hotel, an unprepossessing setting of chipped gilt surrounds and tired hessian wallpaper. Dr Mark Ivor had deliberately asked for it instead of a much larger reception suite; there was nothing worse than talking to a half-empty hall. The main CBI meeting had adjourned; this was one of the fringe symposia and his audience consisted mainly of public affairs specialists, media fixers and their ilk. Over-earnest, mainly young men with a scattering of women, all seated behind green baize-covered tables as if ready, like some school class, to take down everything he said. The chairman introduced him; a spatter of applause greeted him as he stood up to speak. He did not work this sort of group often but his reputation was high and the turnout was a reflection of his scarcity value.

He knew how to catch the audience's attention with educated wit rather than elaborate jokes. He used apparently confidential anecdotes to illustrate how he worked the corridors of power; in reality he gave away no secrets. He explained the spin doctor's techniques for manipulating the legislature, lobbying senior civil servants, playing the media, influencing opinion-formers.

'There are lots of ways of trading favours without straying,' he argued. 'You can ply your trade and make it known what you know without diminishing your reputation for discretion. Let people down by talking too much and you're out. Look at the way the political parties are being packaged in the run-up to the general election. Again and again you'll see that the image of the party leaders wins out over mere questions of policy. Remember Talleyrand: he argued how shocked the electorate would be if they knew by what second-rate men and women nations are ruled. It's all to do with mirrors: the many media reflections of individual political leaders build them up, give them a status way beyond their real competence. Most of those we see nightly on TV are puppets of their image handlers; they're trained to smile nice, look nice, shake hands convincingly, and read their speeches well. Look how, with Ronald Reagan, they made a president out of a B-movie actor. Look how Bell, Reece and the others made the lady from Grantham into a great Prime Minister. Look how they failed with Kinnock. You've got to start with some decent raw material. Remember Laurence Olivier's remark: "If you can fake sincerity you can fake anything".'

At the end of his talk he got enthusiastic applause and a host of questions. A young lady stood up to complain: she was shocked by his cynicism. Ivor should know that politics wasn't really like that. Politicians were there to do their best, to try to right wrongs, get the world to be more humane, more efficient. It was they, not the faceless spin doctors in smoke-filled rooms, who really made the country tick. Ivor had the majority of his audience with him when he answered her question with not a trace of mockery, demonstrating her naivety without putting her down. 'Politics is like acting. But politics is about the only profession for which no training is required. That's why it's the highly expert stage managers, directors, scriptwriters and prompters, who actually set the agenda and win or lose the political fight.'

Questions over, the meeting broke up. Coffee was served in an ante-room. People came up to Ivor to congratulate or to carp. He had provoked a lot of controversy. He looked at his watch: he had an hour to kill before catching the shuttle back to London. He would stroll along Princes Street, perhaps find a bookshop. There was a new book out on the way Britain was said to work, a latter-day *Anatomy of Britain*. He'd heard he was mentioned several times.

As he was leaving, a fair-haired young man he'd noticed in the audience came up and introduced himself.

'Rick Maclean. I enjoyed your talk.' His voice had a strong Scottish edge.

'Thank you. I must —'

'I've been working with CVT — the parliamentary lobbyists.'

'Good company. If you'd excuse me —'

'If you'd give me a moment, Dr Ivor, I could walk with you. I won't keep you long. I want you to give me a job. I think I could help you.'

'I'm not an employer,' Ivor responded curtly as they emerged together into the street.

'I know.'

'I work alone,' he stressed, turning to look at Maclean. Medium height, well turned out, he had a chirpy, almost cheeky approach.

'The best way, in your job, Dr Ivor.' Maclean spoke for effect.

'So?'

34

'You want some back-up, I guess. Research. That sort of thing?'

'I use the Henley people when I need . . .'

Ivor walked rapidly down Frederick Street and turned into Princes Street, jostling in and out amid the crush of shoppers, with Maclean making every effort to keep beside him. To the south, Edinburgh Castle towered, gloomy and very grey.

'I'd pay my way very soon.' Maclean shone with an ambition only just moderated by a natural charm. Ivor was flattered by the young man's persistence.

'Send your CV.'

'I have it here.' Maclean whipped out a white envelope and handed it over.

'Ten for determination.'

'I thought if I didn't strike —'

'All right. I'll call you. But I promise nothing.' They paused among the throng of people on the pavement, shook hands briefly, then went their separate ways.

4

Everybody liked Amanda. She was always being told how popular she was, how reliable, how patient a friend. She failed to see herself in that light: she was impatient with stupidity, got irritated at being used, thought malicious thoughts. But she was good at keeping these things to herself, which was why everybody liked her. She was a good-looking rather than pretty young woman, well turned out, with a sharp clothes sense and lots of poise. Tall, with clear, alive eyes and rich brown hair, she had a quick wit and easy style that had her in constant social demand. Without trying to, men noticed her: perhaps it was the way she tended to stand, shoulders thrown back, breasts and body thrust slightly forward, not provocative but almost so. She had an unhappy history of being attracted to unsuitable drifters, the less rather than more organized men that came into her life.

Right now she felt particularly unlikeable. She was also annoyed, blaming herself for her latest boyfriend's abrupt decision to walk out. Yet she was beginning to realize that Paul's departure was a relief. He had rung later, tersely announcing that he would pick up his things at the weekend. Ten months was a long time: three big, untidy rooms of accumulated mess and memories. While she liked to think her emotions were under control, she could not face him, so she left him to vacate the Pimlico flat on his own, and drove down to Oxford to stay with her mother for the weekend.

Home offered no respite. The sight of the big red-brick house with its overgrown garden, where she had played so happily as a child, failed to arouse any emotion other than a vague gloom.

Her childhood had been a Sunday supplement one, of Habitat stripped pine and dried flowers, all very comfortable if lacking in much emotional warmth. Her adolescence had been equally peaceful and usually happy; she had done well at school and later at York University where she had studied modern languages and fallen in love at least twice. Now, at twenty-nine, she had a lucrative City job with a German bank, her small flat in Pimlico, and, until a day or so ago, a steady boyfriend and tenant. She lived well, travelled a lot and had a good social life. Everybody liked Amanda.

It was fortuitous, if unhappy, that she was there when it happened. She was, in a way, the catalyst. When her academic father had died a few years earlier, it was as if a lid had been lifted off her mother's emotions and temperament. Now she found her at her most stressed, about life in general and money worries in particular. She was also, difficult though it was for Amanda to admit it, drinking heavily. The family house was too big and expensive now, yet her mother could not bear to exchange it for something smaller. Amanda's suggestion of taking in lodgers, students, or letting off part of it, was greeted with complaint and derision. Amanda argued the practicalities of coming to terms with altered circumstance. This caused her to be branded as heartless and only concerned with herself, a stinging parental antidote to the perfect reputation in which she was held elsewhere. A further attempt to reason led to her mother storming out to prune the roses, and slipping on a wet flagstone, falling, knocking herself out and breaking a hip in the process. Doctors and ambulances came and went, followed by long waits in municipal hospital corridors. Amanda threw off any feelings of guilt that she might have contributed to the accident. Her mother, when she came round, had forgotten the quarrel and had too much present pain to think about the immediate past.

After a bleak announcement from an overworked registrar that her mother's convalescence would, because of her age, take several months, Amanda retired to the family home to shut it up until it was needed, to throw out left-over food, to hide valuables and cover up the better pieces of furniture. She worked methodically from room to room. The last one she came to was her father's study. A patina of dust and neglect dressed the books, the papers and other surfaces; it was a room little used since his death. Her mother worked at the kitchen table when she was paying bills or dealing with her correspondence; perhaps it still carried too many memories. By that time it was late in the evening and Amanda was tired. She gave up dusting and turned to browsing, rifling her way through the drawers of her father's big partners desk that stood by the window. She took things out, glanced through them, then returned them carefully to their rightful place. Eventually she came to the sealed brown paper package that lay carefully concealed in the bottom left-hand drawer.

The following story, under the headline 'Right-Wing Pan-European Links Strengthened', appeared in the Daily Telegraph on Tuesday 13th, written by its political correspondent Andrew McBride.

> On arrival back in London late last night from his extensive European tour, noted party hardliner Lord Shand denied that he had been meeting exclusively with right-wing leaders in the five countries he had visited. 'I met social democrats, socialists, former communists, military and trade unions leaders, and, because they exist and we have to keep an eye on and possibly deal with them in the future, some extreme right-wing figures,' Lord Shand angrily told waiting reporters. 'Britain has to cope with world leaders as they are, not what we would like them to be,' added Lord Shand in an exclusive interview with the Telegraph later. (See p. 19.) 'Nationalism is the new problem of the age. We have to be ready to adjust our thinking, our diplomacy, our attitudes, in the new, post-Cold War era. To ignore the new nationalists, call them neo-fascists if you will, would be the utmost folly.' Lord Shand added that he would be reporting on his trip direct

to the Prime Minister and to the Foreign Secretary.

Despite Lord Shand's denials, our own foreign corre-spondents and Reuters confirm that Lord Shand met rep-resentatives of the Russian National League, the Serbian Freedom Party, and the Italian Neo-Fascists in the course of his extensive tour.

He watched the sweat being kleenexed from the man's brow. The make-up girl knew the signs of a flooder, and dusted on a helping of talcum powder before darting back into the shadows. The studio arc lights were already up. The warning indicator on top of the TV camera shone red.

Ivor missed nothing as the taut-skinned, once pretty blonde gave a curt, empty smile. He noticed how ridiculously long her painted fingernails were – too long for good breeding, for fashion, for physical work, for lovemaking. Not that she was there for any of these things. Her role as interviewer was to extract infor-mation, to lure the MP into getting things wrong, losing his cool, making a fool of himself.

They had reached the studio down a decaying alleyway off Old Compton Street. The entrance was next to a tacky strip club, with stairs winding down to the semi-respectability below. As they waited in the garish, poster-hung reception area, Ivor's client, Alan Francis MP, joked: 'Great location. I can use this place as an excuse if the *News of the World* catches me out visiting the girls or shop-ping for exotic porn.' Ivor smiled emptily. Francis was the sort of man who might need such a story, judging from the way he leered at the pretty receptionist who had showed them to the studio.

The face-to-face began effortlessly. Pleasantries were exchanged, reminiscences swapped, well-rehearsed anecdotes retold. Ivor relaxed. A lot had happened over the last week. Maybe he should prune back a bit, cut out one or two fringe clients. The Ramsay Smythe bid, getting Lord Shand accepted by the PM, his other top-flight clients all clamouring for his attention . . . What was he doing stuck here with tedious old Alan Francis MP? It might be a waste of time, but . . .

Ivor acquired his clients with care. He let them select him. 'Reputation has to be weaned, manipulated, cosseted, fed with care. The shelf-life of reputation is insecure and uncertain.' That was the marketing line he used with them. Then he would add: 'A hand wrongly played, just for a moment, can cause you to waken to headlines that scream that your sell-by date has passed.' The suggestion: 'That's why you need me,' was hardly uttered. It spoke for itself.

Ivor's reputation currently rode high. People came to him with problems, unfulfilled ambitions, wounded reputations. They were often told, with polite regret, that his list was full. Yet, in his candid moments, he would admit that to talk of a 'list' was less than exact. He had a core of continuing clients among whom he apportioned most of his working time. He had a fluctuating selection of others, transients and one-off-ers, as he called them, who would ring him, fax him, ask for help and advice on an unpatterned, casual basis. Many of these he neither charged nor would think of charging for his advice, for his lobbying, for his influence. That way he built up his credits, his call-back ability for past favours, his rain-checks for future need. That way his public reputation as a spin doctor, an *éminence grise* without the Cardinal's robes, had been built. He was perceived as a one-man think-tank, a tester of ideas, someone who saw the grey reality between the rigid blacks and whites of commercial or party political dogma. In Dr Mark Ivor's trade, his image was his one and only real asset. He was the producer, director and promoter, never the up-front actor in the play.

Ivor pulled himself out of his reverie at the first warning sign. Alan Francis MP had been having it much too easy. The interviewer, for all her brittleness, had done her homework.

'You say, Mr Francis, that you are opposed to further governmental controls on pollution levels, that it should be left to companies and industries themselves to face up to their responsibilities?'

'That's right.' He smiled confidently.

'But, Mr Francis,' the interviewer's smile had gone, 'as recently as May 1993 you were saying that state regulation was essential. In a speech to your constituency's conservation group –'

'Different times. Different climate. A lot has happened since then.'

'Different audience, Mr Francis? You've changed your stance a hundred and eighty degrees, wouldn't you say?'

'Rubbish. If you don't mind me saying so.' Bands of colour were building up on the victim's cheeks. The powder on his forehead was having a hard time mopping up the rivulets of sweat. 'The degree of responsibility demonstrated by these industries has been increasing steadily. By and large they have proved –'

'I'm sorry,' the interviewer interrupted, 'but is it true, Mr Francis, that in the latest register of MPs' interests you are listed as a consultant to Legate Union, one of the largest chemical companies in Western Europe? Legate, on present count, has fifteen separate major legal suits against it for violation of German and French environmental pollution regulations.'

'What the . . . Exactly what are you implying?'

The MP, heavily flushed, was now poised on the edge of his seat as if ready to walk out. 'I resent most strongly the suggestion –'

'If I may say so, Mr Francis, all I asked was a simple question. Are you, or are you not –'

'To suggest that my legitimate and declared work for Legate Union has anything to do with any changed attitude . . . what I am currently arguing is that our stand on pollution controls –'

'Changed attitude – your words, Mr Francis.' The interviewer smiled, ice-cold. Francis stood, furious. 'Damn you,' he breathed.

The woman interviewer smiled demurely down at her long painted fingernails. Another man was flat out on the doormat of her life.

Ivor stood up rapidly. 'OK. Cut. Cut, I said. That's all for now, team,' he shouted abruptly. 'We'll take ten and do it again.'

He walked over to the MP and took him by the shoulder. 'Anger is the enemy of persuasion, remember. We'll play that

41

back. Thank God it was only a training session. You scored nought out of twenty that time round.'

'Bloody bitch. She provoked me.'

'Which is precisely what you should not allow yourself to be. Which is precisely why you hired me for this training session. Now let's have some coffee and talk through what went wrong.'

The two men moved through to an ante-room and sat down facing each other. The pretty receptionist brought in two mugs of coffee. The MP gradually cooled down. He looked depressed.

'No harm done. We're here to sort this type of thing out.' There was a heavy silence. Then Ivor continued: 'First you've got to learn to sit properly. When you look at the video playback you'll see you were all tensed up, sitting forward with your head buried in your shoulders. The trick is to sit on the tail of your jacket, to keep it down. Otherwise you look as if you don't have a neck. Then, sorry, but you were showing an acre of hairy leg . . . nasty gap between trouser and stocking top. Very distracting on television.'

'Anything more?'

'Watch your hand movements. They're irritating. And the sweat. You'll see it highlighted on the video playback. That tie – more sober perhaps?'

'Did I get anything right?'

'Plenty. You looked straight at the interviewer or the camera. You are coherent –'

'I don't call what I said coherent.'

'Too heated at the end, that's all. You've got to learn to say what *you* want, not what these professionals want to ask. Remember: you're not invited along to show up the superior qualities of the interviewer. So get a few punchy sound bites out that can't be cut or edited. You'll never be allowed long enough on the box to be boring. Keep it short and simple.'

The MP sat brooding. 'That bitch threw me.'

'She's good. I ought to pay her more. I've seen her destroy people who have spent half their lives in front of the cameras. In real life you won't get them being quite so direct. They're too worried about libel or slander, or about you knowing their Editor-in-Chief so well that you can get them sacked afterwards.'

'Good thing too.'

'Work up a number of catch phrases to deal with awkward questions like the one today. Remember Denis Healey. When he got a difficult one he'd say "Now, I think the question you are trying to ask me is . . ." He usually got away with it. Another version is: "The question you should be asking me is . . ." This implies that the interviewer is a prize fool and doesn't understand what he's on about.'

'Perhaps I should take up some other career.'

'Don't worry. I've got more for you. That was the good news.'

'Yes?'

'The bad news is that you're going to have to work on your sincerity.'

'My what?'

'You heard. Shifty's the word. If you can't fix that you're really out for the count.' Ivor smiled. 'We'll sort it out together.'

'Christ, if I have to fix that as well . . .' the man at last grinned back, 'it'll cost me an arm and a leg. How much d'you say you charge for these training sessions?'

'A lot. But in your case –'

'A lot more?'

'Or not. You see, we're in this game together. That's why it's for free.'

'What game?'

'You're a bit slow today, Alan. It's called playing the PM.'

'You're a bastard,' said the MP slowly. 'A real bastard.' He sounded as if he meant it.

Dr Mark Ivor knew exactly his fee for the interview training session. Alan Francis was, after all, the PM's Parliamentary Private Secretary. That meant even more access at Number Ten.

To prove a point, that evening, he was summoned to Downing Street at short notice. His taxi dropped him off just short of the gates at the end of the street. Pushing past a small group of demonstrators — he was not sure what they were protesting about — he gave his name to the police on duty, who swung back the heavy gate to give him entry. He walked up to the famous door. The short street was deserted except for a huddle of cold-looking press photographers and a TV crew in their barriered media position opposite. As he approached, the duty policeman recognized him, reached up and lightly tapped the brass knocker. The door opened at once.

Civil servants, political advisers and image-makers like Ivor enjoyed working for the Prime Minister for the most direct of all reasons: he was a lesser version of them, a political operator of limited intellectual ability, an adequate user of the system, normally uninspired, unless in a tight corner when he became devious. He had a disciplined civil service and kitchen cabinet team round him who guided him as to how he should act and think. Like many weak men he bore the imprint of the latest mind to influence him. Alan Francis had brought Ivor up to date on the post-Brogan, post-ministerial suicide line-up of these confidants, consultants and cronies, increasingly pre-eminent among whom was the Lord Shand.

He met the peer by chance as the one was going in and the other out. They shook hands warily but politely then Shand unexpectedly took him aside.

'You did well. Everyone is grateful. Particularly Soper, of course. A vicious solution though . . .'

'Thanks. I did very little. She walked right in.'

'What's happened to her?' asked Lord Shand.

'Still awaiting trial in Bangkok, I think.'

'Poor girl. Learnt her lesson, d'you think?'

'I'll find out.' Ivor showed no hint of compassion.

'We should have a talk,' the peer volunteered.

'Whenever you're ready. How was your trip? You got a lot of coverage.'

'A lot of misrepresentation in the media as usual. Suggested I was just meeting right-wing extremists. Utter nonsense.'

'Of course.'

'Which is why I'm here now. Reporting back to the PM as requested.'

Ivor waited and Lord Shand continued, 'I'm not possessive about my relationship with the PM. Teamwork's the thing.' Was Lord Shand protesting too much, Ivor wondered.

'You play the game well,' the peer added.

'I know how he reacts to new people and new ideas, when he needs help and when he'll reject it.'

'The civil servants?'

'I've got a workmanlike, if not close, arrangement with Tim Willis, the Private Secretary and Caanan, the Press Secretary.'

'What about Eugene Blackmore?' Shand referred to the head of the Number Ten Policy Unit.

'Yes. Not bad. They and the Secretary to the Cabinet may not actually revel in my access, but they play along,' Ivor responded. 'They make sure I'm reasonably well briefed. I keep them in the picture. We all recognize the dangers of kitchen cabinets being spawned in Downing Street.'

'We all have to make allowances for the PM's ... er ... irresoluteness.'

'Problem is that, once he has decided on a course of action, finally and unassailably, he's likely to change his mind as soon as you've left him, and some other strong personality arrives to place a different slant on his thinking.'

'A minor defect in Her Majesty's First Minister.'

'So I hang around until the ink is dry on a document or a decision has been made public, and is irreversible.'

'Prime Minister says you're a good listener.'

'I relate to his differing needs and moods. Sometimes he's all business. Nothing personal intrudes. Sometimes it's the reverse.'

'I appreciate your help, Mark.' Lord Shand smiled a thin cold smile. Just then a secretary came in to show Ivor to see the PM. 'Let's get together soon. With Ramsay Smythe perhaps? My club if you like.'

'With Ramsay Smythe, sadly, it's more likely to be at his,' said Ivor whimsically, wondering briefly at why Shand would want to meet his tough client. The two men would be most unlikely allies.

Ivor found Her Majesty's First Minister, Michael Wilson, in a mellow frame of mind, with the anxieties over the recent disasters gradually being replaced by the short-term expediency of dealing with the next day's headlines. With the Private Secretary and two diplomats from the Foreign Office present, they dealt quickly with the business in hand, the redrafting of a major policy speech on Europe, then, as Ivor was about to leave, the PM detained him, offering him a drink in the flat at the top of the house.

The PM was not in a mood for serious matters. 'You people don't realize what it's like. I can't go out and buy a tie. I can't take a tube up to Oxford Street. I can't go into Marks and Sparks to buy myself underpants,' the PM said as they walked upstairs. 'I'm in charge, but at what a price! A prisoner of convention and of security.' Michael Wilson was a small, neat man, well groomed, with a clipped, matter-of-fact way of speaking. There was little side to him: what you saw was what you got.

'What do you do?'

'Ties: I get given hundreds. Every new factory visited, they give me a company tie. Sports clubs, regiments, ships, City Livery Companies. Now underpants: that's more difficult. No one presents me with underpants. Eileen gets me them; and socks. Once or twice when I've been caught short, so to speak, I've asked one of my bodyguards. Can you believe it: a copper buying my underpants? All in the name of security, of course.' The PM laughed and Ivor laughed with him. 'Suits, shoes and shirts: no problem. Tailors come to me. Nobody, especially tradesmen, ever turns down an invitation to come to Downing Street to do a fitting for Her Majesty's First Lord of the Treasury.'

'You pay the same?'

'There's a mark-up, I bet. I used to get all my stuff at the sales.'

Ivor sipped the drink he was offered and gazed around the drawing room. It was well furnished in an impersonal sort of way, the official, unofficial London home of the Prime Minister, yet it lacked that individual contribution which would have made it more than a mere hotel suite. There were a few personal belongings, official photographs, knickknacks and gifts with which he had been presented: those and a couple of lurid paperbacks. The pictures, the furniture, the lamps, all had that cared-for, uncaring look of Government.

'It's lonely.'

'They say that about being at the top.'

'I only need pick up a phone and the place would be swarming with exciting people: artists, TV people, film stars.'

Ivor sat back and waited. It was a moment to listen rather than contribute.

'It's difficult to keep or see friends. They pretend to be the same. I pretend to be the same. They know I'm not. I know I'm not. I turn to those living the same sort of life as I do now. Politicians, civil servants, Party people.'

'We're all in danger of abandoning our friends. Not deliberately. Through neglect, through the pressures of the present, through moving on,' volunteered Ivor.

The PM stood and poured his guest another drink. 'Which is why I value occasions like this, Mark. You're not in any pigeonhole.'

'Thanks. If that's a compliment.'

'You're impartial. You give me advice, for me. No policies to push. And . . . thank you for your help on that . . .' The PM paused. 'Will she be all right? I mean . . . she had it coming, but Bangkok . . .'

'My advice: leave it for the moment. The Thai authorities take drugs very seriously. Remember those two young girls? But in a few months, when things have blown over, I'm sure a deal can —'

'I'm sure you're right. Now that the others, my friends, have gone, you're invaluable. We'll fix the fee. I'll have a word with Rupert Shand.'

'Can I put in a word of warning?'

'Well?'

'The unofficial is never liked by the official. Untidy. It upsets the system.'

'I am Prime Minister. They do what I say.'

'To your face, yes. But they have ways of circumventing.'

'Are you talking about the civil servants?'

'Not so much. They're used to changes, to political appointees, to taking orders.'

'Who then?'

'Whoever currently thinks they have your ear. To them I am a usurper. Dangerous.'

'Shand? Surely not. He's much too grand.'

'We get on OK,' said Ivor cautiously. 'I'm glad he's got your ear. But he's a bit like me. Outsiders on the inside track are disliked.'

'I hear what you say. I want you and Rupert Shand to work together. For me. For the party. For the government. We're all in it together. Aren't we?'

'Of course.' Ivor drained his glass and placed it carefully on the table in front of him.

5

Apart from his secretary, Deborah, there was only one permanent woman in his life. She came with a major drawback. She was unavailable to partner Ivor to theatres and concerts, to Wimbledon, to the Derby or Ascot. She was not a public companion. Those less close to him wondered whether his lone, ageing bachelor status was a cover for something else. Even in these still liberal days, if you were someone who had a closet to come out of, it could do your client list considerable harm.

But normal heterosexual passions Ivor had in plenty. The common problem he had with Fiona Lisbourne was that she was married to someone else. So she missed out on Covent Garden, Glyndebourne and Ascot. She was, however, surprisingly content with discreet opportunities as they arose. Fiona had been greatly assisted in her move to infidelity by her husband, a man of monumental self-importance, a legend in his own mind, a financier who worked in the sort of City broking house where this trait passed largely unnoticed by his peers.

Fiona's arrival on Ivor's stage put an end to a complicated line of conquests to which the *Telegraph* article had referred, particularly the very public affair with a Californian soap opera starlet, which had promoted him, for an unwelcome season, into the Benson and Dempster columns and the raunchier pages of the gutter tabloids.

He first met Fiona as she languished with her pompous spouse at a fortieth-birthday party given by a mutual friend near Henley: a mellow, virginia creeper-covered house set in immaculate grounds close by the Thames. The evening was going as slowly as such long-arranged, well-intentioned occasions often do, and Ivor was on the point of playing his old trick of getting himself summoned away by a phone call to some urgent meeting any-where but at Henley, when he spotted her in a corner of the room, partly screened by an oasis of potted plants. Even from a distance he could hear some man, reciting, to a resigned group of listeners, every well-known cliché about the dangers and chal-lenges of further European integration. As Ivor watched, she stood and left the group, possibly to seek the solace of a drink.

He seldom allowed himself feelings that might get out of con-trol, and had little conscience over his active sexuality. Yet even he was unprepared for the suddenness of it all. Falling in love reveals the inadequacies of past relationships. At first, all he noticed was the close-cropped auburn hair, neatly tapered to the back of her neck. There was little else that was boyish about her, with her high-cheekboned face, her lightly tanned skin, amused, dark eyes, fine nose and full lips, the lower one with just a hint of a pout to it, as if looking for something to press itself against. Of medium height, she was wearing a crisp cream dress with a broad sailor collar that cut away to the front over the glimpse of tender skin and an interestingly heavy bust.

There were, to Ivor, two types of attractiveness in women: serenity and vivacity. Go too far in one direction and there was the chance of dullness; in the other, precocity. In Fiona he was to find an attractive in-betweenness that led him straight to aston-ishing feelings of sensual and intellectual lust. He had to get to know her. Immediately. There and then. It was an emotional imperative.

He noticed the provocative way she cocked her head to one side as if to listen more carefully. He remarked certain vowel sounds, telltale signs of a first language that might not have been English. He stood in her way. They smiled at each other. He introduced himself. It was as easy as that.

'That man's boring for England.'

'That man's my husband.' Her eyes swung briefly back in his direction.

'I meant the subject is boring. European integration is, well . . .'

'Boring. Of course you did.'

'Mark Ivor.'

'How do you do? Fiona Lisbourne.'

'Can I get you something?'

'White wine. Thanks. Mark Ivor? You're the famous spin doctor.'

'Hate the expression.'

'It's what you do?'

'In part.'

'The other parts?'

'This and that.'

'Very informative.'

'Let's go outside.'

'My, that's quick.' She laughed.

'It's a bit sticky in here.'

'So it is. I hardly noticed.' She laughed again, an easy sound he found pleasant and slightly teasing.

'If I'm the spin doctor, what do you do?'

'I grow children. This and that otherwise.'

'And?'

'Picture restoration, freelance. A fair amount for the big galleries. I started out as an artist, then decided I'd be better off saving the greats of the past rather than pretending I was going to be one of the greats of the future. I write about it all — as therapy.'

They were outside by now, on a terrace. It was a soft, damp evening in which lanterns threw down occasional pockets of light on the large garden beyond. A few other shadowy couples chatted around them. In the background were the distant sounds of music and laughter.

'Therapy?' He looked at her questioningly, then, when she did not respond, went on: 'I was about to leave. I got back from Hong Kong this morning.'

'Ah, the jet set. I worked there once. After Germany.'

'Germany?'

'I'm an end-of-the-war child. Father: army. Mother: German. The conflict of my childhood was between the accepted evil of half my race and the retrospective morality of the other.'

'Tough on a child.'

'Yes . . .' She paused before changing the subject. 'How was Hong Kong?'

'Still the same. Drinking a lot of champagne, but not laying down a lot of port.'

She laughed and looked hard at him. 'Maybe I should say I'm glad you didn't leave?'

'Why not?'

'Perhaps I will later. Now tell me how you "spin".'

After the buffet they stood outside once again. It had been raining but now the sky had cleared and the night was mild. Fiona's husband had lapsed into an alcoholic limbo and was parked in a corner taking nothing in. She and Ivor were now concentrating exclusively on each other, having reached the stage where neither of them, for the moment, cared if others noticed.

'A down-to-earth friend of mine believes that physical attraction is caused by low-level electric discharges . . . from people's bodies.'

'Stirringly romantic.'

'Sets up an electro-magnetic field. If the fields match . . .'

'What happens?'

'Er . . . attraction.' Her electro-magnetics were doing strange things to the small hairs down his back. He felt a visceral tightening in his groin: the second flush of lust.

'That's all? Doesn't sound exciting.'

'It can be.'

She shivered slightly.

'Cold?'

'No. Maybe you're having that effect on me.'

She looked across suddenly and gave him a long judicious look.

'My line.' He responded. Her hand was resting on a stone

balustrade in front of her, almost in shadow. As a substitute for further talk, he reached out his hand and placed it on top of hers. She made no attempt to move it. The most difficult step in any relationship, the first, had been taken.

*

Amanda was nothing if not resolute. She knew what she wanted, and, with a few enquiries, she knew where to look. It had been a huge shock finding the brown paper package with the letter from the adoption agency and from the Social Services people. But, above all, it had hit her like a lightning bolt in her chest when she found her birth certificate. Who was this woman who had really given birth to her? Who was this man who had sired her? Who were they that had abandoned her to what she now knew were her adoptive parents? The deceit of it all. She had wept for days. She had confided in no one. Now, with resolution in her heart, she would find them; confront them.

After days of searching, with the help of an agency that specialized in such things, she still drew a blank in tracing her mother. But her father's name was unusual. He was the easy part. His telephone number may have been ex-directory, but she soon knew all about Dr Mark Ivor, from newspaper reference libraries and from his entry in *Who's Who*.

*

At a long-planned dinner with Ramsay Smythe, the stress level was high: the take-over bid was about to be launched. For reasons that were, at first, far from clear to Ivor, a bearded Arab dined with them. The Arab's appearance was as totally dominated by facial hair as Ramsay Smythe's was by the lack of it. A crest of eyelashes over hooded eyes and, below, a moustache like a portcullis, under which food had to be levered to allow him to eat. He had a habit of pulling and twisting one corner of it as if trying to train it into a Hercule Poirot crescent.

The dinner did have a purpose, but that, in keeping with Ramsay Smythe's style, was not revealed until the coffee had been served. Till then the conversation had been sparse. Then Ramsay Smythe reached under the table and produced a small gift-wrapped package. He placed it carefully on the table-cloth and, as if reluctant to touch it more than necessary, pushed it with the back of his fingers in Ivor's direction.

'For you.'

'What is it?'

'Rude to ask. From our friend here. He wants you to have it.'

Ivor knew that gifts were like hooks. His working life had been speckled with incidents of social kindnesses, from invitations to the opera or Wimbledon through to barely concealed back-handers or bribes in the form of offers of free flights or holidays in the West Indies. This was too blatant. As he opened the box, even he was taken aback by the vulgar opulence of the diamond-encrusted Patek Philippe it contained.

'I couldn't possibly –'

'No refusals. This doesn't happen twice. I told our friend about traditional British middle-class hypocrisy, what your first reaction would be.'

'Middle class?' Ivor was stunned.

'Members of the upper and lower classes would take it like a flash. Rise above it. You can pay off your overdraft if you cash it in.'

'I . . .'

'Say thank you.' Ramsay Smythe spoke as if prompting a child.

For once Ivor was at a loss for words. The Arab made his only significant contribution to date. 'I take it as a great compliment that my little gift has pleased.' He followed the remark with what Ivor had to presume, by the creasing of his eyes, was a moustache-camouflaged smile.

An hour later, Ivor, having kept up with the others by consuming one brandy to their three – the Arab had few obvious hang-ups about the consumption of alcohol – was happy that his head was still clear. He sipped black coffee as he considered the strategy menu he was being asked to handle.

'It's massive.'

'So is the fee.'

'We'll have to play the unexpected Arab involvement in your bid for the Sigmont Corporation with care.' Ivor paused. 'Tricky when it breaks.'

'That's for you to handle.'

'I . . . of course.' Ivor hesitated.

'All is above board and legal. Not even palm-greasing; not much, anyway. Just good old-fashioned influence-peddling with your contacts, with ministers, with civil servants, with the City. But . . .' Ramsay Smythe paused and Ivor stared at him. 'But first and foremost with those pre-eminent paragons, the guardians of the people's conscience, the newspaper editors.'

Ivor glanced down at the box containing the Patek Philippe. He sensed another moral dilemma, but it would not trouble him for long.

Close to Ivor's table, the hero of Beirut, Fred Cree, ex-*Independent* and now working on the investigative team of an upmarket tabloid, was entertaining a passably pretty bimbo. An observer might have wondered if, in her spray-on dress, she was too foolish to notice what an unappetizing escort she had, or guessed correctly that she had been bought for the occasion. Her chatter did not even reach the level of small talk but it had not stopped Cree devoting some of his attention to her charms for the fleshy delights of the night to come. There was no harm in a judicious mix of business and pleasure. From time to time he pulled his eyes away from her divine cleavage and watched Ivor. He listened intently. He saw the gift being offered and received, and he stored this nugget at the back of his mind for future use. He knew from the head waiter that the table had been booked by Ramsay Smythe. Of the Arab he could discover nothing. But that did not matter to his colleagues on the business pages when he left his lady long enough to telephone his office. They also got excited at the mention of the Sigmont Corporation, a name that had continually cropped up in what he had overheard of the conversation.

Later, when he and his escort followed the three men to the Peacock's Cage, an exotic nightclub to the north of Berkeley

Square, Cree sighed and reluctantly paid the girl off, sending her home by taxi. He would be able to follow them in but the hirsute Arab had been staring at her all evening and would surely have recognized her. Cree's other worry was whether his new editor would accept the Peacock's Cage prices on a receipt as a legitimate business expense. That would depend on the story he came up with.

A busty, under-dressed hat-check girl, a couple of heavy bouncers and an exorbitant entry fee later and Cree was ushered to a small table in a dimly lit alcove between the bar and the stage. As he arrived, a black girl was rotating her topless assets in front of a mixed audience of middle-aged executives, Middle Eastern visitors and a rather more rowdy bunch of Midlands car salesmen up in London for a conference. He ordered a drink which arrived promptly but not as swiftly as the overblown hostess who advanced on his table and sat down unasked. She looked too experienced. He waved her away and sipped thoughtfully at his watered-down Scotch. 'Never take the first on offer,' he thought, then summoned a hovering waiter and indicated a girl perched on a high stool by the bar. In rapid time the leggy redhead glided over and eased herself into the chair beside him. Cree was uneasy. This was not entirely his scene, but as the redhead, who announced that her name was Michelle and that she came from Yugoslavia, turned out to be passably pretty and with a figure that had, like his earlier escort, been enticingly squeezed into an extremely small black dress, he fondled the idea of making up for lost time. But he also had business to attend to in the shape of discovering what the three men in a darkened cubicle on the far side of the room were discussing.

He began working on Michelle in a way that she immediately understood. Fifty-pound notes, if there are enough of them, will buy anything. In any event, she proved chirpy company, an urchin of a girl with big eyes, theatrically pouting lips and sharp little breasts that from time to time peeked mischievously out of the top of her dress. She needed his money.

In the background, the stage show continued. Stripper

followed stripper, black, tan and white, to be succeeded by a conjurer whose ability to make his lady assistant vanish inside mirrored boxes would have entranced any Sunday School audience.

'You like me?' asked Michelle, acting out her demi-monde role. 'You like give me present? I come home with you? Which hotel you stay?'

'I live here,' said Cree.

'You live London?' Michelle was surprised. Men of Cree's age seldom ran astray on their home patch.

'You married?'

'No. Not married.'

'Lonely.'

'Not much.'

'Why here?'

'Business,' he gestured.

'I lead you 'stray or you lead me 'stray?'

'I'm straying nowhere, but I do want you to do me a favour, Michelle.'

'You are nice man. Best for weeks. Why you come here? Too handsome to come here.'

'You can cut the patter. We're talking business, Michelle. Now see those three men over there? Where's your handbag? Look, if you come from the Yugoslavia that was you probably understand what this is. Now I'm going to switch this little box thing on. You hide it in there – under your handkerchief and these funny packets in silver wrappings . . .' He looked at her for a moment and wondered if she understood and what she would be like in bed. Then he stood up. 'There's lots more if you're careful and get it right.'

'You go? I sorry,' said Michelle. She stood too and whispered in his ear. 'You, I like. I do it.'

'Good. I'll be waiting outside. For as long as it takes.'

Michelle shrugged, turned and disappeared rapidly in the direction of the table of three. 'Come back soon,' she said over her shoulder. 'I make you nice time.'

He moved towards the door. If things went wrong, if Michelle mucked it up, he would be able to get away easily. The hat-check girl appeared, his coat pressed against her bust. Then, as he was leaving, out of the corner of his eye he spotted someone he recognized. Cree's luck was there. The man who had just arrived walked quickly past him. Two giggling hostesses approached and were repulsed. Cree could hardly go back, go closer, to confirm his sighting, see where he was going. He looked like a man with a purpose. The hair, the shape of the head, the glimpse of that fierce profile. What on earth was Lord Rupert Shand doing in a place like the Peacock's Cage?

Later, much later, after his money had bought Michelle as well as the tape, he lay in bed and listened to a poor but understandable recording of four men talking serious business. That was one thing. The story would wait. In the meantime he might as well make a few bob on the share price of the Sigmont Corporation. Pay for Michelle and a lot more besides. He picked up the telephone and rang a young City whiz-kid on his portable phone who he knew would recognize a bargain on a plate.

At Hoare Govett, in the City, a nameless young broker came in very early. It was only seven thirty a.m., but the air hostess with whom he had spent an enjoyable, inventive night had thrown him out of her flat before she left for Heathrow and Miami. As he drove in he gave himself a quick shave with the razor he always kept in his BMW. His shirt would have to do another day. He collected a polystyrene cup of coffee from the machine and switched on the Stock Exchange *Topic* Screen at his desk. The picture flickered, then showed last night's closing prices against the listed stock. He had done an amazingly good deal if the tip was correct.

His phone rang. 'This is Framling from Smith New Court.' The voice was rushed and breathless. 'I have a client looking for three million shares in the Sigmont Corporation. They closed at six five three last night; I'll give you nine pounds.'

The young broker was already frantically at work on his hand calculator. That was, he judged, nearly forty per cent premium on the closing price. He looked at his list of stock held.

'I can give you one and a half million at nine,' he said. 'I may have quite a bit more from a private client.'

'Done,' responded Framling, slamming down the telephone.

Behind him, the young broker saw a senior partner who had just drifted in, straight off the night train and a fishing trip in Scotland. He shouted to him, telling him of the sale of Sigmont stock and the premium. The senior partner moved surprisingly fast. He switched on a nearby screen. The *Topic* figures flashed up.

'Pre-Market trading in Sigmont is heavy.'

'A dawn raid?'

'A full-blown take-over bid. I wonder who? Could be Ramsay Smythe's Consortium, I suppose. There were rumours . . . What other Sigmont stock can we get hold of? It's a shoot to the Gods.'

As he spoke, the bid was confirmed on the *Topic* screen. The offer was at nine two five each. The telephones in the dealing room began to go berserk. It still was not eight a.m. The young broker had a satisfied grin on his face all day. His colleagues put it down to his scoring with the air hostess.

A mere two hundred or so men and a tiny number of women hold all the strings of power, turn all the handles of influence in Britain. They are the people who really matter. In business and social life they all know, meet and interact with each other. They are the Establishment. Ministers, civil servants, newspaper tycoons and the captains and the kings of industry, leaders who, in turn, are made or broken by the spin doctors of life, they set the nation's agenda. The rest follow.

At the heart of this web, more important than any minister, and particularly a weak Prime Minister, sits one man, through whose hands and across whose desk run all the threads. 'Secretary to the Cabinet' does not sound a commanding title. Few people know the job exists, fewer know his name. Only a tiny number know him. He is the all-seeing, all-knowing keeper of the nation's conscience, head of the Civil Service, coordinator of the intelligence services, wielder of supreme patronage, fulcrum of the Establishment. There are few events he is not privy to, few trends he does not identify and monitor. Charming, ruthless, supremely imperturbable, even emollient, Sir Caspar Rudd was a true professional in every respect.

Sir Caspar pushed his way through the green baize door that connects Ten Downing Street with the Cabinet Office and paced his unhurried walk along the corridor to his own rooms overlooking Horseguards Parade.

Seated in an armchair by the window, the other man was waiting. Sir Caspar was tall, with fair, thinning hair and a fresh complexion. The other, of equal height, carried a healthy, expensive tan. There was not an ounce of fat about him, and he looked as he was, a leader of men. He rose easily to his feet as Sir Caspar entered and waited for the other man to speak.

'I don't like it. Not at all. Weak men in power are easy prey for the hawks.'

'And the vultures.'

'Yes.' Sir Caspar sighed. 'I don't want to, but I may have to act,' he said. 'I'll need your continuing help.'

Later, when his visitor had gone, Sir Caspar sat at his desk. In the centre, away from the in-trays and piles of Cabinet briefs and minutes, was a red paper file with *Top Secret & Personal* printed at the top and the bottom. He opened the file and read through the several reports it contained. Some were older, some right up-to-date. The three most important ones read:

Top Secret & Personal

TO: *The Secretary to the Cabinet*

FROM: *Chief, C13*

re: **Brogan**

1. Dr Mark Ivor interrogated by SB over knowledge of Brogan's movements prior to assassination. Interviewee volunteered that it was he, repeat he, who

was meeting Brogan at Victoria Station. Interviewee appeared genuinely shocked. We believe did not know that Brogan had been killed until he returned to his office. (See report ZN 0912/92.) Confirm he had no entry re Brogan in his diary. Only Brogan's office (Ivor's PA ruled out as suspect), No 10 (limited distribution) and Party HQ, Smith Square, had knowledge.

2. *Conclusion*: None of the above relate. We are moving our investigation in other directions as specified, since links in Dublin and Londonderry appear to rule out rogue Nationalist or INLA cell operating on their behalf. (See Iraq/Libya report MI6/19900/FQ/92.)

> *Message ends.*

Top Secret & Personal
TO: *The Secretary to the Cabinet*
FROM: *Chief, C13*
re: **Brogan**

1. Regret still no leads. Reports of untraced operative having come in from East Europe are unsubstantiated. We are now convinced no Irish or other known terrorist groups were involved. There has been no claim of responsibility. No possible or believable motive has been even remotely identified. We are still actively investigating but after this length of time we cannot be optimistic about the outcome.

2. On related subject, Consular report ex Bangkok names woman arrested smuggling drugs as same person we were investigating on Brogan's behalf. She claims she was set up.

> *Source comment:* They always do.
> *Message ends.*

Top Secret & Personal
For Addressee's Eyes Only

TO: *The Secretary to the Cabinet*

FROM: *Chief, C13*

re: **Operation Picnic**

1. Following post-JIC meeting Thursday 14 December, you asked for any additional information on those with access to the PM who may be of interest. You know more than we do whom he sees. You also know, given that his wife seldom leaves the constituency (previous report destroyed as requested), that he has felt very deeply both the loss of Brogan and the suicide of one of the few ministers, Maltby, with whom he felt totally at ease.

2. Apart from his Number Ten staff he increasingly uses Dr Mark Ivor as an adviser. (See Report ZN0912/92 and subsequent reports.) We have checked Ivor out extensively. He has no identifiable political agenda; he is a paid adviser on public relations and works for his clients almost irrespective of their standing. (He has been known to refuse briefs from the Libyan and Iraqi Governments and declined to get involved with an Opposition campaign over Health Service administration, because he said it would be a conflict of interests.) He is believed to be fairly loyal in his dealings with the PM and, despite our best efforts, we have found no trace of his breaking any confidences. Our only concern, as previously stated, is in his dealings with Ramsay Smythe (see reports passim). This is something that should be kept under careful review. He also facilitated and encouraged Lord Shand's access (see previous reports), but may now regret this.

3. As to S's growing influence, he has made no secret of his views. In private, he is even more critical

of what he calls Government 'drift' and its frequent 'consensus politics' alliance with the main opposition parties. His recent speech at the Institute for Economic Affairs was widely interpreted by the media as a bid to 'take over where Thatcher left off'. We were, some years ago, concerned by his links, as with Maltby, with the Ceauşescu dictatorship in Romania (reported in JIC Paper 'Funding from overseas for British political figures (1986–1989)'). Now his much-publicized meetings with extreme right-wing leaders in Western and Eastern Europe have led us to believe Special Branch reports that he is the driving force behind the so-called 'Team' which now has been joined, surprisingly, by the retired general, Sir Patrick Gibson MC. (All previous reports on this now reclassified under above codename: 'Operation Picnic'.) There some danger lies in S's increasing access to the PM. (As discussed fully at meeting last Thursday. No record has been kept, as requested.)

Message ends.

6

He had originally asked for the meeting to drum up support for the Sigmont bid. Now the agenda was even more to the point. Ivor usually met editors informally, over a leisurely lunch at somewhere like the Savoy Grill, and it was some time since he had gone direct to a newspaper office. This time there was a need for urgent, immediate action.

The open-plan newsroom with its rank of computer screens was paperless and quiet. Less raucous, no litter, more clinical than he remembered, as banks of shirt-sleeved men and women played on their keyboards. Along one wall, a row of glass-fronted cubicles were for senior subs or executives. It took him back to his student days when he had worked one summer for an insurance company in the States. There the bosses had sat in slightly raised, soundproof glass boxes, the better to survey their colourless rows of troops. Each executive cubicle here had a venetian blind that could be lowered to offer a veil of privacy, but the possession of secrets and the wish for confidentiality is best not paraded, and the blinds were seldom used.

The skimpy blonde escorted him to the editor's office. It was a place apart and retained certain tatty pretensions – a portrait of a florid nineteenth-century editor, a bust of a previous proprietor, a glass-fronted bookcase containing bound copies of the Public Register. Archie MacInnery, a tough wee man who had grown up on Edinburgh's Easter Road, had a lived-in body, a thin smile and tired eyes. On his shoulders chips were said to cluster in sacks, and Ivor knew that his attention span could be as short as any busy editor's had to be. But they knew each other well enough to allow for an opening five minutes of banter. Then there would be another fifteen if he was lucky.

'Who's your paymaster these days, Mark?' It was an easy opening.

'Spread my talents. Diversification's the game.' Ivor smiled.

'The advertising industry's hard hit. That affect you PR boys too?'

'If I were in PR. But PR and my job thrive in hard times. We're cost-effective. Tough times for companies, for political parties, for politicians are when we're needed.'

'Thanks for the lecture. If only I could sell newspapers with PR. Harold Wilson called it "organized lying". D'you know how much I spend on TV advertising?'

'I've seen some figures.'

'Crazy. But if we don't, my proprietor shouts that we'll sink.'

'Change a few things.'

'Tell me. As long as you don't charge for your advice . . .'

'Whatever the reality, you're slipping on the image stakes.'

'We're doing much better than the *Express* and *Today*.'

'If you think so.'

'So?'

'Get yourself on TV. And your senior staff. Become a populist *Today Programme* pundit. *Any Questions*. That stuff. You should be in there every time, Andy.'

'I hate the personality cult. Media triumphalism. People with intellectual incontinence.'

'Stuff the hate. Get out there. Sell yourself. Listeners think you're great so they go and buy your paper.'

'I'll think about it.' MacInnery looked up quickly. 'Tell me, Mark, what carpets are you selling today? Could it be a predator?'

'Define predator. You journalists think in simplistic terms. If you don't know what to think, your bloody editorials end up whining that "further research into the problem is urgently needed".'

'Not fair.'

'OK. Not quite, but Shaw said it: half the time the press can't distinguish between world catastrophe and a bicycle accident. And you don't differentiate between good business practice and bad.'

'Let's see: those who make profits for their shareholders versus those who make profits for themselves. How's that for a start?'

'I'm not joking. You press have pulpits like the churches. You create saints and sinners. Your opinion industry is working on the wrong lines. Your editorials tend to damn take-overs . . .'

MacInnery smiled emptily. He looked at his watch. 'Get on with it Mark. What d'ya want? I've an editorial meeting in ten —'

'The Ramsay Smythe Consortium bid: your City people are hammering it. It's good news. The Sigmont management had gone to sleep. So had their profits.'

'You're paid to say that.'

'Yes.'

'Whose hands are being greased on the way, apart from yours?'

'I'll ignore the tone, Archie.' Ivor was not going to get riled. 'I'm retained.'

'Retained? An elegant, refined word. So? I see what my City people write. I have every trust in them. Forget it, Mark. How does the poem go? "You cannot hope to bribe or twist, thank God, the British journalist."'

Ivor did not smile. 'You've forgotten. It goes on: "But seeing what the man will do, unbribed, there's no occasion to."'

'Look Mark. Joke's over. I've my work to do. The City thinks your people will tear Sigmont apart. You know the game. If you've got a case to put, send it in. We'll file it somewhere.'

Ivor stood. 'You're missing the point.'

'I am?' MacInnery suddenly became aggressive. 'I like hearing that sort of thing. Makes my day.'

'Relax, Archie. I know you too well to waste your time, to come here and argue Ramsay Smythe's case cold. You can write what you want, so long as it's accurate. Level playing fields is all I'm asking for. The Sigmont management are getting all the brownie points. You're printing their press releases almost verbatim.'

'Are you questioning our integrity?' The voice was flat and hard.

'It's not yours. It's one of your staff. I don't know him, but his name is Fred Cree.'

'Cree? One of the best investigative people. Straight up and down.'

'And suddenly very wealthy, so they say.'

A chill silence descended on the room.

'What d'you mean?'

There was a pause of almost a minute. 'Your man Cree has been following two paymasters. You – legitimate, and the Sigmont people.'

'How d'you know, dammit?'

'He bribed someone to bug us the other day. Trouble is, he did it in a nightclub where we were meeting.'

'You're boasting about nightclubbing at your age?'

'Not my scene. But the club, sad for Cree, actually belongs to Mr Ramsay Smythe. I didn't know that either.' Ivor paused. 'By the way, Ramsay Smythe let the hostess keep the money Cree gave her, and doubled it. He thought that was funny.'

Archie MacInnery went and stared out of the window into the dismal street. He did not look at Ivor as he spoke. 'You know, sometimes I'm glad that I'm in this clean, pure profession of journalism . . . Thanks for coming in to teach me ethics, Mark,' he said.

Twenty minutes later, Fred Cree was summoned to the editor's office. He was in there less than a quarter of an hour. When he emerged, he was white-faced and shaking. He slammed the door behind him and went quickly up to the desk of the editor's personal assistant. He reached over, unasked, and seized the large desk diary that was lying in pride of place in the middle.

'Hey, Fred, you can't have that. It's private.'

'Which is why, lady, I bloody well want to look at it,' hissed

Cree. His eyes ran down the entries for that day until he spotted Ivor's name.

'Of course. It had to be him,' he breathed.

'Give me that, Fred. Do you want to get fired?' the personal assistant was standing, shouting at him.

'I was. Again,' said Cree. He threw the diary back down on her desk, then turned and left the room.

Amanda was frightened. She sat, huddled for protection, in the battered armchair that occupied almost a quarter of the tiny Pimlico room. Until now it had been a warm, secure place, where she had felt self-confident, inviolate. But now, on a table cluttered with books, newspapers, and a half empty mug of coffee, the telephone sat, mute and menacing, waiting for her to pick it up and ring.

She was about to unleash something over which she would have no control. She was not sure that she was prepared to contact this Dr Mark Ivor, but the alternative, to leave the evidence sleeping, was not an option. After the initial surprise and shock, after the hurt caused by her adoptive parents' never having told her, it had, with youthful curiosity, been something of a treasure hunt. It was a nervous game, trekking through recent history in the public records office and the library of press cuttings. Who, where, how old, what class and status? Were they alive or dead? All these questions had swept her mind since her discovery of the package. She wanted to know before she made her move. She never asked herself whether she needed to know, nor how much, when she found the truth, she would be helped or wounded.

After an age she picked up the telephone and dialled, apprehension pulsing within her. It rang twice, three times, four . . . Then a man's voice answered.

'My name is Amanda Telforth.' Her whole body was shaking.

'Yes?' The voice at the other end betrayed nothing. There was a pause.

'Is that Dr Mark Ivor?'

When he responded, she blurted out her story, hesitantly, badly. There was a long silence at the other end. She thought that she had made a great mistake and the male voice echoed her feelings.

'Miss, er, Telforth, you are making a great mistake. I have no daughter. No children of any sex or age. I am a bachelor. I have never been married.'

'I believe you are wrong,' she responded quietly. 'About children, I mean.'

'I don't know who you are or who is putting you up to this. If you or they have anything further to say, speak to my lawyer. I will give you his name and telephone number.'

'Nobody else is involved. If you want to deal with it that way . . . I'm sorry. I'll ring off . . . go away . . . leave you in peace.'

There was silence at both ends of the line for some moments, then Ivor said, 'You have to give me some shred of evidence, Miss . . . Who exactly are you? I know of no one called Telford.'

'Telforth. Paul Telforth was the name of the man I always believed was my father. There's no reason why you should have heard of him unless you were a geographer at Oxford – you were PPE, weren't you?'

'I . . . yes.' She had done her homework.

'Telforth isn't a name you'd have any reason to remember. But a French girl, a trainee teacher, I believe, Annette Valais, the Edinburgh Fringe Festival, summer 1962.'

There was a long silence, so long that Amanda had to say 'Hello?' to reassure herself that he had not cut her off. She edged herself deeper into the security of the great armchair and shivered slightly. This was a game best not begun. This was no game.

Mark Ivor's office was cold and dark. In his haste to answer the phone, he had only put on one side light. It was enough to see by, but only just. He shivered as Amanda shivered less than half a mile away, for reasons different or the same. He had had so many other things on his mind and then this. He would have put the receiver down on an obviously unbalanced woman, and yet something in the voice, then the name from the distant past stopped him. How does one deal with someone claiming to be your child, someone you have never heard of, never believed existed? These things do not happen. Unwanted children, yes; illegitimacy; adoption; abortion. 1962 was long before the Abortion Law Reform Act.

Unaccustomed indecision gripped him. What to do now? How does one deal with such a problem? Any problem? Of course. A meeting. Lawyers? A drink? Lunch? Absurd. He played for time. He took her number. He would call her back.

Fiona and he made love, then he told her. 'May I talk?' he began quietly.

She laughed sleepily. 'Talk? That's usually a female request.' But when he started describing the telephone call, Fiona became more alert.

'It can't be true.'

'Right. Some sick hoax. An amazing conversation . . . preposterous.'

'Could some tabloid be trying to set you up? Something to do with the bid for the Sigmont Corporation?' she asked.

'Unbelievable. Unbelievable . . .' His words stuttered repeatedly. But then he remembered the clear female voice that had forced him to take the call more seriously, and the name, Annette.

'I can't even say how I replied. Or recall exactly the name she gave: Amanda . . . Amanda Telford or Telforth.'

Fiona sat up in bed, draped only in a sheet, and looked down at him as he continued. She was still more amused than worried.

'I took her number, said I'd call her back. I started to say where I lived but she coolly told me she already knew.'

He described how he had walked around his office, switching on the lights. He remembered muttering to himself like an old man. Some sort of joke. Unbelievable. Absurd . . . How do you deal with someone who claims . . . who claims to be your daughter? He had walked over to his desk and automatically started shuffling through the bundle of mail and messages that had been left for him. He sat down. A birth, an unknown birth. When?

Who? How long ago? No ... No ... It was a joke. He was being set up. Which friend? No, more likely the *Sun* or the *People* or the *News of the World*, trying to set something on him, something to do with the PM, or to discredit the Ramsay Smythe Consortium. Blackmail? No, it was a case of mistaken identity. Or a girl on the make?

He undid his collar and tie and immersed himself in his relaxation technique. He could always conquer things that way. Count slowly to ten, a breath between each number, then back down to one. Arms out by his sides, fingers slightly splayed, palms turned upwards. His legs were lightly crossed, the ankle of one resting on the hook of the other. After five minutes, he re-emerged with partially regained composure and a state of high curiosity. Then he picked up the telephone and called Walt Tesco.

It had happened to her before, of course, men following her in the street. But this time it was different. The battered Cortina appeared in her wake on a number of occasions. She noticed it first when it crashed the lights in Victoria Street in an effort to keep up. Then, when she stopped suddenly, it nearly hammered into the back of her Polo. Looking in the rear mirror, she glimpsed thick pebble glasses worn by someone so short that he had difficulty seeing over the top of the steering wheel. Later she was aware of the same car parked outside a restaurant in Sydney Street as she and a group of friends emerged after a convivial get-together. Beside it stood its fat and scruffy driver, too engrossed in the women's lingerie display in a darkened boutique window to be genuine. Amanda took in the sighting but it still failed to register properly until she saw the same car, the same man, parked opposite her front door in Pimlico as she left for her office the next morning. This was more than mere coincidence. Now she knew she was being followed. A real bore; more likely a pervert than a potential rapist, but she would take the registration number and report it to the police if she saw the man again.

That evening she drove home after the frustration of shopping at an overcrowded Sainsbury's. It was about seven thirty and pitch dark. She had just found a place to park her Polo when she noticed the Cortina pull in behind. She would have played things more cautiously, but she was tired and irritated so she stormed up and hammered on the driver's window. The man inside wound the window down a few reluctant inches.

'Who the hell are you? Why're you following me? You dirty old man.' She yelled. A passing couple paused to stare curiously before going on their way. From inside the car came a protest of innocence. The man was following no one. Amanda's anger, slow to ignite, exploded. Gone was her normal, cool approach. Rage overcoming her caution, she reached for the handle and pulled the car door sharply open.

'Out!'

'I'll call the police if —' the man began, but Amanda reached inside and tried to pull him by his jacket collar out onto the pavement.

'Hey, I ain't done you no harm.'

'It's me that's going to call the police. What the hell're you up to?' she shouted.

'Hey, not so loud . . . please . . . I'll lose my licence,' the fat little man pleaded.

'Then explain yourself. Now,' barked Amanda. She was scared but he looked even more so.

'Well, Miss Telforth —'

On hearing her name Amanda stepped back in astonishment. 'So you are following me.'

'Look, miss, I'm doing a job. That's all. I don't know . . . Let me get someone to talk to you. I think you'd both prefer that.'

'What the hell's all this? What the fuck are you on about?' She seldom swore but this required it.

'I mean it. You'd prefer —'

'I'd prefer you to come clean.'

'OK. I've a phone in the car.'

The fat little man reached inside his car, unclipped his phone, switched it on and dialled a number. When it answered, he stammered out his explanation. 'Sorry, but you've got to talk to her. Get me out of this.'

'You made a mess of things, Mr Tesco,' said the cool voice at the other end. 'Are you sure it's her?'

'Sure? One hundred per cent.'

'Put her on.'

Walt Tesco thrust the telephone at Amanda, who seized it. 'Who the – who the hell am I talking to?' she shouted. She was aware that, as she spoke, the fat man was attempting to ease off into the darkness.

The voice that answered came as a shock. She recognized it at once. 'I can understand you're annoyed, Miss Telforth,' it said. 'Which is unfortunate in the circumstances. You see . . . I felt I should find out a bit about you . . .' There was a pause, and a slight falter in an otherwise controlled tone. 'Now that I have, I think we should meet.'

Fred Cree was a born misfit. He had a complexion of unappealing texture, the victim of a pockmarking impetigo of childhood, further harmed by a heavy beard growth which gave him a permanently scarred and unshaven appearance. He was a hairy man all over; fringes of coarse black pile sprouted from the cuffs and collars of his shirts. Those who had the misfortune to see more discovered a matted torso, back and front, which accounted for noticeable problems he had with body odour. His unappealing presence otherwise centred on a pair of red and watery little eyes which peered and pried about him with relentless dedication. When drunk, which happened often, he began to look like one of those unfortunate cases who wander the unkempt streets, berating the moon and swearing at lampposts. Had he ended up in prison, well-meaning social workers would doubtless point to his appearance as a mitigating factor in any wrong-doing. When he spoke, through birth or elocution, his voice projected in a peculiarly strangulated way. But what he wrote tended to be both intelligent and far-seeing. He composed well, with a verve and style which few could match. He was, thus, always in demand

73

in a media world that is not always choosy about the lifestyle of its journalists.

Cree's motivation in life was envy: envy of those richer, better placed, better looking, more successful than himself. Like some Victorian beggar, he had his nose pressed enviously against the window of society and privilege. He felt he was always missing out on life, constantly haunted by a regret for things never done, places never visited, people never known. Affectionate relationships were strangers. Bitterness or spite defeated ambition in the confines of his mind. It was inevitable that he should have chosen journalism as his career. When he started out on a story, he liked nothing more than dethroning the good and the great, the wise and well-born, when they became foolish. Profiles, exposés, insights, revelations of all sorts, financial, social, political, sexual, fed his appetite, his grudge against the world. All was revenge-based, the venting of spleen. Newspapers were a God-given vehicle for his spites and vendettas. And in Dr Mark Ivor he now had his supreme target.

He was meticulous and methodical. Working from home as he now had to, he opened a file on Ivor, and against it started building a matrix of names: Ramsay Smythe, Sigmont, Michael Wilson, the Prime Minister, Lord Shand, various newspaper editors, Smedley, Peter Maltby's suicide . . . There was no pattern yet. Not yet. But Cree had plenty of time on his hands.

7

Fiona knew and understood when, later, he told her of that long-forgotten past. Bed had, after all, been a playground. Recreational sex was something neither to be ashamed of wanting nor to apologize for having. Love-making could be part of love or it could stand, so to speak, on its own. Between consenting partners, the straight and the experimental were natural, and in no way the prerogative of the predatory male. He had met too many predatory females, more as he had grown older, women attracted to an unattached man, an increasingly rich man, a man sweetened with the aphrodisiac of power.

Thirty years ago it had been very different. Even among university students in the early sixties, extra-marital, or, more usually, pre-marital activities, were clandestine, at least as far as parents or families were concerned. A growing exception was among the increasingly liberated founders and their groupies of that swinging decade. Many of these came, met and intermingled, minds and bodies, at the cradle of so much bright young talent, the Edinburgh Festival Fringe. And when it came to young French women, well, they had been different long before any such social and sexual freedoms arrived in that wet and windy city.

She had been a sparkling nineteen-year-old gamine, vivacious and full of life. Her faulty English, the way her words came tumbling out in laughter-filled abandon, had captivated the still gawky young man. She was extraordinary in every way, against the background of that grey cold summer. His selective memory played tricks. He had gone with Annette Valais to party after show after party, and they had ended up in bed. A few days, a few weeks, and then she was gone. That was all. He had tried to find her but she had left no forwarding address. Vanished. Only then had he realized that he knew nothing about her beyond the fact that she came from France and was possessed of the most beautiful body and a great range of love-making skills.

He remembered the immediate aftermath, the dejection, as much as the brief affair. How could she have gone without a word? As he pulled these hazy memories back into focus, he recalled the arrangements for them to meet in the afternoon after a sleepless, torrid night. She was going shopping, to see someone, to arrange something. He could not remember. All he did recall was the long wait in the café off Princes Street, then going back to the little student flat he had rented for the Festival, then the frequent returns to the café, the messages left with anyone who might know or remember her. But there was nothing. Even her modest duffel-bag of possessions went with her when she disappeared. He had even gone – now he remembered – with a friend, to a police station. Thirty years is a long time, but he still recalled the laughter, then the sympathetic smile of a police sergeant as he dealt with a runaway lover and the abandoned lovelorn. What more could Ivor bring to mind except that brief, long forgotten passion, that long forgotten face, and a name – Annette Valais? How could anything have come of that brief liaison? How could it emerge *now* in the form of one Amanda Telforth? He would have known. He would have known.

Fred Cree was some weeks behind his prey, but he had a single-mindedness which meant that, very slowly, he was catching up. From his City broker contact – they had both benefited financially from that relationship when the bid for Sigmont broke – he now knew all there was available to the banks about Ramsay Smythe and his team. There were a number of loose ends – what was the scope of Ivor's brief and what his role had been in using the information in the *Securitate* files that had led to Maltby's suicide.

Then he had a lucky break. He met 'by accident' an old Special

Branch contact from the days when he worked on IRA stories who was on the team still working on the Victoria Station bomb that had killed Brogan, the Party Chairman. But accidental meetings between Special Branch and people like Cree do not happen. That soon became clear as the two men sat together in a Vauxhall pub.

'Great to see you, Fred. How are things?'

'Bad to bloody.'

'Out of a job, are you?'

'As it happens.' Cree sipped at his pint. He was beginning to wonder about the chance meeting.

'Why?'

'This and that.'

'Redundancy or . . . ?'

'Ends up the same, without the cash.'

'Wouldn't have anything to do with a Dr Mark Ivor, would it?' The Special Branch contact smiled at Cree's look of amazement. 'Don't ask. It's our business to know things. We just happen to be tracking that man's every movement.'

'Why?' stuttered Cree, and then it all came out. At least some of it did.

'Ivor was waiting to meet Brogan off the train.'

'You don't think he . . . ?' Cree became suddenly alert.

'No way. But he was one of a tiny number who knew Brogan's movements.'

'Ivor's secretary?'

'Called Deborah something. Dead end there too. Loyal, old school. Real tartar. Last sort to suspect.'

'Then?'

'Why are you so interested in Dr Mark Ivor, Fred?'

'A business story . . .'

There was a hostile pause. 'I believe you, Cree.' First names were suddenly dropped.

'Tell me.'

'Who's so close that he would know Ivor's every move?'

'Man called Ramsay Smythe?'

'Clever.'

'You mean . . .'

'I don't mean anything. But that man is bad news. Businesses in Romania, Bulgaria and the former Czechoslovakia – the home of Semtex.'

'The bomber's favourite. But why should he . . . Why are you telling me this?'

'Oh, we don't think Ramsay Smythe had anything directly to do with the bomb either. But his contacts might. And you might just turn up something . . .'

'You've been helpful in the past,' said Fred Cree cautiously.

'One turn deserves another,' his contact responded softly. 'We know you will be too. When we need you.'

In the week leading up to the unbelievable meeting with a girl who claimed to be his daughter, Ivor had a world of reality to face. His diary was packed with meetings with government ministers, ambassadors and industrial leaders. He had to make a speech to a closed meeting of top City brokers and travel to a business meeting in Amsterdam with a Dutch publishing house. Dominating everything, there was the accelerating public relations and lobbying activity for Ramsay Smythe, which was proving more and more fraught as the Sigmont Corporation organized its defences. The fight was getting dirty. They had picked up a specially fed rumour of an American firm of accountants being hired by Sigmont to dig up anything they could on Ramsay Smythe's business and private life. Ivor knew there might be a lot to find but he was not worried by the thought of the accountants. There were different truths to be revealed.

He also had his work for the Prime Minister which included being asked to sit in with Lord Shand on interviews to choose a new Media Manager. The previous press man had left in a hurry after his acute alcoholism became impossible to hide. Ivor was not on the committee that had produced the shortlist. His name appeared nowhere. But the PM wanted him to have a say to ensure that the man chosen – the women had all been eliminated

– would be able to cope with the media pack behind the scenes, as well as sounding convincing on the public stage. Image was more important than substance; there were plenty of researchers and face-workers to do the thinking behind the scenes.

It was ironic because, when the selection committee met at Central Office, Shand's first question to the first candidate was prompted by a briefing note written by Ivor himself.

'I know you'll understand,' was the quiet beginning, 'why we have to ask you about your private life, to conduct what we . . .' – Shand smiled menacingly – 'what we call the *Sun* Test.'

Watching the committee members as they made instant judgements about the tense-looking interviewee who sat alone on the other side of the green baize table, the question inevitably spurred a mixture of anxieties in Ivor. He was alert to the deeply unpleasant strain of vindictiveness that runs through the British character, a twentieth-century version of getting one's kicks by watching the Tyburn gallows at work. The public, ably abetted by the media, liked to build up their public figures; they garlanded them with praise, making them into icons. Then they excitedly joined in the kicking and spitting and back-stabbing as these elevated men and women were dislodged from their pedestals or fell, for one reason or another, into the gutters and sewers of life. Dethroning the famous was a national sport. They fell by accident or design. They jumped or were pushed. Sometimes they were tricked, hoodwinked, set up, stung, usually by the popular as opposed to the 'unpopular' broadsheet newspapers, who catered to the public liking for social executions by revealing the sexual and other peccadilloes of the rich and famous. An illegitimate child suddenly appearing in the life of someone with as many enemies as he had . . . If true they'd have their fun.

Ivor watched and wondered if this particular candidate for the post of Media Manager knew what he was letting himself in for. Probably flattered by getting on the shortlist, little did he realize that if he won it would be goodbye to sleep, to peace of mind, to privacy. Above all, privacy. A private life was impossible in the goldfish bowl of politics. The man straightened both his tie and himself in his chair and struggled to look intelligent. 'I'm not sure I . . .'

'Quite simple really. The Tabloid Test. Is there, ahem, anything in your past or your present, anything at all, that might cause us problems if, say, the *Sun* newspaper were to set their more unsavoury reporters on to investigating you?'

'I don't think –'

'Think hard,' Lord Shand interrupted. He went straight to the point. 'Sex, especially what might be seen as deviant sex . . . extra-marital and so on? No? Good. How about money matters? Lloyds losses? No unpleasantness there? No insider deals or tax matters that might come creeping out of your history? Family problems, prison . . . ?'

'I had a bit of a fuss over an unpaid parking fine . . .'

There was laughter. Ivor looked at Shand. What personal vices might he be hiding? Most people were hiding something; the more straight-laced they looked the more likely it was.

'I don't think we need worry,' said Lord Shand. 'That sort of thing won't turn the media litmus paper purple. Anything else?'

The candidate paused and shook his head.

'I'll have to record this on your file if we decide to appoint you. If anything nasty does emerge, I'm afraid we ditch you. Very publicly. Very fast. No holds barred. The party always comes first. You do understand?' Lord Shand smiled again. Ivor watched. There was no warmth in his eyes. There would be no mercy from that quarter if one slipped from grace.

With his experience of the Washington political scene, Dr Ivor was asked by Michael Wilson to attend the trade strategy group meeting on the following Tuesday. At the end of the session, when the Prime Minister had left the Cabinet Committee Room, Tim Willis, his Principal Private Secretary, took Ivor to one side. 'A word with you, Mark, if you've a moment.'

'You're all quite worked up about this, aren't you?' suggested Ivor.

'US protectionist moves? The PM takes them very seriously.'

Willis was an earnest, studious figure in his early forties, with totally round schoolboy glasses wired flat against his face. But if he looked vague, the reverse was the case. He was a high-flyer who handled the multifaceted problems that flooded across his desk with consummate skill: the best sort of Whitehall Mandarin.

'Things on your mind?' Willis asked.

'One or two.'

'Not as sharp as usual, were we?'

'Late night.'

'Personal problems?'

'How – no.' He checked himself. 'No. Nothing.'

Ivor knew he'd have to kick-start his brain cells now. Willis was so much on the ball that if he noticed intellectual slippage on Ivor's part, the PM would be the first to hear about it.

'You saw the latest MORI opinion poll. Puts the US way down the list in terms of popularity,' Willis volunteered amiably. He was staring at one or two of the other committee members who were slow in leaving the room, and Ivor realized that he was waiting for privacy before moving on to something more important.

'Always has been,' Ivor responded. 'We mock them and their politics, but everyone shares their dreams. Anti-Americanism prospers on both wings of British politics. Until we need their help.'

'Latest Washington trade legislation is hitting British companies very hard. The Trade & Industry Secretary's got a paper for Cabinet.'

'With all that's happening further east – narrow nationalisms – it's not bright of the Americans to turn their backs on the world.'

'They've been badly hurt by our attitude to the Arabs.' Willis looked irritably at his watch. He lived by time, each hour planned to the last minute of a crowded diary. Oblivious, other civil servants still loitered in the Committee Room.

'Not as much as their pockets have been hurt over the oil price.

Their ambassador said as much at that Chatham House seminar. He put on his special "man of destiny" act. He's a man it would be hard to underrate, incidentally.'

'We know the problem. It's like trying to nail a jelly to the wall,' said Willis, with a shrug. 'The PM's Cabinet colleagues – most of them – want the Americans to stew in their own isolation.'

'Some politicians –' Ivor cut his words short as the two men were at last left alone. 'If the Great British Public knew what really inadequate people they were –'

'They'd realize they'd guessed right all along,' said Willis, interrupting. 'Now that we're alone, Mark, I wanted a quiet word.'

'I suspected –'

'Ramsay Smythe.'

'I've made no secret: I'm retained by his consortium.'

'I know that. Which is why I thought it would be useful . . .' Willis paused. 'It's none of the government's business by whom you're employed, you understand. But my job is to protect the Prime Minister . . .'

'What are you saying, Tim?'

'Put it this way: the Opposition could make something of the fact that a close adviser to the PM is also involved with someone who –'

'You have something on Ramsay Smythe?'

'You should be cautious.'

'The Sigmont Corporation's been feeding out dirt.'

'Nothing whatsoever to do with the Sigmont Corporation. This is a – a government source.'

'Can you explain?'

'Sorry, Mark. Classified.'

'An intelligence source?'

'You might speculate.'

'You're warning me but not telling me what you're warning me about?'

'I knew you'd understand, Mark.' Tim Willis allowed himself a waspish smile.

8

An MP he knew slightly was at a table with a woman too attractive and well dressed to be a genuine research assistant, relation, or mere friend. She was the sort it was dangerous to be seen alone with in the Strangers' Dining Room at the House. Maybe the man believed that dining so openly with her would deflect any rumours, or that Parliament was such a club that no one would gossip about what they saw there. At a guess he would be proved wrong on both counts. Reflecting on this, Ivor sat at his corner table waiting for his host, the Financial Secretary to the Treasury, to rejoin him after a vote. Ivor inevitably related the little scene to himself. How would he look tomorrow with his young female companion? What would she be like? Who would those who knew him think she was?

The Financial Secretary, a jovial man beneath whose ebullient exterior, according to his ministerial colleagues in the big spending departments, there beat a heart of ice, wove his way back to the table.

'Waste of time,' he beamed. 'The Opposition aren't really bothering.'

'What was it?'

'Not quite sure. Something on broadcasting legislation. I was doing the lobby fodder bit. Where were we?'

'You were talking about East European requests for food aid.'

'We're going to help, of course. With the Germans. Most of the Europeans.'

'The US?'

'They've gone to ground. Half the Administration think the

Cold War is about to break out again any minute; the other half are so inward-looking they're in danger of vanishing up their own fundaments. Washington's legless and running to put up every trade barrier they can think of.'

'All we do is ignore it?'

'Why not? What's to be gained?'

'What's to be lost? We can't let go of the UK–US link.'

'Why not?' the Financial Secretary repeated. 'It's a delusion. Long has been.'

'It's fundamentally important. The PM thinks –'

'Fundamentally? Really, Mark? I know how close you are to the PM. They say you actually think for him a lot of the time.'

The Financial Secretary was a close friend and always spoke his mind. 'But leave that. Tell me about your campaign to persuade the shareholders that a bid by Ramsay Smythe for the Sigmont Corporation is in their very best interests.' The Financial Secretary paused. 'I have to warn you, I have my doubts.'

The two men stopped talking as a waiter slopped some lukewarm House of Commons Chablis into their glasses. Ivor lowered his voice. 'Before we get to that, you've heard the three-line-whip gossip?'

'Whispers, Mark, only. Tell me more.'

'I'm not interested in the gossip so much as –'

'Which means you are very interested in the gossip.'

Ivor smiled and continued, '. . . so much as the implications for the PM, for the government, if even half the story is true.'

'True, true, truth. Seek truth from "known facts", you keep telling me.'

'It's my profession.'

'And?'

'Fact one: at least one of the tabloids thinks it's onto the biggest ministerial sex scandal for years.'

'I'd heard it was half the Cabinet – the half that isn't impotent, the other way inclined, or geriatric.'

'You're kind to your colleagues.'

'I talk about them as they talk about me – only more so.'

'Seriously.'

'Seriously? OK. Seriously. There's something in it. I hear there are photographs with the man's, or men's heads cut out. Shades of the orgies in Profumo's days.'

'And?'

'And, as you say, so what?'

'If the worst comes to the worst . . .'

'And it all gets out? It won't bring the government down. So far as I'm aware, not even the most salaciously extreme stories suggest that the PM's involved. Of course, there was an earlier story about him. I wonder what happened to the woman . . .' The Financial Secretary laughed unpleasantly.

'I don't think the PM would —' Ivor checked himself. 'All it will do is make us look a bit foolish, give the Opposition and the country something to laugh about, and probably mean that Miss Three-line-whip, or whatever the good lady is called, gets invited onto some chat show to talk about the valuable social services she's offering.'

'You're worried?'

'Not involved. So not worried.'

'OK. I'll forget it. I'm not looking for problems. But you may be wrong.'

The waiter came and cleared away their plates.

'Anything else, Mark? Sweet? Cheese?'

'Just coffee, thanks. And . . . I . . . since you asked about the Sigmont Corporation bid . . .'

The Financial Secretary raised his eyebrows ever so slightly and smiled. 'Tell me,' he said. He was used to working meals where the real meat was only laid on the table right at the end.

'You know I'm retained by Ramsay Smythe. Our proposal offers a very good deal for their shareholders. There's a real heavyweight campaign out there trying to rubbish it. The Sigmont people are spending a hell of a lot of money . . .'

'Standard practice. Not illegal.'

'. . . bribing their way round London.'

'Bribing or just a little heavy PR?'

'Large amounts of money. To senior media people. To . . . politicians.'

'That's a serious accusation, Mark.'

The Financial Secretary spoke quietly. He looked slowly around the room and then stared hard at his guest. He was no longer smiling.

'I hope I know you well enough to expect you to be able to justify that. No gossip, you understand.'

'No gossip. Just the truth.'

'Very well then. Truth. But before we meet again, Mark, just check, will you, that your Mr Ramsay Smythe is whiter than white. It's not what I hear.'

'Everyone's warning me.'

'Then maybe you should take heed, Mark. I'd hate you to deceive yourself. Or, more importantly, me.'

Only once before had he been to Ramsay Smythe's flat. The six foot four minder showed him into the empty oak-panelled study with the message that the Chairman would be with him shortly. Ivor walked over to the big picture window and looked at the tourists and groups of schoolchildren thronging Green Park. He knew the question he had to ask but was not yet sure how to do so. A moment later, Ramsay Smythe burst into the room. He was at his most amiable.

'How's the campaign?'

'I've seen all the broadsheet editors and their City people.'

'What vibes?'

'Breaking both ways. You saw the useful piece in the *Independent* this morning?'

'If anyone reads it.'

'I've sent copies of it to a number of key . . . An independent, *Independent* view is more valuable than any amount of press releases from us.'

'You were behind it?'

'My briefing.'

'Looking for an increase in your fee?'

'I don't work that way.'

'Only joking, Mark,' said Ramsay Smythe in a no-joking voice. 'So why did you want this "couldn't wait till Friday" meeting?'

'You've a lot of enemies.'

'Little people. Sigmont Corporation dirt diggers.'

'Others.'

'Over a long and eventful business life? Yes, lots. They don't worry me. It's my so-called friends that scare me.'

'Can I speak frankly?'

'That's why I pay you.'

'Is there anything I should know?'

'About what, Mark?' Ramsay Smythe's formidable face showed irritation.

'Skeletons?'

'Skeletons? We all have skeletons. Ask your friend Lord Shand about skeletons.'

'You know what I mean.'

'Somebody's been whispering in your ear, have they, Mark? If you're worried, just say so. We can always call a halt to our relationship.'

'I don't mean that.'

'Of course you don't.' Ramsay Smythe came round behind Ivor and placed a huge and far from reassuring arm on his shoulder.

'There's nothing at all to be worried about, Mark. Your reputation is as safe as is mine. Believe me, Mark.'

Ivor felt weak, knew he had been weak. He hoped, as he was shown from the room, that his reassured look appeared suitably genuine.

Business crises he could handle. His few personal crises he could handle. When they both came together it got tense. He was nervous. He arrived early. Why the hell had he rung the girl later and suggested lunch? Absurd. A meeting at his solicitor's chambers would have been cleaner. If it was some set-up, he had no support, no witnesses, nothing. He felt anxious, a feeling alien to him. He knew, of course, that he could not have met her at his lawyer's. Steven Rotenbein was the wrong sort. Steven would have not taken it seriously, or taken it too seriously. He had to do it on his own. He and this Amanda.

Why had he chosen Langan's? Big, noisy, and he wouldn't know too many political people there at lunchtime. He had his usual corner table. He sat down and stared round. No serious faces, though one or two public ones from the show-biz scene. He picked up the menu, taking in nothing beyond noticing that his hand was shaking. New arrivals were analysed one by one. Too old; too young. Could not be her, nor her, nor her. He clung to the belief that it was all a mistake.

Amanda took a long time preparing: hair, clothes, shoes, make-up – which was always minimal – and, above all, mentally. It worked: she looked totally self-controlled though inside she was in turmoil. She arrived precisely on time. Something about her immediately indicated that this had to be Amanda. Tall, poised, an attractive flood of reddish-brown hair, dressed in a well-cut costume, handsome features and a clear, confident look. There was no immediate feeling prompted by her physiognomy; she merely looked the part. He studied her as she paused at the door, as she stared around the room as if looking for a familiar face, as she spoke to the *maître d'hôtel*, as she was ushered between busy tables to where he was sitting.

They shook hands formally as at some business meeting: a firm grip on both sides. She settled into her chair, declining the offer of a pre-lunch drink. He ordered a bottle of Perrier and a glass of house Chablis. He wanted to stare at her, examine how she looked, but he kept his eyes averted, his small talk busy with the trivia of lunch.

She would not have noticed if he had stared; her attention was firmly on the menu. Her attitude now suggested a reluctance to be where she was, a regret at having embarked on her search. She had only a glimpse of him as she came up to the table. There had been no instant recognition, no pang of bonding, nothing wonderful, no physical resemblance to bolster her uncertainties.

88

She had presumed so much, had thought there would be some sign that would announce 'This is it'. There was none.

After a few empty minutes she looked up, determined to get things moving. 'I read your *Who's Who* entry. Why did you never marry?'

'I never found . . .' he began, then checked himself. That was not the agenda. He wanted her answers to *his* questions. 'Before we get to me,' he began, in what he hoped was a reasonably friendly tone, 'tell me why you think I – that is – that is – why you think we are related.' He felt as lame and absurd as the words themselves.

'There's not much doubt about it. Please –' She interrupted herself. 'Don't be shocked. It's happened. I'm trying to be as matter-of-fact about it as possible.'

'Shocked . . .' he breathed. She was more in control than he was, trying to reassure, to pacify him. 'I'm sorry I put that man Tesco on to you.'

'I'd've done the same,' she responded hesitantly.

'If you are so sure, did your mother say . . . ? Did *she* tell you?'

'I've no idea who or where my real mother is. I know little about her apart from her name and that she was French and that she recorded you as my father.'

'Me . . .' He paused, lost for words. Then: 'No trace of her?'

'No trace,' she replied softly.

A waiter arrived to take their order. It gave them a breathing space. When the man had gone, Ivor reasserted himself, looked straight at her for the first time and said, 'Why don't you start from the beginning and tell me exactly what you think you've discovered.'

His emotions were left in disarray. The lunch was polite but distant and ended indecisively. Amanda departed with mixed impressions of a dynamic but up-tight man, full of hang-ups and inhibitions. He saw a superficially poised but vulnerable young woman who was certain of herself at one level but confused at another. He too had looked for a physical connection. She volunteered to send copies of all the documentation to his lawyer. They agreed to meet again. As they stood to say goodbye, their parting exchange was the most realistic.

'I don't know what to think. The evidence is scant,' he said.

'If it's correct, then at least it wasn't hate at first sight.' She smiled thinly.

'You were right to pursue it. I would have done the same. D'you want a blood test or something?'

'I don't . . .'

'Your real mother?'

'I don't know what to do.'

'I don't know what to advise.'

'We'll be in touch.' She had turned away then, disappointed.

'Yes, of course,' he responded automatically. And that was that.

Dr Ivor was neither pedantic nor over-fastidious but he preferred order and neatness. This particularly applied to his working environment. A desk piled with paperwork and a badly organized filing system led to a cluttered mind. The discipline of tidiness kept his thoughts in good order. What aptitude his secretary, Deborah, had lacked in this direction when she had first come to work for him five years earlier, she had soon acquired. She now knew that a work surface with almost no papers on view did not mean that her employer was idle or under-employed. It could signal the reverse: that he had cleared the decks for a crisis on its way. A desk top, its furnishings, its style, says much about the user's work methods. Ivor's partner's desk top was not only neat but also handsome: a serious work station. Good leather blotter and correspondence trays, a pair of matching Pate Peperium jars full of clips and fasteners, an old brass paperweight, an ivory paper-knife, a ceramic jar of carefully sharpened pencils, two sleek black telephones and a cylindrical glass jar of peppermints. Peppermints were one of his weaknesses.

There was no paper on his desk now, apart from a notepad. It was all on his PC. He kept correspondence to a minimum, used fax rather than post, and expected Deborah to do likewise. His most active lobbying exercises generated not a single page of printed record, not, at any rate, until the fee invoices were issued.

Deborah, unhappily single and in her early forties, believed in keeping herself to herself. She liked Ivor, liked working his way, liked the solitary lifestyle in the small but elegant office-apartment in Victoria, liked the fact that her working hours were largely hers to choose. This was particularly so when he was abroad. She was dedicated to her work and to Ivor. She was even a little in love with him, though she would never have admitted it, not even to herself. Since he was a great believer in fast communications, he had provided her with a fax at her flat and a portable telephone for her own use. That way he could get her at any time. An occasional middle of the night call from California was a small price to pay for an agreeable workstyle.

The office had double doors that led to Ivor's flat. It was home base when he was not travelling or at his cottage on the west coast of Scotland. A bedroom, a guest room that was seldom used, an elegant sitting room with some tasteful pieces of furniture and well-collected paintings, his library-study packed ceiling to floor with bookshelves, long windows looking out onto a quiet, tree-lined street; a huge kitchen-dining room. Deborah knew the house rules. The kitchen was hers to use as she would. The bedrooms were out of bounds, as was the sitting room. She would never have thought of invading them, though she supervised the elderly Irish cleaning lady who had done for Ivor since time immemorial in her free run of the entire flat. Deborah was content, and if she had personal hang-ups and anxieties over her social relationships, they never intruded into her employment. He liked and trusted her in return: he was generous over pay, never failing to mark birthdays and Christmases with ever more generous gifts.

All was otherwise well in her life until the end of a busy session with her employer after he returned on a late flight from his trip to Edinburgh. He dictated a pithy memorandum on Eastern Europe. He wrote a few thank-you notes to people whose hospitality he had accepted. He got her to send out a handful of regrets to invitations to attend dinners or to speak at seminars. He gave her a list of telephone calls he wanted her to make, setting up appointments, cancelling others, fixing one or two working lunches, and one working breakfast. She never queried the unexplained blanks in his diary. There was one woman in particular who telephoned and who never left a message. Deborah had her bouts of speculation about his love life but kept her conclusions to herself. As he was not married, there was no reason for secrecy, unless it was the woman who needed to keep the secret.

It was a huge surprise when he told her about Amanda. She was flattered when he said that she was almost the first to know. He seldom chattered to her about his private life; he seldom chattered about anything. When he began talking, Deborah at first linked it to the mysterious telephone calls, but it soon emerged that those must be from someone else. The story came pouring out: his amazement, his initial disbelief, his caution, his doubts, his growing certainty. She was fascinated by the human dimension it suddenly revealed in her employer. She shared his emotions as he laid them bare. Tears came to his eyes. She wanted, for a moment, to hug him in his confusion. That moment evaporated when he ended lamely: 'I'm taking her to the theatre tomorrow night. Can you believe it, Deborah? Me, a father, and . . . and of a daughter.' He paused, turned away, then laughed out loud, suddenly, unexpectedly, almost stridently. She pulled herself together and laughed with him, then poured him a large whisky. She had one too.

There was more to come. 'I much appreciate all that you do for me, Deborah. If I don't always say so, it's meant,' he began. She wondered where this was leading. 'We make an excellent team. But there are a number of leads I miss out on. I often feel I haven't done enough background reading when I write a report to ministers. I'll slip up one day for lack of a crucial fact.'

'What's coming now?' Deborah asked herself. 'Is it something to do with his daughter? Am I being dismissed?'

'The last thing I want you to think . . .' he went on. She knew, from what she had often heard him say in the past, that when people used a phrase like that it meant that they would be bound to think whatever it was. 'I'd hate you to think that I undervalue your work or am pushing you to one side. Thing is . . .' He paused. 'Thing is, I'm contemplating taking on an assistant, mainly on the research side. Useful in seeing people who aren't major players, but who could be valuable. I miss out on some of the charges. Too casual. I know you remind me, but . . . It's not that I'm scrabbling after fees, but I could make more, and do more, a deal more effectively.'

'You have someone in mind? Where would they sit?' The practicalities came from Deborah as he knew they would. Not a word about how she might feel about having her tidy, private office invaded by a stranger.

'I never use the spare room. You might like to go out and buy a desk. Push the bed up against the wall, throw a rug over it and call it a couch. What else? Filing cabinet?'

'A secretary for him? I take it it's a him?'

'God, no. He's just an assistant. I'm not wanting to build an empire. He'll have to be his own secretary, his own PC – yes, it'll be a man. I thought you'd prefer that in any case. You won't mind doing the odd thing for him in an emergency. But, good point, I'll make sure he's computer literate.'

'Who?'

'Oh, yes, who . . . Well, I've been thinking about it for some time. Didn't come across anyone I liked. Then, in Edinburgh, I met someone I took to. Another Scot, I'm afraid. A bit brash, but he'll mature. No decisions yet. I'll have to check him out thoroughly. He'll be ringing to make an appointment. I'm thinking about salary and so on. Gut reaction only: he might suit. Name is Rick Maclean.'

*　　*　　*

Ten days later, everything came together. When the PM, with a majority of only eighteen, and frustrated by the constant climbdowns necessary to appease his rebellious backbenchers, told Ivor that he was thinking of calling a snap general election, Ivor started clearing his diary for the fray. Even Ramsay Smythe was sympathetic. 'Rather the wimps we know . . .' was his response when Ivor indiscreetly hinted at the news.

If bustle and activity were marks of achievement, then Central Office was well on the way to winning. Competent party officials packed the halls, corridors and meeting rooms. Less competent, bright young things of various sexes, including a clutch of plump daughters of the party faithful, 'helping out for Daddy', rushed about with bundles of manifestos, press releases, political biographies, posters and publicity photographs. Earnest researchers pored over opinion polls and computer print-outs, and a few relics of an older generation brayed and buffooned in the background.

Everyone noticed when Ivor arrived. He was a key figure. The Prime Minister was known to listen to him. But Lord Shand, who had unexpectedly been appointed Party Chairman just before the election was announced, now had a different agenda. Ivor may have been the party guru, may have been the architect of the press, publicity and much acclaimed advertising campaign. He may have succeeded last time round. But reputation lived only until something came to kill it. Lord Shand, as he found his way into his new role, was determined to let everyone know who was in charge now. Dr Ivor would have to recognize that.

'Hello, Ivor. We're keeping you busy?' asked a tall, vacuous man, with an inbred face and no chin. Ivor recognized the vice chairman of one of the regional groups. 'Meet the wife, Priscilla.' Ivor and a lady with a bird's nest of hair and a mouth full of buck teeth shook hands politely.

He moved quickly to the chairman's office, shouted his cheerful hellos to the secretaries, and went in, unannounced.

'Hello, Mark. Just on time. Look at some of this briefing material, will you? Not sure the back-room boffins have got the argument right. Bit too strident. What d'you think?' There was no sign of Shand, but a party grandee sat at his crowded desk. He was a charming, old-school figure, with distinguished white hair and avuncular half-moon glasses that kept slipping down his nose.

Ivor took the pages and skimmed expertly through them. Taking out his pen he crossed out the occasional word and phrase, working fast, line by line, spending more time redrafting a punch line at the end. Politics, like instant coffee ads, must have its slogans. The grandee stood over him, watching and feeling relieved and comforted. Ivor would ensure there were no elephant traps for the media to pick on. In the key weeks before the election, they had to watch like hawks that Central Office did not put a foot wrong. The government could win this election unless it did something to lose it. Power was only a ballot box away. The grandee's job was on the line. He wanted his peerage.

Ivor handed the draft back; the old man scarcely glanced at it before pressing a bell to summon an assistant. 'Have it typed,' he ordered. 'Proofread it three times, then it can go out.'

'Now, Mark,' said the grandee. 'Advice, please. Rossiter, that neo-fascist candidate in Gloucestershire, has been spewing a lot of racist rot about forcible repatriation to Jamaica and so on. What do we do? Ignore him? Issue a rebuttal? What d'you think?'

'Two things,' said Ivor decisively. 'Issue a low-key retort — nothing that will stir the press. I'll draft something. Get Rossiter up here today and read him the riot act. Open his mouth once more, and he's out. Hammer him hard.'

'Good. I'll get on to that. I'm sure the PM will agree.'

'I'm sure. The party's a loose coalition. We've got to use heavy-duty paper to cover the cracks until the election's over.'

Lord Shand walked in as Ivor finished speaking. He had his customary look of disapproval, retained even when his mouth split into an approximation of a smile of greeting. Ivor sensed that the grandee seemed embarrassed at having been found with him.

'Polishing up a couple of news releases, Rupert.'

'Excellent. Mark has a great ability with words.'

'A matter of getting the tone . . .' began Ivor. 'I may have my faults but –'

'But being wrong isn't one of them,' said Lord Shand. His mouth was still smiling; his eyes were not.

'*Touché.*' Ivor smiled back. He was aware of an undertone of hostility that he did not quite understand, but it did not worry him unduly. Shand owed him favours.

'You're coming to the main strategy meeting?' asked the grandee. 'Tomorrow at ten? Here?'

'Fine,' said Ivor, looking at his watch. 'God, late for dinner. Black tie. One of those City occasions where a black armband would be more appropriate.'

He said his goodbyes and cheerfully left the room.

'What we would do without Ivor, I don't know,' said the grandee after he'd left. It was the sort of statement put up as a trial balloon to see what flak it would generate.

'I do,' said Lord Shand. 'We'd get to running things as I want them done.'

'What's he done?'

'He's good, but he's like a cockroach. You stand on him and as soon as you remove your heel, he gets up, shakes himself and scuttles away. Too clever by three-quarters. By the way . . .' Shand paused, then said icily, 'in future, use our new Media Manager for drafting and checking your press releases. Dr Ivor works to me.'

'If you say so, Rupert,' said the grandee abjectly.

9

Ivor had seen powerful men, able to cope with every challenge of running some great department of state or public company, brought low by a domestic crisis, a carping wife, a divorce, a child custody case. Companies and advisers did not know how to cope with a chairman or CEO whose poise and detachment withered under such a strain, with a consequent collapse of professional judgement. The private affair corroded the public function. Similarly, he had seen close colleagues, with doting spouses and promising children, casually throw that happiness away by letting business commitments undermine and eventually destroy family bliss. One great chairman of an international airline, who hired and fired without a tremor, who was ruthless, even unscrupulous, in his take-over battles, who constantly picked fights with his competitors, Ivor had once found weeping and distraught, unable to take any professional decision, because his long neglected wife had run off with a much humbler man.

Steven Rotenbein, his lawyer, had heard Ivor hold forth on the subject of public men with private crises and knew, when he got his client's hand-delivered memo, that the practitioner was sick. Ivor seldom rambled. This memo did.

> *She is sincere, there is no doubt. She is acting on her own. She is certain she is right. It is not a set-up and she has described a plausible scenario. A few weeks ago, Steven, I saw a TV programme about Vietnam. You may have watched it. One image stuck and has returned to haunt me. An orphanage, a third-world*

orphanage, where the children were all the black or blond and blue-eyed bastards of countless GIs' penetrations of the brothels of that war-devastated country. A generation with unknown American fathers. OK. It was different times and different circumstances. Women always know when they become mothers. Short of blood tests and DNA there is no similar physical proof for the father. I found Amanda more battered by the revelation that the couple who had brought her up were not her real parents than by the discovery of me. I marvelled at her sang-froid, then realized she was forcing herself to keep control. She is as fragile as hell. I wonder how she saw me.

You'll want to know what conclusions I draw . . . Is she? Is she not? Whatever, her arrival has changed my life. Annette Valais . . . It has to be true. It was a long time ago that Festival fling, but I don't remember other men in the French girl's life . . . Did I say, at the birth, which, as you'll see, took place in the maternity wing of the Brighton hospital nine months later, she clearly recorded my name as the father? (Copies of Birth Certificates and Adoption Papers enclosed — as received.) Tesco, the private detective, has got us a photocopy of the hospital admission record. The statement of paternity was never passed on to me. You will see, Steven, that the other details are quite clear: the baby was adopted within a few weeks of the birth. There is no record of the adoptive parents having had any subsequent contact with Annette. She disappeared, without any forwarding address, doubtless back to France. I have to admit that it was when Amanda began questioning me about Annette Valais, whether I might have a photograph of her, what she had looked like, what her background was, that I began to see physical similarities. I scraped my memory for every *detail I could recall. What do I do now, Steven?*

You will be hearing from Amanda direct. I want it all verified independently, as quickly as possible. Don't worry about the cost. Do it yourself. Keep it to yourself.

Rotenbein rang him just before he went into a meeting. The voice at the other end of the telephone started flip, making light of the whole situation; the nudge-wink, all boys together routine. Ivor cut him very short. On this one jokes were out. Rotenbein, subdued, said he'd come back soon. He'd double-check the Tesco research and see if Annette Valais could be traced.

Later Ivor rang Amanda. 'Hello,' he began, almost apologetically. 'It's, er, Mark Ivor. Look, I've got tickets for the new Ayckbourn play on Friday night. Would you like to join me?'

*

The man in overalls started to appear regularly at the Victoria mansion block that housed Ivor's office. His pass explained that he worked for a security waste company. The hall porter was satisfied, believing the man was employed to remove classified computer print-outs from an office below Ivor's and take them away in his van for secure destruction. The man in overalls was an expert. He knew to leave identical black plastic bags outside Ivor's door in place of the ones he had removed so that no one's suspicions would be aroused.

Going through someone's garbage can be an unpleasant task. It can also be rewarding if one knows precisely what one is looking for.

*

'So we challenge you, come out from behind the double talk, tell the British people the truth, not what you call "the facts". Tell the electorate exactly what these pie-in-the-sky policies of yours would cost the British taxpayer. Our simple message to the leader of the Opposition is: "Come clean."'

99

The screen went blank. Someone threw a switch and the lights went up in the bare Knightsbridge studio. The chairs, of a type that had been fashionable in the seventies, were not for relaxing in. The dozen or so who had been watching the rushes of the final pre-election party political broadcast stretched uncomfortably and turned to see who would react first. About half were from the advertising agency and the production company; the others were Central Office people, the Prime Minister, Lord Shand, the Media Manager, and Mark Ivor. Two teams with very different strips: the party people in pin-striped suits, neat ties, traditional haircuts; even the statutory woman, a key parliamentary candidate, wore a pin-striped costume, her close-cropped hairstyle matching that of her peers. The creative team were, by contrast, in fashionable slept-in clothes, ones that might have been laundered, wrung out by hand and dried without reference to an iron. The agency had its woman too, a pretty production assistant whose main effect had been to keep Lord Shand's attention diverted from the business in hand. Given her come-hither behaviour, she was, if a virgin, unlikely to survive in that state for long.

'Not bad. Not bad at all. In fact, I quite like it. Hard hitting and to the point. What d'you think?' asked the Prime Minister. A mutter of sycophantic agreement rumbled around the room.

'I liked the way you cut in all these damning quotes by Opposition spokesmen. I take it they've all been validated?' asked the Media Manager.

'A straight cut — each one,' a crop-haired man from the production team assured him. His earrings shone as he spun his head. 'No special edit of any of them. They can't complain we've done a dirty tricks.'

'You cut them short I take it?'

'Sure. They ramble. We took the best, or the worst, bits. They damn themselves.'

'What do you think, Rupert?' The Prime Minister turned to Lord Shand, who was fantasising about the production assistant.

'What? Yes, quite. That is, I agree. Good.' He was, for once, caught off guard, but quickly pulled himself together.

'You, Mark?' prompted the Prime Minister. The creative team were apprehensive. They knew Ivor's blessing was essential.

'Sorry to cast a shadow. I've argued before: we must use these party political broadcasts to push *our* policies at the viewers. All this one does is knock the Opposition.'

'We agreed –' interrupted Lord Shand testily.

'The old adage. We don't want to knock the Opposition; they do it so well themselves,' responded Ivor.

'That's what the film is all about,' the film director said in frustration.

'I know,' said Ivor. 'But it doesn't work. Our broadcasts ought to hammer home *our* achievements. By all means have a quick dig at the Opposition on the way, but do it not by making them appear dangerous or devious, but by looking absurd. Get the electorate laughing at them and we're home and dry. Ridicule is more deadly than argument. We've got to stress their inadequacies, programme the public to have a sniggering reaction every time they come into view. Good news: I liked that line about getting a second opinion on the Leader of the Opposition from a taxidermist.'

The political people laughed. The creative team looked dejected.

'OK,' said the Prime Minister. 'Your point taken, Mark. If the creative team can please rework it on those lines. Now,' he looked around the room, 'anyone got anything else? No? Good. Then, thanks for coming. We'll meet again – say – same time Wednesday? Give you enough time?'

He didn't wait for an answer, stood and quickly left the room. Ivor, oblivious to the hostility of the production crew, went with him to an empty office next door. With a last look at the research assistant, Lord Shand moved swiftly to join them. He was not going to be left out.

'Good on you for making that point, Mark. I felt the same. But it came better from you,' the Prime Minister was saying as he entered.

'Anything to help,' Ivor responded, briefly reflecting that the popular image of Her Majesty's First Minister as a cross between a used doormat and the yawn personified was sometimes quite close to the truth.

'What good these broadcasts do, I'm far from sure,' sneered Lord Shand. 'My family walk out as soon as they come on.'

'We can't stop because the Opposition won't stop,' said the Prime Minister inanely.

'They hate them as much as we do and they can afford them less.'

'We're stuck with them. Which is why I feel we should follow the lead of the big advertisers and go all out to entertain.'

Ivor addressed the two politicians. 'Tell our story. But make them laugh, like the lovebirds couple in the coffee ads. The man in that clip had as much passion and fun in his voice as the speaking clock.'

'Politics isn't about *fun*,' corrected the Prime Minister.

'It wasn't at all bad.' Lord Shand was decidedly irritated.

'If it were a captive audience. But, as you've just said, Rupert, we have one that wants to go and put the kettle on or take the dog out.'

'You've made your point, Mark,' retorted Shand, cutting him short. 'Let's see what else they come up with. Now, you wanted to talk.'

Ivor went to the office door, looked outside, satisfied himself that only the PM's bodyguards were outside as he had requested, then shut it behind him. He kept his voice low. 'The News Editor of the *Independent* got onto me less than an hour ago, just before this screening. He tipped me off: the tabloids are about to break that major sex scandal story in tomorrow's editions.'

'Which?' asked the Prime Minister.

'God. Is there more than one scandal?'

'Which tabloid, I mean?'

'The *Mirror*; the others are in close pursuit,' said Ivor. 'I heard some weeks ago that it was coming. If it's as big as they say, they'll all be on it. Even the heavies will have to follow. We won't worry too much about party political broadcasts after that.'

Shand put on his iciest elder statesman act. 'Kind of you to trouble yourself, Mark. As the PM knows I think we can relax. Someone not a million miles away from the Chief Whip's office has had a word with a certain newspaper proprietor. The man's beginning to get knight-starvation. Wants to make his wife a lady, y'see. The Attorney General's been shoving his weight around as well. It caused them to re-think. As the evidence the paper has isn't all that conclusive no one's going to run any story.'

'You put a cap on it?' Ivor was uneasy. That was usually his task.

'The story's dead, Mark. Stone dead. There is no sex scandal.'

'The Opposition? The *Independent*?'

'They have no facts. Only gossip. The *Mirror* was a slight worry.'

'Fine. Just fine,' said Ivor, marvelling, despite his chagrin, at the ways of the British Establishment and their unique ability to protect their own. Then he shook hands with the Prime Minister and Lord Shand, and left the studio.

Lord Shand watched him go. A shadow of distaste fell across his features. Ivor had had his uses. But now, now he was beginning to be too much. Shand believed in customary power, heredity, the ruling class. If he could not rule as his ancestors had ruled and become Her Majesty's First Minister because his Old Etonian and Grenadier Guards background and his peerage set him apart from the modern egalitarian world, it was still his duty to ensure that the country was well governed. As Party Chairman he was now in a key role. He had his agenda and even if it did not suit the left, he was going to see it through. Indirectly, of course. He would act through the little man, the present incumbent of Number Ten Downing Street. Lord Shand had a cunning that many brilliant intellectual minds who laughed openly at the aristocracy could not rival. His voice might have upper class tones but it could still issue razor sharp commands. A natural leader, at one time it would have been a strain to lead from behind. Now he relished the role of puppet master and disliked the thought of any challenges to his new-found position.

It had been Ivor who had recommended Shand to the Prime Minister in the first place. The relationship had started well. Shand had brought style and distinction to a shabby, lightweight administration. Until he established himself, Shand had wanted Ivor on his side in playing the Prime Minister. Michael Wilson had always taken to Ivor, consulting him, ringing him up both late and early. Ivor was less intimidating than the peer: more reassuring. Ivor was a constant guest at both Downing Street and Chequers. Lord Shand had seen Ivor as a useful tool, a moderating influence, a steady hand at the tiller of advice when the political gales began to blow. Then, slowly, after Brogan's assassination and the suicide of Peter Maltby, the PM's closest ministerial friend, he began to want sole access. But Ivor seemed to be always there, the outsider on the inside track. Lord Shand thought himself too proud for jealousy, too patrician for envy, too effortlessly superior to worry. Yet, like a small sore on a gum, his attitude to Ivor had begun to irritate, then suppurate. That indiscreet nightclub meeting with Ramsay Smythe, arranged by Ivor, had added to Shand's growing unease. Ramsay Smythe with all his past East European connections. That too . . . That too . . . Shand now considered Ivor to have influence out of proportion to his station. He had become the peer's rival for that vapid thing, the Prime Minister's mind. In other circumstances Shand would have forced Ivor out into the cold. Later, he would have to go, with no qualms on Shand's part. But not quite yet. There was a deeper game in which Ivor could still be useful.

*

It was a rambling old house on the outskirts of Oxford. Comfortable and clean, if a bit faded. The nurses were friendly. There was a decided odour of nursing home about it but, also, in her 'mother's' room, was that other smell that she had come to recognize since her adoptive father's death. How had she got hold of drink? A friend? Maybe she had bribed a nurse. Amanda thought of taking it up with the matron but decided to leave well alone. There were other more important matters to deal with.

The alcohol had the one-sided effect of anaesthetizing the conversation. Amanda watched someone become visibly older and more crumpled as she fumbled for her words. She had changed so much, or perhaps Amanda's view of her had changed. She looked around the room. Where was the bottle hidden? Probably in the bedside cupboard, within easy reach.

'We were always going to tell you, dear. We ran out of courage. We were . . . I am . . . so fond of you. You were ours, through and through. You do realize that, don't you, dear? I hope you aren't angry. You aren't angry, are you?'

How could she not understand, this poor, sick old woman, hunched up in her hospital bed? Amanda felt a mix of emotions: pity, but also a deep hurt, that a great part of her life had been a fiction, her history a lie. Her whole being had somehow disappeared in one flash of discovery.

She stilled her emotions. There was no point in displaying them now. She had to recreate her past. She stood up and kissed the old lady routinely on both cheeks. She had left the sick-room before the tears welled up to glisten in her eyes. She wiped them roughly away. She had been undecided. Perhaps she should forget Dr Mark Ivor and live with the roots she knew. But no. Not now. She was going to find her family. That past was another country, and she was going to visit it.

10

The Secretary to the Cabinet, Sir Caspar Rudd, sat at his vast partner's desk and looked out towards the lights in Horseguards Parade and the darkness of St James's Park beyond. It was nearly nine o'clock at night and the rest of the office had long gone. In a minute he too would lock his papers away in the safe, then go for a night-cap at the Reform Club, before taking a taxi home to Chelsea. Lady Rudd was away for a week, staying with her sister in Wales. It was like being a bachelor again, able to keep his own working hours without being complained at for always coming home so late. Except that his bachelor days were long, long past. Now he was the keeper of the soul of government.

Once again he took the simple sheet of paper from its red jacketed file and read it carefully.

Top Secret & Personal

TO: *The Secretary to the Cabinet*

FROM: *Chief, C13*

re: **Operation Picnic**

1. Material found in routine searches of Ivor's waste (Authorization on file) over a period of four weeks, shows little, because subject puts little on paper. In other circumstances we would report findings on a financial deal with Bahrain to Inland Revenue, but given security considerations we have not done so. There is a certain amount of background material

on Ramsay Smythe bid for Sigmont (separate report being prepared), and other documentation re a young woman who claims to be his daughter (available for use if required). One possible lead is his employment of a new assistant about whom we have information from a highly delicate source. If Ivor employs this man on a permanent basis, this could prove useful. There is no, repeat no, evidence of Ivor being in any way involved with *The Team* so far. Full watching brief on subject continues.

2. Your request re Lord S, following his surprising appointment as Chairman, has been fully implemented. CIA sources, via MI6, confirm continued contact with right-wing parties in the five East European countries mentioned. *Auswärtiges Amt* and *Deuxième Bureau* sources cross-check with GCHQ material (available to be seen only at this office if required) about the increasingly efficient liaison between these groups. S appears to be playing multiple hand, keeping options open but has regular and secret contact with General Gibson's '*Team*'. One intercept (fragmented) has S talking about ensuring that 'the little man' (his usual term for the PM) does what he is told and 'sees the light'. Updates to follow.

Message ends.

Sir Caspar Rudd sighed, slipped the paper back into its red jacket, stood up, put his papers away in the safe, twirled the combination dial until it locked securely, unhooked his overcoat from the stand, opened the door, switched out the light and left the room. Tomorrow was another day. Tomorrow he would have to put the PM face to face with the facts.

Precisely one week later, Lord Shand was secretly wined and dined by a senior executive director of the Sigmont Corporation in an elegant Belgravia apartment. During the course of the meal he was made an exciting financial proposition. It was expressed in such a roundabout way that no one could ever have taken it as a bribe. No money would change hands. Who would ever know about the change of title deeds for a substantial villa on a tiny West Indian paradise of an island? Lord Shand did not react to the proposal. Not so much as a flicker of an aristocratic eyelid. But the executive director left the dinner table knowing that the peer was enticed, if not yet hooked. What still had to be decided was what Shand's duties might be in return.

Ivor had had a discreet morning meeting at Kensington Palace — his advice had been sought on how to handle the latest matrimonial scandal — and arranged to meet Rick Maclean afterwards at 190 Queen's Gate. The Royal audience finished early; he waited for Maclean in the wood-panelled bar. It was only twelve thirty, but already there were too many noisy Knightsbridge yuppies, Arabs from nearby embassies and fat men discussing contracts. A barman served him a drink as he sat and watched a demure little secretary sipping her white wine, while her ageing boss tried to grope her knee. Beside them, a business woman imperiously ordered lunch for her two male acolytes who hovered nervously around her.

Maclean arrived promptly and they went through to the restaurant. Ivor's cross-questioning began as soon as they had ordered. He was deliberately heavy.

'Your attitudes to further European integration?'

'I adopt a balanced approach. We should only do what's practicable. I'm a Euro-wet except when it comes to the much bigger problem in what to do about the debris of the erstwhile Soviet Empire. An inward-looking Brussels, within its present membership, is madness when we've got the biggest economic slum sitting there, just across the border. Rampant nationalism in Russia and the Balkans –'

'Surely that's just why we need to stick together?'

'Of course. A strong NATO –'

'Germany?'

'The key. As usual. Fascism's rampant there too. German economic and industrial demands will grow and grow. The nineteenth and early twentieth centuries all over again.'

'We have our fascists, our rabid nationalists, here too.'

'General Gibson's crowd used to be dismissed as a bunch of cranks when they first teamed up with the British National Party. Look at them now. Some pretty heavy right-wing Tory supporters, big business money pouring in. Even Lord Shand is said to be flirting with them.'

'You believe that?'

'He's got some strange friends.'

'You're well informed. And?'

'As a result of nationalism elsewhere, neo-fascism in France, the Low Countries, Bosnia, Romania . . .'

'Britain?'

'Naturally. I sympathize in many ways, Dr Ivor. I hope you're not shocked. Margaret Thatcher had a vision. It's been lacking ever since. We need to match the external threat. Believe me, I'm no latter-day Mosley, but the great problem for the rest of this decade, and for the first of the new millennium, will be how to contain extreme nationalism abroad.'

'Worried?'

'This is an interrogation more than an interview.'

'A debate. A catechism.' Ivor smiled at the younger man. 'A mind-cleaning exercise. Sell yourself. How do you stand on Germany?'

'A united Germany has been a recurring nightmare for the last two centuries, for its neighbours, for Britain. It is back at the top of the agenda. While the Cold War existed, Germany had its problems, caused problems, but was not a major problem in itself. Its geographical location, its size, its people, their nature . . .' Maclean's words tumbled out. He was as confident and self-assured as when Ivor had first met him, just stopping just short of being bumptious.

'You believe in national characteristics?'

'Don't you?'

'Unfashionable though it is, there's no question but that the Germans, the French, the Italians, the –'

'The Scots . . .'

'Definitely the Scots . . . all have distinct attitudes to life. Do you get involved in the problems you're asked to work on?' Ivor asked.

'Of course. Very involved.' Maclean spotted the trap. 'But I keep my detachment. I keep the emotion bit out of it.'

'Like the best senior civil servants?'

'Got to watch passion doesn't creep in.'

'Sounds sexy. So . . . So . . . you want to join me?' asked Ivor.

'Very much.'

'Why?'

'You're the best around.'

'Ah! How d'you know?' Ivor was flattered, despite himself.

'Reputation. Your reputation for being influential means that you're influential.'

'I'm a loner.'

'I know. But, as I said when we met in Edinburgh, I can offer back-up, research, first draft of reports. I'm good at picking up gossip.' The young man easily overcame his modesty.

'Where?'

'I'm nearly thirty-one. All my best contemporaries are on rung two of their ladders – politics, Civil Service, the City, academic research institutes, think-tanks.'

'Young Turks.'

'Young Turks.'

Ivor looked at his watch and ordered coffee. 'You haven't convinced me of two things. One: whether I need you . . . or anyone. Two: whether I can afford you.'

'I'll earn it.'

'If enthusiasm were everything . . .'

'I've brought along a bundle of things I've written. I've got some referees you could speak to.' The young man showed the first sign of hesitancy.

'Thank you. That won't be necessary.'

'Oh, I see.' Maclean's disappointment spilled over onto his face.

'You don't think I'd waste my time, and yours, getting you here without having done my homework, do you? Let's see. I've spoken to your old professor, Richards, to Tony Moran at Kleinworts, to the oil people in Aberdeen you worked for last year, to Sir Freddie Blakeley at the Home Office. One or two of them kindly faxed me examples of your work. I've read it. Do you have anything else I might not have seen?' Ivor smiled a touch smugly.

'I, er, maybe I have one.' Maclean was nonplussed for a moment, then smiled chirpily. 'That's the reason I want to work for you. You steal a march.'

'Flattery will get you everywhere.' Ivor stood up. 'I've got to go and sit in on a press conference. Come with me. We can talk further.'

Government cutbacks meant Civil Service buildings had a low priority for redecoration. No ministerial message, put out in such surroundings, would have sparkle and zest. A tired room for a tired occasion. About half the rows of seats were occupied.

'A poor turn-out,' volunteered Rick Maclean.

'You have things still to learn,' teased Ivor. 'There are about fifty people here, four TV crews, twenty or so scribblers and five or six still photographers. That's all the major British media outlets covered. A lot for a domestic press conference.'

A journalist from the *Independent* spotted Ivor and came over. 'What's he going to say, Mark?'

'It may have changed since I last heard.'

'You're not saying?'

'I'm not saying.'

At the top of the table, in front of a banner which announced, with stunning blandness, '*Towards the Year 2000*', a group of press officers from the Department of Health fluttered around like pigeons in Trafalgar Square. A senior figure arrived, coughed and tried the microphones. He tapped one, then spoke. The inevitable feedback whine screeched around the room. The minister, the up and coming Horace Tetchley, was on his way. There was a mini-panic as a sound technician was summoned from a back room. On the far side, a dispute was under way between a camera crew and the men from the COI who were refusing to adjust their arc-lights.

'Why here?' asked Maclean. 'Are you involved in health matters?'

'I'm not. But if we're to win the general election, I need a view on where the government is going wrong on this one.'

'Money, money, money . . .'

'Poor Health Service reorganization. Look at the standard of these Civil Service press people.' He gestured. 'They think that PR is all about events like this or shoving out another boring press release. No wonder they get such stick from the media. They hand it to the Opposition on a plate.'

'What are they doing wrong?'

'If we work together I'll let you into the secrets.' Ivor paused and waved a friendly greeting at a familiar TV cameraman. 'You need to know I'm also here for a more immediate reason.'

'Yes?'

'I've got to make a judgement on how this particular minister, Horace Tetchley, will do if I put, sorry, if the party puts a lot of effort into sending him on a major tour of the marginal constituencies.'

'You know him. You've seen him on the box.'

'I've not seen him work a press conference. That's what matters. How he actually handles himself, deals with questions, makes the journalists relax, gets them to laugh and, above all, puts his points across. That'll make or break him, and the party.'

'His policies —'

'— may be slightly interesting. For five minutes. In the long run — by that I mean longer than tonight's TV news and tomorrow's first editions — it is *how* he says what he has to say, not what he says, that'll count. Here he comes. Watch him, Rick. Mark him out of ten for dress, for style, for timing, for ability to field difficult questions, for keeping the room interested and good natured. Forget substance. Forget content.'

'I knew you were cynical. Not how much.'

'Putting you off?'

'Not at all. But the minister's intelligent. He'll have worked hard at his briefs with his senior officials.'

'Right.'

'Well then?'

'The media's reaction to what he says – *that's* the key. Believe me. He's got to sell it like soap.'

'They know all he's done for the Health Service. Historically –'

'Most journalists' recall of history is who bought them their last drink. Quiet or we'll miss the gems.'

Half an hour later, the minister stood to leave but a handful of journalists crowded around him. Ivor turned to Maclean.

'How did you rate him?'

Maclean glanced down at a notepad he was holding. 'Score six overall. Seven on dress and style, five on question handling and timing. Only three to four on keeping everyone awake. Boring, in fact.'

'What about content?'

'I didn't take much in.'

'Precisely my point, Rick. Your score more or less matches mine.'

'And?'

'Could you improve him if you were his image handler?'

'I'd make him stop fiddling with the coins in his pocket as he spoke. And he was talking into his shirt-front the whole time.'

'Voice down. Here he comes.' Ivor stood as Horace Tetchley himself came towards him.

'Morning, Mark.'

'Morning, Minister. That should make some headlines.'

'How d'you think it went?'

Ivor side-stepped the question. 'Can I introduce my new assistant, Rick Maclean, Minister.'

Maclean showed no emotion as he shook the minister's hand.

A little later, while Ivor stood chatting to one of the BBC TV newsmen, a man came up to Maclean and introduced himself.

'Fred Cree. You work for Mark Ivor?'

'I . . . I suppose . . . yes.'

'Great fixer. Great reputation. I've been following his success for ages.'

'He *is* good.'

'Look . . . we must have lunch sometime. I'll give you a ring. Can I get you at Dr Ivor's office number?' Cree's badly shaven jaw split into something resembling a smile.

'See you,' he said, and moved swiftly away.

Maclean went over and rejoined Ivor.

'Who was that?' Ivor asked.

'Name of Fred Cree, I think.'

'Now working for . . . ?'

'Not quite sure.'

'Yes. I know Cree. Wants careful watching.'

A meeting that the authorities, even with GCHQ's help, were unable to monitor because of the seniority of the figure to whom the property belonged, was held in a house in Lord North Street, Westminster. Lord Shand, two knighted MPs on the extreme right of the party, General Sir Patrick Gibson MC, Mr Ramsay Smythe and the well-known proprietor of a major newspaper empire sat, late one night, discussing their forthcoming strategy if, as predicted, the government held on to power after the election. Shand warmed a brandy goblet in his hands. Ramsay Smythe and the proprietor were sipping whiskies and water. The General did not drink, nor did he say very much. He was a man who held his own council.

'We all agree,' Shand was talking, 'that the external threat is very great given the internal political inertia . . .'

'Cowardice . . . impotence . . .' muttered one of the MPs.

'But a coup, a political coup in the United Kingdom is unthinkable,' said another.

'There is a much cleverer way. And just as effective,' Shand continued. 'I have it in hand.'

'Could you explain?' asked the General, breaking his silence.

'I remember, years ago, in Africa, there was a coup that wasn't,' reminisced Lord Shand. 'The president was in his palace, carrying out his policies. Then a small group of highly motivated men moved in. No shots were fired. No one was arrested. They just took over the president's mind. Policies gradually changed. No one outside noticed for a while. Everything was done gradually, slowly. It was very clever. Even the president did not realize what was happening at first. When he did, when the outside world began to react, it was too late. The new policies – they were much more left wing, but that does not matter, the communists were good at fourth-column work – were the president's policies, expressed and presented in his name. How could he refute or condemn them? He was a prisoner only of the decisions taken in his name.'

'Clever. Very clever,' said Ramsay Smythe.

'A coup from within,' murmured the General thoughtfully.

'But you are not some anonymous figure, Rupert. You are widely known for the views that you hold,' said the newspaper proprietor cautiously. 'We are not in some tin-pot African dictatorship. This is a democratic country. People already suspect your motives, and are jealous of your access to Michael Wilson. They know the PM is weak. They are worried about your influence.'

'That's where you and your newspapers come in,' responded Lord Shand. 'And I have it in mind to take a back seat in the run-up to the election, for all is lost if we lose it.'

'So how . . . ?' began Ramsay Smythe.

'I have the man through whom we can best work. He has access. He has known skills and impartiality. The PM trusts him.'

'Of course, Dr Mark Ivor,' breathed Ramsay Smythe approvingly.

* * *

115

Following this meeting, a short exchange of conversation did become available because General Gibson and Lord Shand continued talking in Gibson's car when the latter dropped Shand back at his flat late that night. Gibson's car had been specially attended to by experts at their trade. At his office in Whitehall, Sir Caspar Rudd read it with the greatest of care.

> **Top Secret & Personal**
> **For Addressee's Eyes Only**
> TO: *The Secretary to the Cabinet*
> FROM: *Chief, C13*
> re: **Operation Picnic**

Following is transcribed conversation (*it became inaudible at times*) between two males on Thursday 29th. Speaker A is believed to be Lord Shand. Speaker B is identified as General Sir Patrick Gibson.

A: Good evening, that was.

B: Interesting.

A: I trust some of our friends as far as I could throw them.

B: Especially RS? He needs handling with a long spoon.

A: We need his money.

B: Media barons are . . .

(*conversation inaudible*)

A: We need more support on the public relations side. We need the hearts and minds to follow.

B: Tell me about your Dr Mark Ivor.

A: All things to all men.

B: Has he really such good access to the PM?

A: Unfortunately.

B: Or fortunately. Is he buyable?

A: With care.

B: How are you going to recruit him?

A: I have my ideas.

B: Keep me in touch, Rupert. I have my contacts too . . . (*conversation became inaudible from then on*).

[*Source Comment* to Chief C13. Dr Ivor's name is now increasingly coming into play re Operation Picnic. He is a clever man but may not, repeat may not, realize how he is to be used.]

Message ends.

11

It was a very male bedroom: dark, rosewood fitted wardrobes neatly filled with well-pressed suits, a panelled dressing area, with long mirrors and a dumb valet, one or two paintings, including a seductive pre-Raphaelite nude above the bed. The bed itself was a great rosewood four-poster.

Mark Ivor's ego was in great shape. He was riding high. He was, in consequence, hyper-randy: his glands, his hormones were in overdrive. He rolled over lazily in the turmoil of the bedding, pushing aside a leather belt that had so recently been put to pleasurable use. Fiona rolled with him, then on top, staring down into his eyes. Her tousled hair fell across a face that was warm with sex and pleasure.

'My young family think sexual intercourse only began in the sixties.'

'Right. Before the Lady Chatterley trial, sex: the second-last taboo.' He thought briefly of Amanda.

'The last?'

'Death.'

'God . . .' Fiona paused to fight away his exploring hand. 'Give me a break.'

'Why? You want. I want.'

'A break, I said. I want to talk.'

'Ugh. That's as much a conversation stopper as "What shall we talk about?"'

'I don't get any talk at home. Husband doesn't speak to me any more, except about the mundane, the domestic. He drinks so much I'm probably suffering from passive alcoholism.'

Ivor laughed. 'What subject?'

'You,' she said. 'I want to get inside your mind, get to know what makes you tick.'

'Cross-examination?'

'If you like. I want answers.'

'Never mix business with —'

She interrupted his words with a kiss. Then: 'For you, your business is your pleasure.' It was a statement.

'I suppose.'

'You enjoy it?'

'Mostly.'

'What?'

'Problem-solving.'

'Other people's problems.'

'They're much easier.'

'You don't have commitments. You don't have too many hang-ups. Lucky . . .'

He looked away for a moment, hesitated as if to say something, then turned back to stare up at her. 'What d'you want to know?'

'What are you working on?'

He feigned a foreign accent: 'Geev me your body, Mata Hari, and I will tell all . . .'

'Go on.'

'Main financial one is the mega take-over of the Sigmont Corporation. You've read about it. I'm paid by the Ramsay Smythe consortium to keep relations with Westminster and the media happy.'

'That's fairly straightforward. And big fees for Dr Ivor . . .'

'It is a good deal, for Sigmont shareholders . . . and for me. But we're faced with a board of directors who don't want to be taken over and who are playing dirty.'

'When it comes to dirty . . .' She laughed, groped lightly at him and the conversation was interrupted for a few moments. Eventually their bodies came back to rest.

'Go on,' she urged.

'I've an on-going arrangement with the Prime Minister and with Central Office.'

'The PM?'

'I don't talk about the PM.'

'Quite right to be discreet. I'm not upset . . . What about Lord Shand?'

'He's one of my colleagues . . . I help him out from time to time.'

'You'd take a brief from the devil if he paid you. I've met him, you know. Socially. The epitome of the British aristocrat. Apart from one thing.'

'Shand? What's odd about him?'

'He had an odd East European wife. Romanian, I think. She died a year or so ago. He was devoted to her.'

'That's a surprise. He's a hard man. But I have my ethics.'

'Your ethics are between your legs.'

'You're vulgar.'

'That's why you like me. What else d'you do for the party? Persuade the electorate to like their health service policies?'

'Not that sort of detail. I persuade the persuaders. I work on opinion-formers – in the press, and in the party too.'

'How?'

'Depends. Suggest to one backbencher that advancement may come by supporting this rather than that; hinting that knighthoods come easier to those who toe lines.'

'It doesn't work that way – does it?'

'It does. Titles, honours, go to those who don't rock the ships of state. Merit plays little part.'

'Will you get a gong?'

Ivor shrugged. 'If I'm on the right side at the right time. Remember the only class that really matters in the UK is the governing class. I'm on the margin. If the window of political opportunity opens as I'm passing . . .'

'I'm serious.'

'So am I. The luck of the draw. Baubles are given out like long service and good conduct medals. Remember the Goon

Show line: "Collect your MBEs as you go out of the door, folks!" '

'Do you see much of the PM?'

'Mmm. Yes. Help on things he doesn't want to put through the usual channels. I don't cry it aloud.'

'And your advice?'

'He sees me as uncluttered by a party or civil service mentality. And that's all even you are going to get out of me on that subject.'

'Modern Machiavelli.'

'They say.'

'He . . . Machiavelli's had a bad press.'

'Unfair. He was only being realistic. He never really argued that the end justifies the means. His Prince was coolly advised. Rationality was in; emotions out.'

'You're against emotion? Does anything pass your nerves and touch your heart?'

'Sounds romantic. Depends on circumstances. If you allow emotions to cloud your judgement you're finished. Become over-committed to a cause, let reason tangle with passion, you're on the street.'

'Passion . . . yum, yum. What other driblets of wisdom have you for me?'

'Lots. Mostly unformulated. One day I'll write a book about manipulation.'

'Of what?'

'Of other people's pride. People's ambition. People's violence against the weak.' He paused as if considering whether to say more, but some long-buried secrets are too deep, too personal, too hurtful to be shared . . . shared with anyone.

Fiona saw, for an instant, something of this, some deep insecurity in Ivor, some relic of past hurt. She saw a flash of tears quickly wiped away. She spoke softly then. 'What about *your* goals? You must have *some* that aren't other people's.'

'You're mocking again. I'll dry up.'

'I'll make you moist.'

'Back to basics, Fiona.' He laughed lightly. The tension she had seen had quickly passed away.

Later he talked about himself, more than he ever did.

'Yes. Manipulating people, situations, not for financial gain, but because I enjoy it. Altering future history: does that sound pompous? I avoid the headlines. People seek publicity or get built up by media hype; then they're massacred when they slip.'

'You enjoy your outsider-insider reputation?' Fiona forced him to keep talking. He tried to get out of it by fooling around, joking, changing the subject, resorting to the physical. She persevered. He began to see in her things he lacked, things he wanted. He gradually revealed his motivations to her, each previously compartmentalized part of his life.

After a time she got up from the bed, slipped on his dressing gown and poured them both a drink.

'So. The political catalyst, making certain decisions become inevitable? You're a power-broker, sometimes a king-maker. Without responsibility.'

'This is Your Life, eh?' he suggested.

'Scottish background . . . a little help from the United States, gives you a classlessness in a still socially stratified British political arena. Mr Presentation Man plus.'

He stood up, naked, stretched and bowed mockingly, then moved across to a side-table and topped up his drink. 'When my biographer sets to work, I'll put you both in touch.'

Fiona turned away. 'You're an enigma. You've no political ambitions, so you say. I believe you: you're not interested in "power" or personal prominence. The game for the sake of the game. But what about your values, Mark? It's them I'm worried about. When I open the cupboard, what's inside?'

'Whew,' he said. 'Not finished yet?'

'Not quite. You see yourself untouched by events. But that's a cop-out, a rejection of responsibility, and a defence mechanism.'

'Not surprising if true. Remember how the press assassinate:

Parkinson, Halpern, Mellor, Yeo. The media fuel the public's malicious pleasure.'

There was a long pause. 'I believe you really think you *are* immune,' Fiona said eventually.

'There's something I wanted to tell you. About all that.'

'You're being serious? At last.' She looked hard at him.

'Never more.'

The telephone rang. He picked it up reluctantly.

'Ivor here,' he said. He listened. 'Tim Willis? Yes, of course. I'll be there in half an hour.'

Ivor put the phone down and turned to Fiona. 'I have to go. That was Number Ten.'

'Name dropper. What were you going to say?'

'I was going to say . . . It's about him. And keeping my impartiality. My values such as they are.'

'Well?'

'I'm suddenly being pressurized. To pressurize him – the PM – and I don't like it.'

'By?'

'Shand. And others. It's as if it's concerted. All part of a plan.'

'What sort of plan?'

'I don't know. Not yet, anyway.'

The two men had a unique relationship, perceived differently by each. Ivor was the cleverer man, just as most men and women on the staff of senior politicians are more able, if less self-assuming, than those they serve. They got on well but would never be close friends. Someone, sometime, had told the PM the story of Père Joseph, the seventeenth century Capuchin friar and confidant of Cardinal Richelieu; the original *éminence grise*. The PM had subsequently compared Ivor to the friar, laughingly contrasting grey religious habit with grey Savile Row suit. Later the story spread to the gossip columns, to Ivor's embarrassment. The Prime Minister was a man whose image scored much higher than his reality. With Ivor's help he had worked on his television performances and had almost perfected the skill of appearing genuine. He had grown in status as he had gained in self-confidence. Senior civil servants thought him a 'good' Cabinet Minister; they liked ones who listened, who read briefs with attention, who were efficient in dealing with submissions, who knew, like them, how to bury contentious issues by handing them over to committees where they could be lost for generations. The Prime Minister did not upset the flow of State business with too many new ideas of his own. He was a first class, third class, operator helped along by good luck. With the press watching like hawks, he was beginning to know how to hold the attention of his political orchestra without turning his back on them. He was good with words; he could slalom down a verbal ski-slope, zigzagging around the rocks of unpalatable truth, and still reach the end of his speech with his audience, even those on the other side of the House, laughing with him, or at least not laughing at him.

The PM was a practical man. He liked plain talking. He said he wanted to know what he ought to hear not what sycophants wanted him to hear. Unfortunately, he took bad news badly, so ministerial colleagues were economical in passing on news of misfortune. That was where Ivor came in. He got away with it. He knew his man. He had no axe to grind, no political point to advocate. His role was to advise the Prime Minister on what was best for him. They had that simple goal in common – until Lord Shand came along.

Ivor reflected that, in the PM's shoes, he too would have chosen an alternate adviser from outside the system, a foil to bounce revolutionary ideas off, to act as burglar of external information, to act as gofer and to communicate beyond the immediate corridors of power. But as an outsider running on the inside track, Ivor knew he needed to keep in with the Establishment, that matrix of individuals who brought about or cancelled change. Now something was shifting: Lord Shand had always appeared like the Establishment personified; he had blown hot then cold, and now once again Shand was courting him.

Michael Wilson was in his top floor sitting room in Downing Street when Ivor was shown in. In open neck shirt, carpet slippers on his feet, he slouched on a sofa surrounded by several open red boxes, which spewed their contents over furniture and floor.

'Fix yourself a drink, Mark. I'll be with you once I've killed these Foreign Office telegrams.'

'Thanks, Michael.' Ivor was on Christian names in private.

Minutes passed, the PM bundled the multi-coloured bundle of briefs and telegrams into their despatch box, slammed the lid and turned the key. He pressed a bell beside him. 'I'll get these taken away, then I'll be with you.' A messenger appeared as he spoke, picked up the boxes and disappeared.

'Now, got a drink? OK. We've got a problem.'

'Yes?'

'Sex scandal.'

'I thought the system had sat on it. Rupert Shand said –'

'Rupert was right. That one we fixed.'

'So?'

'There's more. And we can't use Bangkok again.'

'Leave it all to the Chief Whip, Michael. He knows who's sleeping with whom, who's a pervert, who's merely whore-mongering. He can handle it.'

'The one we killed was about Prentice.'

'I thought his resigning for family reasons was a little sudden. What was it?'

'His mistress is half Iraqi. Links with Baghdad intelligence. Pity. I liked and trusted Prentice. The best ones seem to fall most easily.'

'Prentice can't have had that many secrets.'

'He'd been pushed into doing something stupid on an arms contract, persuaded to sign an export licence for a Middle East shipment that should be going nowhere.'

'Idiot. But even if the papers do pick it up, it's water under the bridge. The government acted promptly and impeccably and all that. I'll be ready with a word for one or two editors: to set the tone.'

'Thanks, but no thanks. I've already handled Prentice.'

'Then who? What?'

'Don't know. But Caanan and his Press Office think the *News of the Screws* are chasing another story.'

'How d'you know?'

'Anonymous phone call. Someone important is being set up. Bondage; under age sex; you name it.'

'*Another* Cabinet Minister? You're not keeping them busy enough.'

'This isn't funny. Politics used to be cleaner.'

'Never was clean. Sex and politics are too similar. Lust and deceit; great pretensions of loyalty; the subordination of straight behaviour to expediency fuelled by desire. Too many powerful and rabid men; too many young women ready to surrender their virginity on repeated occasions either for money or as a career move.'

'Heavy stuff.'

'Sex and truth are rotten bedfellows. If the first's around, the second gets forgotten.'

'We have to kill it.'

'You can't hush up a sex scandal.'

'I'm warning all my colleagues at tomorrow's Cabinet.'

'Tomorrow's a whole night of passion away. The environs of Parliament are filled with semi-ladies. *Les Grandes Horizontales* . . .'

'The mistake is out there waiting to be made. What do I do?'

'Let it run.'

'I said this isn't a joke, Mark. I'm about to announce the damned date for the General Election. I can't have any more nasty stories.'

'No, Prime Minister. But you know as well as I do that the press have always got about a dozen parliamentary scandals that they *don't* run. Let's stop and ask: who is putting them up to running them just now? And why?'

Ivor went back to his office and worked hard on the telephone for the next few hours. He got through to a number of respectable and far from respectable journalists whom he knew he could at least partially trust, if only because they needed him more than he needed them. He drew a blank. He rang a famous gossip columnist and a paparazzo photographer for whom he'd once done a considerable favour when the man was arrested for trespassing on the property of a Hollywood superstar. It was this last call that gave him what he was looking for.

There was a stakeout. A house close to St Pancras was being watched night and day. Telephoto lenses monitored all from a room rented by the *News of the World*. It was said to be a Cabinet Minister. There were rumours as to who it was, but no one was sure. The next time the victim came to whet his sexual appetite, they would be waiting.

Ivor rang the Prime Minister on his private line and told him. Then he decided to call it a day. But he was a man who always noticed detail and, just as he was leaving, he spotted that the mahogany veneer was coming away from the back of his large partner's desk. He was meticulous about the condition of his furniture. He leant across to look. The blemish, like a dark shadow, ran just under the edge, where the desk top sat on one of its heavy pedestals. He would fix it himself unless it was a more serious fault, in which case he would call his French polisher . . . But there was nothing wrong with the veneer. It was a small, wood-coloured block, no more than an inch across and half an inch deep. It was hanging loose, attached to the underside of the desk by a thin piece of wire. It must be a piece of jointing, a wedge meant to hold the desk top steady on its base. His fingers reached towards it, then something made him stop. He stood up, walked round to the other side of the desk, opened a drawer and took out a thin pencil torch, then returned to examine his find. The underside of the little block had detached itself from the woodwork. One of the two sharp pins that were meant to be embedded in the underside of the desk was bent, perhaps in the haste of being quickly planted there. But it wasn't the pins that he saw first; it was the sheen of dull metal, the tiny coils of wire, the two round, long-life batteries such as one finds in some makes of watch.

Ivor knew a bug when he saw one.

*   *   *

The next day there was a terse exchange between Chief, C13 and F.R.S./17.

> **Top Secret & Personal**
> TO: *Chief, C13*
> FROM: *F.R.S./17*
>
> Subject has discovered a listening device in his office. He may start making a fuss.
>
> *Message ends.*

> **Top Secret & Personal**
> TO: *F.R.S./17*
> FROM: *Chief, C13*
>
> Most displeased. How did it happen? *Fullest* report required.
>
> *Message ends.*

> **Top Secret & Personal**
> TO: *Chief, C13*
> FROM: *F.R.S./17*
>
> Regret previous message incomplete. Device has nothing, repeat nothing, to do with us. We are investigating. Urgently.
>
> *Message ends.*

Later, when Sir Caspar Rudd heard about it from the Chief of C13, he was more than usually alarmed. He knew Dr Mark Ivor. He knew how close he was to the PM. If Ivor's office had been bugged, how many of Number Ten's secrets were now more widely known? It was all getting out of hand.

12

Mirrors reflected mirrors into infinity. If he moved his head slightly, he could see part of his face and the back of his head in multiples, as the hairdresser's thousand scissors made their final cuts. Hands pulled the towels away. Ivor stood up and the man brushed him down. It was then that he spotted Walt Tesco, perched on a chair by the door, browsing through a magazine. He quelled a momentary flash of anger, paid the bill, leaving more of a tip than he had intended, then walked briskly towards the door. Tesco jumped up, tossed the magazine aside and followed him into Jermyn Street.

'We arranged to meet at my office tomorrow at ten. Why now?'

'Had to, Dr Ivor,' said Tesco, beaming up at him.

'How the hell did you know where I was?' Ivor forced himself to keep cool.

Tesco came back at him vigorously. 'First: Ramsay Smythe rang an hour ago. Told me sharpish he wanted us to get together. Like immediately. You'll find a similar message at your office. Second: I'm a private detective. But it doesn't need that to ring your secretary, explain the problem, and track you down.'

'I'm not prepared to –'

'Look, Ivor, I know you're an important man, but just remember, please, that I've already apologized for upsetting your Amanda –'

'Leave the girl out of it,' Ivor interrupted. They stood facing each other on the narrow Jermyn Street pavement.

'Fine. I just want to make my point. You're treating me like public enemy number one without any justification. You ought to know how demanding Ramsay Smythe can be. With him, now means now.'

'Let's go to my office,' said Ivor, softening a fraction. He made to hail a taxi.

'Let's not,' responded Tesco. 'Let's go walkabout. Never know who might be listening . . . in your office . . .'

Ivor looked sharply at Tesco but he showed no sign of following up on his remark. They walked down to St James's Square, across Pall Mall, past Carlton House Terrace and into St James's Park.

'Nice girl. Sorry I messed it up,' Tesco volunteered.

'I said – leave her out of it.'

'OK. OK. Well, look. I don't know what Ramsay Smythe has told you, but –'

'I work for him as a PR consultant. I'm involved in the bid for the Sigmont Corporation – media and political lobbying. That's it.'

'You don't know about Ramsay Smythe himself?'

'A bit. But I'm not going to gossip to you.'

'Lay off the aggression, if you don't mind.'

'Very well, I'm sorry.' Ivor felt he had overreacted. 'But . . . Amanda . . . It is a huge surprise, Mr Tesco.'

'You said it, let's stick to Ramsay Smythe. As to gossip, well, I know more than's healthy for one person to know about another. I've been working for him for a long time.'

They walked on through St James's Park. In the background, a cluster of dejected pelicans stood under some trees by the lake.

'What's his problem?' asked Ivor.

'He keeps getting little messages, including ones from you, that the government knows something. Leaves a nasty taste. He wants people to like him.'

'Like him?' Ivor laughed. 'Yes, I did get warned.'

'It's not something dug up by the Sigmont Corporation's dirty tricks department, you know.'

'I was given no details. What is it about him?'

'He told me to put you in the picture. More or less.'

'Why not himself?'

'Maybe – odd thought – he's embarrassed. By asking a favour. When he usually commands.'

'Favour?'

'Let's find a park bench and sit down for a bit. I'll tell you about it.'

A casual observer might have thought the two men seated on the park bench remarkably ill-matched. Beside them an elderly lady was feeding an assortment of ducks, pigeons and sparrows. The immaculate Ivor was uneasy until the story hooked him; Tesco, bulging out of his badly fitting suit, was animated, almost cheerful. An eavesdropper would have heard how Tesco had arranged to buy illicit material from the Romanian *Securitate* archives: a confidential file about Ramsay Smythe and his activities in East-West trade, along with another one that contained the dirt on Peter Maltby, which had led to the minister's suicide.

'We both had a hand in that; not much to be proud of there,' volunteered Tesco. 'But a lot of money changed hands over the years. Ramsay Smythe also received substantial retainers, and not just from the Romanians. And why not? Behind the old Iron Curtain backhanders were the only way to do business. It's no use HMG getting all moralistic now.'

'If that's all, why's he so concerned, so sensitive?' Ivor asked. 'It's all history.'

'A documented file is different. Ramsay Smythe realizes there must be more material now held by MI5 or MI6. Probably transcripts and interrogation reports. They're much less easy to forget. And then there's the amounts of money involved. Ramsay Smythe thinks the Inland Revenue could go for him in a big way if there's hard evidence.'

'Go on,' encouraged Ivor.

Tesco laughed. 'Ramsay Smythe is very much a family man. Cares about his wife and children. He really does. In Bucharest, away from the domestic nest, things were different. You understand, Dr Ivor. In the wrong hands, the evidence of a varied amount of sexual dalliance could have provided first-class blackmail material. So far, only the East Europeans themselves and Western Intelligence have been interested in what's buried in the *Securitate*, the Stasi, the Czech, let alone the Soviet KGB files.'

'Yes,' said Ivor, taking it all in. 'I suppose that if all their contents became openly available, the potential for extortion would be enormous.'

'I've been over before,' Tesco admitted. 'I thought of going over and bribing them to let me browse through some more files. If only someone would finance the trip. There are a lot of other skeletons, a lot of bigger fish, if you'll excuse the mixed metaphor,' he added darkly.

'Is Ramsay Smythe asking me to broker an amnesty for him? With the government?'

'Something like that.'

'Why didn't he ask me himself?' Ivor asked again.

'I tell you: he's shy.'

'Both you and I, Mr Tesco, know that this is one great big lie.'

'He doesn't want his past interfering with the present.' Tesco hesitated. 'He thinks it's all so unfair. He's being singled out, branded as some sort of double dealer, while others get away with it.'

'Peter Maltby didn't get away with it.'

'No,' said Tesco slowly. 'But Lord Shand seems to have done.'

'I don't understand,' said Ivor. 'I thought Ramsay Smythe and Lord Shand were in bed together, that they thought as one.'

'Oh yes they do. But you see, Ramsay Smythe always likes an insurance policy. He wants to keep in with the Establishment. Just in case Lord Shand . . .'

'Loses?' asked Ivor thoughtfully.

*

Caley Perkins was like no other of Ivor's friends. An overgrown child of a man, he was in his late fifties, almost bald with a sparkling, if puckered, face. He was also an outstanding psephologist. A former Professor of Statistics at Manchester, he had turned to polling late in life and now ran P-Poll, one of the most successful public opinion polling companies in Britain. He knew how politicians and the media tended to revile public opinion polls, but secretly took account of them. Caley Perkins knew everything there was to know about public and group opinion.

He was also an outstandingly good cook, never giving a moment's thought to taking most of the day off prior to entertaining friends at his cluttered Kensington apartment. Ivor went there not just to eat but for an experience. This time he was on his own. The meal, a cold cucumber soup, a soufflé, and then a dish of duck on a bed of wild rice, was five star.

Caley was sparing with the drink until the meal had ended. He did not want his guest distracted. One glass of Sancerre, one glass of a rich Australian Cabernet Sauvignon. But after the dinner was cleared away to his oak-dressered kitchen, the wine was allowed to flow freely.

'How did you find the time?'

'Finding time is an attitude of mind. You're dominated by your watch, Mark. You tell me. How do *you* find the time? All your projects . . .' Caley Perkins began opening a second bottle of the red. 'Like to finish the Sancerre?'

'I'll stick to the Cabernet. I'm sure the white will keep.'

'Not in this house, it won't. There aren't such things as half empty bottles in my fridge.'

'How do I find the time? You know how I work.'

'I know the results you're said to get. I know whom I've seen you with, your myriad conspiracies.'

'Conspiracies . . . that's not very nice,' responded Ivor, looking across benignly at his friend. There was already a slur to his voice. 'Plots. Talking of which, I've always wanted to write a novel. Having to deal with reality all day does it. With a novel you can ignore reality, put in as fact precisely what you want to be fact. If you say that this incident is a fact, then it stands, unchallenged. You can create characters with as much depth or passion, generosity or corruption, modesty or ambition, as you please. You can give them the most extreme opinions, put ideas or statements of the most stupendous insolence into their mouths, then disown every element of them. A novelist can blend truth and fiction, build warm, sexy relationships. A novelist is a creator, a little god.'

'I believe, my friend, that you are getting a little pissed,' said Caley Perkins.

'You held back on the booze.'

'You've made up for it.'

'I'm talking sense,' Ivor said, a touch aggressively.

'Of course you are.'

'I come here . . . to relax.' He splayed himself out in his chair.

'You should do it more. Anyway, I asked you how you fit in everything.'

'I go for those who can advance or veto strategy. Very few of them, I can tell you. They control the pressure points. I try not to waste time. I avoid those with no discernible gifts or –'

'What bloody arrogance, Mark. You've become like that type of intellectual who only knows what he wants to know or recognize.'

'I'm not being élitist. Merely practical.'

'Politics is élitist. I know that. And it never fails to disgust.' Caley Perkins grimaced.

'You live off it too.'

'I do. And I see that the difference between greatness and stupidity in politics is that greatness has its limits.'

'Precisely my point. I build access to the decision makers, not those who hold a title. I persuade them that what I want them to do is their idea. I concentrate on one issue at a time. More dilutes the chances of success. I know my allies and my enemies. Finally, I keep it brief. Beware boredom.'

'You – boring!' Caley Perkins joked. 'Not a bad list. I imagine that's how you play the Prime Minister.'

'I don't play the PM. I advise him.' Ivor slopped more wine, unasked, into his own glass.

'Listen, will you, Mark. You may think you know everything. Think again. There's more than one who dislikes your influence, your access. But they want to use you. So that they can use the

PM. I hear stories. Politics is full of opportunists who let you get on with it until you stop playing their way. Stop and you'll soon feel the steel-tipped boots style of politics.'

Through the wine, Ivor was aware that Caley Perkins was also giving him some sort of warning. But he felt too relaxed to get serious. '*They*, Caley? Assassins, the heavy mob, the Bow Group, the Young Conservatives, far left, far right . . . ?'

'I don't think that Lord Shand is your greatest friend.'

'Never have thought of Rupert Shand as particularly cuddly. But he needs me.'

'At the moment.'

'I can handle him. I know a lot about him. Knowledge is power, all that junk . . . He's just a bit proprietorial, that's all. Anyway, he's not one of the steel-capped brigade. Barkers or Gucci shoes for him.' Ivor was aware of a slight slurring of his words.

'If properly applied, Mark, a Gucci toe can cause a lot of pain.'

'Listen, Caley. I'm not in the mood,' said Ivor.

'Very well. But I'm warning –'

Ivor briefly pulled himself together. 'Look, Caley. I know I've got to watch it. I know people want to know what I know. I know people want to use me. How am I sure? Well, it comes home to you hard when you find out that your office has been very professionally bugged. Now, are you going to open another bottle of this excellent plonk or are you not?'

There was no record whatsoever kept of a secret meeting between the increasingly determined Sir Caspar Rudd, Secretary to the Cabinet, and the Chief C13, at which only one other man was present, where anxieties were shared about Lord Shand's growing influence over the Prime Minister. It was also noted, from covert intelligence sources, how generous Mr Ramsay Smythe was being in helping with party funding. The Secretary to the Cabinet later had to use special powers to ensure that the Political Honours Scrutiny Committee did not allow the proposed CBE for Mr Ramsay Smythe. Additional lobbying had been noted via Caanan, the Press Secretary at Number Ten, from the proprietor of a major newspaper group. Written reports on the activities of *The Team* were not discussed. They were hardly necessary when excellent first-hand evidence was available. The activities of the spin doctor Mark Ivor were also reviewed. Had he been aware of what happened next, Ivor would have realized that, in Sir Caspar Rudd, he had an easy equal at his game.

13

The faces of the people thronging a theatre foyer say something about the play. A light comedy, a drama, a musical: each category has its own style of audience. The heavier, more difficult plays self-select a more intense-looking clientele. The lighter ones attract the Home Counties, up-in-the-town-for-the-night crowd, and the tourists, the life-blood of the West End theatre.

The Ayckbourn play, a drama of clever words and little action, had attracted an in-between category. Amanda saw a problem for the two dozen apparently unilingual Japanese tourists who chattered amongst themselves in the front row of the stalls. She had plenty of time to ponder; late that afternoon he had phoned from Number Ten to say he would be delayed. Her ticket would be at the box office. She was to go in and take her seat. She was not impressed. It was a bad beginning.

In the event, he slipped into his seat beside her as the house lights dimmed. 'Sorry,' he whispered. 'It couldn't have been a worse day.'

'Not to worry,' she responded. Ill at ease, she was glad she would not have to talk. She judged he was tired from the way he slumped low in his seat and, as the evening progressed, she also noticed that, from time to time, he would produce a sweet from his pocket and slip it furtively into his mouth. It was a human touch, yet he did not offer her one.

The play was thoughtful but light enough to be entertaining. The combination lubricated the uneasy minutes of their conversation during the interval. He was seldom at a loss for words. Words had always come easily to him: they chose him, sounding perfect in place and time. Except tonight. Tonight words came hard.

He had studied all the legal documents. Rotenbein assured him that they would stand up in court in any paternity case. In between talking about Ramsay Smythe, Tesco had indignantly confirmed the certainties of his investigations. She was his. There was no doubt.

She asked for white wine; he bought a large gin and tonic to see if it would help slip him into gear. By the time the interval ended they were beginning to explain to each other what they liked, what they did when they were not working, revealing, layer under layer, how they lived. But it had to wait until dinner at Joe Allen's for them to cut through.

The cellar restaurant, with its undressed brick walls, its red-checked table cloths, its self-assured bustle, was packed, but he had a table well protected in a corner. They sat at an angle to each other, able to watch the room. As they settled in, Kathy Turvey, the TV presenter, was leaving the restaurant. She spotted Ivor, came and gushed all over him, kissing him effusively on both cheeks. He introduced Amanda without explaining her, before she whirled off, surrounded by a coterie of admirers with a flurry of 'we must have lunch soon'.

There was a moment's silence, then Amanda opened: 'What was she like? Annette?'

'The memory's a bit hazy. Close-cropped urchin's haircut, big mouth, generous smile. I think I was in love.'

'I'm glad. If you hadn't been ... well ... I might have felt I'd come cheaply.' Amanda paused, then: 'Why did she leave?'

'I don't know. No rows. No harsh words that I remember. We hadn't reached that stage. I never discovered. I tried to find her for a while. Life moves on.'

'Maybe because she discovered she was pregnant?'

'Perhaps.'

'She may still be around?'

'I suppose ... You want to find her?'

'I'm having a hard enough time finding you.'

'Thanks.' He smiled.

'I didn't mean it quite that way.'

'It's been a shock for me too. And I've had longer not knowing anything about you than you have.' For the first time he looked at her hard and long. She stared away from him across the crowded restaurant, aware that he was studying her. She gave him time, not spoiling it by turning and picking up his gaze.

'What do you see?' she asked, still looking away.

'Nice girl.'

'You sound like a date.'

'We'd make quite a presentable couple.'

'Younger girl; older man. Quite acceptable. The other way round and it's wrong. Why?'

'Life's unfair.'

'I've seen press photographs of you. Your partners are much more glamorous.'

'Entirely the wrong impression. No one in gossip column shots ever has a spot. But the beautiful are always blemished.'

'The daughter in the Ayckbourn play gave her parents a hard time.'

'I suppose . . . realistic. I've no experience.'

'Your parents? What was your father?' She hesitated as she saw his face stiffen.

The answer was a long time coming. 'One day,' he began, then stopped. 'One day I may . . . may be able to tell you.'

'What?'

'Sometimes it can be better to be adopted . . . be . . . be an orphan than to go through . . .' He stopped again and shook his head. 'Not now,' he said.

'I'm too old to give you problems.' She tried, lightly, to change the subject.

'You've given me one – pleasurable – just by appearing.'

'I didn't mean . . . There were periods with my parents – I mean with my . . .' She dried up temporarily, then almost shouted. 'You do realize, don't you, what an empty, bloody hole appears when you discover that your every root is false, is a bloody lie?'

'I do.'

Tears welled up in her eyes. She fumbled in her handbag. It was a most natural thing for him to offer her his handkerchief. As she reached out, he took her hand, gently but firmly. She smiled at him through her tears. It was odd for them both. Not close but not remote.

For the second time in as many days he found himself being catechized by a woman about his beliefs. Amanda was also more interested in principles than in practice. How could he live an all-things-to-all-men life? Where were his loyalties?

'My bond is to client rather than cause. If I don't like the cause, or the client, I don't take their shilling. I'm no more morally compromised than any politician or civil servant. We're all faced, daily, with presenting cases with which we don't necessarily agree. That is how it is in public service.'

Amanda was gentle but not persuaded. 'It's letting expediency win.'

'You misunderstand,' he remonstrated. 'I don't only think money, I don't always accept the status quo, or authority. I've come to realize that authority isn't always worthy of respect. It can behave very badly indeed.'

'So what *are* your values?'

'Like most people's. All the full-stop words.'

'Full-stop?'

'You can't argue against "Justice", "Liberty", "Peace". "Decency", "Motherhood".

'Ah! Motherhood.'

'Bad choice. Delete motherhood.'

Amanda laughed. 'I didn't mean to start off criticizing –'

'We all have conflicts. Your work for a German investment bank, for instance. A lot of people would find reasons to complain about you doing even that. Not only Little Englanders or Second World War veterans.'

'Why on earth?'

141

'Banks are seen as fair-weather friends. Kind in times of plenty and enemies in times of need. And German banks: well . . .'

'Cruel. And untrue.'

'A matter of perception. Just as you make judgements on what I do, so I was setting up similar ones about your international capitalist role. Both are wrong.' He smiled.

'Cliché?'

'Clichés have a habit of being true.'

'I read an article by you: you argued that if someone says "Everyone knows" you must blast back with "Everyone may know it, but is it true?"'

'Done your homework.'

'I've a lot of homework to do.' She said it simply but confidently and it elevated his senses to a pitch he had seldom experienced before.

'In most social life, you don't get to know people – only their idiosyncrasies,' he volunteered.

'We're well beyond that already, aren't we?'

*

Some days later, in the late afternoon, Ivor sat with Rick Maclean in the back of a chauffeur-driven Volvo, returning from a two-day seminar on international affairs. Maclean sat in silence; this was not a moment either for small-talk or for a further parading of silence. Be silent and the other side will, eventually, feel forced to fill it with talk. Silence, well handled, could suggest deep thought. Maclean knew his place.

Ivor was consulting his most important professional tool – his address book. Addresses, telephone and fax numbers. A coded list of private lines, an asterisk marking those of his contacts who did not mind being rung out of hours at home. He made a few calls on the car phone, then for about five minutes, he sat, oblivious to everything. Maclean waited, aware that his employer was on some deep relaxation trip.

Ivor eventually stretched, and turned. 'What did you get out of that seminar?' he asked.

'Not much.'

'Not much fact. But you'll learn, when you get to know more MPs like that triumvirate, that greed keeps politics alive.'

'They're not corrupt.'

'No. Two of them probably not, though Adams would sell his grandmother for a handful of silver. A lot of nasty gossip around about him and undeclared private contracts. Like all politicians, they're hungry for private finance, if not for themselves, for their causes, their constituencies. They'll go anywhere, do anything, to achieve it. Conflicts of interest ooze under every Westminster door.'

'You're cynical about that too?'

'Keep an eye on the networks that link business and politics. Every day, public policy is corrupted by money. Why shouldn't it be the same further down the dung heap? Money and sex. By the way, you must meet Ramsay Smythe. No connection of course.' Ivor smiled.

The car wove through the dense traffic at Hyde Park Corner and turned down Constitution Hill.

'Lord Shand was quite supportive,' Maclean volunteered.

'Shand. Yes . . . I suppose. He's hard to read. He wasn't too pleased with my relationship with the PM. I'm an interloper.' Ivor laughed mirthlessly. There was a lengthy pause. 'For a while I thought our relationship was going bad. Now I'm back on his IN-list. Not quite sure why, or if I want to be.'

'This next meeting?' asked Maclean, changing the subject.

'Foreign Office. I should have briefed you, but there's been little time. I'm more interested in you getting to know my style. Take notes. Say nothing. This one's interesting. And difficult. Subject: Nationalism, neo-fascism and all that.'

'I'm listening.'

'The Foreign Office is the best-staffed department in Whitehall. The people you'll meet are all high-flyers. Or follow the cult of the high-flyer. From the Planning Staff and the European Depart-ments. They're as jealous as Shand is of outsiders. Only they *know*. On the other hand they're flattered by reputation. They recognize reputation in others. So I'm not entirely unwelcome, particularly where new subjects are concerned.'

'Extreme nationalism's no new subject.'

'Absolutely not. Top of the list of world diplomatic problems for hundreds of years then went dormant. Now we've won the Cold War, it's back with a vengeance.'

'Not an original thought. I mean –'

'You're right, Rick. Not original. But we have to start thinking about it in an original way. That's why the PM wanted to meet these diplomats.'

'And will we talk about neo-fascist nationalism here in the UK?'

'I'll bring it up. They'll say – the FO people – "I say, old chap, not our patch . . ."' Ivor laughed.

'And you'll . . . ?'

'And I'll bring in the evidence of pan-European networking.'

'You'll mention Shand?'

'Certainly not. Too many ears at that meeting. Shand and I need each other too much just now for tales to be told about me discussing him behind his back. Wouldn't do, Rick. Not at all.'

A much criticized amount of money had been spent in restoring the conference room to its former glory. Huge paintings of forgotten heroes of the Raj stared imperiously from the walls. Unwashed folds of bomb-proof net curtains draped untidily over the long windows that overlooked St James's Park. This, coupled with the fact that the chandeliers seemed to have been fitted with minimum voltage bulbs, succeeded in ensuring that all the expensive grandeur was dulled by an institutional gloom.

At the head of the green baize table sat Tony Harper, the Minister of State for Foreign and Commonwealth Affairs, a modest little man with, as someone had said, much to be modest about. Round him sat his officials, ready to protect him from the folly of his remarks. Ivor and Maclean were the only outsiders. Once the formalities were over – Harper read almost without a mistake from the brief in front of him – the discussion largely took place between the mercurial Stanley Vickers, the Head of Planning Staff, and Ivor himself. Each man recognized the other's talents; neither was prepared to subordinate them to his own.

'We and the Federal Authorities speak as one in deploring the rise of —'

'Could we agree to keep the public polemic out, otherwise we'll run out of time,' said Ivor softly.

'I was setting the parameters,' said Vickers aggressively. Not one of the sweetness and light brigade, he looked as if he was on permanent guard against enemies. When he got angry or carried away, a high flush appeared on his cheeks, his chin thrust out aggressively, while his crop of carrot-red hair bobbed about in erratic sympathy.

'Ground rules. Background, that sort of thing,' echoed the minister, nodding sagely.

'Could we take that as read?'

'With respect . . .' said Vickers.

'Which usually means with absolutely no respect,' said Ivor to Maclean in an almost audible stage whisper.

'. . . we ought to rehearse how we see the position at present,' said Harper on cue.

'As you please.' Ivor shrugged, smiling politely. He had done his best. He would now resign himself to listening to parameters being defined all over the place. For the next half hour, phrases like 'historical perspective', 'narrow nationalism' and 'unrestricted immigration fuelling the tide of neo-fascism' came and went around the dull confines of the room.

'Most interesting,' Ivor said eventually. 'Most interesting,' he repeated, as if to ensure that he was believed.

'Well then, Mark,' said Tony Harper in a vapid attempt at chairmanship, 'how d'you . . . er . . . think . . . er . . . we should progress?'

'The problems lie east of the Oder-Neisse line. Third World immigration we can control. The East European flood has only just begun: starving refugees, economic migrants, fuelling extreme nationalism, the terror attacks we've seen on refugee camps and so on . . . The problem is accelerating rapidly.'

'Your turn to define parameters,' smiled Vickers with a touch of malice. 'We know all that.'

'Quite,' parroted the minister.

Ivor ignored the interruption. 'What more should we do about keeping close to Germany, making sure we act as one with her, not letting the problem get out of hand, containing nationalism without pandering to it?'

'We do know the questions, Mark. They were all set out in the recent Joint Intelligence Committee paper.'

'Thank you for letting me see it. Good analytical piece – even the bit about anti-Semitism.'

'Is this a run-up to something, Mark? Why are you stalling?' asked Vickers.

'You're worried about extreme right-wing links.'

'Yes.'

'Yet there's an unwillingness to face the fact that much of the driving force is coming out of the UK.'

'Not our patch,' said Vickers.

Ivor turned to Maclean and smiled.

'Quite so,' said the Minister of State.

'Which is why – only a suggestion – perhaps this isn't the right forum in which to be discussing this.'

'We are extremely interested –'

'Of course you are. But we may need to act internally.'

'Very tricky,' interrupted the Minister of State. 'Take Lord Shand for example. Very close to the PM and very close to some rather nasty –'

'I think, Minister, we might wrap the meeting up now,' said Vickers hurriedly. He was getting out of his depth. 'Perhaps Mark has a point.'

Tony Harper looked at his watch. He was a man who had gone to sleep on the back of a little past reputation after he had won a famous by-election. His attention span was notoriously short. 'Yes, of course. I'll report your view to the Foreign Secretary, Mark. He may then have a word with the PM.'

'Thank you, Minister,' said Ivor quietly. 'You may find that they already know what I think.'

The meeting broke up. The minister disappeared. Maclean loitered out of earshot as Vickers pulled Ivor to one side.

'I wish you hadn't sprung that UK fascist links thing on us, Mark. So much of the material is very highly classified.'

'It's getting quite nasty. You'd be better out of it.'

'We need to be kept in the picture, Mark,' said Vickers. He hesitated then asked: 'By the way, how's your Sigmont Corporation bid going?'

'Problem with the Monopolies & Mergers people. It's delaying matters.'

'And Mr Ramsay Smythe? I understand he's not someone who believes in sitting around, operating by the book.'

'You too . . . you've heard something?' Ivor tried not to sound curious. Vickers was not misled.

'So have you, I gather.'

'He employs me. Nothing precise.'

'Watch your fingers. Can't have it both ways.'

'What d'you mean?'

'Intelligence contacts are worried. Shouldn't be saying any of this to you. But your Mr Ramsay Smythe may actually be funding some of the activity we've just been talking about.'

'I don't believe that for a moment,' said Ivor quickly.

'I hope you're not as much a fool as you're pretending to be,' responded Stanley Vickers quietly.

Ivor always said it would be interesting to write a study of the sociology of the official cocktail party. Particularly, the diplomatic reception. What good did they do? Was there an international conspiracy to keep them alive? Why did Germans and Russians, French and Arabs, Americans and Chinese, and the British, all continue with diplomatic entertaining? Were secrets really traded; were deals done; was influence peddled; were they worth the money, even if the drink came duty-free? If, on the surface, he was cynical about them, Ivor realized that because they existed, he had to take account of them. If invited, he usually went. When there, he was adept at talking only to those he wanted to talk to; he had developed a high skill in avoiding those whom he wished to avoid.

'If you think the diplomatic round is glamorous, come along to this evening's batch,' he suggested to Amanda. 'They're not there to be enjoyed.'

'I haven't been invited.'

'If I turn up with a partner, no one is going to turn a hair. But I will call the Americans. Security . . . so they have you on their list.'

'You really have three different invites for one evening?'

'Bit of an exception, but yes.'

'And you're going to all of them?'

'I'll give the Emirates a miss. It's dry. They serve fruit juice and mineral water. But the Dorchester know how to handle Arab receptions. The Western diplomatic soaks crowd a corner of the room next to the servery. The waiters sneak in with trays of juice and, buried among them, the hard stuff. Everyone knows what's going on. It's all a game.'

'So?'

'The American Ambassador's residence in Regent's Park first. A bit of business if you don't mind. There's a party of Senators here. I want to get alongside one of their Foreign Affairs people. Besides, it's a beautiful house. Then on to the Irish in Belgravia. It'll be different.'

'In what way?'

'A good party. Guinness, Irish Mist, plus the expat Irish gift-of-the-gabbers from television. Cheerful, if nothing else.'

They turned off the Regent's Park ring road and into the Winfield House drive. Marine guards at the gates checked under the car with their mirrors before they were allowed in.

'The burdens of democratic freedom,' Ivor remarked.

There was a receiving line: the ambassador and his wife, the deputy chairman of the Senate Foreign Relations Committee and a political counsellor from the embassy. A junior embassy diplomat announced them as they came in.

'Sir Malcolm Morgan MP. The Ambassador of Norway. The Lord Mayor of London and the Lady Mayoress. Dr Mark Ivor and Miss Ivor.'

Hands were shaken, a few words exchanged, then the guests moved into the milling crowd. Waiters stood with trays of drinks. Ivor helped himself to an American-style gin and tonic, solid with ice; Amanda took a glass of orange juice, then turned to him. 'That *was* a surprise.'

'What?'

'You know perfectly well. *Miss Ivor.* Is that . . . the name you gave them?'

'Isn't that you?'

'Easier when I'm with you. I don't want to be identified as a mere escort, do I?' She smiled sweetly. 'Tell me though: why have you brought me?'

He took her hand. It was a natural thing to do. 'I want to introduce you to one or two people. Want them to meet my . . . er . . . family.' He smiled. 'There's a woman over there, for example. I knew her well once, before she became a major TV star. She'll be *very* surprised to meet my daughter.'

'Could you chart me out a list of your life and loves? Wouldn't want to put my foot in it, would I?'

Later she watched and listened as he lobbied the Senator. All was subtle, understated, low key. The point came after several minutes of lively small-talk about American football, the election, the weather. She was impressed at his technique: there were jokes – no, not jokes; educated wit. People laughed *with* Ivor. She stood back and watched faces, monitored reactions rather than listening to the words. Even with the great and the good, this stranger, her father, tended to become the focus of attention. Was it pride that she was feeling? Whatever it was, it was new and exciting. It broadened horizons in a way that a new love in her life would never have emulated. At one moment Ivor turned unexpectedly and caught her watching him. He flashed a secret smile at her, quick and genuine. Amanda felt a rush of warmth

149

towards him. She had been brought up in a family where love had been little expressed; she had never, that she remembered, seen her adoptive parents touch, let alone hold each other. They had been kind and understanding, but always distant. Now she wanted to go over and touch him in public and to hold his hand. He would be a thread of brightness in her life from now on. She had a lot to catch up.

As they were leaving the Residence and she stood waiting in the hallway while he retrieved their coats, Amanda became aware of someone watching her. She turned and saw a tall, sparse man surveying her from the doorway. His face was familiar but she could not quite place him. Arrogant, icy and aloof; was he looking at or a hundred miles through her? As he looked away he appeared totally devoid of emotion, but then, as she studied him, she sensed a hint of a repressed passion beneath. It was strangely fascinating. She shivered.

Her father appeared, clutching their coats. He saw her look towards the other man.

'Oh, there's Rupert. Hello. Look, can I introduce you to my daughter, Amanda. Amanda – this is Lord Shand.'

'Your daughter, Mark? I . . . delighted to meet you, Amanda. I didn't . . .'

As she shook the dry, leathery hand, Amanda felt herself being stripped bare by his eyes. She recognized him now: he was a man who would take sex for the sex alone.

Later that night, at the Irish Embassy, after all the laughter and drink had cheered her into a good humour, she admitted to her father her mixed impressions about Lord Shand.

'I've heard some women react that way with him. Bit of a cold fish. But his heart's in the right place,' he responded benignly.

'His heart?' asked Amanda. 'I wonder . . .'

'Wouldn't be too dramatic about Rupert Shand. He's cold and aloof, but his judgement is good.' Ivor heard himself say the words, but her remark had something of the flavour of what

Caley Perkins and others had said recently. An interesting coincidence, but only that.

Amanda meanwhile felt deep down that her father was, for the first time since they had met, very wrong indeed.

14

Ivor stood silently in front of the long mirrors in his bedroom and dressed himself with care but a shade more casually than usual. He then spent an inordinate amount of time adjusting the appearance of his flat. He kept consulting his watch. He poured himself a stiff gin and tonic but left it untouched. He sat down for a few moments, then almost immediately stood and began pacing about the room.

He had to go through with it. He was about to introduce a mistress, with whom he was deeply infatuated, to a newly discovered daughter. He was a man who always had everything in perfect order within a meticulously planned existence, yet they had exploded his attitude to himself. Fiona knew about Amanda. The day before, he had bitten the other bullet and told Amanda that he was having an affair with a married woman. She shrugged and appeared to take it well. If she did not entirely approve of the disruption of another marriage, she did not let it show. She could hardly make demands on a lifestyle newly discovered.

Ivor sat down again and looked accusingly at his watch. They were late: neither would want to be the first. Perhaps they would not turn up at all. Why should they? He was their link. They had no need of each other.

The bell rang. He heard laughter. When he opened the door they were both there; having met on the stairs, they were already talking to each other, only interrupting their flow to greet him. He was glad, then almost jealous, for, once they had sat down, and with drinks in their hands, they continued talking to each other rather than to him. Uneasily, he left them and went to the kitchen to get the tray of canapés that Deborah had prepared. On his return he stood outside the door listening for a moment before re-entering the sitting room. They were still chatting about many things but not about him. He felt ignored. But it was a delusion; he *was* their catalyst. He began to talk about the strangeness he felt but when they both turned and stared at him he dried up; there was no need to explain anything. All was self-evident.

They were together for less than an hour. Then Fiona announced that she had to leave; she must get home. As such encounters went, if there were such, it had gone well. They had spent most of the time talking not about themselves but about any common interests they could discover, such as Germany: Amanda's work, Fiona's half-German parentage, Ivor's worries about neo-fascism there and elsewhere in Europe. When Fiona stood to go, the others stood with her. She kissed Amanda on the cheek and Ivor on the mouth. 'I look forward to us getting to know each other. First I have to sort out my life,' she said simply.

The two women left with differing perspectives of what had happened. For Amanda it was simpler: she saw her father as having gone through an emotional clearing exercise, setting the record straight for her, making sure she knew everything there was to know. By so doing he had demonstrated his need to start with a clean sheet. For one so heavily involved with the posturing of the politically committed, he had to reassure himself that there was absolutely nothing false in their relationship, right from the beginning. Amanda in her turn was only interested in her developing link with him. She thought briefly that she might have been jealous of this Fiona. That she instantly liked the other woman was an added bonus.

Fiona's attentions were still focused on the inevitable dangers of having an affair, now that Amanda had been allowed into the conspiracy. In the end it could only cause suffering to her atrophied marriage, to Mark and, inevitably, to herself. She had liked Amanda, a pleasant, natural girl, but wished she could have arrived at a later stage in her relationship with Mark. She was not jealous of Amanda but she might become jealous of the time and attention Amanda would require of her father.

Ivor himself was left behind at his most clumsy and unsure. The two women had got on well. He appreciated that. But it introduced massively unsettling elements. That would not have mattered in other circumstances. But it meant that he was not as alert as he should have been when a greater entrapment came along.

Top Secret & Personal
For Addressee's Eyes Only
TO: *The Secretary to the Cabinet*
(No, repeat no, further distribution
without authorization)
FROM: *Chief, C13*
re: **Operation Picnic**

Following is Priority information (Code: Zealot Plus). Full transcript of latter part of meeting is submitted *in toto* as it gives a great deal of info re characters involved. Meeting took place: Shand/ Gibson/Ramsay Smythe, followed by these three being joined by Dr Mark Ivor, at RS's Green Park flat. All spoke openly because RS assured them he had anti-bugging system in place. (GCHQ have been able to circumvent that particular US device for almost five years: see Counterint/Tech/1990/MR855).

The three *Team* members began by discussing reluctance of newspaper proprietor to go along with some of their recent moves. S was particularly concerned about leakage. RS felt problem was minimal. (How wrong they were can be seen from report from the editor, MacInnery, reporting his proprietor's views: copy on file.) Lord S suggested this was all the more reason to bring in Dr Mark Ivor to help on the PR and strategy front. 'We need', he said, 'to win hearts and minds. Ivor's good at that. Let's get him on board.' RS agreed that he should be brought more fully into the picture. 'I'm already paying him, after all.'

They would present it to Ivor, Shand suggested (his language is precise) as a 'simple battle for access, for territory, staking out a part of the political landscape. That territory is the largely barren but essential one, the mind of the Prime Minister.'

Throughout the subsequent meeting, Dr Ivor was not as sharp and up to the mark as we have come to expect. He seemed preoccupied. (See separate report on his private life: copy on file.)

>*Verbatim transcript as follows (Certain sections and words were inaudible):*

Ivor: The PM feels . . .

Shand: What you tell him to feel.

Ivor: Unjust. He has a mind of his own.

R.S.: OK. But . . . (*inaudible*)

All present laughed.

Ivor: The PM asks me what I think. I tell him.

G.: And he listens, which is why we invited you to come and talk to us.

Ivor: You three are . . . er . . . working together?

Shand: We have a common agenda. A common bond – representing politics, industry . . .

R.S.: You are already on my payroll, remember . . .

Ivor: Your agenda?

Shand: To stop the drift. To help the PM win the general election by concentrating his mind on the real issues: firm government . . .

G.: Law and order, a strong defence and overseas policy –

R.S.: (*interrupted*) The trouble is – he's a wimp. He doesn't stand for anything. He has no mission, no vision, no determination. Those politicians around him may like him, but none respects him. At best they're looking for jobs, for his remaining patronage. But . . .

Shand: We cannot replace him at present, before the election, and if things work out properly we may not need to do so.

Ivor: I don't quite . . .

Shand: We play him. We work through him. He needs us . . . or will need us.

Ivor: A puppet?

Shand: Disraeli's 'Phantom Prime Minister'. If you like, Mark. We can't continue sitting around and watching this man, who ought not to be where he is, who got there by accident –

Ivor: But was democratically –

Shand: Democracy! It's junk if that's all it can come up with. We're here to give that little man the strength he doesn't have.

R.S.: Until we can find someone better.

Ivor: You're hijacking him. A sort of internal coup.

(*Source comment: there was a long silence at this point. At least, no sound was identifiable*)

Shand: I couldn't have put it better myself, Mark. That's why we need you.

Ivor: What about the others round him in Cabinet?

Shand: The weak are a long time in politics. The strong have gone.

Ivor: Brogan . . . the other ministers . . . Maltby's suicide . . . those close to him . . . they have gone. You're going to imprison . . .

Shand: Only his mind. And his will. We knew you'd get there in the end, Mark. We *have* to fill the commanding vacuum. We want you on board.

The meeting ended shortly thereafter. Ivor was tasked to bring the newspapers and public opinion into line as and when required. Ivor reacted cautiously. We have no evidence yet of whether he is now in with *The Team* or simply playing for time. This will be closely monitored.

Message ends.

* * *

Top Secret & Personal
TO: *Chief, C13*
FROM: *The Secretary to the Cabinet*
URGENT. URGENT. URGENT.

You have full authority to warn Ivor off. Please expedite and report back soonest.

Message ends.

Dr Mark Ivor's view of what happened at that meeting was somewhat different from that suggested by the words of the transcript. So much of the exchange was lost to its secret readers. They could not see the faces, could not read the body language, or hear the tone and paralanguage of the exchange. For the first time Ivor understood clearly what was happening. His face reflected some of his growing concerns until he deliberately controlled it as the enormity of the plot was unfolded. He would certainly have agreed with the intelligence assessment that he had been much distracted of late by Amanda's appearance, but he was alert enough to realize that Lord Shand was the driving force and that Ramsay Smythe was the provider of funds. He could not read the motivation of the soldier: General Sir Patrick Gibson, an ageing but still athletic-looking man, looked somewhat out of place in such a conspiracy, but Ivor had long since ceased to marvel at other people's private habits and deeply held beliefs.

Ivor left the meeting giving as few undertakings as he could get away with. He was deeply uneasy. But, while his loyalty was being sorely tested, Ramsay Smythe was still his client, and Lord Shand and he were meant to have the best interests of Michael Wilson at heart. He said he would do his best.

They sat at a corner table in the Coffee Room at the Garrick. Its dark blood-coloured walls were festooned with paintings of famous and not so famous actors and actresses of past centuries.

'Splendid.'

'Best club in London. Best food too. Have you ever eaten in any of the Pall Mall or St James's clubs?'

'Men's clubs aren't my scene. Though a boyfriend did, after a drunken dinner party, take me to a topless club . . . *The Gaslight*, was it?'

'Different sort of men.'

'Oh . . . I don't know. The same species. Just a little bit more subdued here.'

To give the lie to her remark, a guffaw of laughter came from a group of men seated at the long club table in the centre of the room. The word 'daughter' rang clearly through, and one man turned in his chair to stare briefly at them both.

At drinks beforehand they had been waylaid by two old friends of Ivor's, one an elderly actor, the other a High Court judge, both of whom were already well into their cups.

'Amanda . . . well . . . pleased to meet you. I didn't know . . . well . . .' said the one with considerable lack of clarity.

'Daughter, eh . . .' echoed the other, winking and nudging Ivor heavily in the ribs, knocking him against a glass display case full of theatrical artefacts. 'Daughter . . . well, well. Used to be nieces, didn't it? No offence, I hope, my dear? Well, well, you are a dark horse, Mark.' The old men's laughter had echoed behind them as Ivor and his daughter went down the great staircase to dinner.

'Sorry about that,' Ivor had said.

'I thought they were rather jolly. I've seen the actor . . . what's his name . . . in plays and on TV. I suppose we may get quite a bit of this. A confirmed bachelor, in the real sense of the term, suddenly turning up with female progeny.'

Over dinner their conversation took on a tougher flavour.

'I don't have power. I told you: only influence,' he argued.

'A quibble.'

'Not at all. Power implies ability to enforce. I can't insist if someone doesn't do what I say.'

'People act on what you advise.' Amanda was intense in her bid to find out what her father thought.

'Often. Not always.'

'You're a bit ruthless. That worries me.'

'Not ruthless, Amanda. I like certain things to be done. I keep my identity and values. Why should that worry you?'

'Maybe I've inherited some of your traits.'

'You're painting me bad.'

'Predatory.' She hesitated as the word came out.

'I'm going to get angry if you push that line. I never have been dishonest and you don't know enough about me even to suggest that.' Ivor felt more hurt than irritated.

'Sorry. I mean you go single-mindedly in support of your client, whatever the ethics.'

'I've warned you about the careless use of "ethics".'

'You get people's hackles up.' Amanda was blunt.

'I don't change tack to court popularity. Memories are short when things work.'

'Ends justify means.'

'If they want someone weak and sycophantic, they don't employ me. And, back to your ethics, I'm just about to turn down the biggest, toughest and most unethical offer I've ever been made.' Ivor looked as worried as she had ever seen him.

159

'Are you going to tell me about it?'

'Not everything. For your own good.'

'Sounds sinister . . .' She tried a smile but he did not react.

'I used to believe advocates of the conspiracy theory of history were crazy. My experience of politics was that most things happened by muddle, by accident. I was wrong. Naïve. People in politics naturally conspire. They want to contrive things behind the scenes, in the corridors rather than in the debating chambers. The latter is for the public, gesturing once the deed is done. I'm a late convert to the conspiracy theory,' Ivor continued in sombre mood, speaking in a low voice.

'And you cater for the needs of the conspirators,' commented Amanda.

'Don't get me wrong. Conspiracies can be benevolent, totally altruistic. Often are. Most people are charitably disposed. They actually want to improve the lot of their fellow men.'

'And their own lot in the process.'

'Of course.'

'So who is this group?' she asked.

'An intelligent, determined, highly motivated team . . .'

'Sounds OK to me.'

'Who're set on hijacking the Prime Minister.'

'Taking him where? You can't be serious?'

'Taking him nowhere. They keep him where he is but surround him with their own people.' Ivor paused as a waiter came up and refilled their glasses.

'What about his civil servants? The Cabinet?'

'Gradually, gently isolating him from them; it nearly happened in Harold Wilson's days, remember?'

'I don't remember . . . You're being a little overdramatic.'

'I would have said that . . . before . . .'

'Are you going to tell me about it?' Amanda asked gently.

After dinner he dropped her off at her Pimlico flat by taxi, kissed her goodnight, then decided to walk back to his own house in Victoria. As he crossed Vauxhall Bridge Road and turned down one of the little side streets behind Westminster Cathedral he was aware of a large black car coming up behind him. It looked official so he paid little attention until it pulled up beside him as he walked along. A window was opened and a voice called out, presumably to ask for directions. Instead the voice addressed him by name.

'Dr Ivor. Would you mind getting in, please. We want to talk to you. Don't worry. You're quite safe with us.'

Sir Caspar Rudd frowned as he read through the report that had just landed on his desk. He disapproved strongly of physical violence. They had not been very clever.

> **Top Secret & Personal**
>
> TO: *The Secretary of the Cabinet*
> FROM: *Chief, C13*
> re: **Operation Picnic**
>
> With some difficulty, subject, who struggled at first – he thought he was being kidnapped – was persuaded of our good intentions. Demanded to know who 'we' were. Eventually he told us what he knew. Subject taken aback when we said we knew it all already. He assured us he was not, repeat was not, going to co-operate with *The Team*. He has reluctantly agreed however not to reveal this to them for the time being. We have arranged discreet mechanism for keeping in contact.
>
> Subject's motives appear reasonable. He points out that he is still employed by RS. Wants continued watching.
>
> *Message ends.*

Sir Caspar Rudd reached across for the secure red telephone. It was more than just watching that was needed. He would have to sharpen C13 up a bit.

'Now you're working for me you'd better know everything,' Ivor said, and then uncharacteristically told Rick Maclean what had happened to him the previous night. 'The authorities know more than I do. They've been monitoring Shand, Gibson and Ramsay Smythe for a long time. They told me what I was only just beginning to realize. I was being used: swallowing hook, line, sinker, the lot. Damned bloody foolish I've been . . .'

'What are you going to do?' asked Maclean slowly. 'I'd be cautious.'

'You're damn right. I go along with it . . . playing for *The Team* as if nothing had happened. I don't like it, but I've no alternative.'

'Dangerous . . . if they found out.'

'They won't find out,' said Ivor confidently.

Had Ivor been more alert, he would have realized subsequently that more was going on round about him, and at a faster rate, than was healthy. Once, then twice, he was excluded from meetings at Number Ten that he would have expected to attend. Then a week passed without him having heard from the Prime Minister. But he was occupied on other matters and thought little of it until later. Then, out of the blue, the Prime Minister, on the private advice of Lord Shand himself, rang him to ask him to go to Washington on an urgent and important mission.

15

Fred Cree was unfailingly, unambiguously bitter. He was one of the duffel-coated sixties school who had come to maturity believing that society owed him a living; that society was malevolent, prejudiced and unfair. His gripes about life had begun, way back, with the name he had been burdened with: 'Fred' was common and there was something about 'Cree' that lacked any distinction. His God-given physique and appearance were further reasons for grievance. All in all, in the poker school of life, he felt he had been dealt a dud, shabby hand. It left him, according to one of his very few friends, 'with more greasy chips on his shoulder than an Australian on an off day.' He had a life-long urge to get even: 'even' with whom it did not matter. When he set to such work, 'he made Janus look single-faced': his friend again. His was the whinge of unfairness, the voice of envy.

Now on the general election campaign trail, all his hang-ups, his unspoken vendettas, his personal cyanide wars, were fed and fattened, taking on a new dimension. He was the cynical observer, untroubled by the need to win votes, yet for once courted by those who did. He was in his element. Clever poison dripped daily from his pen. His new editor and the readers loved his stuff. The party press people were afraid, yet catered to him, though they realized that few brownie points would be gained by being kind or helpful. Fred Cree was vicious; friend to no one, enemy to all. And in particular to Dr Mark Ivor. So when, to his surprise, his proprietor arranged a private meeting between him and Lord Shand, it was especially welcome.

It was as a result of this that Cree now stood watching a

helicopter land in the middle of a school playing field in a cloud of dust and a storm of free-blown grass. A curious crowd of teachers and school children cheered, then turned away as eyes and faces were swept with swirling debris. A group of four sober-suited men and a neat girl secretary emerged from the helicopter's side and, bending low to avoid the still whirling blades, walked across the pitch to the waiting bus. They climbed aboard and, almost immediately, it started up and drove away.

It was no ordinary bus. It was a Battle Bus, donated and fitted out by a rich Midlands businessman to serve as a mobile party headquarters for the election campaign. Inside were desks, word processors, a large map-board, a rack of mobile phones, a bar, even a couch on which to rest between forays into constituency war-fields. The couch, less properly, had most recently been used by the neat girl secretary and the new Media Manager, who had forgotten all the warnings about the *Sun* test, but that was another matter; such fleeting passions were inevitable if not forgivable in the heat of battle.

The bus parked in a side street near the Birmingham hall where the election rally was to take place. Inside, the four men and the girl sat round a conference table. Outside, on the pavement, the bus driver stood talking to the minister's Protection Squad officer. It gave them a chance to have a quiet smoke and those inside the confidentiality and security required.

'Seven meetings in a day: that's going some,' complained the Minister of Health, Horace Tetchley, to his PPS. 'All miles apart. Even with this bus and the helicopter, well, I mean . . .'

'We can manage. I've timed it pretty accurately,' said the political agent.

'What sort of number have you?' asked Ivor.

'Not many. A hundred at the outside.'

'Press?'

'That's the good news. Both BBC and ITN, and at least a dozen others.'

'Excellent,' said Tetchley.

'Not bad,' said Ivor. 'Bunch the audience as far forward and as central in the hall as possible. The TV crews conspire with us on that. Like studio audiences at talk shows. Adds life. They can get their reaction shots.'

'Done already, Mark,' said the political agent.

The minister's protection officer climbed into the bus and coughed discreetly.

'Yes, Terry?'

'Journalist outside, sir. Wants a quick word.'

'I haven't time for interviews before the election meeting. Maybe afterwards,' said the minister.

'Says he's doing some in-depth background piece. Wants to talk to the agent.'

'I'll go see,' said the political agent and disappeared. By the time he came back, the minister and Ivor were stuck in a last-minute drafting session on the speech. Ivor did not, therefore, give his full attention to the political agent when the latter returned and explained: 'That journalist's been producing some pretty heavy stuff. This time all he wants is to write a gentle background piece. He says. The hard work the party team put into the campaign, behind the scenes . . . Can he eavesdrop on our sessions in the Battle Bus . . . ? No secrets, no confidences broken. He'll work on lobby terms. Mood piece. He says he's spoken to Central Office who've given their blessing.'

Ivor's attention was focused on the minister's speech. 'No views,' he muttered. 'If Central Office has no objections, and you, Minister, of course . . .' He made the critical mistake of not asking the journalist's name.

The minister's thoughts were also on the speech. 'So long as he doesn't get in the way. Re-check with Central Office . . . Now, Mark, how about my last remarks? Are they punchy, upbeat enough? A joke, perhaps? Send them home laughing? How about the one about the frog and the Social Democrats?'

Bad decisions, casually taken because they appear to be of little significance at the time, are signposts to the graveyard of politics. One phone call to an overstretched press man at Central Office, and Fred Cree became, for two days, a fly on the wall, watching the campaign team at work and play. Despite himself, Cree increasingly came to admire the way Ivor handled the party people, the press, the ministers. They all seemed to accept not his authority but his judgement. They did things not because he demanded or cajoled: he pointed out the options, weighting his preferred one, then left them to make the inevitable move. Cree was attracted by the technique, jealous of it, wanted to emulate it. Here was someone Cree would wish to be. Ivor was not even aware of any of this; it was not that he was dismissive or antagonistic towards Cree; there were always a lot of journalists around; he knew what Cree had done in the past, but if he spent his life worrying about all the journalists he didn't trust, he'd have little time for anything else. Cree was on the fringes; neither participant nor player. He was irrelevant. And that, to Cree, was an additional massive hurt.

A front-page exclusive about a political intrigue, like a sex scandal, carries real weight if the timing is right. The timing for anything out of the ordinary, anything embarrassing to candidates or party on the last few days before a general election, is bound to be excellent. Excellent for the Opposition; even more so for the circulation figures of the newspaper with the scoop. Two and a half weeks to go to election day: that meant, Cree calculated, two weeks till the optimum time to publish. Two weeks and a hell of a lot of work still to be done if his story was to build up, if the dirt was to stick.

He'd arranged to take Amanda to meet some of his friends, so he had to ring her and cancel when he got his instructions.

'I have to go to Washington.'

'When?'

'Tomorrow. They have my tickets already.'

'Is it always like this?'

'Sometimes.'

'Stop for a moment. Is it all worth it?' Amanda asked.

Ivor paused. 'One day, yes, I'll stop and ask myself just that.'

'Don't leave it too late,' she responded with concern.

Amanda thought it odd when Lord Shand rang her at the office immediately after her father had left for the States.

'Rupert Shand — you remember we met at the American Ambassador's? I'm an old colleague of your father's. Look, I hope you don't mind but if you had time, could we meet up? There's something I'd like to talk to you about.'

Lord Shand was at his most charming. In spite of her first impression of the man, Amanda was flattered and intrigued. She accepted.

An air traffic controllers' go-slow, and Concorde arrived at JFK an hour and a half late. Ivor was doubly privileged, not just by flying supersonic, but because he had no onward connections to worry about. A private plane provided by an enthusiastic expatriate supporter of the government was waiting to fly him direct to Washington. He arrived on the sort of fresh spring day that suits that city so well, and it made him feel buoyant and confident.

He had been invited to dine alone with the British Ambassador, Sir Andrew Huggins, that evening, and to stay at the distinguished Lutyens residence on Massachusetts Avenue. A stretch limo met him at the airport and took him straight to the embassy, up the short driveway and in under the covered arch. A white-jacketed butler greeted him, collected his bags and showed him up the circular stone staircase that led to his suite. Left alone, he made a number of telephone calls to confirm his meetings for the next day, unpacked, took a shower and then, wrapped in a towelling bath robe, stretched out on a chaise longue to relieve his backache, and to unwind. He would not sleep. It was now past midnight, London time, but he had long ago forced himself to ignore jet lag and hit local time running. Within a few seconds he had projected himself into his usual state of relaxation, shutting out noise, anxieties, work. The counting. The breathing, regular and deep. Ten minutes of mind suspension, then he came to, fully alert and ready for everything.

He looked at the elegance around him. Some time ago the PM had casually suggested that he himself might like an ambassa-

dorial appointment. It had been vetoed by the Foreign Office, of
course, but the thought had been there. Not that he really wanted
to give up his London work, and in any case he felt that diplomatic disciplines would be too constraining for his individualistic
lifestyle. Besides, he had no wife. A wife was essential to an
ambassador even in this enlightened age; a wife needed to keep
house, to run the hotel which was what most big embassy resi-
dences were, to field the non-stop through-put of ministers, MPs,
civil servants, minor Royals and other VIPs.

Ivor was an unofficial guest, one of the ambassador's oldest
friends. But he was also there at short notice and the ambassador
was curious. It was his job to be curious.

'Delightful dinner, Andrew.'

'The sous-chef is French. I don't boast about that.' The
ambassador was a tall, angular man with hooded, intelligent eyes
and an icy wit.

'You keep a good cellar. This claret . . .'

'My *frais* gets eaten away by the heavy drinkers, to coin a
phrase.'

'Still enjoy it?'

'Every minute. But then I've decided to enjoy everything
between now and death. Not Joanna, though. She's staying with
friends in Maine. Can't get away quick enough.'

'How long to go?'

'Eighteen months. Why? Looking for my job?'

'You heard the gossip?'

'I did. The PM was right not to push it. Wouldn't have done
him or you any good. You're a loner. You'd have to suffer a
creaking system and a hell of a lot of fools. Need patience, self-
control, team-work. Need to lie abroad for your country. And
lie convincingly.'

'My detractors say I'm good at dissembling.'

'Avoiding the truth. So why are you here?'

'Re-establishing old contacts . . .'

'Like with the Chairman of the Senate Foreign Affairs Committee?'

'That's intelligent of you, Andrew.'

'No. Well informed. Maybe Bill Crespini at the White House?'

'Deputy Chief of Staff to the President is an important guy to keep tabs on.'

'Particularly if you want the President to make a few helpful, low-key, remarks in support of HMG in the last few days before the general election. By the way, I'm giving an election-night party. Do stay and come to it. Just a few close friends. About eighty.' The ambassador laughed mirthlessly.

'I have to get back.'

'I know. You've got Britain to run.'

'A little help from the government . . .' Ivor paused. 'How the hell d'you know who I'm seeing?'

'The Foreign Editor of the *Washington Post*? A good "pro-the-present-British-government-because-they're-pro-America" editorial for the British press corps here to pick up and report back? Should swing a few votes.' The ambassador was teasing.

'You always were quick and alert, Andrew. For a diplomat. How d'you get my programme?'

'Not my staff. Not my contacts at the White House nor on the Hill. Not the *Washington Post*.'

'Mystery story . . .'

'A call from London. A man called Fred Cree. A journalist. Did you know he's writing an in-depth piece on you?'

'Cree . . . I know him. He rang you?' Ivor was, despite the claret and the time-lag, suddenly alert.

'He asked a lot about you. I replied with my usual plentiful stock of platitudes. He knew we were old friends, asked what you were doing while you're over here. Then he told me. He told me you were lobbying these Americans for election support for HMG. He *was* well informed.'

'He was, wasn't he?' Ivor fell silent.

'Somebody talking out of turn?' asked the ambassador.

'More. Looks as if he's seen my diary.'

'A tricky story if it breaks.'

'Minor stuff,' said Ivor dismissively. But alarm bells were

ringing hard. This was one of those times when Deborah was going to have her sleep disturbed.

The meetings at the *Washington Post* and with the Senate Foreign Relations Committee were cautiously successful. The senator and the foreign editor were sympathetic and said that they would do what they could, within the constraints of not interfering too much with a foreign country's electoral process. If they were curious at Ivor's unofficial role, they kept their doubts to themselves.

The White House was different. He went in by the side gate, through the rigorous electronic security procedures, then waited until a staffer came to pick him up and take him to Bill Crespini. The Deputy Chief of Staff's office was to one side of the entrance hall, with a partial view of the rose garden and the permanent patrol of Secret Service agents flitting about in the grounds beyond. Crespini he had known from the days when they had both participated in a Harvard seminar on some now-forgotten East-West topic. They had been in the same syndicate, dealing with a conceptual problem the seminar staff had set them, and there had been a lot of 'bonding' under pressure. They had kept in touch. They were pleased to see each other.

'How you been?' asked the Italian-American. 'Still running little old England?'

'Keeping the Anglo-Saxon flag flying.'

'Not too many of them here these days. We're all Latins now, or Pacific Rimmers.'

'I'll forgive you.'

'You're committed to your government party now? I always felt you were a woolly liberal.'

'We grow older, we grow wiser . . . Slithering across the political spectrum from left to right.'

'Not too far right. You're a paid-up member of the party?'

'An employee; what you people call a facilitator. Open doors for other people to get together.'

'You lobby.'

'I lobby. We haven't got it down to such a fine art as you have here in Washington. More low key. More subtle.'

'There ain't a hell of a bundle of subtlety about you crashing into the White House to lobby for your people's re-election.' A wary note had crept into Crespini's voice.

'We're not expecting the President to stand up and say who to vote for. But –'

'But a little bit of gentler stuff wouldn't come amiss. Right?'

'Right.'

'Like now?'

'When talking to British journalists here. On the lines of what's good for them is good for us. I'm not asking for any knocking of the Opposition.'

'Of course you're not, Mark. Of course you're not.' He paused. 'You remember me. I measure statements by their truth content. But . . .'

'But what?'

'You're here to ask favours. I know the President would have done what he could. Discreetly. He likes your Prime Minister. He really does. But he has to do it very carefully, for your sake and his. Particularly if anyone knows he's been asked to help.'

'Which no one will.'

'Which they do already, Mark. You've slipped. Someone's slipped. Badly. I'm afraid any help from here has gone down the drain.'

'What d'you mean?' Ivor already knew what the answer was going to be.

'A man. Fred Cree? Got through to me yesterday. God knows how he got past my staff. Knows all about your trip. Had I been able to reach you, Mark, I would have warned you. And I would have cancelled our meeting. For both our sakes, you understand.'

Bill Crespini paused and then stood. The meeting was at an end. 'Nice to see you, Mark. Real nice. We must keep in touch.'

16

Top Secret & Personal

TO: *The Secretary to the Cabinet*

FROM: *Chief, C13*

re: **Operation Picnic**

The Team have been meeting regularly, usually around Westminster. For some reason, they have now employed Logan (ex GCHQ) and we have consequently been unable to access information. Use of other methods now in preparation.

Message ends.

The Secretary to the Cabinet, Sir Caspar Rudd, was, as was usual with him, somewhat ahead of the game. He dictated his brief reply.

Top Secret & Personal

TO: *Chief, C13*

FROM: *The Secretary to the Cabinet*

re: **Operation Picnic**

Evidence from other Cabinet Office sources suggests the reason for their increased security: Ivor has inadvertently revealed to someone, identity still unknown, who has in turn told the members of *The*

Team, about your past interception successes. He now, equally extraordinarily, is in Washington on party business. On a related matter: what do you know about a journalist, Fred Cree, who is working on some exposé of Ivor? Reply required soonest.

Message ends.

Back at the ambassador's residence, the butler waylaid him and handed him several messages: one from Tim Willis, the Private Secretary to the PM, one from Caley Perkins, and one from Fred Cree. All were marked urgent. He got through to Willis first, who spoke with barely concealed anger.

'He wants you home. Straight away. See no one else. Talk to no one else. The press are on to what you've been doing: lining up the Americans to support the party. As soon as the Opposition cotton on, we'll have a right old scandal.'

'I'm only a messenger, Tim. You know that.'

'What I know, I know,' said the voice at the other end coldly. 'I'm not apportioning blame. I'm on a damage-limitation exercise and I don't like it. Remember: I'm a civil servant, not a party man.' He rang off.

When Ivor, who rapidly realized the implications of the phone calls from London and the implicit dangers for him, eventually got through to Caley Perkins, he heard the same sort of noises and was warned that there was a trampling stampede of people getting out from under: the 'it's not my responsibility' brigade were running for cover.

'Dealing with the weak-kneed, with known enemies, is all in a day's work,' said Ivor.

'It's the unknown ones that spell destruction,' was Perkins' enigmatic reply.

Thus his major mistake: he returned Fred Cree's call. He was determined to defend himself. The telephone conversation was all sweet reasonableness. Ivor flew home overnight, believing he'd put everything on ice until his return to London.

He arrived back at Heathrow tired but relaxed. He would have a shower, change his clothes, be ready for anything the day would throw at him. He was wrong again and knew it as soon as he saw Deborah standing with a chauffeur, waiting for him. She had never done that before. She looked prim, efficient, very concerned, and had a bundle of the morning's newspapers under her arm.

'It's bad,' were her opening words.

'How bad?'

'Start with the article by Cree. The others have picked up from him.'

'I thought I'd killed it.'

'Your US trip is only one part. You're the spin doctor. The Opposition are jumping up and down with glee. The PM wants to talk urgently.'

'I'll go see him.'

'No . . .' She paused. 'He doesn't want that. Mr Willis said that you were not to be seen.'

'Ship of State deserting the sinking bloody rat,' growled Ivor as they piled into the back of the car. He picked up the newspaper and began to read.

'Your . . . er . . . daughter and your friend Fiona both rang. Can you call them?' Deborah ventured. He did not respond. For the first time she saw his hands shaking.

The headlines screamed: *'Who runs Britain?'* Under Fred Cree's byline, the opening paragraph set the tone. In normal circumstances no serious newspaper would have carried such a bitter and detailed attack on someone so relatively unknown. These were no normal circumstances. Quite apart from the double-edged machinations of which he was still totally unaware, Ivor was a perfect weapon with which to attack the party.

Cree had prepared the ground meticulously well. There were no innuendoes, no paragraphs of speculation, no flights of unsubstantiated gossip. It was all hard, witnessed evidence. Fact and more fact. When Cree had put the draft in front of his editor, the latter was in a receptive frame of mind. Neither man had any reason to feel charitable towards Ivor and a quick telephone call from their proprietor supported the hardness of their line. The newspaper's libel lawyers, despite some traditional sucking of teeth, did not stand in their way.

With the general election only days away, the timing was perfect. There was no question of entrapment: Ivor had walked into it with his eyes wide open. After all his years of success he had made a number of small but crucial errors of judgement, he who was always so sure-footed, he who had made a profession of helping others avoid the banana skins of life. He was about to perform the glissade of all time. The newspaper carried an editorial drawing on the article. Printed in bold type and written in the best holier-than-thou style, it read:

> *This newspaper has always campaigned fearlessly to applaud achievement and to expose wrongdoing. We have never been frightened to tell the truth even when huge pressures have been put on us, proprietor, editor or journalists, to do otherwise. Democracy is a delicate plant. Now we have a blatant attempt to relinquish power and responsibility to the unelected.*
>
> *In this regard we have no hesitation in naming the spin doctor: Mark Ivor, a man for whom responsibility is an alien concept. Dr Ivor, to those of our readers who are unfamiliar with his name, is a political lobbyist. That is a perfectly proper function; they are, or should be, known about, declared, above board, though their methods may, by definition, be far from obvious.*
>
> *So what is wrong with the activities of Dr Mark Ivor? Is he bribing anybody? The answer to that, as far as we are aware, is no. Is he doing anything illegal? Strictly speaking, no. Is he working for unscrupulous causes? Again no. Are his methods, in pursuit of the goals he is paid to achieve, questionable? Here's the rub. No one is accusing Dr Ivor of wrongdoing. What we do claim, however, is that the way he is being allowed to operate*

is wrong. He has power and influence way beyond what any unelected citizen ought to have. No wonder Opposition leaders are clamouring and questioning who is really running Britain: questioning a Prime Minister who allows Dr Ivor to spread rumours that influence votes at the Party Conference, to direct every detail of their current election campaign, to be sent to Washington to lobby the US President and Administration to ensure American support, to play along with suspect right-wing groups. The strains of such conflicts of interest have gone well beyond breaking point.

Professional advisers have always had their place in Westminster, in Whitehall, in Number Ten. Prime Ministers are allowed their gurus. Churchill had Brendan Bracken and Bob Boothby. Macmillan had his John Wyndham. Harold Wilson had Joe Haines and Marcia Williams. Margaret Thatcher had her Tim Bell and Alan Walters. But this Prime Minister is different. At a time when more and more power has moved from Parliament, from Ministers, to a Presidential-style Prime Minister's office, the present incumbent is not just taking advice, not merely operating a Kitchen Cabinet. He appears to have handed over responsibility, authority, decision-taking, to the man whom he himself calls his Modern Machiavelli, Dr Mark Ivor.

Dr Ivor has no portfolio but is widely believed to have more power than any Minister, more influence over the affairs of the nation than any single member of the Cabinet. Is this not abhorrent to the British system? We believe it is. We tell the Prime Minister to reject Dr Ivor and disown his activities. If they do not, then in a few days' time, the British Electorate will reject him.

Most of the other papers took up Cree's story and ran with it. Some editorials attached no blame to Ivor whatsoever. '*All he is,*' the *Independent*'s editorial read, '*is a resourceful, charismatic and doubtless effective adviser. Otherwise he would not be where he is today. But is he checked sufficiently? Who controls him? Who pays him? How does he keep his separate interests apart? It is those who have allowed this situation to develop who are the ones worthy of real blame.*' The *Sun*, by contrast, had its front-page lead under the banner headline '*Secret Love Child of PM's crony.*'

A lengthy traffic jam on the M4 meant that by the time the chauffeur had got them back to central London, Ivor had read all the articles and profiles that Deborah had flagged up for him. He had been totally silent all the way, and eventually, when he spoke, his voice was subdued. 'That's news creation for you,' he said. 'The press are great at building people up only to destroy them. The only thing with me is that they've done both, all within one day's editions.'

'It's not you they're getting at. It's the party . . .' began Deborah.

'I can live with it. Live with most of it. Except this man Cree's piece, the profile on the back page. Most of them are using me and my semi-mythical role to attack the government. He . . . he's attacking me. A real vendetta piece. All this about my "personal lifestyle", my "late conversion to the existence of a daughter", and again, my "illegitimate daughter". Damn Cree. That's vicious grudge. I can take all the professional dirt he can throw. But . . . hurting Amanda, that hurts me. And he knows it.'

Deborah looked quickly across at her employer. 'You're bad at thinking about what your own advice to a client would be in such circumstances . . .' she began. Then she checked herself. Even in the dark light in the back of the car, she could see tears of anger glistening in his eyes.

One bearded paparazzo photographer was sent flying by another in a cacophony of clattering camera gear and attendant imprecations. Two tabloid journalists had a minor punch-up as they pushed and shoved for the best position by the doorway to the fury of the camera team from ITN which until then had had an uninterrupted line of sight. A policeman appeared from nowhere, talking urgently into his microphone as he sought instructions from his headquarters at Rochester Row. Someone had tipped off the press corps. They knew to the minute when Ivor was due back at his office in Victoria.

He had telephoned Number Ten from the car. The PM wasn't available to talk, but Willis warned him the press were out looking for him. Despite years of watching politicians hounded by the pack, it still came as a shock to see twenty or thirty of them camped outside his door. Had he thought it through he would have gone to ground until he had time to gather his thoughts. He knew only too well that he should pull up and collect himself but he was brimming with anger at the way the story had been built up. Caution, eroded by tiredness and the overnight flight, was dismissed in favour of a dangerous bravado. He would face them out.

Deborah tried to warn him. 'Look at them,' she began. 'D'you think you should stop a little short of the door?' The driver, watching in the rear-view mirror, started to slow down, waiting for instructions.

In his fury and confusion he ignored her advice. 'No. Go on. Go on. I'm not going to my office. I've a lot of calls to make. They're only bloody press. They won't trouble me.' It was always easy to bear the misfortunes of others; the test came on home territory. When he looked back on it later, he realized that he had been much more shaken than he admitted; that when one's judgement slipped once, it could set in train a pattern of miscalculation.

The brittle, fickle, cynical media circus pounced. Before he was out of the car, they were around him, pushing, shoving, hardly giving him space to open the car door. The flashes of the cameras, the aggrieved shouts of TV crews whose lens shots were blocked by the milling throng, the shouted demands of reporters, microphones, note pads and tape recorders thrust in front of him, aggressive and frightening. He tried to smile.

'I'm afraid I have nothing to say.' His words were drowned in a competitive babble of questions.

'Dr Ivor, have you seen the press reports that the PM does exactly as you tell him?'

'Dr Ivor, we're from the *Newsnight* team. Could we ask you a few —?'

'Have you anything to say about the matter of the ministerial sex —?'

'The Leader of the Opposition has issued a statement, condemning —'

'Dr Ivor, your illegitimate daughter . . .'

Ivor resolutely fought his way through the crowd, trying to hold his temper, trying to keep something approaching a cool, good-natured look on his face. He tried again: 'A storm in a teacup . . . I have nothing to say . . .' Such is the nature of press competition that they all lost out in their struggle for a picture. Eventually he made the short distance from the car to the door. He was vaguely aware that Rick Maclean had appeared and was helping to shepherd him and Deborah to safety. Rick Maclean. The man had a nervous look to him — or was it Ivor's imagination? The details of his trip to Washington . . . Fred Cree . . . there had been something about Rick and Fred Cree . . . He suppressed the thought.

'Hi, Rick. Fun welcome home, isn't it?'

Maclean smiled an uneasy smile.

Inside the flat the office lines and his private telephone were all ringing. He picked up the ex-directory receiver. It was Amanda.

'Why didn't you warn me?' She burst out. 'Why . . . how are they on to me?'

'I'm sorry. It took me by surprise. I just don't know.'

'I've nothing to do with your work. Have you read what they're saying about you . . . me? And we've only just met. It's bloody ironic, isn't it?' She was uptight and angry, not so much at him as at the situation.

'Are you all right?' He was too shaken to be able to respond effectively.

'Are you?'

'So far.'

'I've a clutch of press camped outside the office. They followed me this morning. I tried to ring.'

'I've just got back. I'm sorry,' he repeated.

'Don't keep saying that. My boss is being very good. I told him about it.

'By the way,' she added, 'there's something I meant to mention to you. Your new assistant, Rick Maclean: I met him the other day.'

'Yes?' he asked.

'Found his way about for an Edinburgh lad. I was at the Tate Gallery for a lecture on Friday. A friend and I walked from there back towards Westminster. I saw him coming out of a door, just by Smith Square. He seemed embarrassed to see me . . .'

'I don't suppose –' Ivor began.

'He was with, of all people, Lord Shand. Wasn't that a little odd, given what you've told me?'

'Thanks. Look, I've got to go, Amanda. I'll ring you later.' He put the phone down, feeling doubly inadequate; he had let her down as well. Then he began to realize how it had been.

As he finished the call, he heard Deborah and Rick Maclean saying almost identical things on both his office lines. No, Dr Ivor was not available for interview. No, he had no statement to make. No, they had no idea whether there would be a statement later.

'Take the phones off the hook,' Ivor shouted. 'I'll work from my private line. I have to talk to the PM. I need to think.'

'I'm sorry . . .' Maclean was repeating as Ivor shut the door firmly behind him.

Alone in his study Ivor stared aggressively down at his desk. He had to pull the various threads together. Then he stood up, resolved to deal with one immediate, unpleasant part of the problem. He threw open the door of his study and stalked over to confront Maclean. The younger man was sitting working at his desk. Ivor towered over him.

'Precisely what did you want to say you were sorry about, Rick? Would you like to tell me?' Ivor paused, then went on: 'Who did you talk to about what I was doing? Who did you give my programme to? Was it Ramsay Smythe? Lord Shand perhaps? Or did you go straight to Fred Cree?'

Maclean looked up at Ivor, saw the look on his face, said nothing, stood up, coolly put some papers in his briefcase, then walked towards the door and left the office. Deborah watched the scene in silence, before going to the kitchen to put the kettle on for coffee.

17

Even though he was sometimes in error, Lord Shand was a man who was never in doubt. The Prime Minister was far from reassured by him, but feared him as a pigeon does a bird of prey. After the comforting presence of Mark Ivor, Rupert Shand's claws seemed increasingly there to pierce and seize on any business that failed to meet his demands. His hooded eyes would flash, the sneer in his voice would become even more contemptuous. Then would come the stillness, the unspoken disapproval, until the PM did what he was required to do.

'Shared hatreds are the best basis for political alliances. We must play that for all it's worth,' dictated Shand.

'Of course, Rupert. You put it well. Which . . . er . . . ?'

' "Back to basics" failed as a policy because there was no force behind it. In the new cut-throat world alliances are fine, provided our own national strength is reinforced.'

'Defence . . .'

'And Law and Order, and a strong Foreign Policy. Real issues that the people understand. They've had a drift, they've had puny consensus politics. They want strong leadership. You have to seize the opportunity.'

'They say, the press that is, that I lack the resourcefulness. I admit it. I'm not a confrontational sort. I go for compromise.'

'And quite right too, Prime Minister, when compromise is really the best policy. But from now on we're going to work hard to put a much more positive message across. Perception is reality. You've got to work on how you say what you say. More force,

more punch. I'll get you better lines to read. That speechwriter
. . . I'm not sure your chaps Willis and Caanan are really up to
it. What d'you think? Good fellows. Safe pairs of hands, both
of them. But maybe outstayed their usefulness? Come to think
of it, I have one chap who might be just what you need . . .'

'Have to talk to the Secretary to the Cabinet, Rupert.'

'Oh, I'm sure he'll be open to your suggestions, Prime Minister.
You set the agenda, say who you want, and he'll go along with
it. He is Mr Compromise personified. Does everything by the
book. No side to him. By the way, he's fairly close to retirement
too, isn't he?'

'I . . . yes . . . I believe so. But we mustn't rush these things,
Rupert.'

'How right you are, Prime Minister. But we can always plan
for eventualities . . .'

In Ivor's brief experience of him, Walt Tesco had the discon-
certing habit of turning up when least expected. This was no
exception. Since he arrived back from the States, he had played
cat and mouse with the press, but was determined, as far as he
could, to carry on a normal existence. This included attending a
policy studies seminar in a discreet building in a street behind
Westminster Abbey. As he was leaving the seminar, the security
guard at the door warned him that someone had come to reception asking if he was in the building. A glance through a window
into the street confirmed that a press photographer, with another
man in tow, was loitering to one side, while a number of others,
probably press as well, were waiting in a car parked on the other
side of the road.

'Is there a back entrance?' Ivor asked his hosts. While the
security guard was sent outside to tell his driver to meet him at
a street corner half a block away, he waited a few minutes, then
was let out by a tradesmen's entrance into a quiet mews lane.
Tesco was waiting for him.

'How the . . . ?' Ivor began.

'These press guys are so thick. I saw your chauffeur being sent off, so what more natural than you might have plans to leave other than by the front door.'

'All right. Clever. But I don't . . . we don't need each other any more, Tesco. What d'you want this time? Amanda's fine . . . my Ramsay Smythe contract is dead, I gather . . .'

Tesco ignored Ivor's remarks. 'You're having a hard time,' he volunteered.

'My problem.'

'Sure. Sure it is.' Tesco looked from side to side, grinning as usual. 'Got your car waiting somewhere?'

'Yes . . .'

'I'll walk with you. Maybe you'll give me a lift.'

'Maybe I won't.'

'I can help.'

'I don't need help. Anyway, why should you?'

'That's my business. You go for the cock-up theory of what's just happened? All these press stories?'

'Politicians always conspire, but in this case, yes. Helped along by human deviousness.'

'I wouldn't blame yourself.'

'Did I say I was?' They had reached the entrance to the mews, where it turned into a main road.

'Your car? Left or right?'

'Left. Maybe fifty yards. Beside a pub.'

'I'll check for you,' volunteered Tesco. 'Make sure that the gentlemen of the press haven't suddenly got clever.' He started out of the mews entrance and looked around cautiously. 'OK. Clear, I think. I can see your car.'

The two men emerged and walked rapidly down towards the waiting car. Ivor's driver had the engine running. Tesco looked at the other man enquiringly.

'OK. Get in,' said Ivor reluctantly.

When they had settled into the back seat and Ivor had given the driver his instructions, he turned irritably and demanded: 'Explain. What do you want now? What can you tell me?'

'Cree was put up to doing that story.'

'Journalists don't need encouragement to be malicious.'

'They need encouragement to believe there's a story to write in the first place. You were set up.'

'I have enemies. Why are you telling me? Are you looking for favours?'

'From you?' Tesco was genuinely surprised. 'Oh no. Nothing to do with you.'

'Well, would you mind telling me then what you're on about?'

'It's like this. Cree . . . I know him a bit. Done some sleuthing for him in the past. Asked me to do some on you. I listened, then said no. Conflict of interests, I said.'

'Are you looking for money?'

'Me?' Tesco looked genuinely hurt. 'Look, his proprietor put Lord Shand on to him –'

'When?' Ivor was suddenly much more attentive.

'They set up the whole thing together. Cree was working on a nuts and bolts piece about you. Then came the Battle Bus, the stuff about you and the PM, the Washington trip . . . You have an assistant, a young Scot –'

'Had.'

'He and Shand . . . I'm not quite sure, but someone's been paying him.'

'Rupert Shand is pretty devious, but even he wouldn't go as far as that.'

'Shand is jealous of you. It was him all the way. Wanted you out. And he's succeeding.' Tesco paused, then continued, 'Do you really want him to win? If not, I know where to find out a lot about Lord Rupert Shand.'

Ivor would not have been surprised by the tense and bad-tempered meeting that was taking place at that very moment at Number Ten, Downing Street. With the PM and his Private and Press Secretaries, Tom Willis and Denis Caanan, were the Chief Whip, Lord Shand and Sir Caspar Rudd. Had circumstances been otherwise, Ivor would have been present as well.

The six men stood rather than sat around the table, instinctively knowing it would be over quicker that way. The PM was speaking. 'He was most valuable to us, to the party, to me.' The past tense had its significance. If his attitude appeared irresolute, it was because it was based on the varied resolution of the others.

'Has been,' said Lord Shand, rubbing it home.

'Now an albatross.'

'I feel a certain loyalty . . .' the PM tried again.

'To the party first, I hope,' Jeffreys, the Chief Whip, interjected. 'On top of it all, this funny business about a daughter. Suspicious. Unsavoury. How could the man not know he had a daughter!'

'We're talking about his work,' muttered the PM.

'Work and play always run together. In my experience, that sort of thing says a lot about a man's character.'

'I can hardly believe . . .' began the Chief Whip, then thought better of it, as Lord Shand continued.

'That sort of scandal just adds spice to the tabloids' version of events. I don't judge a man by his sex life, but there are just too many unsound people in his life.' The word 'unsound' was damning in the extreme.

'Of course, I hadn't realized he was . . .' the Prime Minister hesitated.

'The backbenchers, to a man, or woman, want us to cut him out . . . you to pack him off, Prime Minister. Knock him for six. Straight into touch,' said Jeffreys, rubbing his hands together in a Pilate-like gesture.

A good mixed metaphor, thought Willis, but not very appropriate. Constant sporting allusions were among the silliest oddities of British political life.

'The phones at Number Twelve have been red hot since the story broke. A delegation from the 1922 Committee is coming in two hours' time,' the Chief Whip continued. A great intriguer, he was nicknamed The Cobra, from his habit of swinging his head from side to side as he talked, as if wishing to hypnotize his audience into submission.

'We have an election to win. This whole bloody thing is God's gift to the Opposition. Davies has been on TV non-stop, accusing us of allowing Ivor to run an alternative government.' Lord Shand punched his points home.

'It's rubbish,' said the PM weakly.

'The press are used to creating facts out of less than this,' Caanan chimed in. 'It'll be the only subject at my midday Lobby briefing.'

'He has been very useful to us. I agree.' The Chief Whip tried to be fair. 'What are you going to say to the press?' he asked.

'Stonewall. Rubbish it. Downplay Ivor. He was in a minor advisory capacity, and so on.' Caanan had already worked on his script.

'That go far enough?' asked Lord Shand.

'No,' said Caanan, with a shrug of resignation. 'It's what they'll expect me to say. They'll discount it before I open my mouth.'

'Where are our media friends?' asked the Chief Whip, looking enquiringly round the room as if expecting to find them sitting there.

'Nowhere, when a story like this is running. At best we'll get "*Vote for the government despite . . .*" sort of editorials,' answered Caanan.

There was a pause. Everyone waited to see who would speak next.

'You must go all the way,' said Lord Shand coldly. 'The future of the government is at stake.'

'What are you driving at, Rupert?' asked the PM. He was staring back at Shand, sensing the answer already.

'Ivor was only an adviser. Your adviser. He had a lot of access. Influential, but a man inflated by his ego, his reputation. He wasn't averse to having it widely talked about. Good for business – his, not ours.'

'He went too far,' echoed the Chief Whip. 'Much too far.'

Tim Willis caught the eye of his colleague, Caanan. Both were thinking as one about the expediency of politics, the short-term deviousness of its practitioners and wondering who would wield the dagger. Meanwhile Sir Caspar Rudd was watching them all in silence.

Lord Shand continued to press his advantage: 'He exceeded his brief.'

'We all knew what Mark was doing,' the Prime Minister insisted, aware that they were backsliding, with those shiftily distant expressions that betrayal lays on otherwise honest faces. 'We've used him. He's been a key figure. The architect of the whole election PR campaign. He knows all the strategy.'

'Accepted,' said Lord Shand, 'that he played a part. But the rest of us have done a little, have we not?' He smiled the sort of smile that had left a lot of bodies strewn along the wayside of his life.

'Invaluable aide, for us all ... We were all, apart from the civil servants, privy to where he was going, what we asked him to do in Washington.' The Chief Whip tried to soften his words to find a compromise with the Prime Minister. There was another long silence.

'But ... we have an election to win. This could easily tip the balance. Prime Minister, you've got to instruct Caanan to reflect this discussion in his briefing, that Ivor is no longer in our employ, or ...' Lord Shand hesitated.

'Or what?' asked the PM.

A chill of crisis swept through a room that was used to crises. Shand stood, unbeatable in his ability to manipulate those who stood in awe of his title.

'Or you and the party can do without my future service. I regret to have to say this. You cannot allow an alternative government like this. He was a paid lobbyist who went too far. He exceeded his brief. Prime Minister, you have a choice.'

'This leaves us ... me ... with a serious ... a major problem.' The PM made one last attempt. 'The party signed his cheques, Rupert. Now we're ditching him. God, after all he's done ...'

'If I may say so, Prime Minister, he ditched you.' Lord Shand raised his voice at last. 'He knows the penalty.'

Caanan looked at his watch. 'I'll have to go, Prime Minister.

The Lobby will be seething.' He stood, waiting for guidance.

'Go ahead,' said the Prime Minister. His eyes were staring down, fixed on the table in front of him. 'Just go ahead.'

Only Sir Caspar Rudd had not spoken. No one was surprised, since he seldom spoke unless he had to. His expression gave nothing away but he had already decided on his next course of action.

When he was in difficulties, when he needed unprejudiced advice, Ivor turned to his friend Caley Perkins. One of the keys to understanding Ivor lay in his relationship with Perkins; each was the whetstone for the other's wit; they got on well and agreed about almost everything except the relevance of public opinion to political life. In Ivor's view the public were so fickle, so open to influence by the last opinion-former to harangue them, so swayed by the day's headlines, that their 'organized hypocrisy' ought to play almost no part in enlightened political judgement. Not unnaturally, Perkins disagreed; beyond, he argued that to go against the findings of the polls too often or for too long, and a political party was doomed.

'Well, but . . .' Ivor would argue back.

Then they would defuse the situation by turning to discuss the latest production of *Turandot* at the English National Opera, and such minor disagreements would quickly fade. But Ivor continued to believe in élites, in identifying them, in cultivating them, the mere two or three hundred people that really mattered in contemporary Britain. He backed up his case by defining a simple geographical imperative. The seat of government, the location of almost all serious political, social and financial decision-taking was not the South East, not even Greater London, but a small number of locations in a very small part of London. The top really was very small. He believed in élitism, that persuading, enticing, forcing, infuriating the élite into action was the only way to achieve real progress. His genuflexion in the direction of the ballot box and of democracy was a gesture. His faith lay in the meritocracy, a wise legislature, a benevolent dictatorship.

Let the elected representatives of the people worry about the people. They were not his concern.

When he launched into such an argument, Perkins' eyes would sparkle and light up his cherubic face. He would frown momentarily and appear shocked.

'Come off it, Mark. You don't believe all that rubbish. You know it's the people, the electorate, who matter in the end.' Then he would smile his 'you cannot be serious' smile.

'I mean it, Caley. I really do. A few hundred men. Hardly any women. They set the tasks. They define the agenda. They make progress. They impede it. Know them and you know what makes Britain tick. The rest are spectators.'

'You, Mark? Spectator or player?'

'Me? I'm the Strategy Man, remember?'

That was all in the past. This evening it was different. There was no banter, no wit in Ivor's voice when he rang his friend. 'Can you come round?' he asked simply. 'Please, now.'

Perkins was at Ivor's flat within half an hour. Deborah showed him into the study and shut the door behind her.

'I've been set up,' began Ivor.

'As you say, we know the problem. It's the answers that are tricky. Which would you rather face now, my public, the incompetent, unthinking many, or your corrupt, clever, few?' Perkins threw himself into a chair in the corner of the room.

'I'm not into theorizing right now, Caley.'

'You've got to theorize. Look at your problem as if you were advising others. You've handled news creation before.'

'Not right on top of a general election, I haven't.' Ivor paced the carpet nervously.

'OK. Let me help. Your élite: what are they going to do?'

'Ditch me.'

'One way or another. Right. That's what you'd have advised them to do?'

'Yes.' It was more of a grunt.

'You live by the élite. You die when they throw you out.'

'Charming.'

'You know what I mean. You've only got them. You've got no wider constituency of support, no public to appeal to, no fan club. The press won't back you even though they disturb the democratic process every day far more than you ever could.'

'If I had supporters, what could I say?'

'What would you say?'

'Defend me . . .'

'Of course.'

'Without damaging the party and its election chances?' Caley Perkins got to his feet, walked to the window and looked out, unseeing.

'Any more than has been done.'

'I don't need this, Caley.'

'Yes you do. The catechism approach. Talk it through. Talk it out. Facts, parameters, strategies, conclusion.'

'Your options. One: do nothing. Two: defend yourself. Three: blame everyone else. Four: attack.'

'Depends on what the PM, the others do?'

'You know that already. From what you've told me about him, the PM will wriggle for a bit, then run for cover like the rest.'

'Shand? I now know he was behind it from the start.' Ivor was surprised by the bitterness in his own voice.

'It doesn't matter who set you up. The deed is done. Now, which option is it to be?'

At that moment Deborah came into the study. 'I have Number Ten on the line. The PM wants to talk.'

'I'll be a moment, Caley,' said Ivor as he left the room. When he returned a few short minutes later, any remaining anger or bitterness had been replaced by despondency.

'You're right. The Number Ten Lobby briefing has kicked me in the crutch. They've thrown me out, and with a real vengeance. I'm yesterday's man.'

'Dramatic stuff. All the more reason. You've got to fight. Defend yourself. You did nothing wrong. You did as you were asked.'

'Cree's right. By and large I did as I was asked, but it was action that I had proposed in the first place.'

'You didn't have a free run?'

'There were things I couldn't do.'

'Modest as always.' Caley Perkins smiled reassuringly, and Ivor tried to smile back. It didn't quite work.

'I can't fight back. There's a real conspiracy afoot in Lord Shand and his *Team*. But not now. I have other stories . . . but it would only hurt the PM and the party.'

'They deserve such loyalty?'

'They're going to get it.'

'You've got your future, yourself and your daughter to think of.'

'God . . . Amanda. She's really upset. All this press attention is so new to her. Guilt, loss of face.'

'Surviving families is a tricky business. You've had it too good for too long. What did the PM say, if you don't mind my asking?' Perkins stared hard at his friend, waiting for the answer.

'Said he was sorry, would you believe it? That I was off their books as from now. Said he was advised to tell me to lie low. Advised to –'

'Who by, now?'

'Doesn't matter.' Ivor shrugged.

'Someone else who's valuable, impregnable, irreplaceable?'

'Probably. Just like me.'

18

Ivor kept his own counsel, believing he had bigger things to worry about than the treachery or folly of a temporary assistant. He believed that until the *Spectator* hit the news-stands on the Friday when Maclean, getting everything he could out of his brief exposure to Ivor, proved himself equally adept at kicking a man when he was down. The lead article was entitled '*Working with Machiavelli*', and was real Judas stuff.

'Sue!' hissed Deborah in such a vicious tone of voice that it startled him.

'No, no and no. I've always advised clients not to sue. It gives status. It adds currency to the accusation. Even if you win, the judgment never rectifies the insult.'

'Plenty of insults around.'

'It'll die. Even with Shand's help, the story has a short shelf-life. Unless the government loses the election. Then I'll be one of the factors. If they win, I'll be able to slip into well-deserved obscurity.'

'How can you take it so lightly? That creep's betrayed you. It's lies.' All Deborah's long pent-up loyalty and devotion boiled to the surface.

'Lies among the truth. Maclean should learn that you have to have a good memory to be a good liar. But if I let that cheap little man get to me, Deborah, that day I'll give in. And it's not just him. It's those who put him up to it. I won't let it get to me.'

'They were jealous of your access.' Her eyes glistened.

'Most misery in the world is caused by the exploitation of envy. Now . . . I don't get mad. I get even.'

'That's better.' His secretary smiled. 'With whom? Maclean? Shand? The PM? The party?'

'None worth the strife. I need to get even with the system. My part in it.'

'Can I get you a drink? Whisky?' Deborah, not fully understanding, stood, prim and neat, then started bustling around the office.

'Thanks. Not that either. So easy to slip into that trap. Drowning problems.'

'So what?'

'So we're going to take a break, Deborah. I want you to take a holiday till after the election.'

'You've got so much on.'

'Cancel it out. Not out of weakness, you understand. It's just that anything I do now would be misconstrued, used to keep the wicked guru story running.'

'Your clients?'

'My good clients will understand. They'll wait. My bad clients will ditch me anyway. Remember what happened to a man I knew once, Mike Deaver, Deputy Chief of Staff to President Reagan? He had the President's ear, and, more importantly, Nancy's. He was everywhere. Fixed everything. Made policy. Acted as gofer. Eyes and ears and mouth of the President. A real American spin doctor. Then he slipped on a few banana skins.'

'I seem to remember,' said Deborah.

'Leaving the White House, he set himself up as a consultant. Made the cover of *Time* magazine: a picture of him on the phone. The caption read something like "*Who is this man telephoning?*" – what they were getting at was that as a private consultant, with lots of overseas consultancy fees, he still had direct access to Reagan. That smelt. Suddenly the most sought-after man in Washington didn't have any friends. His enemies – he had more than some – pounced. Charged with unethical activities. I forget the details. All I know, Deborah, is I'm not going to put my foot into that trap.'

'What could they do?'

'Easy. Suppose I started setting up any of my clients with MPs or ministers just now. With friends like Cree and Maclean around, I'd keep my limelight, and no one would touch me. No. As they say: my future isn't what it used to be! But it'll swing back. So, I'm off. Close the shop, Deborah. We'll redraw the map later.'

It was the last Sunday before the election; for the politicians, a lull, a rest day. Almost. Ivor was packed for Scotland, aiming to take the lunch-time shuttle to Glasgow. The early-morning call from the Prime Minister was totally unexpected, the voice at the other end tired and dejected. Ivor changed his plans and drove to Chequers.

He remained in the library, well out of sight, as civil servants and party men came and went. The two men had a late meal together, then went for a stroll in the grounds. There was a late spring chill in the air but the trees were beginning to bud. Over lunch, with domestic staff hovering around, they had talked strategy, analysed the day's batch of opinion polls, almost like old times. Now it was different. In the background, police bodyguards with dogs patrolled the perimeter fence of the Prime Minister's country residence.

'I used to be paranoid. Whenever I saw an armed man like that one over there, I wondered: bodyguard or assassin? Now I don't think about it. Too many enemies.'

'You're not that vulnerable.'

'Well protected, but not from my real opponents.'

'Which ones are real? Do you ever know?'

'The ones sitting on the Opposition benches I can see. It's the ones on the benches behind me I worry about. It's the friendly fire that kills. Remember Margaret.'

'Politics is never about kindness.'

'You've got up-to-the-minute experience, Mark. I'm sorry

about what's happened. Colleagues felt . . . maybe I didn't fight hard enough for you . . .'

'Hard enough.' Ivor glanced across at the man walking beside him, saw how ordinary he was, how weak and unsure.

'We've been ungrateful . . . as dicey as accepting a drink from a urologist.'

The Prime Minister laughed briefly. 'I relied on you.'

'That's what they're complaining about.'

'I need advice, unfettered by Civil Service or political bias. Thank God for Rupert Shand.'

'If you think so.'

'He's not self-seeking.'

Ivor walked in silence.

'I just wanted to say I'm sorry,' the PM repeated.

'B-movie dialogue.'

'I mean it.'

'Thanks.'

They walked back towards the house. As they approached, the imperious figure of Shand appeared at a doorway, watching them.

'Christ! He's an hour early,' said the PM, looking and sounding like a schoolboy caught by the Headmaster smoking behind the gym. Shand's smile had a heart of ice.

'No one saw you coming here?' were his first words. He ignored the Prime Minister with the effortless arrogance of his class, leaving Ivor wondering if he would add something like 'I'll talk to *you* later.'

Ivor shook his head. 'The secret is safe.'

'This is no joke, Ivor. We advised the PM not to be seen with you. You, of all people, must realize –'

'I realize the whole thing, Rupert. The sound of skins being saved.'

'I thought you big enough not to be bitter.'

'Bitter: no. Wiser: yes.'

'You're not going to do anything foolish, I hope.'

'Memoirs? Sell my soul to the *Sun*? Set up Fred Cree perhaps?

Like you, Rupert? This time it could be twenty things you didn't know about Lord Shand. What secrets are you hiding, Rupert? Or I could ring my Scots friend, Rick Maclean . . .'

Lord Shand stared down at Ivor with loathing.

'One more thing, Rupert. As the new keeper of the conscience of the Prime Minister, I hope you live well with your own.' He spoke as if the PM were not even there.

'I'll ignore that, Ivor. You're under pressure. We all know what game we're in, otherwise we wouldn't be here. I warn you . . .' Shand's tone was viciously unpleasant.

'About?'

'Dirt-dealing. Old stories . . .'

'Old stories? About you? You make me curious, Rupert. But relax. I'm disappearing. Best wishes for the election. I shall watch from afar.'

'Where?' Shand looked surprised.

'My business. You don't need me, surely?'

At the top of the steps Lord Shand turned to go back into the house. There was an aristocratic angling of his back that excluded Ivor from further discussion.

'Prime Minister, if you don't mind. I think we should get down to work. Your Eve of Election speech.'

The Prime Minister threw a sheep-like glance towards Ivor, nodded imperceptibly, then meekly followed the peer inside. Ivor stared after them, contempt more than anger welling inside him. Then he turned and walked briskly towards his car.

There were two more events of significance before he eventually flew to Scotland late on the Monday. His solicitor, Steven Rotenbein, rang with the news that he had traced the where-abouts of Annette Valais. She was living in a converted farm-house near St Malo with her schoolteacher husband and four children.

'I'll talk to Amanda. But not now. Do nothing further, Steven. No contact. Nothing. Not now.'

The other thing was that he had been so infuriated by his

encounter with Shand, had blurted out the unintended question about his secret life, that despite his promise to himself, he picked up the phone and dialled Tesco. When the other end answered, he asked: 'You remember when we last met, you made me an offer?' He paused. 'What's it going to cost to go out and get the files?'

> **Top Secret & Personal**
>
> FROM: *The Secretary to the Cabinet*
>
> re: **Operation Picnic**
>
> *Note for the record of conversation with*
>
> *PM – 10:30 am Tuesday 23rd November*
>
> 1. I raised with the PM the anxieties that existed over the degree of access to Number Ten and to sensitive policy papers which he had recently allowed to Lord Shand. I argued that the in-house team of civil servants, Willis, Caanan and myself, along with the Policy Unit, were surely sufficient to his purpose. He reacted angrily. He said that following Ivor's departure he needed a source of personal advice, uncluttered by civil service or party dogma. Lord Shand fulfilled this role extremely well.
>
> 2. I attempted to point to the evidence of doubt about Lord Shand's background, extreme political leanings, and recent activities. I stressed the added unease that his relations with Ramsay Smythe had also caused. This information was rejected out of hand. 'I was advised that you would say this,' were the PM's actual words. 'You have a choice: accept the situation or we could bring your retirement date forward if you prefer.'

When he had finished dictating the note, Sir Caspar Rudd went and sat at his desk. Outside he watched the double file of

Horseguards riding off the Parade onto the road that led up to the Mall. It was a brave sight. The spring sunshine sparkled on their helmets as a group of Japanese tourists turned to watch and applaud. All was well with the world out there; it was up to him to make sure the same applied inside the walls of Ten Downing Street.

19

Even the dawn came late that day, a dawn of leaden skies and sweeping sheets of rain. Mark Ivor got up briefly, peered through a misted window and returned to bed. What had he to get dressed for except to pick up the milk at the gate and go, later, to get whatever London papers had reached the village shop? Did he want newspapers? The thought made him pull the quilt tightly over his head to shut the outside world away. He heard the telephone ring distantly, forced himself to ignore it, and eventually drifted fitfully back into a dream-filled sleep. His depression matured later when he got up and stood under a shower so lukewarm that it could not ease his back. A few thousand spent on a new hot water system was long overdue. The extra burden of thinking about that minor domestic matter plunged him further into a burgeoning gloom.

He was alone at the cottage. Alone, inactive, almost incapable of action. He had determined he would not use the telephone or the fax unless driven to it. He was still sufficiently determined to stick to it and he had only been there for forty-eight hours. Usually he revelled in the wildness, the aloneness, the exhilaration of long, windblown walks along a deserted shore with only rabbits, seals and seabirds for company. He had always had a profound envy of those who were more effortlessly casual than himself. He coped well with order but the random unsettled him. Remote Scotland gave him a necessary fix away from conformity. Usually. Now, apart from stocking up with food and drink in the village shop, he had done nothing, gone nowhere, not even to see his crofting friends down the hill by the shore, where he would be sure of uncomplicated, boisterous talk and serious drinking. Even the old black and white television had given up the ghost. Radio Four was his link with the real or phoney world outside his cottage retreat. Here was a different pace, a gentler rhythm, a world where the old joke rang true about *mañana* being too urgent a word for those Highland ways and places.

He settled down in a deep armchair for his mind-suspension routine. Arms out; palms facing upwards; body and limbs relaxed. He started counting and breathing regularly. His mind wandered. He started again. He veered off. It wasn't working. Damn Shand! What was he doing running away up here, while that arrogant bastard took over the reins ... the campaign ... the mind of the Prime Minister? He tried again. The telephone rang four times then cut. It rang again immediately, a signal that it was Deborah. He forced himself out of the chair and picked up the receiver.

'How are you?' Her voice was anxious. 'The press are looking for you. Heavies want an interview; tabloids are looking for photographs of Amanda.'

'Am I that important?'

'Today, yes. Tomorrow ... ? Who knows. They have tunnel vision.'

'How's Amanda?'

'Taking after you, she said. Relishing giving them the slip. She said to say she'd ring you tomorrow at ten.'

'I'll be waiting.'

'I like her. I mean ... You're very fortunate, both of you.' Deborah rang off in embarrassment at letting her personal feelings show.

Left alone, he felt emptiness, but emptiness weighed down with *ennui*. Depression was replaced by apathy until depression took its place once again. He was restless, then he sat still for an age. When he found himself getting worked up again about Shand, he pulled on an anorak and wellington boots and walked the mile to the village. The London papers had not arrived. He picked up the *Herald* and the *Oban Times*, bought some bread, and turned to walk home. Rain blanketed down. He deliberately pulled off the hood of his anorak to let the elements wash his thrown-back face and hair. The brief exhilaration was soon replaced by a cold, dull chill, as rain found its way in rivulets down his neck. One boot leaked, mulching with a sock that kept slipping, with infuriating relentlessness, down leg and foot towards the toe. He would have a blister on his heel by the time he arrived back at the cottage.

A red Post Office van splashed towards him. It slowed, then stopped as the postman, recognizing him, leaned out for a brief chat.

'Not a bad day.'

'Bloody awful day.'

'You should have been here last week.' The postman came from South Uist and had a soft musical lilt to his voice. He grinned suddenly. 'It was you I was seeing on the television the other day. Was it not you? If you are to be running the country like they say, and this election thing, what are you doing at Ardmore?'

'They can manage without me.'

'Can they indeed? I was not thinking that they were doing so very well.' The odd negative added a gentle poignancy to the remark.

'Taking a break.'

'Funny time to take it.'

'It's a funny old world, as Mrs Thatcher once said.'

The van drove off, cascading along the potholed lane.

Left behind, he piled up the last two hundred yards of hill towards home, forcing himself to walk fast. Damn Shand! He put his head back and started singing out loud, to the clouds, to the rain, to the empty lane. He laughed briefly until he lost his breath. Then came a brief dizzy spell and a tightness across his chest, which made him stumble out of control against a dripping hedgerow. It was as if he were, for a moment, crazily drunk.

He arrived back, gasping for air, but now surprisingly detached and unworried. The walk had done him good. He pulled off wet clothes and the irritating socks, and slipped into a thick-knit polo neck, corduroys and slippers, then lit a soon-blazing fire in the huge grate. He looked at his watch. It was well past midday. He opened a bottle of red wine and poured himself a generous glass. Then he settled in the great wing chair, warming his feet by the fire, to browse through the worthiness of the good Scots press.

They were full of the election. The problems of a neo-fascist Eastern Europe and the tensions in the Middle East were relegated to inside pages, with the exception of a local story about a boat, fishing off the West Coast of Scotland, losing all its nets to a mystery submarine. On the election, the Opposition had caught up fast but the opinion polls were swinging wildly in every direction. Caley Perkins of P-Poll was quoted extensively, speculating that the government could easily lose by thirty or forty seats. There was a long profile of Lord Shand, the PM's closest adviser, a piece obviously placed by Central Office, judging by how crammed it was with platitudes. Why should he carp? He had done that sort of thing often enough himself.

He saw his own name, once, twice, three times. The Opposition having accused him of having held the tiller of the campaign, were now sarcastically commenting that the government's campaign was rudderless. 'We criticized. They dropped Dr Ivor like a stone. They compounded their folly. Now they only have themselves to blame.' He could have been flattered, but knew he was merely a stick to be used in an increasingly dirty campaign. The *Oban Times* had a short profile on him, commenting mainly on the fact that he had a second home at Ardmore. Why then had the national press not tracked him down? Was he yesterday's news already?

Ivor made himself a sandwich and poured another glass of wine. As he did so, he caught sight of himself in a long-case mirror. A hollow-eyed, unshaven figure. No sign now of the polished, elegant personality who had been equally at home in Downing Street and the White House, at Covent Garden and at Ascot. He laughed briefly at the reflection, remembering a long-forgotten glimpse he had once had of Sir Alec Douglas-Home, the day after he had resigned as Prime Minister, standing, in baggy tweeds and a worn pullover, waiting for a tube train at Westminster underground station. Public life missed important people for no more than an hour or so after they departed. Shelf life in the public memory was seldom longer than that of a carton of milk.

He ate the sandwich, helped himself to a tub of yoghurt and poured a third glass of wine. He noted, dispassionately, that the bottle was already two-thirds empty or one-third full and it was not yet one o'clock. Still, why not? He was, today, answerable to no one, not even himself. He tried his relaxation technique once more, the counting, the deep breathing, the conjuring up of easy images. It failed him or he failed it. He switched on the radio and listened to the lunchtime news. It was all election. On and on and on. He, who would have been so involved, working a twenty-hour day, hardly sleeping, advising, plotting, drafting speeches, briefing political correspondents, sitting the long night hours through with the PM, was as if a thousand miles and hours away from all that had been his reality. It was another life.

'I don't miss it,' he suddenly shouted out aloud at the empty room. Then, shocked at his echoing words, he slumped back in his chair and wept.

Later, he drank more and more and eventually poured himself into bed with the quilt over his head. It was fortunate, for when the press car turned up and the two journalists got out, knocked on the door and then walked round the cottage before leaving to report to their editors that while his car was there, there was no sign of him, he heard nothing. Had he wakened, gone out to meet them, he would have presented a wild, drunken image that would have made a splendid picture story and the sort of headlines that make people laugh or weep. The gods were with him and he slept till dusk.

He staggered up, rebuilt the fire and fed cassette after cassette into the music player, sound turned up too high, with, in the background, the whistle of a rising wind and the splatter of a rainstorm struggling to get in at windows and door. Bach's violin concertos, Tchaikovsky's Symphony No 6, Dvořák, Sibelius,

Wagner and more Wagner. Wagner suited the moment and the post-triumphal despair that embraced him as he sat in self-inflicted hangover and misery.

The telephone rang. It stood on a battered table in the cramped inner hall. He let it ring on. It rang twelve times, then stopped. After a few moments it started again. Six further rings and he went and picked it up.

'You didn't answer.' It was Fiona.

'I was out getting wood,' he lied.

'Are you all right?'

'Yes, I am. No, I'm not.'

'You shouldn't be on your own.'

'Without you? Perhaps not.'

'That's not very welcoming.'

'Welcoming?'

'I'm coming up, if you want me.'

'Want you? How . . . ?'

'He's gone to the States. For ten days. Unexpected. I've had the children invited to friends for half-term. I thought I'd go and see that elderly aunt of mine in Perth – for about five minutes, since we don't much like each other – then . . . You'll have to pick me up somewhere.'

There was a long silence.

'You want me to come, don't you?'

'Yes . . . yes, of course.'

'The way you sound, I need to come.'

'Bring warm clothes,' he growled, wondering where the aspirins were.

'OK. But no nightdress.'

*

A stalactite of lime dripped onto the top shelf from the rotting concrete roof. Below, racks of steel shelving stretched away into the half-light offered by the few naked bulbs. Hundreds upon hundreds of yards of files, each tied in rough brown cardboard folders, each containing the life histories, the petty indiscretions, the would-be treacheries, the transcripts of interviews, the interrogations, the intimate bugged conversations, that the demented rulers of the *Securitate* had decreed should be kept to hold a nation in thrall.

Walt Tesco, who had bribed his way in, as he had done in the past, was not interested in files about the Romanians. Besides, his knowledge of the language was nil. His guide, an elderly, whey-faced man who had something wrong with his feet, shuffled ahead of him into the gloom. His condition matched his tale of having been an archivist for almost forty years in this ugly, abandoned place, in a barbed-wire compound on the outskirts of Bucharest.

The overseas section was in a vast warren of its own, labelled by country, by date, by name. These files had lain undisturbed for many years. For the last vile decade of Ceauşescu's reign, all the new data were logged on the most advanced, Japanese-made, computer files. Tesco was not interested in the modern stuff. The file he was after had been a long time sleeping.

Diplomats, politicians, businessmen, visiting dignitaries: tailed, watched, listened to, enticed with sexual and financial favours, bribed and, occasionally, blackmailed.

Italia ... Statele Unite ... Anglia ... Anglia ... Why did foreigners always talk about England? Why not *Marea Britannia*? There were many shelves for *Anglia*, organized alphabetically and by date. Tesco took a sheet of paper from his pocket and consulted his notes – September and October 1977. Eventually, with the help of the archivist, who was more alert than he first appeared, he found the two files he was looking for. He turned the sheets of cheap paper on their string bindings. Much of the material was in Romanian but there were lengthy transcripts in English of what looked like telephone conversations or whispered confidences recorded in hotel bedrooms. He noted one or two or three very familiar British and American names. There was material here that could, if cleverly used, help solve Romania's balance of payments problem. As always, the contents, even after Tesco's cursory glance, showed that many men in the highest positions, apparently tried and tested, have no more scruples about national allegiances than lesser mortals, if they are enticingly enough tempted by sex or by money. And if they are confident that they will not be found out.

The files slipped easily into the nondescript plastic bag. The archivist's lingering doubts about letting Tesco take them away were soothed with the help of another envelope filled with US dollars. After all, after the Revolution, who in Romania would notice? Who would miss them? What did it matter any more?

Late the following afternoon, Romanian Airways flight RO121 disgorged its few occupants. Those who could afford it flew British Airways. Tesco walked faster than the rest. He carried a small blue canvas holdall and a battered plastic bag – the same bag, but the brown cardboard file cover had been removed and burnt and the contents had been cleverly separated and interleaved with a long technical report on the building and financing of a new domestic appliances factory in Bucharest. It had been a precautionary measure only. The Romanian customs officials were a shadow of their former selves, mainly on the lookout for plundered antiquities and works of art. And the British customs – the only printed or written material that they were usually interested in was pornography. It was too early for the Romanians to have got seriously into that game yet. Nonetheless . . .

Walt Tesco presented his British passport to the immigration officer who looked hard at him and immediately waved him through. He picked up his battered Samsonite suitcase from the luggage carousel and made his way through the green, nothing to declare, channel. He was almost through when a young, pleasant-faced customs man stopped him.

'Could I have a look in your case, sir?'

'Of course.'

The officer opened the case and worked his way efficiently through the contents which seemed largely to consist of crumpled shorts and underwear.

'Bucharest isn't hot on laundries,' said Tesco apologetically.

'I quite understand, sir.' The officer neatly reclosed the suitcase. 'Your hand luggage, and that plastic bag, sir, if you don't mind.' Again, the contents were swiftly and expertly scrutinized. 'Been abroad on business, have we, sir?'

'Helping the Romanians move into the twentieth century — fridges, cookers, that sort of thing.'

'Thank you, sir. Welcome back.'

The smiling customs man waved him through.

'Thank you.' Tesco picked up the suitcase, the blue canvas holdall and the plastic bag and followed the other arriving passengers out of the Customs hall.

Outside, he was greeted by the noise and turmoil of the Terminal Two Arrivals area. A barrier separated passengers from those waiting to greet them. A television camera crew and some photographers, in their perennial pursuit of compassion and sentimentality, jostled around a young couple carrying a child. The adults were smiling and laughing; the child was crying desolately. At a guess it was the climax of another heart-rending Romanian Aids baby adoption saga. Tesco pushed irritably past and on through the crowd towards the exit door and the taxi rank. He would be glad to get home.

*

He picked Fiona up in Glasgow, city of culture, red sandstone tenements and great sprawling cemeteries. The storms of the past days had cleared away, to be replaced by the crisp, clear spring weather that showed Scotland to best advantage. They drove up a mirror-like Loch Lomond on a road seasonally uncluttered by tourists, and turned off left at Tarbet towards Inveraray and the west. The drive to the cottage took over two hours with a brief stop for a bar lunch in a little loch-side pub that glowed welcoming with its open fires. Ivor remained remote on the journey, unsure both of himself and of their relationship now that they were out of their smooth metropolitan environment. She had never seen him subdued and unkempt. He had always been so much in control of himself and his Savile Row appearance. She had admired that but she was also pulled to this other, darker side. His sullenness was a challenge. She was in a thoughtful, emotional mood as she too adjusted to being out of her boring, domestic normality. Suddenly, feeling both free and trapped by her emotions, she felt like molesting him, teasing him, seducing him, as he sat beside her, hands tensely clenched on the steering wheel. But she forced herself to wait; she knew him, but not enough to know if he might reject such a blatant advance. Besides, the road was twisted and narrow there, with a sheer drop to a boisterous, white foamed river, far below.

She saw the cottage as he had done when he had first come there. He told her that he had bought it on the spot, using his portable telephone to place an instant offer with the Glasgow solicitors. At that time portable phones were a rarity in that part of Scotland. The solicitor had been fascinated: it was a chance freak of reception, standing at the top of the wind-swept hill, that had allowed the call to go through.

As they drove up the narrow track, Fiona saw the desolate beauty of the place, the tough, stone built cottage clinging to the side of the bracken- and heather-clad hill. She took to it immediately. This was somewhere she could feel for, feel at home. Down below clustered the grey stone and whitewashed village beside the sweep of the sea loch. Beyond, an unrepeatable view of water and hills and mountains stretched on and on in a hundred misty shades of blue and grey, away to the Outer Isles. Fiona's feelings for him helped colour her view and made it marvellous and enchanting. For the moment, the hardship and misery that such a bleak and barren landscape could also offer was ignored.

'Magnificent.'

'My emotional lung.' He stared at the view as if he too was seeing it for the first time. It was suddenly very important to him that she liked it as well. He took her inside to the fire-smoke warmth. She found it small, friendly, more than a little battered, with bits and pieces of furniture, carpets, pictures picked up from here and there over the years. Around the windows and by the fireside were the flotsam and jetsam of his walks and rambles along shores and across mountains. Strangely shaped stones, glass fishing floats, wind- and sea-sculpted wood that had appealed, all lovingly collected in a happy clutter. On the crowded mantelpiece, beside the candlesticks and the postcards, the boxes of matches and a clock that had long since ceased to work, pride of place was given to a large glass jar of peppermints, smooth Scots pan drops, which he bought in bulk in the village shop. She took all this in and more as he went outside to bring in her bags. She saw the pin-board of photographs in the kitchen, smiling holiday faces, laughter-filled parties, one in fancy dress. There were women, pretty women, intelligent flushed expressions. One in particular appeared several times; she was often draped round him. The kitchen was small but tidy. Fiona saw the empty bottles. He had been there for only four days. She thought briefly of her husband and how he had begun to drink. Perhaps the bottles were left-overs from previous visits. Perhaps not.

'Men want a virgin who's a whore.'

'Who told you that?' he asked, leaning on an elbow and looking at her.

'Some man in my past.'

'Coming into the world by the route we do, makes us always want to get back in the same way.'

'Part of you's not doing too badly.' She gyrated her hips seductively, moved over and he lay back on the pillow moaning gently. 'Therapy's working. You look better already,' she added, bending low and pressing her twinned nakedness against his chest. Her hair brushed his face and he stifled a sneeze.

'Very romantic. Sorry.'

'I liked that little extra spasm.'

'Anything for a kick. Even a sneeze.' They both laughed and turned together, entwining and interlocking, arms, legs and bodies in a heap of joy. The bed gave them enough room; it was by far the largest piece of furniture in the house, occupying most of the space in the upstairs bedroom.

'How did you get it in?' she panted.

'Usual way. Between your thighs. Hadn't you noticed?'

'The bed, idiot.' She laughed, pinching him playfully.

'Came in bits. Built in. Nailed to the floor. Supported on beams. Impregnable. Indestructible. Even with us on top of it.'

'Doesn't squeak, thank God. I hate beds that squeak. They usually do, and out of sync.'

'Try music. Try it to music.'

'What? Pomp and Circumstance? People of my age need the right sort of timing if we're making love to music. Slow, slow, quick, quick, slow.'

'Or, in your case . . .' There was a pause in their chatter as action demanded all their breath.

'I like you out of context,' she gasped, eventually.

'This *is* my context.'

'No, it's not. Back to the womb. Escaping.'

'I left London deliberately.'

'That wasn't leaving. That was flight.'

'I'm not scared.'

''Course not. Pride wounded. Deeply. A question of status.'

'You don't understand, Fiona.'

'I understand very well.'

He started to withdraw, physically and emotionally. She read his irritation and abandoned any further serious talk. He was not in the mood to be humoured; she would resort to a slower seduction. This time it would be subtle, less the feverish tearing off of clothes, the flood-gates of passion. Now it would be sexual and intellectual game-playing, the association of the two to create a heightened one. She began by getting up and slipping on her clothes.

'Where are you going?'

'I'm cold. Need a break.'

'Come back.'

'And I need to eat. You haven't offered me anything since I arrived.'

'Haven't I? Oh . . . OK. I'll have to get some firewood in

anyway, before it gets too dark.' He pulled himself off the devastated bedding, climbed into warm clothes and went out into the crisp cold of the twilight.

While he was outside, a telephone rang. A moment's hesitation and Fiona answered it.

'Yes?' she asked. 'Who do you want? Oh, no. Too late, I'm afraid. He was here. He's gone off, back to London, I think. Me? Oh, me. No, I'm just a neighbour.' She put the telephone down and turned to find him watching her from the open door. His arms were full of logs.

'Who?'

'*Sunday Times.*'

'I might have wanted to speak to them.'

'I knew you didn't.'

'Just a neighbour . . . You lie well.' He said it kindly.

'Since we've met, I've learned a lot about subterfuge.'

'D'you feel guilty being here?' He shut the door behind him. A log dropped noisily onto the floor and rolled into a corner.

'Betrayal of family and so on? Certainly not. If my other half is sober enough in New York, he's probably doing much worse things.'

'Like . . . ?' He bent and arranged the logs in a huge wickerwork basket by the fireside.

'I don't want to talk about it.'

'We always talk about me and my problems.'

'I prefer it that way. Mine are all the usual things, the boredom of marriage, frustration, loneliness . . .'

'Loneliness?'

'Of course. It's the loneliest thing, a marriage. If it continues when it's terminal.'

They sat down opposite each other at either side of the hearth.

'I used to think of women as beasts of prey. Were you on the prowl when we met?'

'Certainly not. I was going in search of a drink, I seem to remember. Intending to anaesthetise my emotions with gin.'

'Would you like a drink now?'

'Would you?'

'Perhaps.'

'You drink a lot? On your own?'

'Don't begin . . . No, not usually. But over the last days . . . Poured myself into bed. You spotted the bottles?'

'Why?'

'Do I need to explain? I'm not going the same way as your husband, if that's what you mean.'

'I'll have a gentle drink then, please. It ought to be whisky.' She was looking hard at him. His eyes were burrowing into the roaring flames of the fire. He looked up. 'No, wait,' she said. 'Stay there. I'll get it. I want to wait on you.' She walked over to the oak sideboard and poured two large measures of whisky. 'Water?'

'Half and half.' He followed her every graceful move as she brought the glasses over and handed him his. She stood over him, so close that if he had bent forward in his chair he could have kissed her midriff.

'No, don't move.' She reached forward and clinked her glass against his.

'*Slainte!*'

'*Slainte!* You've learned quickly.'

'I knew a Scots Guardsman once.'

'And?'

'Thick as two haggises . . . No! Don't get up. I'm your hand-maiden. I do everything for you now.'

'Fantasies.'

'Yes. Mine. Play my game. Please.'

Remaining close she placed her glass on the mantelpiece then dropped her arms to her sides as if in total, abject, submission. She looked down towards the floor, eyes and eyelashes acting total modesty.

'What?'

'Hush. Don't spoil it, Mark,' she whispered.

'Actions that, in the first steps from innocence, might be

thought perversions, take on a new, more acceptable reputation once they have been experienced. "Safe sex", the contemporary, Aids-related clarion call, can unleash ways of fulfilling desires that older generations only dreamed about.'

'Tell me.'

'Virtue is its own reward; traditional forms of copulation reap the same,' lectured Ivor. 'Gentle, consenting exploration of the wilder shores can release deeper passion, even overwhelming love to back the lust.'

'Go on,' she whispered.

A night of deep feeling was being kindled by fantasy, then filled by enticing that fantasy to resolution. The games men and women play run on strange routes. The sphincter of desire was binding tight. Thus Mark and Fiona.

They slept late and when they awoke, the house was cold. It was to be a morning of practicality after a night of joy.

'Eggs and bacon. If you're still my slave, I demand.' He sat up in bed, pulling the quilt off her still recumbent, naked back.

'Jeeze, it's cold. Please, Mark. Let me sleep. We had so little . . .'

'I have to go chop logs. We used them all last night. The stove in the kitchen should still be warm enough.'

He darted naked from the bed and went through to the bathroom to sluice himself down under the tepid shower. 'I'd stay dirty for a while, Fiona,' he shouted through to her; 'until the water heats up.'

A little later, a thick towelling dressing gown over her jerseys and jeans, she made her way down to the kitchen and began preparing breakfast. Outside, under a clear blue sky, the day was brisk and inviting. She could hear, in the distance, the evocative sound of seagulls and waves breaking on the shore. He had promised her a long seaside walk after breakfast. She was very happy.

In the lean-to woodshed at the end of the croft, he was setting to his task. Inherited from the previous owner, a huge piece of tree trunk, almost three feet across and two feet thick, served as the chopping block. It was some hard, foreign wood, washed on to the shore and brought, with great effort because of its weight, up there to serve its purpose. He was proud of his wood-chopping abilities. He would place a log on the block, then, with both hands apart, swing the long-handled axe high above his head. As he brought the axe down, he slipped the hand nearer the axehead down the shaft, till it hit the other at the heel, giving maximum momentum and power with minimum effort. His aim was good. Pine logs and other soft wood split neatly in two, the halves tumbling off into the corners of the shed to be collected later.

It wasn't getting any easier as he grew older. He was overweight and took too little regular exercise: those working lunches, dinners and chauffeur-driven cars. Of course all the intellectual activity burned up energy and kept him sort of fit . . . But did it? After only five or six logs he was breathing heavily. Too heavily. He paused for a moment and then started again. Axe swung high, hands coming together at the top of the crest and then down. Crack. The weight of the axe should do most of the work. Not too much strain . . .

His breath suddenly seemed to cut, choking in his throat, as a great force clamped around his chest. It was only for a moment, the deep heavy pain. He stumbled where he stood, then sat down, involuntarily, on the wooden chopping block. His face and body were pouring with sweat. He felt the shirt inside his heavy fisherman's jersey suddenly cold, as it stuck to the skin of his back. And then it was over. He sat still for five, maybe ten minutes. Damn! He wouldn't put it off any longer. He would go for a check-up. He knew he must.

Fiona came out looking for him. 'You're all right?'

'Yes. Fine. Just a bit out of condition, that's all.'

'Don't strain yourself. Come on in. Breakfast's ready.'

'Won't be a moment,' he said. 'I'll just stack these logs and I'll be with you.'

*   *   *

Two seals, looking like grey lobster-pot floats, bobbed their inquisitive whiskered heads up and down with the waves, watching the two solitary figures. The shoreline, a perfectly white semicircle, stretched towards a distant cluster of rocks by the point. The sand was so soft and fine that it had, in past centuries, been collected and sold as the blotting sand for quill-pen users in far-away Edinburgh and London. The wind blew it lightly over an occasional flail of seaweed and, now and then, an indentation that signalled some half-buried shell or piece of flotsam. Down by the water's edge, where the sand was heavily damp, erupted heaps betrayed where lugworms had buried themselves away from the long beaks of the sandpipers and other sea waders. They walked, hand in hand or arm in arm, laughing, pushing and pulling each other like two truant schoolchildren. In their wellingtons, they splashed along the edge of the foaming surf, she crying out loud with mock rage when one more daring wave swamped over the top of her boot. Eventually they came to the outcrop of rocks.

'Come, let me show you something.' He grabbed her hand and pulled her behind the largest of them, where he took her in his arms and kissed her, long and deep.

They only paused for breath when she, opening her eyes for a moment, pushed him away.

'Look,' she said. 'They're watching.' They turned to see that the voyeur seals, sensing an incipient mating game, had come close in and were straining high in the water in their curiosity.

'Shall we give them something to shock them?' Fiona said mischievously.

'No, wait. I want to show you . . . Here. Behind here.' He led her on over the wet, seaweed-draped rocks, to a little alcove, where a quirk of nature had trapped a multicoloured hoard of pebbles. Just as they reached it the sun came out from behind a cloud and lit up the little treasure trove.

'How beautiful,' exclaimed Fiona, bending forward to collect the brightest in her hand. He bent beside her, intent on adding the sea-polished best of them to a collection he had in a jar on his mantelpiece.

As he leant forward, he felt giddy. Then there was no muscular reflex to hold him upright. Suddenly, there was a new vice-like pain behind his breast bone, a pain that shot to his arms and neck, crushing him into oblivion. He seemed to fall for an age, like a felled tree, collapsing prone in front of her. His head and shoulder cracked on a seaweed padded rock. It was a sound that she would always remember.

He recalled nothing of how, in near panic, she had pulled his face clear of a rocky pool, how she somehow tied her anorak around his head to protect it, and had pulled him slowly, so slowly, back along the gentle sandy shore. Near a croft on the shore, a journey of almost half a mile that took her ten times longer than it had taken them to walk, she left him for a few desperate minutes. He was still unconscious, with a weak pulse, but breathing regularly, as she laid him in the lee of a thick clump of couch grass. She ran all the way. It was the croft that belonged to his friends. Fortunately, they were at home, but had no telephone so the woman of the house had to climb up to Ivor's cottage to call an ambulance from there.

The crofter came with her, pulling after him a rusty two-wheeled dinghy cart, which he used for bringing his rowing boat to and from the water. Together they rigged it as a wheeled stretcher and brought him to the croft. It took another half an hour before the ambulance arrived.

Ramsay Smythe was a powerful man. But like many bullies he was a coward at heart. He was always accompanied by one of a team of ex-Marine bodyguards, but the trouble with that was that while such bodyguards are excellent in dealing with dangers from the outside world, they are of very little value to the person they are meant to be protecting if the State is the threat. Old loyalties can be made to outweigh the new. The bodyguard, in consequence, was not there when Ramsay Smythe, a blonde on his arm, emerged from his club a little the worse for wear in the early hours of the morning. What little resistance he offered was swiftly overcome as he was bundled into the back of a waiting van. The terrified blonde was given her taxi fare home and told not to talk on pain of a fate worse than death.

Top Secret & Personal

TO: *The Secretary to the Cabinet*

FROM: *Chief, C13*

re: **Operation Picnic**

Ramsay Smythe picked up as authorized. (A powerful man and it was an ugly scene inside until we made him see sense.) This morning he was confronted with the duplicate copy of his own *Securitate* file. (See ZN1587/93 and other folios.) He started whimpering then. When we got round to plea-bargaining, he began to see reason. It was, for him, a good offer, considering the alternative: a long prison term for espionage, blackmail, extortion and a lot else, or, if he turned Queen's Evidence, freedom, a guarantee that his file would be shredded, his bid for Sigmont would get the government's blessing, and maybe a knighthood would come along in the course of time. He is not stupid; he saw sense; he's singing like a bird about *The Team*. My operatives doubt, however, that they will ever be able to extract the truth about their involvement in Brogan's death even though we are now convinced that it was inspired or financed by them. Such an admission would be too much, even for R.S., and without our using means you are not prepared to authorize, we must close that line of enquiry. Whatever, Shand, with your other key agent's help, is now isolated. Over to you.

Message ends.

Tesco expected a round of applause when he telephoned Ivor with news of what he had brought out. It surpassed his wildest expectations. There was only an answering machine. He left a grudging, disappointed message: 'Tell him I've got the crown jewels. They're here when he wants them,' he said.

Meanwhile, when the editor buzzed him, Fred Cree mentally went over his most recent entertainment claim. Had it been one that he had embellished? But all the man wanted was for him to ring Lord Shand. And the peer in turn suggested that he might take the night train to Glasgow.

20

Above the bed a rack of devices was arrayed to measure blood pressure, to hold drip feeds, to summon assistance. There were respirators, switches, red warning lights, radio selectors and panic buttons. Along with X-rays and radiographs, the inevitable record chart was there too: what the patient was allowed and forbidden to eat, details of medicines, of pulse, temperature and bowel movements. The rubber-wheeled bed itself was a multi-faceted contraption which allowed the occupant to be raised or lowered, penned in with bars like a child's cot, or swivelled around for ease of examination.

Mark Ivor gradually took in these and other things as he lay in the private room in the Glasgow hospital. He was draped with catheters; bandages and plasters on his arms and body covered the entry incisions for drip-tubes. Through a drug-soaked mind he could hardly recall the drive from the local cottage hospital, the vice-like pain, the exhaustion of the long, bumpy ambulance ride. He had only ever been seen by white, Anglo-Saxon medics in the past, so the Nigerian doctor with strong traces of Glaswegian in his speech pattern who appeared regularly by his bedside was another new experience. Apart from nearly dying, that was.

With the sympathetic connivance of his crofter friends, Fiona had taken the journey back to Glasgow with him in the ambulance. She stayed with him for twenty-four hours, then common sense, if not emotion, forced her to return to her family. She had desperately wanted to stay, to be with him, to tend to him, but he was in good hands and she had her own life to sort out for the future. Even before his attack, she had come to realize that it now lay entirely with him: he was unique, mesmeric, someone with whom she wanted to share her all. From his sickbed he summoned back reality sufficiently to urge her that no good would come of adding the immediate strain of a divorce to that of his own health.

Amanda replaced her that same afternoon. She breezed in full of cheer, with bunches of flowers and bags of fruit.

'I've also bought you these,' she said, placing a large bag of peppermints by his bed. 'I hope you're allowed.'

'Angina. I'm too young for this,' were his laboured words of greeting.

'Obviously not,' she responded. 'Far be it for this new daughter to start off by urging a more slim-line father, but I did notice your trouser top was taking too much strain.'

'Learning the hard way.'

'Opportunity to make good.'

'I was . . . we were just walking on the shore . . .'

'What else? No, don't tell me.'

'It's endemic in public life. By the time we've made it, most of us are past it.' His illness had not removed his sense of the absurd.

'Nonsense. You know what –'

'What?'

'A fresh start.' Amanda looked hard at him, relishing a future ability to bully her father for his own good.

'Tell me.' He tried to move up the bed so that he could look at her more easily. She bent over and rearranged the pillows behind his head. 'To be in hospital is to have the finality of life thrust before you. But . . . But, I have to get fit. It wasn't a stroke. My intellect is as sharp as ever.'

'Modest, my father.' She smiled gently. 'The love affair between you and your intellect will run and run. And they call mine the "me" generation . . . egotistical . . . self-centred.'

'You're being serious.'

'A little. I've been talking to Dr Adebanjo and he told me what to say.'

'Which is?'

'Easy and more easy. Diet, exercise and no strain.'

'Tensions kept me alert.'

'You'll have to find other ways. If you do, prognosis is good.' A nurse came in to give him an injection. Amanda kissed him on the forehead and left. He settled back to sleep.

He was so sedated, so cocooned in his hospital environment, that he barely realized it was the eve of the election. In his enforced isolation he was allowed no newspapers. Television was available but he felt too tired to watch, to take anything in. The medical parameters removed the need to act; every function was taken care of; the day was planned with no room for self-expression.

When the two men came into his room he was on the point of sleep. He stirred himself sufficiently to presume they were hospital staff. In his daze he noticed they were not wearing white coats and one of them was carrying a strange-looking aluminium case. They looked too scruffy to be hygienic.

'Feeling better, Dr Ivor?'

'I . . . yes, thanks,' he whispered. The injection was working; his brain was just ticking over. He was very tired. Why didn't they go away and let him sleep? Why were they there? One seemed to be unpacking a camera from the case. A camera?

'A few questions, Dr Ivor.'

'My medical records. You have my medical records,' he whispered weakly. Why wouldn't they leave him alone? He so much wanted to sleep.

'The Prime Minister knows you were a paid consultant on the Ramsay Smythe bid for Sigmont. Did he promise to help? Was money mentioned?'

Something felt wrong. Damn the injection. It made him so remote, so unclear. What were they asking? He was sick. He had had a heart attack.

'You must answer, Dr Ivor. Here, let me sit you up a bit. Fred here wants a nice bright photograph of you. Good and alert, you know. Want to look your best for our exclusive, don't you?'

The man was pulling him upwards, straightening the sheets,

222

tugging at the white night-gown he was wearing. He felt a pain. Not much, but a warning. He mustn't move. They mustn't . . . He felt so doped, but not enough not to react to the camera, the flash and, suddenly, to understand the question.

'Are you saying the PM helped with the Ramsay Smythe bid? How much money was involved, Dr Ivor? You've got to answer, you know.'

Slowly he reached his hand out under the bedclothes. Slowly. Slowly. He knew he must get there. Out from under the bed-clothes. They were making a fuss about getting him to sit up and look alert. It was around there somewhere on the side table. Somewhere.

'We know all about it, Dr Ivor. All we need is your confirmation. See I've got my tape recorder here. It's running, Dr Ivor. There, be a good guy. The truth – we just need you to say it in your own words.'

His hand found the emergency call button. He pressed. He kept his finger on it. The journalists did not relate to the alarm bell ringing a corridor away. He remembered Dr Adebanjo running in, a Charge Nurse close behind him.

'What the hell are you people doing here?' He heard the shout. Then he drifted into a deep sleep.

A general election is the means by which the British electorate, every five years, is allowed to choose, on a rough and ready basis, who is to rule them in the period between. It is a conflict of interests pretending to be a conflict of principles. One party wins, usually due to the faults and inadequacies of the other. Democracy is a fragile plant. The electors vote for the *status quo* or for change, without any clear idea of what those elected are going to do once put into office. Elections are occasions for politicians to succumb, even more than usual, to the aphrodisiac of the press and of the television cameras. The media caters to their whims. The election takes on the trappings of a Miss World competition, with the leaders proclaiming that they want world peace, freedom, justice, but never that their principal aim is to save their seats. Elections, like wars and Royal scandals, help sell news-papers. A good election in the eyes of the public is one where there is a lot of high-tempered abuse. In wars, the British reserve their hate for the Hitlers, the Galtieris, the Saddam Husseins. In peace they reserve it for each other.

Largely unrecognized by Ivor, this particular general election came and went, and the government and its Prime Minister were returned to office with a tiny, almost unworkable, majority. There would have to be another election – probably within the year. In his life these were all minor events. The sex scandal that Ivor had worried about had also broken, but the public were already satiated with that mix of political scandal and it too was quickly forgotten except by the MP and his wife whose marriage was destroyed, and the foolish girl who had her story and her topless picture paraded across most of the tabloids, without get-ting a penny for her pains. One of the Sundays tried to run an Eve of Election story about the PM, Dr Ivor and the Ramsay Smythe Consortium, suggesting that money had been offered, if not changed hands, and that unless the matter was cleared up, the electors should cast their votes elsewhere. It backfired. Amanda, showing an inherited skill and determination, arranged a press conference. With the help of the hospital authorities, and Dr Adebanjo in particular, she told, with great feeling, what had happened when the two journalists had tricked their way into the Intensive Care Unit. There was some mention in one of the broadsheets of Fred Cree's involvement. But dog doesn't eat dog in the media world, and so the story died.

It was a long, slow three months as spring moved into late sum-mer. He worked hard at his physical recuperation, first in hospi-tal, then at the convalescent home, then with an exercise bicycle at his flat in London. He regained his ability to relax, to count and deep-breathe himself into a state of suspended animation. It worked better now than it ever had. He felt recharged. He determined to make it stick. He would cut back on his workload and control his innate competitiveness. The women in his life,

Amanda, Fiona and Deborah, conspired, became a troika, determining where and what he should do and, more importantly, what he should not do. The Scottish cottage was out of bounds. There was too much potential strain there. That could come again later. Gradually, as he regained his health, Ivor wanted to return to the fray. He wanted to drink, to dine, to intrigue, to lavish affection on Amanda, to make rapturous love to Fiona, to dictate influential letters to Deborah. He fretted when they said no. He worried that, when they at last let him off the leash, he would have lost the talent and forgotten the skills.

The gentle aftermath of work done in the past was sometimes allowed to intrude. A remarkably subdued Ramsay Smythe came in secret one day to tell him that an agreed, friendly merger with the Sigmont Corporation had been signed and sealed, with the blessing of Her Majesty's Government and the Monopolies & Mergers people. Ivor, for Ramsay Smythe's new long-term reasons, was credited with having helped engineer the deal. The cheque was one that could not be refused without causing grave offence. Somewhere along the line, Fred Cree had this leaked to him and became apoplectic with fury. He made the mistake of writing about it, this giving currency to the rumour that, even on his death bed, Ivor retained his Machiavellian skills. The *Mail on Sunday* did a profile on him, how he had nearly died, the lot. In the public mind, Ivor was back in business.

One day he had an unexpected visitor. Someone he had almost forgotten about. Deborah just managed to camouflage her distaste as she ushered Walt Tesco into Ivor's office. In his scruffy, stained clothes, and with a liberal sprinkling of dandruff around his shoulders, he was hardly a typical visitor. To his surprise, Ivor's greeting was almost warm.

'When did you get back?'

'Quite some time ago. I thought you'd disappeared, then I got the news from Amanda. How are you keeping?'

'Better and better.'

'Lost a bit of weight?'

'That too.'

'I could do with some of that.'

'I can't recommend angina. Do I owe you some money?'

'Don't you want to know what I've got first? I have it here.' Tesco lovingly patted a fat, brown envelope he was holding.

'Tell me.'

'I'll leave it with you. It makes fun bedtime reading. Lots of it is intercepted conversations in English. I had other bits translated from Romanian.'

'And?'

'You want to destroy him? You have the weapon.'

Later, much later, when he had finished reading his way through the meticulously recorded details in the file, Ivor stood up and walked over to fix himself all that his doctors allowed – a very watery whisky. He had learned about a man and his weaknesses. But what did any of it matter now? It was all over and done with. Let it lie buried along with the Cold War. He would pay off Tesco tomorrow and that would be that. Ivor took a large brown envelope from his desk, slipped the file into it, sealed it, then locked it away in the safe that was concealed behind a row of leather-bound books in a corner of his study. The past was the past. Any other course of action would be pure vindictiveness.

About the same time, he decided to put out his own individual marker that he was back, that rumours of his departure from the political limelight had been premature. The grit in the oyster factor was at work. He accepted an invitation to appear on the live TV discussion programme *Behind the Headlines*. Deborah was concerned that he might find it a strain and quietly consulted Fiona and Amanda. Unbeknown to him, they met, discussed him at length, spoke to his doctors, and gave the go-ahead.

The BBC sent a car to bring him to the Television Centre at Shepherds Bush. A production assistant led him along the labyrinthine corridors to the green room where the programme's other participants were already gathered. He knew two of them.

There was Rothwell, a Professor of Politics from the LSE, whose mind, reflected by his way of dressing, had developed little since the revolutionary sixties; Alan Parkin, a journalist from the *Observer*, was of the same bleeding hearts vintage; and then there was a Tessa Downes MP, who was famous for being famous and particularly known for her rent-a-quote opinions on everything, which she was always ready to offer in a boundless sea of sentences. The subject for the evening's discussion was whether good communicating skills mattered to leaders. Looking at his fellows, Ivor wondered whether he had made a mistake. On the other hand it might allow him to shine.

He was wheeled off to make-up where a bright girl, who he felt would have done better on the programme than any of them, set about blending his face, covering up blemishes he hardly realized were there. A tiny mole on his left cheek was powdered and painted into oblivion, his five o'clock shadow became as pink as the rest of his face, his hair combed and sprayed to perfection.

The programme began well: the tough woman presenter kept the discussion disciplined; the MP, in particular, had her inanities strictly rationed. The discussion revolved around Professor Rothwell and Ivor, the former arguing that substance in a political leader was what mattered and that how things were said had little or no importance. This allowed Ivor to pursue a favourite topic: of course content mattered, but too many populist leaders had the power of speech but failed to communicate, to get their points across. Too many were wet-finger leaders, following rather than leading, watching the way the wind was blowing before deciding on a course of action.

This gave Professor Rothwell the opening he was obviously waiting for. 'Dr Ivor has had a lot of experience in dealing with weak, opportunistic leaders. No names, no accusations, if you know what I mean.'

The presenter picked up this reference to Ivor's past connection with the Prime Minister. 'Did the PM,' she asked, 'spend a lot of time on his image? Or was he all nuts and bolts politics?'

Ivor generalized his answer away from his former client: 'Leaders become icons, prisoners of their reputations. Close to, they are ordinary men and women doing a job to the best of their ability. They're frequently chosen not for their ability to lead . . .' he looked directly at the camera lens, 'but for their ability to read their parts well. They have to be actors. Look at President Reagan. If they can fake their sincerity, they can fake anything.' The others round the table laughed politely. 'Too many political leaders are programmed to appear great by their image makers. A warm smile, a firm handshake; these are as important to leadership as any policy. Illusion and reality; the triumph of packaging over substance.'

'Much depends on the team behind a leader, don't you think?' suggested the professor.

'Sure. Even the great need back-up. Good handlers.'

'You look on such people as handlers?' The professor kept after him.

'In a way, yes,' said Ivor carefully. 'Handlers of a leader's time, the access to him, the advice he receives, the briefing material he's given to read. They monitor his press, make sure he realizes that merely generating press cuttings is not a mark of greatness.'

'Censoring?' asked the journalist.

'Weeding out the unnecessary.'

'Hidden puppet masters?' the woman MP butted in.

Ivor reacted quickly. 'Few leaders are anyone's puppets. They don't last long if they are.'

'Some people argue that these spin doctors, as Americans call them, do all the scripting and directing. They have one interest: keeping their leader in power. Keeping others — rivals — out.' Professor Rothwell gave his best academic pundit look for the benefit of the cameras.

'In this country there are too many checks and balances to allow that to happen for long,' Ivor responded. 'There are always competing power groups out there waiting to challenge any adviser who gets into . . .'

The show was going out live. Perhaps the professor had been

put up to it because audience ratings were flagging. Suddenly he personalized it. The programme presenter made no attempt to stop him. 'Was that why they got rid of you, Dr Ivor? We're told Lord Shand and other "Party Grandees" slipped the knife in.'

Everyone stared at Ivor, waiting for him to react. He was aware of producers and floor managers moving rapidly about behind the television arc lights. Would he explode? Would he explain? It could be great television. But Ivor was ready.

'I thought you might lead the conversation down that route, Professor Rothwell,' he smiled. 'I always tell trainee interviewees to beware the barbed wire that their interrogators try to ring around them. I also tell them that in question and answer sessions never worry about the questions. It's the answers that count.'

'We're waiting,' responded the professor dryly.

Ivor knew that producer and audience were waiting for indiscretions that would produce headlines. Discretion, by contrast, would not add to the press cuttings, but would signal to those whom he respected that nothing had changed. Loyalty remained his style.

'Wait on, Professor. I'm sure the viewers out there will agree with me that when you've held a position of trust, you stick with it. You don't reveal confidences. Out of bounds, that question, Professor. But . . . I would say that he who controls the door to authority controls that authority. Now . . .' Ivor turned slightly in his chair and smiled mischievously at the presenter. 'Now . . . I've been talking too much. I do apologize.'

What could the presenter do but move the discussion on to other things?

Lord Shand caught the end of the TV programme as he came back from the House of Lords. He had missed much of it but got the gist and saw how much in control of himself, and of others, Mark Ivor still was. The man looked healthier than he had been when last seen. Shand was not someone who ever rested in the assumption that battles won meant the end of the war. In the army he had learned that an enemy is an enemy until he's dead.

21

When he had got back to his office, Deborah handed Ivor a *Private & Confidential* fax from Steven Rotenbein. They had employed one of the best French agencies, working discreetly, making no direct contacts. The agency was, Rotenbein assured him, 'good at the human side of things'. The human side of things ... Attached to the fax was a translation of the Agency Report.

> *Subject in her late forties, lives, as previously reported, with her husband, a Headmaster, in a converted farmhouse on the outskirts of a small village which lies some fifteen kilometres south of St Malo. She has four children, two boys and two girls, all in their middle to late teens. The family live comfortably: they are popular in the community.*
>
> *Subject is much involved in local social and charitable work and has written and published a small history of the area. The family are conventional in behaviour, and are regular church-goers. It is this Agency's view that any contact or revelation about the existence of an earlier child of the subject, born out of wedlock, many years before her now apparently happy and faithful marriage, would not be beneficial to any of the parties concerned. If, however, the presumed offspring and her father wish to pursue the matter further, it is strongly advised that they discuss the matter with the Agency first.*

When he had finished reading, Ivor closed the door of his study and rang Amanda.

'Is this a good moment?'

'As any.'

'I've had the report from France.'

'Read it to me.'

When he had done so she said: 'You don't need to ask, I've gone this far . . . we've gone this far. I want to go over. And soon.'

'I've a meeting in Paris next week. It's a long way round, but I could meet you in St Malo somehow.'

'I'll take my car. Take the ferry. Meet you there.'

'Let's talk tonight.'

'I have a meeting.'

'I'll pick you up. Where will you be?'

Ivor and his daughter had let each other into much about their individual interests and involvements. But, so far, they had skirted around the quicksand of party political alliances because they wanted common interests to bond them, and realized that politics might introduce friction. She recognized that in his past work for the government and Prime Minister he was more interested in the techniques of power than power itself. She accepted he was probably far from committed to the policies of the party itself. He, in his turn, recognized youthful liberal instincts, and knew that most of her friends were even further to the left. She had told him that she had briefly been a member of the Greens, but that its utopian lack of organization had driven her to resign. Now she went to occasional meetings when attracted by a particular cause. She took her issues one by one, as the radicalism of youth began to wear thin.

Her current cause was holding a rally at the Central Hall, Westminster. He was early, proceedings were still in progress, and he slipped in quietly at the back to listen. He wished he'd brought a raincoat to hide the conspicuousness of his business suit amid the egalitarian throng. He slouched low in his chair, watched, and was taken back to his own youth.

A woman with a strident voice on the platform was proclaiming some great world injustice. She spoke in all-embracing clichés, offering little from which to dissent. Another accent, another clothes shop, another audience, and what she was advocating about humanity and justice and peace would have been in perfect harmony at any Conservative gathering. Just as Tory meetings had their manners and their mores, so did this one. The true blue uniforms, the hats, the twinsets, the regimental ties, the creases in the trousers, the well-polished shoes, gave place to a different but distinct uniformity of its own. Professionally discontented women in shapeless upper garments and long trailing skirts of dark crushed material; shapeless Doc Martens; hair ungroomed; round-lensed, horn-rimmed spectacles chosen as if to reflect indignation as they caught the hall lights. And the men, the anoraks, the beards, the jeans, the trainers, the rucksacks. Both sexes, faces pale from following correct eating patterns, digesting worthy, low-cholesterol, nutritional meals. This crowd had the advantage of youth, though there was a strong leavening of sixties throw-back culture, an ageing generation of protest and dissent.

The Germaine Greerist call of the next speaker further fuelled the mood. The words, in Ivor's ears, were time-warp words, of envy and of dated advocacies of past class wars. The subject of the rally was conservation and anti-pollution, all worthy enough. But the voices were ones that echoed the revolutionary slogans of his youth: 'unthinking capitalism', 'international conglomerates', and 'privilege, ravaging our national heritage'. He waited for them to stand and sing 'The Red Flag' or 'The Internationale' but it never came. They did not even join in 'We Shall Overcome'.

Amanda, dressed in similar uniform, turned intuitively and spotted him. She got up and walked back quickly to sit beside him. 'Sorry. It's running on. We can go if you like,' she whispered.

'No hurry. You don't mind being seen with me dressed like this?'

'They might think you are from MI5.'

'No. I know all about that. MI5 are clever. They have the

233

biggest beards, the most torn jeans, the shabbiest sandals.' He smiled and she giggled.

'Are you making fun?'

'Absolutely not. So far I've not heard a single thing I've disagreed with.'

'Hush,' said a woman in the row in front, turning to stare.

Father and daughter stood up then and quietly left the hall.

'What did you really think?' she asked, once they were outside.

'I have nothing against the cause. It's the speakers I can't stand. Don't get me wrong. All political meetings — right, left or centre — they're all the same: earnest, committed, self-opinionated, strident . . .'

'They believe —'

'Of course they believe.'

'That woman spoke well.'

'She spoke loudly. She spoke fluently. What did she actually say?'

'If you listened —'

'Of course I listened. I always listen. You should know that by now. But I don't *remember* unless anything interesting is said.'

'Cynic.'

'With much to be cynical about.'

'You haven't changed.'

'I hope not.'

'Your morality, it's all . . . expediency. It makes me so . . . I wish you'd stop. Change . . . go for something less competitive . . . Please . . .'

As her irritation grew, Amanda saw she had begun to annoy him too. She had hoped his illness would have mellowed him, but a flush of colour had appeared on his upper cheeks, visible, even by the yellow of the street lights, as they made their way towards his parked car. She backed off.

'Sorry,' she began. 'What I meant was —'

'What you meant was what you said, Amanda.' He spoke slowly and precisely. 'I came to pick you up at your meeting and you immediately start expecting me to find fault. I'm not interested in spiky moral indignation. I'm not kick-starting that sort of debate with you. I've had a lifetime of watching people manicuring their injured liberal principles in front of audiences. I'm not going to be moved by them. Don't misjudge my motives on that.'

She would not withdraw. His critics were right: he was so damned convinced by himself. He was so bloody stubborn, so impregnable in his beliefs. For a moment her irritation welled up into real anger. But it evaporated as quickly as it began, as, on an impulse, he took her arm, pulled her towards him and kissed her lightly on the cheek.

'Growing pains,' he said softly.

'Yes,' she nodded as they both got into the car. 'We'll have to learn.'

The next day he went to listen to a hearing in Committee Room 10, at the House of Commons. It was on proposed new monopolies legislation and he wanted to get up to date again on current political thinking. A mass of party point-scoring had to be got through, and it dragged on until nearly eight o'clock in the evening. Fortunately he had no dinner engagement and Fiona was off being domestic with her children. He had intended to go straight home and relax, but on his way out he was hijacked by his old pupil, Alan Francis MP, the PM's Parliamentary Private Secretary, who steered him to the Strangers' Bar for a drink. Francis was already heavily lubricated, but he had had many years of training and so remained coherent if somewhat long-winded in what he had to say.

'Thing is, Mark. Don't trust most of my colleagues these days. Want a bit of advice. Strategy. That sort of thing.'

'If I can.'

'Thing is. Well, you know . . . well, the PM . . . I'm being kept right out these days. Hardly see him any more. Never asks my advice. Don't mind my talking off the record, do you? Some of us, well, think Rupert Shand has far too much of a hold. Him and that fascist Gibson.'

'I heard.'

'Thing is: bad thing. Bad for the country, that sort of thing. Too much a belief in his own divine leadership qualities, Rupert Shand. Out of the trenches, over the top and at 'em. Not what we want at the moment. My Lord Shand wouldn't know what the needs of the country were if they came and slapped him in the face.'

'I know what you mean.'

'Besides . . .' Francis lowered his voice and glowered round the bar. 'Besides. Can't stand the bastard. Dealing with him ought to carry a government health warning. Count your fingers after you've shaken hands with him. That sort of thing.'

'I know what you mean,' Ivor repeated. He was cautious, but was listening intently.

'Thing is . . . thought you might know how to scupper that particular exercise.'

'I'm not sure . . .'

'Which means you are sure.'

'How many of you feel this way?'

'A lot. 1922 Committee. A lot.'

'Why not confront the PM or the Chief Whip or the Party Chairman? With your tiny majority, he'll cave in in a flash.'

'You know the answer. If we did that, it would bring things out into the open. Chaps would start taking sides. The Opposition and the press would have a field day. He'd call our bluff and we'd certainly lose the election. The PM may be weak but if he is serious, it could make him dig his toes in, particularly if Shand, who's never one to hide himself under a bushel, is standing on them. Could you . . . think of something?'

'I already am,' said Ivor carefully.

'I knew I could rely on you, Mark. More than a heart attack to bring down the modern Machiavelli . . . Eh?'

Alan Francis's request might not have taken on the same urgency had it not been for a separate event that took place two days later. As people grow older and older, they gradually outlive all but the most robust of friends and colleagues, thus ensuring that only descendants turn up to see them cremated or interred. Others find that if friends and colleagues fall by the wayside or die, they do not bother to replace them. It is all too much trouble. But the great and good are different. They are publicly remembered. They have memorial services, the social gatherings of those who would salute them; parties held for people no longer there to attend them. It was thus, shortly after his return, that Ivor attended one such great occasion in Westminster Abbey. The Queen and other members of the Royal Family were represented by the Lord Chamberlain and by their Equerries; the Abbey was packed with others of the great and the good from present and past generations. Former Prime Ministers, elder statesmen, mere politicians, many of whom had themselves long been considered dead by the younger members of the congregation, clustered in black ties and morning coats like so many decrepit penguins. The Archbishop of Canterbury took the service, a famous peer gave the rose-tinted address, a choir sang, the organ played, and the reading from Corinthians moved many to tears, not out of any grief at the passing, but because the words were so cathartic.

Ivor sat towards the rear, between a retired bishop and a former Ambassador to Paris.

'Keeping better?' He was greeted by the latter.

'Much, thanks.' He wondered again at how so many followed the ill-health as well as the ill-fortune of others.

As the service ended he stood to leave and join the crush by the Great West Door. But first the family and the most important mourners, led by a procession of crucifix-bearing clergy in full regalia, had to be allowed to depart. As he stood by the end of the pew, he saw many familiar faces pass him by. Some recognized and greeted him; some recognized and looked the other way, doubtful in their charity if he was still acceptable to be known. Then came the Prime Minister. He was flanked by the Bishop of London and shadowed by an ever-alert bodyguard. Behind the PM, an arm's reach away, processed the Lord Shand. The fixed followed by the fixer. Ivor watched the peer as he looked to right and to left, registering everyone and everything, never letting the PM get too far ahead. For a lucid moment Ivor thought that if he had ever been the PM's Machiavelli, Shand surely was Rasputin. But Rasputin never had that patrician presence, or, to change the historical reference, those eyes of a Caligula.

The Prime Minister spotted Ivor at the same moment as Lord Shand. Alert and knowing members of the congregation tried to anticipate what was coming. Would the PM or would he not? Would Shand reach out and pull his little protégé out of harm's way?

Malleable though he was, the PM was courageous in his own small way. He stopped his processing, shook Ivor's hand warmly and said loudly: 'Good to see you. We've been worried about you, very worried.' He turned to embrace Lord Shand in his remark with the Bishop of London as his witness. 'Haven't we been worried, Rupert?'

'Of course,' said Lord Shand, with the reluctant warmth of an icicle.

'I'll be in touch, Mark. Good to see you. You're looking well.' The Prime Minister moved on. Lord Shand delayed for a brief moment. There was just sufficient time for him to hiss 'Keep well away,' before he too walked towards the Great West Door.

Since his heart attack, Ivor had tried to keep his promise to himself and those close to him to adopt a more relaxed, more healthy, less competitive lifestyle. In part he had been successful, but now, though he had never been a vindictive man, with three little words, uttered with such vitriol, Lord Shand had reignited all his dormant drive and determination.

* * *

Top Secret & Personal

TO: *Chief, C13*

FROM: *The Secretary to the Cabinet*

Thank you for the full update (ZN3114/94). Regret cannot reopen discussion with the PM on the subject of Lord Shand. His mind is closed. He argues that it is an entirely party political matter of no concern to civil servants. On the last occasion he was most hostile and I have to safeguard my own position. You could, however, without prejudice, ensure that Dr Mark Ivor, if he has recovered sufficiently, is fully informed, to allow him to make the running. This must, given past experience, be handled with the greatest discretion.

Message ends.

Sir Caspar was not waving the white flag of surrender by sending such a message. He was merely clearing the decks. He still had shots to fire.

22

'I watched a television quiz show the other night — about all my brain is up to these days. The girls: very pretty. Some young sylph was asked who I was. What I'd done. They didn't know but one of them said she thought I'd died around 1980. The quizmaster called me a Statesman. Nearly as bad. A former politician in his dotage.' That Grand Old Man, Lord Blakestone, who everyone said had modelled himself on the ancient Harold Macmillan, laughed, tears of mirth sparkling in deep-set, wicked eyes. Ivor laughed with him and thought, momentarily, that politicians, or statesmen, didn't come this way any more. Maybe some had it in them but could not flaunt it freely until they had shuffled off from centre stage into the eventide homes of public life.

Lord Blakestone really was a Grand Old Man, as the political gossip columnists had tagged him. Ivor had seen him at the memorial service, which was what had prompted him into his present course of action, but he had never met him before, since they had, respectively, been too junior and too senior in his host's heyday. Eighty-seven, but as sparkling as someone thirty years younger. Still the malicious tease, the caustic reputation that his opponents had dreaded, of being attacked by his barbs of political invective or assassinated by his famous mockery. Ridicule from his mouth was something few politicians could stand against for long. More deadly than argument, to sneer as he had done, to make people laugh or snigger every time a particular rival was mentioned, was, for his victims, the political end. Lord Blakestone had been an expert. In retirement, he revelled in it still.

He came out to greet Ivor wearing an ancient, darned pullover, carpet slippers on his feet. He stood, beaming, at the door of the great house, a splendid place, crammed with everything from the rarest antiques to kitsch mementoes of his public past. In the panelled drawing room, a place of musty, faded taste, silver framed photographs of kings, queens and presidents were arranged in tarnished glory all over a dust-covered grand piano. A huge fire burned in the grate, in front of which an overweight Labrador slumbered, untroubled by the visitor's arrival.

Lord Blakestone, unasked, poured them both huge tumblerfuls of Scotch, though it was still mid-morning. Then they settled into leather club chairs that spewed their stuffing and broken springs on each side of the hearth. As the day progressed, Ivor wished he had brought a tape machine to record his encounter with this most famous man.

'Key to public life, my boy . . .' – the 'my boy' came without pretension, as if it was the most contemporary expression – 'key is to know who hates whom. Once you know that you know about politics. Friends are few. Loyalty, non-existent. Gratitude dies stillborn. People proclaim the party but all they really care about is *me* . . . *me*. That's rule number one. Know what number two is?' Blakestone took a large swig from his glass and Ivor marvelled that, if his host constantly indulged in such a way, then it was a myth that excess alcohol damages the system. He realized that a reply was not required as the old man continued: 'Rumour . . . that's it: rumour. More important than any newspaper, any television report. Rumour vanquishes fact, destroys credibility, is the assassin of reputation. I hear stories about government ministers at the moment, by the way. True, are they? People still come and tell me, you know. Reminds me of the old days, the Vassals, the Profumos, the Lambtons. Sex, sex and sex. Delicious stuff. Covered up, maybe. But a sex scandal never goes away. An unburied corpse. Stinks to high heaven.' Lord Blakestone paused for breath. 'People still playing that little man at Number Ten. That bastard Shand? No, not a bastard. A shit.

That's him. Always was. And his father before him. Any scandal about him?'

'I'm not . . .' Ivor hesitated.

'It'll come. It'll come. Unless . . . One has to grasp rumour and throttle it through libel actions galore. Nasty. Untidy. Very public. Very dangerous. Particularly if a story's true.' He laughed excitedly. 'Know what? My experience: most rumours to do with sex and politics are true. Driving force of Parliament, along with ambition. Neither can be removed from the bloodstream except by embalming fluid. Who was it said that? Me, probably.' The Grand Old Man peered maliciously across at Ivor. 'Now, my boy, you wanted . . . ?'

'Thank you for seeing me.'

'Have another drink first. No? Don't mind if I do, d'you?'

'I want your advice.'

'Always available, my boy. Comes free. What can this old fellow do? You were the PM's . . . that little arse's gofer, weren't you? Go for this, go for that?'

'Sort of. I fixed a bit.'

'Then you lost out. Thrown out. Modern Machiavelli, eh? Spin doctor – hate the term. That was you, wasn't it?' He paused, eyes suddenly steely and suspicious. 'What can I do?'

'I thought you might use your influence. I know you don't come up to London much these days, but I'd welcome your support.'

'You'd welcome. Why the hell?'

'Some things need saying . . .'

'Write my lines for me as well, no doubt?'

A touch of bitchiness was creeping into his voice, fuelled by the generous intake of whisky. 'What's your agenda?' He paused again and stared hard at Ivor. 'What're you up to, my boy? Heard of you. Read about you. What agenda?'

'The PM's flailing . . .'

'Failing . . . sure he is.' The old man deliberately misheard.

'It's worse than that. He's in the wrong hands. A hostage . . . Almost . . .'

'Is this you talking, Dr Ivor, or is it . . . ?'

'I've been talking to some backbenchers, then . . . the Secretary to the Cabinet suggested . . .'

'Clever of him. You're a sharp man, Dr Ivor, and a shrewd man. And a flatterer. What could I really do? I am eighty-seven.'

'You would be listened to. Lots of TV and newspaper coverage. You are one of Britain's last great orators.'

'Sound convincing, you mean?'

'I envisage —'

'Thought so. You're doing the envisaging?'

'I can assure you —'

'Whatever.' Lord Blakestone waved his hand dismissively. 'Dr Ivor, you want to cater to my vanity. You think I might want recognition once again. Before I pass away?'

'You were indispensable. You carry a lot of weight. Still.'

'De Gaulle said it: "*The graveyards are full of indispensable men.*" What would you want me to say?'

'Bring up the honours of the past; the spectre of the hard right run riot . . .'

'Out of the mouth of the grave comes the voice of the future? Come off it, Dr Ivor. What do you really want?'

'I want you to make a speech in the House of Lords. Just one . . .'

'Ah, so now we have it . . .'

On his way back up to London, Ivor sat back in the driving seat and relished his day. He had been forced to stay on for a schoolboy lunch of mince and potatoes followed by steamed pudding and custard. The accompanying claret had been excellent, if too heavy and soporific for a lunch. Lord Blakestone had captivated him with lively anecdotes of politics long since gone. He brought the past to a life it probably never quite had, lightening it with splendid fantasies such as how he would have loved to have juxtaposed General de Gaulle and Mrs Thatcher in time. He would have given anything to see how each, with their own peculiar brand of nationalism, would have coped with the other and the European dream. This led him to discuss the shelf life of politicians, larding his reminiscences with whimsical vignettes of many of his contemporaries. He quoted Enoch Powell, that all political life ends in failure. Then he qualified it: some kept their influence after they relinquished their place at the Cabinet table; others disappeared without trace the moment they handed over their seals of office.

'Shelf life, my boy, is the key to the history books – whether you are to be an ephemeral footnote or whether, just *par chance*, there is a touch of greatness around.'

'Which is why I'm here.'

'Right, to the purpose of your visit.' He pushed plates, glasses and a wine carafe away from in front of him to clear a space among the debris of lunch. Then, reaching over to a side table, he produced a pad of paper and a pencil. 'Why don't you tell me what you want me to say in this speech. I'm not promising, you know. I'll sleep on it. You've got to send a car for me. I might just relish a trip back into the limelight, if only to prove to that charming girl in that TV quiz programme that I've not yet gone to meet my Maker.' Lord Blakestone smiled across at Ivor. Then he winked.

*

'I'll be very careful.'

'I promise you. I talked to two specialists. I'm right as rain. It won't do me any harm. Quite the reverse.' After a long abstinence, Ivor was again being impelled by his loins.

'I'll be careful,' repeated Fiona.

'Boring.'

'Is that a challenge?'

'Love-play me.'

He lay naked across the bed. Fiona draped herself gently over him, brought her head down and kissed him deeply. Coming up for breath, she whispered, 'I'm about to give new meaning to the word fondle.'

'Happy to be experimented on. Anything . . .'

'Anything?'

'Anything.'

A little later she whispered again, 'You know, it's still new to me, but I could drown myself in my obsession with you.' She was, she felt, even more deeply in love with him than she had been, if that was conceivable; living without him would be impossible, and the mess of a divorce was now inevitable.

'We're getting good at gentle extensions of sex,' he responded, turning over and reaching down to the floor to pick up something which had been used and abandoned only a little while before. He held it up before her.

'Look,' he said. 'Say please.'

'Please . . .'

'Again.' He could not look at her without fantasy.

'Please.'

'Maybe it's the German in you.'

'German, British . . . it's just me. Styles of sex don't have national boundaries.'

'From your researches . . . your years of experience,' he teased, but then he was taking up the leather and bringing it up slowly to caress her body. She let out a sensuous little gasp of pleasure. He found her gentle pleading acutely erotic. He was demanding and hard, yet catering to what she wanted by catering to himself. It built up the bond between them, more and more intense, more and more varied, more and more passionate. Then came the flame, the eruption, the volcano and shuddering aftermath.

Later she said, 'Your Lord Shand rang me a week ago. God knows how he got my number. I met him once; I think I told you. Said he wanted to meet me again. Said he had heard about you and me . . . God knows how he found out.'

'Shand? Really? He has his eyes everywhere.'

'I made some excuse. Then he started. Wanted me to make sure you retired. Said if you didn't, it would kill you.'

'And . . . ?'

'I said you had all the professional help you needed. If he had any message he could speak to you direct. Then he said that it would be tragic for you, and me, if the press were to get hold of the news of our affair . . .'

'Even Shand wouldn't go that far. He really has it in for me.'

'I wouldn't be too sure. He sounded very tense.'

'Then?'

'Then I put the phone down on him. It's strange, politics is rather like sex: the same lusts, the same desires, ambitions and betrayals. Didn't you tell me that?'

'Betrayals? D'you still feel you're betraying?'

'Husband? No, not at all. There isn't even debris left in my marriage. Nothing so dramatic. Long familiarity, long boredom, total indifference. And the children . . . Well, they know already. They're old enough; they won't harm. When we do split, I don't think we'll feel much. Except relief. All of us.'

'When you split?'

'When we split. Like soon.'

'Then?'

'Tell me. Tell me. Tell me we'll be together.'

Like a mirror of Harold Macmillan, who, at ninety, stood in the House of Lords for the last time to condemn Mrs Thatcher for the 'selling of the family silver', so the Grand Old Man, Lord Blakestone, stood to address a hushed house. Every seat was taken, the galleries were full — MPs from the other place, journalists, and television carried it live. No one knew what he was going to say, but Ivor had done his homework and everyone was on tenterhooks.

He did not disappoint. Among the contemporary political midgets he appeared a giant. The voice had lost a little of its strength, there were a few quavers, but the resonance, the cadences and, above all, the wit were still there.

Extract from front page story in *The Times*, dated 23rd of March. By our Political Staff.

The atmosphere was electric. There was no noise as his audience strained to catch even his softest words. He spoke of the dangers to the nation, not of drift, not of indecisiveness, but, in an obvious reference to the Prime Minister himself, of a weak leadership controlled by the hands of darkness. Only someone of his vintage could have used such emotive language. And it worked. He named no names but it was clear to all those listening that he was referring, when he spoke of 'baleful influences', to the Prime Minister's new kitchen cabinet and personal advisers such as Lord Shand, whom he felt were 'leading the leadership', and by appealing to 'the most vicious narrow nationalism', moving us in the direction that had led the countries of Europe towards the catastrophe of the Second World War.

'These,' said Lord Shand dismissively, 'were the ramblings of an old mind, a man in his dotage, seeking past glories . . .'

'He's got amazing coverage.' The Prime Minister's voice came close to a whimper.

'A two-day event. Put it out of your mind. The press will soon forget – when the men in white coats take him back to his hospice . . .'

Mark Ivor caught the flight to Paris with moments to spare and he squeezed himself, panting, into the last remaining seat. With his exercise programme he was fitter than he had been for years, but there was still a long way to go. He fastened his seatbelt and prepared for immediate departure.

Ahead of him in the half empty plane he was aware of a man getting up and moving over to sit beside him.

'After all that's happened, I hope you don't mind,' said a voice. Ivor half turned in his seat but did not immediately recognize the man from his profile. 'I can move back to my own seat if you like, but it's only an hour's flight. How are you keeping, Dr Ivor?'

'Thanks, much better. I'm afraid I've forgotten . . .' He looked again. The face was familiar but not the name.

'Fred Cree. You remember me?'

'I do indeed.' Ivor sometimes forgave his enemies, but never forgot their names. He turned away.

Cree did not let up. 'You bear a grudge?' he asked aggressively.

'I seldom bear grudges,' responded Ivor, without attempting to look again at the man beside him. 'But . . .' he went on, 'but with you, maybe I'll make an exception.' He shut his eyes. He began to count: one to ten, very slowly, each number broken by a long deep breath. He relaxed, shutting out the plane, and Cree.

Brittany was, to Ivor, the best of France. Paris was great for a weekend and the south was tolerable with friends. But Brittany he had always loved: the varied coastline, the stone and slate villages in their gentle coatings of moss and lichen.

He met Amanda at St Malo, straight off the ferry from Portsmouth. They had arranged to go directly to the Agency offices which were situated in a side street, under the shadow of the town's ramparts. The middle-aged French lady dealing with their case looked severe, hair pulled into a tight bun. She listened in silence as they gave further background in a clumsy mixture of French and English. She showed no signs of astonishment: all life's delinquencies had been paraded before her in the past, but gradually she displayed some sympathy, though retaining a certain professional aloofness. When she came to question them, she revealed almost perfect English.

'Why do you want to meet?'

'She exists. She is part of me,' Amanda began.

'It will come as a great shock to her, her husband, her children. Think of her children.'

'Think of me. I've lived a lie.'

'I understand, Mademoiselle. I am merely making sure you do. It could, and I have had experience of this, lead to the break-up of a happy home. It could offer you little satisfaction in the end.'

'Perhaps I could get in touch without her family knowing?'

'Difficult. If she is an honourable woman, it may be emotionally impossible for her to keep such a secret.' The case worker spoke slowly and sensibly.

'She knows I exist.'

'She knows deep down. But if she is like others I have dealt with, she has it well buried, if not forgotten. Certainly there was guilt. It was a long time ago. Twenty, nearly thirty years. You cannot live with guilt that long and stay sane.'

'Perhaps she tried to find me?' Amanda was pleading. 'British adoption laws are strict; even more difficult for a foreigner to negotiate. They would not tell her where I was.'

'Speculation. I do not know. You do not know. Only Annette Valais knows.'

'You put Amanda . . . us both . . . in a very difficult position,' said Ivor.

'That position started long ago. We are looking, how do you say, for solutions. We know the problem.'

'So what should I do, Madame?' asked Amanda.

'I do not know you well enough to judge. You have found your father. You may ask yourselves if that happiness is not enough. I do not mean to sound melodramatic, but happiness, tempered by the creation of misery, could wipe out happiness.'

'I know,' said Amanda. 'I just don't think . . .' She started to break and Ivor put his arm round her and held her. She laid her head momentarily against his chest.

'See. You have happiness,' said the case worker, a kinder tone mellowing her voice. 'Think hard, may I suggest. Meanwhile I have these photographs of Annette Valais and her family, from the local paper: when her husband was appointed headmaster, and here, when her *Petite Histoire de Cette Région* was published.' She handed her two visitors some newspaper cuttings. They were far from clear but one showed a bearded, bespectacled man standing beside a woman. She was quite short, almost dumpy, with looks that were striking, if eroded by the years. There was another picture of her standing with someone with a *tricolore* band across his chest – perhaps the local mayor. A third, dated several years ago, showed her smiling at the camera, surrounded by a number of small children.

In the dim office light Amanda strained to look at the photographs. She was desperate to see something that would tell her, as on her first meeting with her father, what she was looking for, some feature, some resonance, some recognition. She was disappointed but far from beaten. 'I can't see . . .' she faltered. 'They are . . . press photographs. It is difficult.'

Ivor took them from his daughter's hand and he too studied them under the light. Was his memory playing tricks? All memories are selective about what is retained. Was he deceiving himself now? He looked hard and long, then he handed the cuttings back to the case worker.

'Thank you, Madame, but even after all these years, I am sure this is not Annette Valais.'

The case worker was confused, then indignant, then confused again. The neat order of her case was under threat. The British papers must be at fault. She began to suggest that Ivor's memory, after all it was nearly three decades, was warped by the distance of time. The *Directeur* of the Agency was summoned, and one of the other case workers. Papers and files were scrutinized. Ivor and Amanda were left alone while a whispered case conference was held in an adjoining room. The case worker returned and said that if they came back the following morning, additional checks would be made.

It was certainly not religious feeling that led them into the little church. They had gone for a walk after a dinner in the hotel where they were staying, and had come across it by accident, through an archway in a narrow cobbled side street. It started to rain and as he had no coat, they went in to seek shelter. The lights were all on inside; a service had just concluded. Groups of robed nuns stood talking quietly together. It was warm and welcoming, hundreds of candles guttering in front of the many shrines.

They walked up the centre aisle and stood together before the rich altar, staring up at a great ornate crucifix that hung above it.

'Do you want to go ahead, Amanda?' he asked eventually.

'Are you saying stop?'

'Of course not. It's just . . .'

'I need your help just now, not your doubts. Please.' She turned and looked imploringly at him. Her face looked drawn in the flickering light. 'It was you, for Christ's sake, that made all this, made me . . .'

People turned to stare at the alien sound of the raised, English voice.

There was a long pause, then suddenly she said, 'I know so little about you still. Are you religious?'

'I understand the feelings that religion can give rise to. Plato said: "It was a wise man who invented God".'

'I don't follow.'

'Just . . . It's a good invention at times of stress.'

'Like now?'

'Like now. It would be convenient to believe.'

She turned to face him. 'There is something I should have told you.'

'Go on.'

'Lord Shand, Rupert . . . I had dinner with him a few weeks back. I met him a couple of times later. He tried to –'

'I don't want to know.' Ivor's voice was suddenly cold.

'I was flattered when he first asked me. I once told you . . . he has that viciously sensual look. I found –'

'I really would prefer . . .' He looked away and Amanda could not see the expression on his face, but she sensed his discomfort.

'Wait. Later, when I got to know him better, I realized it wasn't my body he was after. He tried to get me to persuade you to pack it all in after your illness. He sees you as the major threat to his position. When I reacted with hostility, he started to threaten. He said he'd destroy you before you destroyed yourself. I felt that this time it was a more physical warning: destroy meant destroy.'

'You too? He tried to get to Fiona as well. Was that really why he asked you?'

'I think . . . the last time I saw him he started to make a pass, but it was too late. I left him at the dinner table. At one time, I remember, you too felt there was no harm in him. When you were so ill there was sense in what he was saying.'

'Was there?'

'He started to tell me something else.'

'About me?'

'Yes.'

'Before you ask then . . . Yes, it's true. Some of it.'

She was silent for a moment, then: 'It can't be. How do you know what I was going to say?'

'There's only one story Rupert Shand could get me on: the story of that junior minister – Soper and the girl.'

'You . . . set up the girl. She was arrested . . . by the Thai police.'

'She should be on her way home any day now.'

'Fourteen months later. I cannot believe –'

'You don't know the circumstances.'

'No circumstances could possibly justify that.'

'Perhaps you're right. With hindsight, yes, it was wrong of me, very wrong. But remember: she was trying to blackmail Soper, to destroy him. A quarter of a million pounds, or she'd sell her story to the *Mirror*.'

'One wrong doesn't even begin . . .' Amanda paused, lost for words. Had she so totally misjudged this man she asked herself.

'The alternative scenario –'

'Scenario – you sound as if you're talking about a bloody TV series,' she hissed.

'. . . was that the government were going to call in the Attorney General. She'd have got ten years at least.'

'And Soper would have been thrown out.'

'Perhaps, perhaps not. The Great British Public don't like blackmailers. And she was on drugs, hard drugs.'

'So you suggested . . .'

'I suggested nothing.'

'You got someone to suggest to her, some crappy journalist, that the police were on to her, that she could still blackmail, still sell her story from the safety, say, of Bangkok.'

'That's how greed works.'

'Damn,' whispered Amanda. 'You were too good to be true.'

Ivor turned and looked hard at her. 'I played a part. I admit it. Shand himself did the dirty bit but I'm not proud of my contribution. Yes . . . You make me ashamed. It was wrong. Even evil. At the time, at any crucial time of crisis, I have always believed that ends justify means. Recently, well . . . never again, that I promise you.'

It was only then that he told her of an enforced hill walk nearly four decades earlier, a hill walk with his father, his damned, accursed, vile father with his constant, evil smelling, sexual demands. The steep climb up a mountain ridge where he trailed behind, his father yelling at him to keep up, mocking him, chiding him, then when they reached the top, reaching obscenely towards his groin . . .

Ivor stopped for a moment, not looking at his daughter. Tears ran freely down his face. 'Ahead of me . . . He was ahead of me . . . when his foot slipped on the scree. He caught briefly on a thin ledge of rock and reached his hand up screaming at me to pull him to safety. I turned away. I waited, and then he was gone. And I was glad.'

After a while she whispered, 'I'm glad you told me. Is there more?' She shared his tears as she spoke.

'Not like that.'

'I'm glad you came.' She paused. 'Here with me, I mean. I'm not sure I could have done it on my own.'

'It may be just as painful.' He put her arm round his daughter as they continued to stand in front of the altar.

'You quote Plato. I quote Aristotle. He argued that women are fonder of their children than men because they are certain they are theirs.' He shook his head gently as Amanda continued. 'But in this case he was wrong, wasn't he? D'you know something? I'm here, I dragged you here because . . . I'm curious, I want to know. But if you ask me if I "care", well, I'm not sure that I do. Why should I? I've been deracinated. My life's been a drama these last short weeks and months, and it's getting very mixed reviews. I've not lacked reasons for tears, but, you know, I've hardly cried. I've been happy.' She stared hard at him. 'Yes . . . you.' He took her hand as if she were a child and they left the church together.

After a night spent in their largely deserted seafront hotel, father and daughter presented themselves once again at the Agency. The *Directeur*, with the case worker flanking him, was conciliatory, almost apologetic. Without revealing reasons, they had made enquiries with the police, at the *Mairie*, and with the local social services department. The outcome was clear, sad, and very final.

The graveyard on the outskirts of the town was a pretty one, even in winter. Surrounded by an ancient stone wall, the ground inside was almost a metre higher, testimony to how many had been buried there across the centuries. Close by the walls, the willows drooped down to touch the dense yew hedges which gave their own evergreen protection. The occasion was as poignant as the faded roses on the graves. Ancient stones of granite, softened by moss and lichen, stood or leaned in among those of more modern marble. Here and there, carved angels and ornate cruci-fixes had toppled and fallen in a tangle of last year's long grass.

The case worker went with them. She wore dark clothes. The British couple were less sombrely dressed since they had come unprepared for death. The headstone was of black marble with raised metal lettering. Two women, distant cousins with the same year of birth, both of them named Annette Valais after the same ancient matriarch. One still alive and with four children; the other, Amanda's mother, four years dead, with no children recorded on the grave.

A light wind from the sea gently rustled the willows. Father and daughter shook hands with the case worker and all three turned and walked away.

*

From outside he heard the telephone ringing as he arrived back. It kept on ringing as he unlocked the doors, switched on the lights and went and picked up the receiver.

'You've been so long.' It was Fiona. 'We're here together, at home, my husband and the children . . .'

'What?'

'The press, the damn, bloody press . . . We're besieged. They know about us. I've had to tell my . . . Why like this, Mark? Why? Couldn't I have broken it quietly?'

He heard her voice, usually so quiet, was at breaking point. Then came the crying.

'There's one, Cree, offered to buy my story. It was Shand wasn't it? It had to be Shand . . .'

Inside Mark Ivor something snapped.

*

'Who is this man?' demanded Lord Shand, staring down at Tesco with the disdain that only centuries of breeding and in-breeding could muster.

'A colleague,' said Ivor coldly.

'You have five minutes. No more.' He reluctantly ushered them into the immaculate study of his Mayfair town house.

'A little more than that.'

'You're on sufferance, Ivor. Say what you have to say, then . . .'

'I am trying to keep cool after what you . . .' Ivor checked himself. 'If you want to play differently, just let me know.'

'I'm not playing. You're a meddler, Ivor. I told you: stay away from the PM. You've done enough damage.' Shand remained at his most icy and aloof. He stared at his visitors, and waited. 'Well?'

'Not about the PM. About you,' responded Ivor. 'One word.'

'What d'you mean?'

255

'Romania.'

There was a long silence, then Lord Shand started to talk with unaccustomed rapidity. 'My long connections with Romania, and East Europe, are well known. You may not like some of my recent right-wing ... But the Foreign Office is fully aware ...'

'Not right-wing. Not recent. Very left and a long time sleeping. When were Ceauşescu and his wife assassinated, executed? Christmas, eighty-nine?'

'I know nothing. The Foreign Office —'

'The Foreign Office haven't had the benefit of having read your *Securitate* file.' Ivor held out a brown envelope towards the other man but the offer was ignored. There was another long silence. Shand sat down heavily by his desk. Ivor had discussed with Tesco what his reaction might be. They had opted for fury or blustering denials. They were wrong.

'So ... so you know.' The voice was shockingly altered, almost inaudible. 'I supposed any file, any evidence, had been burnt or ... or forgotten. Ramsay Smythe once warned me of his experience ... and there were these too ... in high places not just with Romanian links but Czech, East German ... but life moves on ... So ...' He looked up at them, ashen-faced. 'So ... what do you want? Retribution or ... blackmail?'

Unasked Ivor and Walt Tesco also sat down and waited. Eventually Ivor spoke. 'Why don't you talk about it? Your betrayal?'

'Betrayal!' Shand laughed mirthlessly. 'A ridiculously dramatic word.'

'A man deceives rather than betrays a wife, family, friends, business colleagues. Betrayal, Shand, like treason, affects cause or country. It's an act that's never forgiven. After the long frost of the Cold War, you may think we can call it something cleaner, more sanitized, but in my book ... the word sticks.'

Shand sat in silence, staring ahead of him. After a while, Ivor began talking, quietly at first, then with increasing force.

'Betrayal, like espionage, the most secret of all vices. The majority of you who betrayed your country were never found out. Your secrets were only known to those grey intelligence organizations to whom you'd sold your souls. Then came the end. Were you shocked by its completeness, Shand? The collapse of Communism? The death of the secret state? Did you ask yourself: were your secrets safe? Who might reveal who had betrayed whom?' Ivor paused to look at the peer who was staring down, hands clasped in front of him. 'Personal files freed from hidden archives, uncovered . . . heinous crimes, or, now that the Cold War is no more, irrelevant footnotes to history?'

Ivor pulled the rough cardboard-covered file out of its brown envelope and begun to shuffle through it. 'The translation . . . it's a methodical record by the way . . . a fifteen-year period, ending with Ceaușescu's execution in December 1989. Let's see. In return for substantial payments and access to sexual favours, your services were available to them. Not for you dead-letter boxes, codes, cyphers, secret transmitters. Not for you the leaking of state secrets, weapon dispositions, military movements, strategies. Not even commercial secrets. No. Lord Shand was too grand for all that. You were among the élite in the hall of betrayal. See – they called you an *Agent of Influence*, paid or recompensed – females are not strictly payment, I suppose – for your influence on the highest political decisions. You were their man.' Ivor waved the file high. 'You were indeed . . .'

The defence was unexpected and simple.

'Quasi-intellectuals like you admit to only one version of the truth,' said Shand when he had recovered some of his composure.

'One version of the truth?' said Ivor. 'No. I've never agreed with that: don't you remember a conversation we once had, at Covent Garden? Fact and truth: there are always so many varieties depending on whom it comes from.'

'Then . . . You have read my file. I've not had the privilege of seeing what I'm alleged to have done. But I am denying nothing.'

'So?'

'So why did I do it?' Shand volunteered.

'We've established that,' interjected Tesco.

Shand ignored him. 'You read sex. You read money.' He directed his remarks entirely at Ivor. 'Even your little man here,

257

your "colleague",' the words emerged with contempt, 'will recognize that I've never lacked either.' He paused. 'That may be the *Securitate*'s explanation. Perhaps it helped their accounting practices, left them money for their own purposes. I don't deny what I've done. The reasons ... the reasons ... I would never have stooped to that.'

'So?' Ivor waited. When the explanation came, it too was unexpected and plausible. It came like a lecture.

'The plight of the Hungarian minority in Romanian Transylvania has been a source of bitterness across the centuries. They were always persecuted. They were discriminated against. Particularly under Ceauşescu and his Communist forerunners. A beautiful Hungarian girl manages to flee to the West and, eventually, in a London nightclub, she acquires a real catch, a peer of the realm. There was love. There was joy. There was great happiness. Then, in the sixties, she was approached; she agreed to work for Romanian intelligence in return for the release of her widowed mother and her younger sister. Until ... ? The mid-seventies. Yes ... Only then did I become aware of this double life. She was still beautiful. I was still in love. We tried to break free, but the *Securitate* were ready to expose the wife of a prominent member of the House of Lords. I found ...' tears glistened in his hard eyes, 'I found myself increasingly sucked into the web of ... betrayal – your word – to protect us both. Once swallowed, the hook pulls downwards in a spiral of greater and greater demand. Then ... she died.' His voice dropped. 'From cancer, a mere six months before Ceauşescu's fall. Maybe, Ivor, with your recent discovery, you understand more about family loyalties. Now ...' he said, suddenly standing and reasserting his authority. 'I asked you: is it retribution or is it blackmail?'

*   *   *

Top Secret & Personal

TO: *Chief, C13*

FROM: *The Secretary to the Cabinet*

re: **Operation Picnic**

1. Shand has struck his tent. He has gone abroad — to the West Indies I believe. (See report on Sigmont Corporation and Shand: FQ2368/93.) He told the PM that he felt he had made his contribution, that it was time for others, for a new team. I will explain about General Sir Patrick Gibson's role in due course. Dr Ivor is now back in the swing at Number Ten. Suggest close Operation Picnic. Open personal file on last named: on a contingency basis only. Please confirm.

2. On the related issue (RV19/PPR/71) woman was released two weeks ago after representations to Thai authorities. She is now believed to be back in Britain. She says she will not talk. Since the alternative was 25 years that seems sensible. Whether we can enforce this in the future is, however, debatable.

Message ends.

When he had finished dictating, Sir Caspar Rudd told his secretary to show in his visitor. The tall, bronzed man with the military bearing strode into the room, hand outstretched. Sir Caspar grasped it warmly.

'I'm glad it worked out in other ways. It could have been dangerous.'

'I enjoyed it. I always thought I'd make a good actor,' said the other man. 'Now I suppose I'll have to go back to the cottage. And the gardening. Wife says the weeds are . . .'

'We're very grateful. I'm glad we didn't have to ask you to break your cover, Sir Patrick. It's much better that way, don't you think?'

ENDNOTE

A charity gala at the Royal Opera House a mere ten months
later. The Mandarin Class is there in force. The men, well
groomed, with metallic, educated voices; the women, their
appearances reflecting only the generosity of their partner's
cheque books. The rich, the wise and the bland. Faces straining
to look for the next important person at the expense of the
present. Bonhomie and bombast. Elegant talk and sycophantic
laughter. A visitor from Bolton might wonder that such people
still existed.

They survive because they avoid causing offence. They reach
high office when stronger candidates would cause irreparable
splits within the party. When they eventually fall, they are forgotten by the time the newsprint has been used to wrap the chips.
So when the freed woman eventually spilled her venom, one
faceless Prime Minister fell and another took his place. The scandal was huge for a few days; a sacrifice was made; those on the
fringes stumbled but remained where they were.

As there is no Royal in the Royal Box this evening, the seat
of honour is taken by Her Majesty's newly elected Prime Minister
who, with his wife, is placed beside the Chairman of the Council.
The parties may change; the government may change: *plus c'est
la même chose*. Behind him, because new Prime Ministers need
wise and experienced heads to guide them, and because spin
doctors leave Vicars of Bray green of jealousy, sits Dr Mark Ivor.
His daughter, Amanda, is in the seat beside him. Amanda is
leaving for St Malo tomorrow to seek relations, photographs,
relics, letters. He will leave that to her. A few weeks later and it

might have been Fiona beside him but the divorce proceedings have just begun and the legal processes may be long. In another box, a little away, a contented Secretary to the Cabinet, one of the most important men in Britain, the safest pair of hands, the central pillar of the Establishment, sits with his charming wife and another anonymous couple, she warm and bubbly, he with the disciplined bearing of an old soldier.

In the orchestra stalls below, the Lord Shand, sun-tanned from a long vacation, sits with his young female companion. An alert eye might recognize the pretty production assistant from the TV company which produced the party political broadcast. Lord Shand is still aggrieved at losing out on many things in life, but he is a man to whom sex can be a great solace, and he is already looking forward to the aftermath of the opera. Just before the performance begins, Lord Shand looks up and sees General Sir Patrick Gibson MC and his distinguished companion, and also takes in the scene in the Royal Box. He looks quickly away, a cold blade of fury in his heart.

For a split second Ivor catches that distant eye, but no expression escapes. Gently, Ivor rustles in his pocket, extracts a peppermint and, like a schoolboy, smuggles it into his mouth. It is inward contentment rather than malicious pleasure he feels as the conductor appears on the podium to take his applause.

The following pages contain
an excerpt from

THE BRITISH
AMBASSADOR

Michael Shea's new political thriller

NOW AVAILABLE IN HARDBACK

ISBN 0 00 225234 1

'Michael Shea knows all about political
intrigue . . . his fiction bears a disturbing
resemblance to fact.'
Sunday Times

Saturday 26 November 1966

The last faint light in the western sky brought an end to the short Norwegian day. A disconsolate, solitary gull perched in precarious warmth on a rusting steel stanchion by a vent near the wheelhouse door. Ahead, a crust of ice anchored the larger, broken floes until the reinforced steel bow of the ferry ploughed and shredded everything asunder. From where he watched by the rail, the resultant slivers were overwhelmed then submerged by the relentless grey waves that swirled below him.

He was almost home, almost happy. In the distance he could just make out the shape of the high, snow-covered mountains lining the fjord with, here and there, the faint lights of some remote farm or fishing township. To an outsider it was a bleak and inhospitable prospect, but, like any Norwegian, he was proudly patriotic, and he knew that warmth and love awaited him nearby. An hour at the most and he would be at the door of the pretty painted wooden house amid the snowdrifts on the outskirts of Bergen. His wife, his seven-year-old daughter, the new spaniel puppy he had heard about but had never seen: they would not be expecting him for a few days yet. He would surprise them. His wife would be overjoyed and only a little upset. She would have preferred to have had an appointment with the hairdresser before he arrived; there would be little festive food and wine in the house. She would fuss around and quickly rustle up a meal worthy of the occasion, washed down with too much beer and aquavit. Then there was his daughter . . . He could hardly wait.

His wife would be in even more celebratory mood when he told her the best news of all: this was to be his last trip. No more urgent, stomach-churning calls in the middle of the night; no more unexpected departures; no more tearful farewells; no more weeks

I

of uncertainty, of her not knowing where he was and whether he was safe. No more pointless, pleading telephone calls to the contact at his 'office', asking how he was and when she might expect him. His sole foray into anger had been when he heard later that she had been doing that, but he soon forgave her because he loved her.

Even when he had come home in the past – and she knew enough of his work to realize that his was the most dangerous of all professions – she expected, from long experience, that he would say next to nothing about where he had been or what he had been doing. Only once, when he had returned with severe frostbite in his feet and some of his blistered and blackened toes had had to be amputated in hospital, had he whispered something of having had to lie hidden for days in a makeshift bivouac somewhere in the unforgiving tundra of the north. When she had asked why, he had laughed and said that it was better to lose a few toes than to be shot, or, worse, tortured into some sort of confession before being thrown into an anonymous Soviet gulag to rot for an eternity.

A bearded crewman in thick fisherman's jersey, bareheaded and with no gloves on his huge hands, who seemed totally oblivious to the cold, appeared and manhandled a crate of tinned fish towards a cargo hatch. He left it there, ready to be unloaded, then disappeared down a companionway to the oily warmth of the quarters below. That was where all sensible travellers were, away from the relentless, biting wind.

The two thick-set men, in leather coats with fleece-lined collars and knitted woollen hats, had boarded the ferry at Ålesund. Each carried a heavy suitcase; too heavy, a percipient observer might have thought. They came, still with their suitcases, to flank him as he stood alone by the ferry's rail. He paid little attention to them. He was safe in Norwegian territorial waters. He was home.

A thin strand of piano wire, strung almost unnoticed between the two suitcases' handles, strangled his cry before it was uttered. Three heavy splashes passed unheard on the now abandoned deck. The wire and the weights would hold the body until it disintegrated in the ice-grey winter sea.

1

'You're much better informed than I am about current Anglo–US tensions, Ma'am.' He hoped he did not sound condescending.

'Suppose one ought to be. After all, one's been reading Foreign Office telegrams for well over forty years. A horrid thought . . . It would be a bit remiss . . . don't you think?' The Queen flashed a quick smile.

Sir Martin Milner struggled for a suitable response. Should he perhaps be drawing the audience to an end or would that be against protocol?

'What do you think of the President, Ma'am?' he ventured.

'Bit difficult to make a judgement after only one or two highly formal meetings. Wife seems bright enough. I suppose . . . like everyone else . . . one gets most of one's impressions from his television image.'

'Television's a great equalizer; makes small men great and humbles some of the would-be great,' Milner responded.

'I was saying to the Prime Minister the other day – not mentioning any names of course – that some of his colleagues would better serve their party if they kept *off* the box.' The Queen laughed out loud, a wicked glint in her eyes. Milner thought, once again, how much her subjects underrated her intelligence.

Reaching down for her handbag which had been strategically placed by the side of the gold lacquered chair, she rose to her feet and hooked the handle of the bag over her arm. The audience was at an end. Sir Martin Milner, his wife, Annabel, beside him, stood and moved back a pace. He was aware that a footman, an elegant, gold-braided equerry and a formidable lady-in-waiting, whom they had met earlier while they had been waiting for their

3

audience, had suddenly reappeared through the double doors of the Bow Room.

The Queen came forward and formally shook first Annabel's hand and then his own. 'Good luck,' she said, rather lamely. Then, 'You may have us descending on you, you know. A state visit's on the cards . . .'

There followed bows, curtseys, a retiral towards the doors, then a final bow and curtsey. The ceremony of Kissing of Hands by the new British Ambassador to Washington was over.

Shown out through the Grand Entrance, they said their good-byes to the members of the Household, then were whisked out and away in the drab Foreign Office cars, through the quadrangle, out past the guard changing by the Privy Purse Gate, and into the bustle of real-life London.

After a few moments Annabel turned to him. 'Wise old bird,' she said.

'Seen it all,' responded her husband. 'Sharp political mind.'

'What did she mean by the *other candidate*?' asked Annabel suspiciously. Her steel-grey hair was meticulously styled and tapered; she may have begun giving way to ever more matronly habits, her body expanding from the lithe figure he had married some twenty-five years earlier, but her mind was still as sharp as a scalpel. Wherever they had been posted she was more respected – and feared – by junior embassy staff and their wives than he was.

'Something let slip that I am not supposed to know about,' Milner muttered.

'I thought you were going to tell me everything when it came to future postings.' Her voice was suddenly shrill. He read the danger signals and played it cool.

'Don't know all the details but office gossip has it that when Robinson had his heart attack and I was meant to be going to Ottawa, the Party pushed hard for a political appointment. According to a source not a million miles away from the Head of Personnel, the PM and the Foreign Secretary actually agreed that Vincent, the former Party Chairman, should get the job. Then in stormed the Chief Whip. They looked at the size of their

4

Commons majority, the risks of losing a by-election in Vincent's constituency and at the long-term uncertainties over the next election, and decided on the soft option. Me.' Milner paused, waiting for his wife's reaction. When none was forthcoming he went on. 'I gather Vincent – or more correctly his pretentious wife – is pissed off. He was looking forward to a couple of glamorous years in Washington. Then his peerage.'

'Pretentious . . . is that what they say about her.' Annabel sniffed in a way that was less than approving. He waited, expecting a further barb . . . and it came. 'And us, Martin?' His wife turned in the seat to stare at him. He looked away. 'A couple of glamorous years in Washington, or are you all set for your usual workaholic act once you get there, leaving me as social asset and nanny to the young embassy wives?'

'I am what I am.' It was one of his full-stop phrases. Milner was not going to allow her to draw him into a spat, especially with the Foreign Office chauffeur eavesdropping. Husband and wife lapsed into their customary, hostile silence.

The car turned from the Mall down past Horseguards Parade towards Birdcage Walk. The traffic was heavy in Parliament Square but they were soon into Whitehall, King Charles Street and the sanctity of the Office itself. It was twelve-thirty. A lot had happened, but the day was far from over.

In a bleak little changing room he slipped out of his morning coat and striped trousers, the accepted dress for Buckingham Palace. How he hated the stiff white collar, though it was, he supposed, a shade better than struggling into diplomatic uniform as he had had to do in the past. Annabel had left him at the door. They had brushed each other's cheeks with a formal kiss but neither could wait to escape from the other's presence. Had it not been for the need for such a senior ambassador to appear to have a stable, happy marriage, and because their partnership suited them both well in terms of his ambition and her liking for the glamour of diplomatic life, they would have divorced long since.

Annabel was meeting her sister for lunch. He, by contrast, had a demanding afternoon of briefing meetings ahead of him, arranged by the Heads of Mission Section, to prepare him prior to his departure for Washington. He knew much of the background already. In Brussels, his last post, he had seen most of the important telegrams, knew several of the key people, was familiar with the major crisis points. Once he got to Washington he realized only too well that much of the work would be far from glamorous. It was not just the core diplomatic tasks; it was all the protocol and entertaining that went with being an ambassador there. Outsiders thought it must be fun. Sometimes it was, but little did they realize what a high degree of physical stamina was needed to wine and dine the great and the good for Britain, and to act as a first-class hotelier to the constant stream of official visitors, royalty, ministers, MPs and others, who treated the Washington residence as a home from home. Half of any ambassador's life was either that or acting as a postbox for other people's ideas. The other half, the work that he relished, was adding his expert touch to lubricate the business of what was modern international diplomacy.

Sir Martin Milner also knew that, this time round – he had served there as a junior diplomat – Washington would be very different. The last time, as a mere First Secretary, he had dealt largely with one subject: NATO and the Western Alliance in general. He hadn't needed to know much about US internal politics, trade, cultural or consular matters. This time there was nothing that the embassy and its staff were involved in that he could ignore. In those days he had analysed and given advice to his seniors. Now he would be in charge. There were real problems to solve, minor disputes threatening to suppurate into major crises, as weak political leaders on both sides of the Atlantic dug themselves into ever deeper holes, posturing themselves into ever more intransigent positions. Each problem that arose was inflamed by the media, not because the newspapers and television were particularly malicious, but because they were there not only to seek out truth but to look for cracks, to identify scandal, to unearth dispute and division. The media thrived on bad news, and current Anglo–American relations offered a lot of that.

He changed rapidly into his business suit, packed away the

morning dress in its hanging bag, then went through to the temporary office he had been allocated. He had half a dozen telephone calls to make, including arrangements for a lunch with his son, David, later that week. He would take him to the Travellers Club. He was looking forward to a heart-to-heart with David. The young man's life seemed to be a bit unsettled following an uneasy move from the freedom of university to the disciplines of a City desk, and maybe a reassuring, fatherly word would be helpful, particularly as they would see so much less of each other now that he was Washington-bound. David: the clone of himself, in looks, in build, in character. David: Annabel's darling.

Was that really true? Was David a clone of himself? Certainly they looked very much alike. He, the father, tall, fair hair turning to grey at the temples, with a long taut face, slightly hooked nose, and lips that Annabel had once called sensuous. Now she was more likely to brand his look as contemptuous. To outsiders, his clear blue eyes were his most fascinating feature. Unlike many intelligent people, he looked intently at others when they spoke to him and they felt almost hypnotized by the strength of his gaze, the eyes under their heavy hooded lids, staring at or through them. In his youth he had had as powerful a body as David's, but now it was slightly stooped as a result of his habit of bending down to talk to people of lesser height. That, along with his half-moon reading glasses that seemed always to be perched halfway down his nose, gave him something of an academic look.

Yet under his clothes, he was proud of the fact that he had not let himself slip, as so many of his colleagues had done, into middle-aged overweight. His waist was as trim as it had been twenty years earlier. He took sufficient exercise to keep his figure that way but, more importantly, he knew how to resist the temptation to overindulge in the best wines and the superb cuisine that were constantly on offer in the diplomatic circuit. He was not an out and out aesthete though many thought him so. But he was highly disciplined, and, as Annabel had complained on their drive back from the Palace, was also something of a workaholic. He took some time off, but did not believe in letting work pile up around him. He had one rule: he liked to see a day's tasks properly completed before he retired for the night.

Of his other physical attributes, perhaps the most noticeable things about him after his eyes were his hands. They were long-fingered, finely formed with carefully manicured nails. There was something almost feminine about them, about the way he would carefully pick up a pen and meticulously amend a draft, or write a letter. His handwriting too said much about him: a firm italic, clear, precise with almost no errors. He thought carefully before tracing any line of ink on paper. And it always was ink. He abhorred biro. Yes, as Annabel had said, he did work too hard. Yes, he still had ambition and knew he was going to have to be relentless in Washington in order to succeed. Yes, he was what he was.

He made a couple of telephone calls, one to arrange to see the Defence Secretary on current problems with the Americans about the NATO Rapid Reaction Group and another to the Department of Industry to arrange to brief himself on protectionist moves in Congress that threatened to disrupt the progress on the new GATT agreement. Those completed, he pushed all his papers into his briefcase, took his coat from the hook behind the door and was just about to leave the room when the telephone rang. He looked at his watch, sighed briefly since he would be late for his next meeting. He hated keeping people waiting. Reluctantly he picked up the telephone.

'Sir Martin Milner?' a female voice asked.

'Who's speaking?'

'It's not necessary you should know.' The woman sounded unidentifiably foreign.

'I don't accept anonymous calls. I'm going to ring off.' He was uneasy and abrupt.

'You will listen when I tell you. This is a warning. I . . . we now know about you. We may hate you for it . . . But they . . . they are people who like to cut the strings. All the strings.'

There was a noise in the background and the line went dead. Milner slammed the telephone down. Damn it. What the hell was that about? He looked again at his watch. He *was* late. He had

8

more important things to do and would force the unsettling telephone call out of his mind.

Alexander was not one of the great lights of the British diplomatic service but he had an inbuilt cunning which made him an effective Head of American Department. It was at a meeting with him that Milner was due next. In his shabby office Alexander rose to greet him with a grimace. 'Just when we thought everything bad on the Anglo–American front had hit us, along comes today's hassle.' He flapped a telegram in Milner's direction, somewhat nervous of his distinguished colleague. Alexander was much the junior of the two men even though he would draft the instructions that the ambassador would later have to act upon when he got to Washington. As a defence mechanism against his nervousness, Alexander adopted a light-hearted approach to the difficult political decisions that his department currently were having to deal with.

'What this time?' he was asked.

'Pulling their contingent out of the peace-keeping force. Like next week.' Alexander draped himself in what he believed was a relaxed posture over his office chair.

'We expected it.' Milner pulled up another chair and sat opposite, upright and still.

'Yes, but they could have had the courtesy to warn us when. We sent a gentle protest; they more or less told us to get stuffed.'

'Too gentle . . . That's our problem. We're too nice. Our political leaders smile too much. Thatcher didn't go around grinning and people listened. When she and Tebbit smiled, grown men shuddered and crept away. We need more steel.' Milner knew the office style: kid gloves and not a steel fist in sight.

Alexander laughed. 'The President's a bit of a smile nice, talk nice, do nothing man too. Except when it comes to us . . .'

'What's biting him?' It was a question that Milner would ask many people.

'The Brits appear to be public enemy number one in the President's eyes. It's all in that file.' Alexander pointed to a brown-covered folder on his desk. 'It gets thicker and thicker by the day.'

'A personal thing? The President, I mean.'

'That's your reading; that's my reading. To the media, thank God, it's still the Americans lashing out at everyone to take attention away from their own domestic inadequacies.'

'What was Robinson's guess – before his heart attack, I mean – of what drives the President?' Milner was genuinely curious.

'Never have had it our own way. Special Relationship . . . always a bit of a myth even with Reagan and Bush . . . then with Clinton. But, by and large, there were far more ups than downs. Now this guy comes along.' Alexander was flailing around.

'He's part Irish.' Milner volunteered a prompt line while knowing the answer.

'Nobody's ever suggested that as a reason. There are packs of people far more extreme than him on Irish issues, in the Senate and in the House, and, in any case, everything's looking rosy on that front. Gone through his past with a tooth comb, but we've never come up with serious anti-British comments on that score.'

'So what moves him?' Milner kept pressing his colleague. He wasn't going to get the answer of answers from Alexander but it helped his own thoughts to develop.

'That's why they appointed you ambassador. To find out.' Alexander paused, wondering if he was being too cheeky. But what he had said was true enough. The department and Sir Martin's predecessors had all drawn a blank. 'Nevertheless . . .' he went on hurriedly. 'Before you settle down with these files, let me take you through some of the other big headaches . . .'

Extract from the Court Circular in *The Times*, Wednesday 23 April

Buckingham Palace, Tuesday 22 April.
Sir Martin Milner had the honour of being received by Her Majesty The Queen and kissed hands on his appointment as Her Majesty's Ambassador to Washington. Lady Milner also had the honour of being received by The Queen.

Somewhere in north London, where neither buying *The Times* nor paying attention to the Court Circular was common, the announcement was read out loud by a man to a woman. The man affected an upper-class accent; his audience of one shivered involuntarily.

'Kissed hands. Can you believe . . . ?'

'What else should he be kissing?' the woman asked nervously, not quite understanding.

'The coffin lid,' said the man with a chilling sneer.

*

Like most people he had a view of himself that was not shared by others. Martin Milner thought of himself as astute, hard-working and approachable. The last of these he was certainly not. He had never been someone a junior colleague would rush to in search of solace. If it was not his intention to be remote, it was how he was universally perceived to be.

Between the public and the private man there was a void. There was no in-between with Milner. He would have been shocked to be told, if anyone could bring himself to tell him, that he had few real friends: there were plenty of acquaintances of course, but not many too close. He was, to the outside world, a deeply reserved man, fired by his professionalism and his personal resolve. Those hooded blue eyes of his, according to one less than sympathetic colleague, were like darkened windows on a limousine, allowing him to see out but preventing outsiders looking in. For a diplomat, his background was impeccably correct. Good middle-class professional family, public school, and New College, Oxford. His file in the Personnel Department charted a high-flyer's rise through his career, helped by a mixture of talent and good fortune. It noted his admission to being a slave to the Protestant work ethic: nothing should be left undone at close of play; a tidy working style was the mark of a tidy mind; sleep was a just sleep only when the day's tasks were well completed. That was his self-assessment and it was too kindly; to colleagues who had to work with or for him, he had an over-pernickety attention to the minutest detail. Admittedly his preference for official technocracy over politics as a means of getting things done had served him well throughout his career. Additionally, on the up side, he did not harbour grievances. Once he had told a junior diplomat off for some misdeed or omission, he moved on to other things. He was a present and future man; he talked little about his past. He did not reminisce. Small-talk did not come easily to him.

Yet to mere acquaintances he was not perceived as being totally arid, because he forced himself, as his profession demanded, to socialize, to make merry in a disciplined sort of way. He was good at networking. He was a smooth diplomatic host. He made amusing, pungent speeches; he was clear and fair in his dealings with his staff; and in social conversation he worked hard not to be boring or to talk shop all the time. With his wife, Annabel, as in so many marriages, the end of sex had come early, and now, with various highly emotional lapses, they were more business partners than man and wife. In public she too was efficient and hospitable if not warm, in a world where high entertaining, place-ment and protocol, were still of key importance. Her only openly expressed and justifiable complaint was that in Washington it would be non-stop: constant formal meals, VIP guests, receptions, the day-to-day work that equated itself more to running a five-star hotel than operating a diplomatic establishment. In private she was very different: in turn moody and demanding, and a constant thorn in his flesh. But both hid their conflicts well and few guessed at the stresses and strains that tore at the hearts of this outwardly successful couple.

For this and for other reasons, from time to time even the self-sufficient Sir Martin Milner needed someone else to turn to. It was not that Dr Mark Ivor was his guru nor one who strived to find out much, though he might have guessed, about the strains of the marriage with Annabel. Neither man would have claimed that the one depended on the other except in the comradely way of men with similar intellects and goals. But Mark Ivor was the better listener, a man of reasonable integrity who offered wise advice. To outsiders, they were lifelong friends, though both had gone their very separate ways. Ivor, whom the British media had branded the Modern Machiavelli, the spin doctor supreme, had a largely justified reputation of influencing the minds of more men and women in apparent authority than any other in British political life. He was someone who shared many of Martin Milner's ideas and aspirations, but who acted behind the panoply of state rather than on the public platform as his diplomat friend had done. Ivor read and understood the passions of British domestic politicians, their whims, their transitory views, their fickleness. He knew how to work the London Establishment, that small matrix of people who exercised power through their social connections as much as across a boardroom table or desk. He knew because he was part of that élite.

Physically too they were very different. Milner, tall, fair, stooping, like an ill-placed Oxbridge don. Ivor was darker, shorter and more naturally gregarious. To alert outsiders, both men displayed their strengths through their shared sense of vision coupled with the body language of the powerful. What at a less elevated level the two men enjoyed most, however, was basic political gossip, the plots, the verbal assassinations, the scheming, the tactics, the making of decisions that the tribal leaders of the various political packs appeared to take. Martin Milner and Mark Ivor, so different but both so successful in their chosen fields, had dinner, *à deux*, that late-April evening at the Garrick Club.

Throughout the meal, at a small side table in the dark, portrait-hung Coffee Room, and later, at Mark Ivor's flat in Westminster, as they made considerable inroads into a bottle of vintage Macallan, the spin doctor adopted a style of catechism. He asked; Martin Milner responded. He prodded; the other explained. He interrogated; the newly-appointed Ambassador to Washington expounded. Ivor was Milner's catalyst; both men recognizing and relishing their separate roles as evening wore on into the early hours of the next day.

'The diplomatic profession is not what it was.' Ivor opened the game.

'Cliché.' Milner shrugged, sipping cautiously at his glass.

'You are now well-paid postmen. The work is done by fax, E-mail and phone, from head of state to head of state, from capital to capital.'

'You've been reading the *Spectator*, or the *Daily Express* more likely.'

'The scribbleati have it in for you, I agree. But they're almost right. Most diplomacy is now of the shuttle variety: ministers and top civil servants flying in and out. Or it's done multilaterally in Brussels or the UN.' Ivor was trying to provoke his friend. It was an old battle.

'Who lays the groundwork? When the Secretary of State arrives in some capital, you don't think he starts negotiating then, do you?' Milner was aroused.

'Sure: a lot of preparatory work has gone on behind the scenes.'

'*All the work* has gone on behind the scenes. The Secretary of State has been negotiating, via the ambassador, long before he arrives. He's put his *imprimatur* on the document, on the treaty or whatever, before he steps off the plane. The rest is window-dressing.' Milner stood, stretched his legs and helped himself, unasked, to a refill of Macallan.

'My point precisely. All you're doing is fixing.'

'That's what diplomacy is.'

'Is it going to be any different for you in Washington?' Ivor began adding more bite to his questioning.

'Depends on the personalities. On me, I suppose. Some ambassadors *are* mere postmen. Smile warmly, dress well, have attractive wives who choose good chefs and deliver good dinner parties. We impress by attending all the right receptions and shaking the right hands. We don't put a foot wrong. We don't say a word out of place. But that's not enough in real international life. Some, like you, Mark, make things move. As in all societies, all governments, all diplomatic services, it depends on the individual. Take the present government . . .' Milner gestured with a theatrical sweep of his arm to the otherwise empty room.

'You can take the present government as far as I am concerned.' Ivor laughed.

'Be serious. It's weak. It drifts into crises without knowing where it's heading. It's not got a proper roadmap . . . nor agenda . . . With the present bunch of inadequate ministers, impelled by the system rather than directing it, the people behind the scenes make all the running. People like you . . .' Milner gestured again, this time at his host.

'It certainly makes our tasks easier, we puppet masters, not having our devious plots and ploys interfered with by real people.' Ivor again laughed out loud at his own remark.

'What's true in internal British politics at the moment is also true in American politics.' Milner injected a different note. 'Look at Washington's constant battle between domestic policies and foreign issues. Again and again in the Foreign Office files I see reports from our embassy of how those round the President try to manipulate him in one direction or another . . .'

'The Secret State runs things. Everything is all really governed by civil servants. And by us spin doctors of course.' Ivor stared up at the other man.

'To a great extent, true. Occasionally political figures like Margaret Thatcher emerge who do actually have an agenda, who do actually take decisions, though even she was largely run by her kitchen cabinet . . . Charles Powell, Bernard Ingham, Tim Bell and so on. Just as you, Mark, are reputed to mould the Prime Minister, Michael Wilson's mind . . .' Milner said slowly.

'Is that what they say? Come, come, Martin . . . The PM has a mind of his own.' Ivor glanced down at his empty glass.

'Of course he does. It's just that he gives too much free access to it. Like a rudderless boat he swings with the waves. No stout hand on the helm and all that.' Milner began pacing the room.

'Sit down, Martin. You make me nervous. Back to your American President. Tell me all about him.'

Milner crashed back into his chair. He knew he was getting a little drunk. 'At first, when I started reading all the speeches and telegrams about him, he seemed like an empty suit if ever there was one. I felt I would have to examine the team behind him to know what was making America tick. Then . . .'

'You know what makes America tick? At the moment? If you do you're the only one,' Ivor interrupted.

'Which is what I'm getting at. I don't pretend to understand what's got into the White House, particularly its anti-British stand. That's what I've been asked to find out. Who's pushing the President?' Milner sounded almost plaintive.

'Are you sure he's being pushed? He may be a simple man on the surface, but simple men – remember Ronald Reagan, and Michael Wilson for that matter – often have simplistic agendas which they stick to like limpets.'

'You know that Wilson is completely programmed, Mark. Which is exactly why I want to look at the inner team in Washington. Some of the White House staff are top quality; when they're running things, they really are running things. Take Antonio Delgadi, the Secretary of State . . . There are plenty of placeholders of course, but the good people like him make things happen.' Milner was now more than a little flushed in his enthusiasm.

'And you? You're going to make things happen?' asked Ivor. He was at least two drinks behind his guest.

'My reputation often frightens me.'

'You don't like your advice being ignored,' Ivor prompted.

'Who does? You?' Milner pointed a finger at Ivor.

'A lot of people put up with it. Like me. My advice is often ignored. But they pay me for giving it. I agree on one thing: you and your image match each other. You're a go-getter, Martin. You'll have your effect on Anglo–American relations . . . for good or ill. Which is why . . .' Ivor paused and watched as Milner stood up and went back over to a sideboard and picked up the bottle of Macallan. 'Do you really need another?' he asked gently.

'It goes down well. One for the journey.' Milner paused, then replaced the bottle on the tray. 'No, perhaps that's enough for tonight,' he said remotely. Then . . . 'Which is why what?' he asked.

Another man might have prevaricated, would have held his peace. But Ivor had lots of reasons why he wanted his friend to know what he had done. 'Which is why I pushed your name on the PM. You are the best.'

Milner looked to see whether the other man was joking. 'You're serious,' he said eventually. 'You got me this job? You're the bloody king-maker? Thanks . . .'

'King . . . Ambassador . . . Once your name was in front of him, the choice was obvious.' Ivor shrugged.

'Well, well,' said Milner. 'I do owe you a favour.' It put his friend in a very different light though, and through the haze of alcohol he was not altogether happy. He began to say something but Ivor stopped him.

'Yes, I put your name forward. I trust your ability after all – and value your friendship. Known you a long time, though I still feel I don't . . . know you.'

As he spoke Ivor wondered if he now had gone too far. Emboldened by his own, lesser, quota of alcohol, he decided to press on. It was true what he had said. He did not know this other man, this Martin Milner. Of course he knew what he had achieved, his successes and the way he went about his business. He liked the cut and thrust of their discussions together. He revelled in the other man's acerbic wit: the way he would build up and destroy the reputations of political figures with a smile or a word. But there was another side to Milner: his obsessive industry, his secretiveness, his aloofness with others which, though it might have been initially born out of shyness, was off-putting to many. Had he been a psychologist, Ivor would probably have gone for some theory about anal retentiveness. Yet there was more upside to his friend – he called him his friend to others – than there was downside. Milner was successful in everything he had ever done in his career. If his family life was not everything that the career managers might have wished, that too was, to a large extent, a private matter. It had been the one shadow when he had proposed his friend's name for the Washington embassy, and it had not seemed to matter.

'Who knows anyone?' Milner slurred his words a little.

'You know what I mean,' said Ivor. 'I still don't know what

17

pushes you, what motivates you. It's no longer ambition: you've got all the rewards, reached all the pinnacles you could wish for. After Washington, probably the House of Lords, but as you know you're bound to get that in the end, you've stopped trying. No, it's not ambition. What makes you tick?'

'Same thing as most people: job satisfaction; comfortable life; not too much hassle; duty-free booze; the knowledge that one can sleep well without worrying. And talking of sleep, I must . . .' Milner was beginning to mumble with a mixture of alcohol and tiredness.

'Balls.'

'If you say so. But no different from anyone else.'

'There's something deeper, Martin. If I were a conspiracy theorist, I would guess that deep inside you there's a secret.'

'Murdered my grandmother?' Milner allowed himself a tired smile. 'Come to think of it, I was tempted. She was a bad-tempered old bitch . . .'

'No joking. I don't know, but I don't think it's anything sexual. You may have fantasies, I suppose, but you keep yourself under control. I'm talking about something else . . .' Mark Ivor hesitated. 'Something more brutal . . .'

The other man was silent for a long time. He stared down at his glass of whisky, hands cupped round the glass. Then eventually, without looking up, Milner said, 'Why did you say that?' He suddenly sounded alert and very sober.

'I don't know. The whisky, I suppose. Forget it.'

'Can I forget it?' Milner insisted.

'Is it true?'

Again there was a long pause. 'I don't think so. No,' said the diplomat.

'You remember Marlowe's *Dr Faustus*?' Ivor asked.

'A bit . . .'

'He's sold his soul to the devil . . . eventually the devil came for him . . . You remember? What was the Latin? *"O lente, lente currite noctis equi"* – *"Run slowly, slowly, horses of the night"*. He's working late. At midnight, Lucifer comes for his soul.' Ivor smiled a hesitant smile. He suddenly felt ill-at-ease with his analogy.

'I remember something . . . Had to learn it at school,' Milner muttered.

'I can't quite recall how it finishes but there's another line where he pleads for "*a year, a month, a week, a natural day that Faustus may repent and save his soul*".'

'What are you getting at?' said Milner irritably, rising to his feet.

'Have you a soul that needs to be saved, Martin?' Mark Ivor paused, looked grim for a moment, then smiled. 'Aw, forget it,' he said again. 'Have one last one. Then I'll go order you a taxi.'

At lunchtime two days later Sir Martin Milner stood at the door of the Travellers Club in Pall Mall waiting for his son David to arrive. He glanced at his watch: David was late. He had taken the day off from his City job, borrowed his father's car since his own old banger was in for repair; he would be stuck in traffic somewhere. Milner greeted one of his Foreign Office colleagues, currently British Ambassador in Riyadh, on home leave, who came bounding up the steps towards him.

'Hello, Patrick. Good to see you. How's Saudi Arabia?' They shook hands warmly.

'Same as Saudi always is. Dry, dry, dry. And you? It must have been a whopping surprise getting Washington instead of going to quiet old Ottawa?'

'A bit.' Milner stared beyond him, down Pall Mall, looking for a familiar figure.

'Nasty time to be taking over. Beautiful residence though . . . Lutyens and all that.'

'It's bound to get better,' Milner suggested.

'Why?'

'Things always do.'

'You haven't been in Jeddah recently.' His colleague nodded and made his way on into the club.

Milner looked at his watch again, went inside and beckoned to the hall porter. 'Sure there are no messages for me?'

'No, Sir Martin, nothing.'

'Damn.' He went back towards the door. In the distance, the air was filled with the sounds of screaming sirens and hooting cars.

'It's getting worse, sir,' said the porter, coming out to join him. 'All these roadworks . . . Driving, were they?'

'My son. Borrowed my car. Hellish area to find a parking place. Should have been here ten minutes ago,' grumbled Milner.

'Can't judge how long any journey is going to take these days. Bloody marvel anyone gets anywhere any more,' said the hall porter.

An hour later, having tried without avail to reach David at the family flat or, because he might have changed his mind about going into work, his office, he had lunch at the centre table sitting beside the ambassador home from Saudi Arabia, then made his way back to the Foreign Office. He was not too concerned; David was usually so prompt and there was doubtless some very good reason for his non-appearance. There would be a message waiting back at the office.

At around three o'clock he was thinking of trying to get hold of Annabel to ask if she had heard anything, when the phone on his desk rang.

The voice at the end was hesitant. 'Sir Martin Milner?'

'Yes. What is it?'

'Foreign Office Security, sir. Somebody to see you, sir. Can I bring him up?'

'Who is it?'

He heard other voices in the background, then: 'Sir . . . I think he'd better explain himself, sir, when he comes, sir.'

An unusual sense of apprehension engulfed Milner. He was someone who was always totally in control of his actions, of his feelings, of life's events. He was not one to believe in premonitions but, on top of the strange phone call the other day, there was something not right ... He waited. After some moments there was a firm knock on the door.

'In ...' he ordered.

Two men came into the room. One was a police sergeant in uniform, the other had policeman stamped all over him, but was younger, leaner and fitter; at a guess, a plain-clothes detective. In the background hovered the Foreign Office Security man.

'Sir Martin?'

He stood up. 'What is it?' he asked, suddenly afraid.

'Some bad news for you, sir.'

'It's my son. It's David, isn't it?'

'Sir. I'm afraid so, sir.'

'How ... where is he? He's been in a car accident, is that it?'

'No, sir. A shooting, sir.'

'A shooting?' Milner gasped, uncomprehending.

'He's been shot, sir. As he was getting into his car.' The younger policeman was surprisingly nervous at being the bearer of the dramatic news.

'My car ... Is he ... ? Is he ... ?'

'No, sir. Still alive, bad injuries ... Punctured lung. Other wounds in the cheek, shoulder and groin.'

'Groin ... Oh, Christ! Where? When?' Milner's words spattered out.

'Outside your flat, sir. Before lunch.'

'I was waiting for him, you know,' he said inanely.

'I gather, sir.'

'Where is he? Come on, let's ...'

'In emergency, sir. St Thomas's. We'll take you over now, sir.'

'What the hell's happened? Who would shoot ... ?' His voice broke as he spoke.

'As far as we can make out, sir, he was getting into the car ... your car ... He was shot several times by a man who was riding pillion on a motorcycle. They didn't stop. Got clear away.'

'Who would shoot my David . . . ?' Why didn't the stupid policeman understand his simple question?

'That's the point, sir. It has all the hallmarks of a very professional hit,' came the shattering response.

The Polish Officer

Alan Furst

'Excellent . . . beautifully written, intensely atmospheric and dramatically convincing. *The Polish Officer* is a work of quiet subtlety that will niggle in the memory far longer than most novels of espionage.'   *Sunday Times*

In 1939, as the German army ravages his country, Captain Alexander de Milja enlists in the newly formed Polish underground and undertakes the first of many daring acts of defiance and disruption: transporting Poland's gold reserves to safety hidden on board a refugee train. As the war continues duty takes him, under a series of false identities, from Warsaw to Paris and the frozen Ukraine – enduring a life of dark shadows and perpetual deception, always on the run, always just one step ahead of death.

'A page-turner, yes, but also one of the most evocative works of history I have come across. Read and learn.'
                                                                Observer

'Wonderfully written . . . Furst is the laureate of the vast, mysterious tracts of Eastern Europe. An extraordinarily fine novel.'   *Glasgow Herald*

ISBN 0 00 649356 4

The Heart of Danger

Gerald Seymour

'Unmissable' *The Times*

In a wrecked Croat village, a mass grave is uncovered and the mutilated body of a young Englishwoman, Dorrie Mowat, is exhumed.

Her mother, who loathed Dorrie in life, becomes obsessed by the need to find out about her death. But with civil war tearing apart the former Yugoslavia, none of the authorities there or in Britain are interested in a 'minor' war crime.

So she turns to Bill Penn, private investigator, MI5 reject. For him this looks like a quick trip to safe Zagreb, the writing of a useless report and a good fee at the end of it. But once there he finds himself drawn inexorably towards the killing ground behind the lines, to find the truth of the young woman's death and, perhaps, the truth of himself.

Penn's search for evidence that could, one day, convict a war criminal in a court of law becomes an epic journey into a merciless war where the odds are stacked high against him.

'It's impossible to find fault with this book, which builds relentlessly to its climax. It has an intense feeling of authenticity and it's well written'

NICHOLAS FLEMING, *Spectator*

'Vivid stuff. I write a fortnight after finishing the book and some of the scenes of pursuit and mindless cruelty still return to me'   DOUGLAS HURD, *Daily Telegraph*

ISBN 0 00 649033 6

Provo
Gordon Stevens

Two women. One war. No rules.

Catcher
is the codename of Cathy Nolan, working undercover for
MI5 in Northern Ireland, fighting against not only a major
IRA threat, but also the internal politics of her own side.

Sleeper
is the perfect assassin, put in place years ago, unknown even
to the top-ranking members of the Provisionals' Army
Council.

PinMan
is the target of this, the ultimate coup. Now there is no way
of stopping the mission.

Provo
is the novel that redefines the modern thriller. From
Whitehall to Belfast, Hereford to South Armagh, it is
an adrenaline-pumping, white-knuckle ride behind the
headlines to a land of danger and betrayal.

ISBN 0 00 647632 5